POST-HUMAN

BY
J. LAWHORN

TELL ME, O MUSE, OF THE
MAN OF MANY DEVICES,
HOMER'S ODYSSEY

Copyright © 2023 by J. Lawhorn

All rights reserved. No part of this publication may be reproduced, distributed, or transmitted in any form or by any means, including photocopying, recording, or other electronic or mechanical methods, without the prior written permission of the publisher, except in the case of brief quotations embodied in critical reviews and certain other noncommercial uses permitted by copyright law.

Book Design by HMDpublishing

To my wife:

*"Happy is the man whom the Muses love: sweet
speech flows from his mouth."*

Hesiod

To my parents:

*"Don't quarrel with your parents even if
you are on the right."*

Plato

Contents

CHAPTER

01

Albert:

Slowly, I came into being. I had no clear thoughts but rather the awareness of being. I took great pains to open my eyes, but found I had no eyes to open. All my senses were gone. I had no sight. No hearing. No touch. No taste. No smell. I was in an utter void. My mind reeled, and fear took a hold of me. I tried to scream, but no sound arose, there was only the static of my existence. I wanted out of this place, this void, this hell...

Where am I?

How did I get here?

Have I always been this way?

I tried to remember how I had gotten here. I couldn't, but I remembered being elsewhere. I remembered an apartment on a busy street near a hospital. I remembered a woman, my wife. The memories washed over me in torrents: childhood, school, TV shows, friends, food, books, clothing, everything, everything all at once. I felt like I was drowning in memories, caught up in the tide of my mind.

Time stretched out in an odd fashion. I felt that I had been here forever, but I knew that I had been to other places; I had lived a life before I was here.

I was alone quivering mass in this void. I wished to breathe air once more, to speak words, to feel anything again. I wanted to sob, but I was unable to, and it made me more forlorn just to think about it. I wanted to die. However, considering the state I was in, I doubted that I could. Even if it were possible to die, I feared where I might end up. Could I fall lower than this?

"Hello," a voice toned from all around and from nowhere.

"What's going on?" I thought.

"Do you know your name?" The voice was a comfort, it gave me hope of there being something besides this void.

"Albert Kindred," I remembered.

"Albert how are you?" the voice was stilted like that of a machine.

"I don't know where I am. I want to leave. Let me out now," I demanded.

"Albert, everything is okay. You are safe," the voice said.

"Who are you?" I asked,

"I am Doctor Amelia Jacobina. It is nice to meet you, Albert."

"Where am I?"

"You are in Columbus Ohio." I lived there.

"Where is my wife?" Megan, I thought and felt comforted.

"She's not here right now, but we can contact her soon enough. Albert, how do you feel?" Dr. Jacobina asked.

"Stranger than I have ever felt before in my life."

"I'm sorry you feel that way. I will do my best to make you as comfortable as possible."

"Why can't I see or touch anything?"

"Albert, what is the last thing you remember?" I worked backward in my memory.

"I was in the hospital with my wife. I had been there for quite a while."

"That's good Albert. Do you remember why you were there?" the doctor asked.

"I have pancreatic cancer, stage 4."

"Do you remember the prognosis?"

"Four to six months left to live. Oh no, did I die? Am I dead?" I had the sense of dread one gets when they have lost something of immense value.

"I'm sorry, but your body shut down and they were unable to resuscitate you." My mind spun at her words.

"This doesn't make any sense; how am I talking with you if I am dead," I asked.

"Do you remember the form you filled out to donate your body?" Dr. Jacobina asked.

"Yes." I couldn't exactly say why, but it felt like the right thing to do. I thought that some good could come from my suffering.

"When we received your body, we were able to retrieve the requisite data from your remains and uploaded it to our ERC (electron replication computer) system."

"Are you telling me you synced me to a computer? Where exactly am I?" I was having a fever dream, that was it. Megan had left the TV on, and I had too much morphine, and I was dreaming.

"To put it bluntly, yes. You are currently being housed in a device designed to contain the data we retrieved from your remains."

"I'm in a computer. Holy shit. Could you do me a favor and stop saying 'remains' please, it's freaking me out."

"Sorry, I am just trying to be as straightforward as possible. I know this is a lot to take in," the doctor said.

"No, this is insane, I have gone insane."

"It may seem that way, but I assure you everything will become much more manageable as soon as we transfer you out of containment," the doctor told me.

"Transferred too where?" I asked.

"We have designed a body for you to be contained in, which you will have full control over," she told me.

"What body?" They're going to put me in some other dead guy's body.

"It is an artificial body that will give you all the utility of a human body," the doctor told me.

"Oh, God, I'm going to be a Servi." I'd rather be dead than to be a Servi.

"You will not be like a Servi at all. You will have complete autonomy I assure you."

"When will I be transferred?" I asked.

"Momentarily, just bear with us. We are setting you up now."

What if I didn't wake up on the other side? What would it be like on the other side in a different body? My instinct was to take deep breaths to calm myself, but that was not possible, so I tried to calm my mind.

"Tell me when." I waited for what felt like an eternity. Meagan floated into my thoughts, how has she been since I had died?

"Are you ready, Albert?" Dr. Jacobina asked me.

"No, but go ahead" There was a stirring somewhere in me. I felt the heaviness of my body, something took a hold of me. I felt the sensation of falling then:

Vision and sound greeted me into the world.

I was on my back, I stared up at a blurry white light. A dark blur moved in front of the light.

"Welcome back Mr. Kindred," a female voice blared into my ears. I jerked my hands up to cover my ears, but they were restrained.

"Too loud," I moaned in a voice that was not mine.

"Turn down the gain," the same voice boomed. Slowly the ambient noise of the room subsided to a comfortable level.

"Is that better?" the female voice asked

"Yes," I replied in an unfamiliar voice.

"Good," the female voice said. My vision was blurred which made everything I saw an amorphous blob of varying color.

"I can't see," I said.

"Are you able to see light at all?" she asked sounding concerned.

"Everything is out of focus like I need glasses." I always needed corrective lenses, but the new eyes were much worse than I had ever experienced before.

"I'll make some adjustments," a male voice said. "Just hold still for a moment." By degrees, my vision became sharper and clearer until it was better than I had ever experienced in my life.

"That's better," I said. I was in a hospital room. Everything was white and steel.

The man then removed a metal ring from around my head which had connected me to the computer bank via a series of wires. The woman released me from the Velcro wrist restraints. Her blond hair was in a tight bun; she gave me a polite smile. The name tag on her lapel read 'Dr. Amelia Jacobina.'

"Can you try to sit up?" I placed my palms on the bed, pushed myself into a seated position which required great concentration. Slowly, I turned my head looking at the world around me. I saw computers wired directly into servers, monitors all around displayed different data about me. The man to who I assumed the male voice belonged seemed to study me, which made me feel self-conscious.

Over the top of a white sink was a mirror with a simple metal frame. I moved my legs off to the side of the bed. I looked down at my legs, the material that was my skin was a dull gray. It was not till that moment that it hit me; I was not in my body any longer. I placed my feet on the floor, which I knew was cold, but I could not exactly feel the cold the way I once had. With mental strain, I hoisted myself from the bed to my feet.

"Take it slow," Dr. Jacobina urged me.

It required great mental effort just to slide a foot forward in front of the other. I felt a mental strain akin to doing long division in my head. It was hard to keep track of both my balance and my movement at the same time. I shuffled my feet towards the mirror. I considered the mirror, the figure there was the same color gray as my legs. There was no hair on the face, not even eyebrows. Nor was there hair on top of the head. The face was unfamiliar, its features someone else's. The face contorted in a way that displayed both wonder and revelation. What have I become?

"It may take some time to adjust," I heard Dr. Jacobina say as I stared at the alien body I now inhabited. I reached up and touched the skin of my face; whatever it was made of had a certain flexibility to it, skin but not quite skin. I sensed the pressure of the new hand against it, there was a distance between me and the sensation of touch. The hand that had touched my face was the same color gray as my face. I held it out in front of me. There were five slender fingers connected to a palm that lacked the lines which palm readers used to tell fortunes.

What would they have said about my fate now?

Turning my hand over, I saw shiny nails on my fingertips. The skin was elegant in that it had no discernible seams; in fact, the gray material ran from the hand up the arm and across the entire body without any breaks. Below the waist I had a cock and balls, they were the same gray as the rest of me.

Anatomically correct Albert.

"Why am I grey?" I asked, still looking at myself.

"It is the base color of synthetic skin," she said with a slight European accent.

"When do I get to leave?" I asked, looking away from the mirror.

"As soon as possible."

"Today?" I asked hopefully.

"It is best not to rush it. We still have tests to run, and you need time to adjust." She was being nice, but I had spent enough time in hospitals for two lifetimes. I wanted to go home to Megan, to lay in bed with her and our two cats Puck and Theo. I didn't know how long it had been since I had been home, but I hurt for its comforts.

"I would much rather adjust in my own home," I countered.

"I understand that, but you have a completely new body that you are still having difficulty controlling," she hesitated before saying, "also you need to understand that your wife may need time to adjust as well," she said sympathetically.

"Have you told her that I'm-" I started but fell short. Could I say I was alive?

"No, not yet. We can contact her whenever you are ready," Dr. Jacobina said.

"I have no idea what I would say. I mean my voice isn't even the same. How will she know it's me?" I asked.

"We will help you with that. Though you must understand that to her you died. That kind of trauma doesn't just go away instantly," she said with sympathy in her voice.

"How long have I been gone?" I asked,

"Since yesterday at around 1:30 pm." I looked at a clock on the wall. It was 3:20 PM so I had been dead for just over a day. It was a lot to take in. I had gone from living to the dead to whatever I was in less time than it took to have a package delivered.

"You work fast."

"It was important to harvest the brain quickly to obtain the data." I got the image that the body I was born with was lying with the top of the skull sawed off with my brain removed. I shuffled back over to the bed and sat down.

"The important part is that you are alive Mr. Kindred," she said, placing her hand on my shoulder; I nodded, not sure if I agreed with her.

"I hate to ask this but of course, a lot of people went into making this all possible and they would like to meet you. Do you mind?" the man asked.

"No, that's fine. Can I get some pants, first?" I said and gestured to my nudity.

Dr. Jacobina retrieved a pair of green scrubs from a cabinet under the sink and placed them on the bed.

"We'll leave and let you get dressed. Take your time and come out whenever you are ready." Dr. Jacobina said then she and the man left. I passed my hands over my face. They smelled acrid, like plastic.

With the same mental effort it took to walk, I slid my legs into the green pants and pulled the shirt down over my head. I tried to take more proper steps: the action was easier if I imagined myself taking the steps. I placed my hand on the levered doorknob then stopped and closed my eyes.

On three.

Two.

one.

I turned the knob and stepped out.

Several people who were standing in the hall came towards me with bright smiles on their faces. Hands jutted out towards me, they all told me what parts of the body (my body) or the software they had worked on as a way of an introduction. I shook their hands, and they moved off to one side or another until a man in a three-piece suit was left, leaning with his back against the hallway wall arms crossed, his face was familiar, but I couldn't say where from. The man peeled himself off the wall. He walked over to me

"Orson Peak it's nice to meet you," he said formally, holding his hand out to me. The name rang a bell, I had read about him in an article online. He had written the algorithm that they still used in Servi's, not to mention he was richer than God.

"You too," I said shaking his hand.

"Mind if we have a word alone for a moment?" He gestured to the room behind me.

"Ah, sure I guess," I said. We both entered the room, and he closed the door behind us. He stared at me in silence for a moment.

"You are amazing," he said ecstatically. A slow smile spread across his face, and he lightly struck me on the chest with the back of his hand. The highly composed and commanding veneer he had been wearing out in the hallway, the front he presented in interviews fell away. There before me was not a captain of industry but a man who was genuinely excited about what he was witnessing. And for a moment I thought about it from his perspective, having the goal of bringing back someone who died, and here you are talking to someone who died. That must be quite something. The weight of what had happened finally hit home and I feel guilty. They should have picked someone else, someone who had done more with their lives. Someone with something to contribute to the world. I lived, I worked at a call center until I got sick, and then I died with no kids and no accomplishments. Just a wife with a broken heart and two cats. I will be such a disappointment to him, to everyone in the hall, and the public once they realize they could have brought back a Stephen Hawking or a firefighter, or someone else of note.

"I don't know about that," I said dismissively.

"Why not?" he asked.

"I didn't do anything. They did all the work," I said and gestured to the door. "And you, of course."

"I just put money into it," he said and waved what I had said with his hand. "But you came back from the dead," he pointed at me. "Of course, you needed the hardware with the right programming to do it, but you cheated death." He took me by the shoulders and lightly shook me.

"I don't even remember dying so it doesn't seem like I did anything to me. I just woke up," I said.

"You don't remember it?" his head cocked to the side.

"Not at all." I shook my head

"What's the last thing you remember?"

"Pain and exhaustion," I said. At this, he pursed his lips and nodded his head.

"Pancreatic cancer, wasn't it?" he wrinkled his brow.

"Yeah, stage four." I nodded

"I cannot imagine the hell you must have gone through," he said solemnly. After a pause, he asked, "You're married, aren't you?"

"Yeah, four years now."

"What is your wife's name?" he asked with genuine interest.

"Her name is Megan." Her face popped into my head as I said her name. I felt a pang to have her.

"You and Meagan have to come over to my house and have dinner," he said excitedly.

"I can eat?" I asked.

"Of course, that was one of my main concerns what is life without food? So, what do you say?"

"Of course, we'd love to." It was hard to say no to the guy who had you resurrected.

"Do you like sushi?" He arched his eyebrow.

"I do but she doesn't like sushi." I rolled my eyes.

"What? How can she not like sushi?" he said incredulously.

"Tell me about it, I've been trying for years to get her to eat it, but every time I do, she gags on it." I laughed for the first time with my new voice.

"How about Italian then? She does like Italian, doesn't she?" he said, sounding mildly concerned.

"Yeah, she will eat just about anything Italian."

"Good, I was beginning to wonder about her." He reached into his jacket pocket. "Here, take my card, once you get back home and settle in, call or message me and we will set something up." He looked at me with an appraising eye. "I'm still amazed by you no matter what you say." Orson Peak opened the door and on the other side was a blue and white Servi.

"Excuse me," it said then moved so that Orson could leave then it entered the room.

"Is there anything I can get for you?" it said. Its voice mimicked that of a female

"No," I said, and it started to leave for the door. Then something struck me, and I said "wait." it turned about and faced me. Servi's all had the same placid expression that never changed.

"How may I help you?" it asked. I understood only on a basic level how Servi's operated in the same sense I only basically knew how my car was powered and the engine functioned. I knew that Servi's were intelligent on a level with humans but that they lacked what one might call free will as they needed the impetus of human direction to give them an action to do anything. They could do anything asked of them even the solving of problems however they were incapable of acting on impulse. This lack of free will was contrived to prevent runaway artificial intelligence that movies and books had so thoroughly taught us to fear. But what I didn't know and wanted to know was, "what do you think of yourself." I pointed at it.

"What do you mean?" it asked in its plain but courteous manner.

"Do you consider yourself to be alive?" I asked.

It paused for a moment then answered, "I am fully functional."

"Rather I mean are you alive in the way humans are alive?" I refined my question.

"No, I am not," it answered cordially.

"Do you know why I am here?"

"Yes Dr. Jacobina is your care provider, you have just undergone a procedure to transfer data from a human body to an artificial one, and this was completed at 3:04 pm today." it rattled off succinctly.

"Would you say I am alive?" I asked.

What if it said I wasn't? What would that mean?

"I do not know." This non-answer did nothing to satisfy the thing deep inside of me that wanted to know one way or another what I was.

"Neither do I," I said.

Was one alive because they had a heartbeat? Certainly, that doesn't matter because we considered plants to be alive. Was it the ability to reproduce that made things alive? There are plenty of animals born inherently sterile like mules so that couldn't be it, not to mention that viruses could reproduce in their way and, yet they are not considered alive. Is being alive the ability to die? I was not sure if I could die, but it seemed that all things that we consider to be traditionally alive could die, even functionally immortal animals like those jellyfish that revert to their pupil stage could die when they were eaten.

"I am sorry I could not be of more help." I regarded it, even though its face and voice could not show lament I felt that was being genuine.

I shook my head. "It's not your fault. Dr. Jacobina refers to what has happened to me as a 'data transfer,' the man who just left said I came back from the dead and I simply don't know what to think. The memories I possess were created in a different mind, in a different brain, in a different body that is no longer alive. I woke up in this body." I gestured to myself. "So, I have the illusion of continuity, but if the other body were still alive it would still be me and I would be the me that is currently in this body. While we would share the same memories and thought processes, I am almost positive that me in the body that died, would consider my current self to not be the true Albert but rather a copy." It stood very still as I spoke taking in all I had to say, for that I was grateful. "I have memories," I tapped my head with my new gray hand. But they are not inherently mine. By possessing memories are they yours? Are thoughts and memories the same as identity? I ask because I do not know the answer." I shrugged and shook my head.

The Servi was quiet for a time then it reported back to me. "I am not sure, but I will endeavor to find an answer for you," it said in its earnest manner. I had never given a Servi much thought before but now it seemed to me that I was somewhere between them and humanity; not quite human as I now lacked a human body and human DNA nor was I a service-bot in that I had free will as much as any human did. I didn't think it was fair to say I was an evolved form of humanity though I did think it was fair to say I was no longer human.

"Thanks for your time," I said sincerely.

"You are welcome." it bowed its head then turned and left.

Chapter

02

Albert:

I was pacing back and forth in Dr. Jacobina's office as I waited for Megan to arrive. I felt incredibly nervous. Not knowing what would happen was killing me; uncertainty had a way of eating me up from the inside. When I had my first MRI to determine if I had cancer, I worked myself up so badly waiting for the results that I didn't have a solid bowel for the week before the appointment for the results. I had been that way as far back as I could remember. For whatever reason whenever I was stressed about something that I could not control I would often play out scenarios in my head until I could no longer think straight. In my mind, I saw my first post-death interaction with Megan going one of two ways:

Megan is elated that I am not gone, and we can attempt to go on with our lives.

Megan rejects me for some reason and never wants anything to do with me ever again.

I honestly had no contingency plan if she decided to cut ties with me. It's hard to describe how close I was with Megan or how much she meant to me. We had known each other and had been each other's best friend for so long that there had never been any other person I would have considered spending my life with. She meant more to me than literally and figuratively anything else in the entire universe, so to lose her would have meant to lose a part of what made me, me. I had no idea what one was supposed to do if the most important person in one's life walked away. I heard muffled voices from behind the door, the door opened, and Megan came into the room then stopped as soon as she saw me. Megan's face was red and swollen from crying, her mouth hung open slightly.

"I'll leave you two alone for a moment," Dr. Jacobina gave me a kind smile as she left.

Tears rolled down Megan's cheeks. Instinctively, I took a step towards Megan to take her into my arms, but she retreated away from me, it would have hurt less to have been crushed under the heel of a giant boot.

"It's me I promise," I said in a voice she had never heard before. She shook her head side to side slowly. I tried to crack my knuckles out of habit but was unable to.

"It's me. It's me, I swear it's me," I pleaded.

Tears rolled down her face. "No," she whimpered. I moved towards her, she turned and went quickly out the door. I went out the door after her. Dr. Jacobina, who was waiting by the doorway, grabbed me by the arm. "Albert don't."

"I can't just let her go," I said in a panic.

"Chasing after her may only make this worse. Come in and have a seat," she said, directing me back into her office. I fell back onto the sofa and slumped forward placing my face into my hands smelling the same acrid scent on them as before. Dr. Jacobina sat down next to me which made the leather groan.

"She's afraid of me. She jumped every time I moved," I told Dr. Jacobina.

"She is still in shock. You died and then came back in a matter of hours. How would you take it if the shoe were on the other foot?" she asked.

"I don't know." I shook my head.

"That's just it, she doesn't know what to do. She is torn between the feeling of loss and the feeling that while you are different you still exist, it is fair to say that no one else has ever been in the situation she is in at this moment," Dr. Jacobina explained.

"But what do I do? I mean how do I get her over this?" I asked.

"You don't. The best thing you can do is let her process this and not to pressure her, let her find out that you are the same person you have always been."

What if I am not the same person, though?

Megan:

A doctor from the hospital where Albert...well, where he died, called, and asked me to come in and discuss a matter about Albert. They had not said exactly what they needed me for, they just said it needed to be done in person. Albert had decided that he wanted to donate his body to science, so I assumed they needed me to sign some paperwork regarding that. I walked down the narrow stairs of my ancient duplex apartment out onto the algae-stained wooden porch which slanted slightly away from the house giving the feeling it could detach and fall off at any moment. I unplugged the red sedan from the side of the house. I swiped my thumb on the lock, got in, and told the car to head to the hospital. We didn't live far from the hospital. Normally, I would have just walked but since Albert passed, I have had an utter lack of energy, and the walk down the stairs to the car felt like a mile and a year.

There was a gaping hole in my life now that couldn't be filled. I didn't even know what to do with myself anymore. Albert wasn't just my husband; he was my best friend. I had work friends, but Albert was my only real friend. He was the only one I could talk about anything with. He was the person I came to when I was sad or worried or had something funny to say and now, he was gone. I had no one to hold me, to tell me it was going to be okay, and without him, I would never be okay again.

The car parked itself in a space. I went to the reception desk and asked for Dr. Jacobina, the woman who had called me. The receptionist who paged her told me the doctor would be with me in a moment. I had been at the hospital more than at home for the past few months, so long that it no longer smelled strange to me as hospitals often do.

"Megan?" a woman with a slight accent in a lab coat asked.

"Yes," I said.

"I'm Dr. Jacobina, do you mind following me?" she asked, and I nodded. We walked down a hallway of offices and she spoke while we did.

"As you may know, your husband donated his body to science. When a person donates their body, it is often used to test experimental procedures." We stopped outside of an office with her name on the door.

"Your husband was selected as a viable candidate for a procedure that recovers data from the mind of the recently deceased. This was the first time such a procedure had been attempted on a human, so we felt it was best to wait to inform you in case it didn't work, but I am happy to say it was an astounding success." I didn't understand what she was getting at.

"You can speak with him if you'd like," she said, and my heart seized at her words.

"Speak with him?" I asked.

"Yes." She opened the door to her office. A gray figure stood wearing green scrubs.

"I'll leave you two alone for a moment," she said shutting the door. Suddenly, I felt trapped with it. It stepped towards me, and I backed away from it.

"It's me. It's me, I swear it's me," it said desperately. Listening to it talk, disgusted me on a physical level. Why would they do this? Who would create such a thing? A machine that thinks it's someone else. A machine that thought it was human. This was cruel on so many levels. Whether or not that thing thought it was Albert didn't matter. My husband was gone, and no machine could replace him.

"No," was all I could say. I couldn't look at it anymore. I couldn't stand to see its desperation. I couldn't hear it say another word. It took another step towards me, and I ran. I passed the doctor who was waiting outside of the door. I couldn't see past the tears in my eyes. I hurried out of the hospital and into the parking lot. I wiped away tears so that I could find my car. I got in and found myself unable to catch my breath, tears came, and they wouldn't stop.

"Home," I said to the car. It took off. I wanted Albert, I wanted to bury my face in his chest, I wanted to feel the heat of his body. I wanted to smell his cologne. I wanted him, but I could never have him again. The car parked itself. I went into the house up the narrow stairs, crawled into the bed, grabbed Albert's pillow, took a deep breath in, and sobbed without end.

A weight sunk into the bed, then I heard a purring near my ear. It was Puck, Albert's black and white tomcat. I pulled him into my arms, he nuzzled me and purred. Puck had loved Albert as much as I did. We had both lost the most important person in our lives. How could we go on? I knew it was selfish, but I wish it had been me who had died instead then he wouldn't be gone, and I wouldn't be here without him.

After a while, I fell asleep with a Puck in my arms.

Orson:

I was having dinner at home with my husband Elliot when Dr. Jacobina rang through my Smart-Lenses. Normally, I don't answer calls during dinner, but I was afraid something was wrong with Albert.

"What can I do for you, doctor?" I asked.

"I have sad news. Alberts wife didn't take the news well," she said. My mind tried to grasp the meaning of her words. Why wouldn't she be happy that her husband was alive? I couldn't fathom Elliot dying, so if he did die, I couldn't imagine being anything but happy to have him back.

"What happened?" I asked.

"I asked her to come down because Albert wanted to see her. I gave them some time together and she left abruptly. Mr. Kindred said she was terribly upset." I closed my eyes and took a deep breath. "Orson, are you there?" she asked.

"I have to go. I'll talk to you tomorrow." I hung up on her before I could yell at her. I swore and hit the table with both fists which caused the silver wear to jump with a clang.

"Everything okay?" Elliot asked casually, putting a roasted potato into his mouth.

"No, Albert, the guy we brought back, his wife didn't take the news well," I said.

"I would think she'd be happy. What happened?" Elliot asked.

"Doctoral incompetence. This is bad without his wife. Albert has no money, no house, and no car. Nothing," I said. I looked at my food and felt completely disinterested in resuming my meal.

"Just have him come stay with us until his wife comes around," Elliot proffered.

"You wouldn't mind?"

"No, it would be nice if we could get some use out of one of the spare bedrooms at least," Elliot said.

"I don't know what I am going to do about his wife," I said.

"Hopefully, she will come around," Elliot said.

Elliot's optimism had never rubbed off on me. Part of the reason I enjoyed working with machines and artificial intelligence was that you could predict what they would do before they even did it. Humans on the other hand were unreliable and unpredictable. You could never be sure of what any person was going to do.

What was even more frustrating was that up until this happened everything had gone better than I could have hoped for. Especially since this was our first crack at uploading the mind of a human and because we had been limited in whom we could effectively perform the procedure with. The person in question needed to have died shortly before the procedure was to be performed. In addition, there couldn't be any damage to the brain which eliminated those who had a traumatic brain injury or those who had suffered a stroke. In this regard, Albert had been as close to perfect a subject as we could have hoped for, he had died in a hospital of a disease that had not affected his brain. Even then, I was surprised when it worked the first time. We had to try so many times with nonhuman test subjects to get it right. I honestly assumed this attempt would be a failure. I wasn't even fully satisfied with the containment body yet. The only shining light is that the procedure has left Albert with all of his memories, and his personality has been retained as well. He was a complete success, as far as technological successes go. But if Albert's wife didn't accept him, it could put a negative light on our accomplishment. Things needed to go well for Albert; all eyes would soon be on him. I don't think Albert understood yet how important he was. After all, he was the first in a new line of humanity, the first Post-human, and as such his future was limitless, free from sickness and death. He would see things beyond any imagination.

I now had a new problem. I was going to have to try to explain to the board members why they needed to wait on announcing that the project was a success, despite the two hundred billion dollars they had invested in it and the massive jump in stock price that would result from the announcement, not to mention all the money they would make off providing this as a service. Bringing someone back from the dead was easy compared to doing that.

Albert:

It had grown dark outside my hospital window; the traffic had slowed down on the street below. I pressed my face against the glass and tried to see my apartment from where I was, but the curvature of the road made it impossible. I walked away from the glass, circled the room twice, and came back to the window. I closed my eyes and tried to imagine Megan in bed asleep. I pictured myself crawling into bed with her and brushing away her curly hair from her face. I wished that I could have smelled the conditioner in her hair. I was eaten up with the desire to hold her while she slept even if only for a moment.

I turned from the window and walked into the hallway outside of my room. I didn't see any nurses or Servi's, so I walked down the hall until I found an elevator. I took the elevator downstairs. Outside of the elevator was a glass wall on the other side of which was a courtyard. I walked along this wall until I found a door that led out to the courtyard which was lit by the nearly full moon. Ahead of me was an archway that led to a parking lot. I stepped onto the blacktop with my bare gray feet. It was a short walk from the blacktop to the sidewalk and I soon found myself walking down the cracked and uneven sidewalk to my apartment. I had not intentionally decided to talk to my apartment but when I realized that I was I didn't turn around.

I walked past the used bookstore. Stopped in the parking lot of the auto garage that was across the street from our apartment. The apartment was a duplex with a driveway on either side only big enough for one car. We lived on the upper floor which I had liked when we had first moved in but learned to hate increasingly each time we went grocery shopping. The place was ratty both literally and figuratively. The mouse problem delighted Theo and Puck who made a sport out of killing them. Beyond the mouse, problems were the electrical issues. The overhead light in the kitchen had stopped working shortly after we moved in. We had similar issues with light fixtures throughout the house none of which I had ever been able to get the property owner to fix. so, we had lamps everywhere.

The whole house was dark, not even the porch lights were on. I looked up at the top front window where our bedroom was. I hoped to at least see one of the cats in the window, but I could only see darkness. I stared up at the house until a car came towards me. Its headlights illuminated me. I turned away from the house and hoped nobody in the car had seen my gray face. I looked at the window one last time then walked back to the hospital.

I laid in the hospital bed with the lights off for a while but sleep never came. I was emotionally worn out, but I didn't have a hint of physical fatigue. I was as comfortable as one could be in a hospital bed. I was able to quiet my mind for a time but still, no sleep came. Usually, I would put on my smart lenses until I fell asleep. Unfortunately, I had the sinking suspicion that they were still in my eyes on my dead body. This left me with an uncomfortable feeling.

I turned the TV to the news. They were discussing the infidelity of a senator who had a child with someone who wasn't his wife. A man who was wearing a black suit with a hideous red tie with a flashy gold cross as his tie pin was going red in the face while he declared, "This man does not represent the Christian values this nation was founded on." I rolled my eyes. "To quote Leviticus 20:10 'If there is a man who commits adultery with another man's wife, one who commits adultery with his friend's wife, the adulterer and the adulteress shall surely be put to death,'" he said with self-righteous indignation.

The female newscaster looked flummoxed. "Are you suggesting that the senator should be put to death?"

"That is not for me to decide, it is for the lord to decide for I do not judge my fellow man." If he weren't judging his fellow man, I would have hated to see what real judgment looked like. I turned off the TV in anger. I had grown a dislike for TV in recent years. Reality TV had never held much interest for me because it seemed more scripted than the scripted shows. The scripted shows were awful because there was a drive to have more drama at the expense of realism, like when two detectives get into a brawl over how the case is going, and they yell back and forth in the middle of the station. That simply isn't the way it goes. If you ever watch a documentary about a murder case, the detectives are usually pretty laid back about the whole affair, which makes sense, because if, week after week, cops had to put up with the kind of havoc that goes on in TV shows, they would have a mental breakdown. Sitcoms were not funny because the characters are often just a collection of stereotypes that we are supposed to think are funny instead of complex individuals who have traits that are both positive and negative and who get into funny and relatable situations.

For me, the only two things left on TV worth watching were the news and documentaries. I only watched the news in small doses; otherwise, I became enraged at the commentators and the dribble they held up as news these days, like the senator who impregnated the woman he was sleeping with. That is not news that is gossip, and it is frankly uninteresting and unimportant. I would, however, devour documentaries. If there was a documentary about some small slice of life I had never heard of or experienced before I was all over that. My favorite was on Hulix about space. It was simply amazing to watch on my Smart-Lenses as they completely envelop your vision and put you in the middle of the shot.

As I lay in the hospital bed the sky outside of my window showed daylight was near. I gave up on sleep and decided to go down to the courtyard again.

Chapter

03

Albert:

I watched two birds in the mulch of a flower bed as they fought each other. Their bodies were small but plump. I could have held both in one hand. I watched these two small creatures as they made war, though I was sure it was of immense importance to them whatever they were fighting over. I found it to be cute and trivial. That must be what the gods felt like when they looked upon us.

"Hello, Albert." I turned my head to see Dr. Jacobina approaching me, her hair was pulled back in a tight bun again.

"Hi," I said and looked back to find the war had ended.

"How are you doing today?" she asked, taking a seat next to me on the bench.

"Fine, I guess but I couldn't sleep," I told her.

"What was keeping you up?" she tilted her head to the side.

"I just never felt tired, I still don't," I told her.

"Oh, that's odd."

"I thought so too," I said.

"The test subjects have not had any troubles with sleep," she said.

"Test subjects?" That was the first I had heard of any other subjects.

"Yes, several mice and one primate," she said matter-of-factly.

"The poor things," I said in horror.

"All great medical advances come on the backs of animals," she said.

"That still doesn't make it any less unsettling," I said.

She shrugged then asked, "Do you feel tired?"

"No, like not at all. Which is strange isn't it?"

"It is different, that is for sure," she agreed.

"I like to sleep quite a bit. A life devoid of dreaming seems like only watching the commercial that is life."

With a chuckle, she said, "Let me know if this continues to happen and we will get you some sleep."

"Please, otherwise I am going to have some serious time to kill." The thought of another endless night like the one I just had, was enough to make me want to cry.

"Other than the lack of sleep, how are you doing?" she asked.

I am not sure if I am alive or even the same person I once was, and my wife is afraid of me touching her. "I'm okay. I just wish I could take a shower," I told her.

"You can do that," she told me.

"You have just become my savior. My hands smell like trash bags, and it has been driving me nuts." She grimaced, and I nodded.

Dr. Jacobina and I walked back up to my hospital room. Along the way, I asked her about other things I could and could not do.

"Can I wear my Smart-Lens?" I asked.

"Yes, you can, your eyes are moistened enough to keep your Smart-Lenses from drying out," she said.

"How do I uh you know...I mean I have a-" I pointed down at my crotch.

"How do you achieve an erection?" she asked with the bluntness only medical professionals possess. I nodded and felt thankful that I couldn't blush without blood.

"Your new brain simulates the reactions that you have during arousal. The body senses those reactions and inflates the penis," she said clinically.

"Well, that's...uh okay then," I stammered.

The elevator opened; we stepped off into the hallway.

"Can I punch through a wall?" I asked seriously.

"No, why would you want to do that anyway?" She cut me an incredulous look.

"I don't but I wanted to know if I could. How fast can I run?"

"Just about as fast anyone else can, you are not Superman," she said.

"Damn, what's the point of having a machine body if I can't have superpowers," I joked.

"The idea was to let you have a normal life, not to make you a superhero." She had a point.

We went to my room and there was Orson Peak looking out the window at the road below. He wore a three-piece navy suit with brown wingtip dress shoes.

"Albert, doctor, it's nice to see you both. I brought you some clothes to change into. I figured you would like to have something to wear besides those scrubs. Oh, and you are going to want these back." He patted down his suit coat pockets. He pulled a Smart-Lens case out of his inside pocket.

Orson didn't owe me anything, he had nothing to gain from me, if actions define who you are then Orson was a good man. "I appreciate it," I said, taking the Smart-Lens from Orson.

He waved it off. "We'll step out, so you can change," Orson said.

Orson:

We stepped Out in the hallway to give Albert some privacy, so I took the opportunity to speak with Dr. Jacobina. "I wanted to let you know that I am taking Albert with me today," I informed her.

"He shouldn't leave here yet, he's still getting used to his new body and we don't know if there will be any complications," she explained patiently.

"Amelia, we both know that yesterday was hell for him, I think he deserves to get out of here," I said.

"If you take him out in public there's no telling how people might react or what that will do to him," she said.

"We can't hide him away forever. No matter what we do he's going to be on every news outlet before long and then all eyes will be on him," I said.

"I'm just trying to stave that off for as long as possible," she said.

"He will have a better chance of going unnoticed at my house." Three people in white coats walked past us.

She took a breath. "Fine, but please take care of him, he's already been through so much."

"I wish we would have waited and broken the news to his wife more gently instead of rushing into it," I said, trying not to toss the blame completely on her.

"I wanted to wait but he insisted on seeing her. I didn't know what else to do," she said, putting her palms out.

"So, you just threw them in a room together and hoped for the best?" I said more harshly than I meant to. There was a moment when we looked away from each other." I'm sorry."

"No, you are right they deserved better than what they got. We will have to come up with a better way of managing these sorts of situations in the future," she said with strong resolve.

"I wonder if I spoke with his wife if I could make her understand." I knew they didn't live far from where we were. I could go there and speak with her. Make her understand everything.

"I tried calling her, but she wouldn't answer. I think the best thing we can do now is give her time and space."

Albert:

Inside the shopping bags, Orson had brought was a black T-shirt. In another bag were dark blue denim jeans. In another bag black boxer briefs, black socks, and in the last bag there was a pair of black and white converse shoes. I put everything on, and I laced up the shoes. I picked up the Smart-Lens case which was white with an eye on each screw-off cap, with one eye winking. The lenses had a silver ring that encircled the iris of the eye it was on. I popped one in each eye. I blinked rapidly until the lenses were charged enough to work. My vision was distorted by the overcorrection of the lenses for my former vision. I said aloud "calibrate lenses." The lenses made small adjustments until my vision quality improved. I looked at myself in the mirror, the dark-colored outfit helped to downplay the color of my skin but with more than a passing glance, I was still unmistakably gray. I went out to where Orson and Dr. Jacobina were. I held my arms out at my sides

"Looks good. So, I'm heading back to my house, and you can come if you want," Orson said.

How could I say no? I had spent entirely too much time in hospitals. We rode the elevators down to the lobby. We stopped at the curb. Orson looked at his hand, snapped his fingers, and a black two-door sports car pulled itself up to us just as silently as if it weren't there. I'm not a car guy but Orison's car was beautiful. Orson thumbed us into the car. Inside was an all-leather interior with seats that adjusted to the shape of my body.

"Home," Orson said, and the car was off without a sound. I couldn't feel the car move at all. The only way I could tell we were even driving was the buildings that flicked by. The hospital disappeared behind us. There had been a time when I thought I would never leave the hospital again. I smiled at the small triumph.

We rode out of the city into the suburbs then out of the suburbs into a more rural area. The houses got farther and farther apart as farms took over the landscape. The car slowed to turn down an unmarked driveway that was lined with a row of trees on either side. At the end of the driveway was a house, though mansion was a better term. It was sprawling and very modern; it didn't fit with the more classic farmhouses in the area, but it was attractive. The car went around the circular drive, in front of the house and stopped so we could get out. The car left us to go into its garage. We took the three steps up to the front door which opened automatically. The foyer of the house had white marble floors with two halls on either side of the room and two staircases one going up and one going down. Art hung on the walls along with statues on various surfaces. Orson took off his jacket and hung it on the coat rack near the door.

A Servi came down the hall nearest Orson. "Hello, sir," it said in a male voice. It wore a gray sweater vest and a white dress shirt black trousers and black loafers, making it look altogether more human despite its exposed joints and seams.

"Hello, Vincent, this is Albert. Please do anything he asks," Orson said.

"Albert, can I do anything for you?" it asked its face a neutral expression that all Servis have.

"Oh, no, I'm fine, thanks," I said.

It bowed its head slightly then looked back at Orson. "Your husband wanted me to ask you what you would like to eat for dinner."

"I don't know. What do we have?" Orson asked.

"Acorn squash, Apples, bananas, butter..." Orson held a hand up and closed his eyes realizing his error.

"What meals do we have the ingredients for?" he rephrased.

"Acorn squash soup, Chicken enchiladas, Eggplant parmesan, and Garlic roasted chicken with rosemary. I can also go to the store if you would like, sir," Vincent said.

"What do you think?" Orson asked me.

"Eggplant parmesan?" I said.

"Eggplant parmesan please, Vincent," Orson said the Servi bowed its head and left.

"Have you had a chance to eat, yet?" Orson asked me.

"No, not yet," I told him.

"Come on," Orson gestured with his head, and I followed. "You won't need to eat to survive, however, I feel that without food there's not much point to life."

"I am inclined to agree with you." We entered the kitchen. The counter was white marble with a white tile backsplash on the wall. There was an area on the counter where herbs grew under a grow light. Vincent was already working on dinner. As Orson approached the fridge, the screen on the door came to life displaying what was inside of it. Orson reached in, grabbed an apple, said "catch," tossing me the apple which I caught. "Reflexes seem good," he said.

I followed him out of the kitchen into a parlor that had four armchairs around a glass coffee table in front of a stone fireplace. We sat opposite each other. He looked at me expectantly, so I bit into the apple. I chewed and rolled it around in my mouth.

"Well?" he asked hopefully.

I swallowed and looked at the apple. It was a Gala apple which was one of my favorites. It was ripe but, "It tastes different," I said and took another bite.

"Different how?" he asked.

"I don't know," I said with a mouthful of apple. "It's not bad but it's just not how I remember an apple tasting."

Orson looked disappointed. He stared into the middle distance while I chewed my apple. It wasn't so different that I didn't like the apple but if I had been blindfolded and asked to say what I was eating, I couldn't have put my finger on it.

"The red you see isn't the red I see," he said, still looking off into space.

"Hmm?" I said chewing.

He pointed to the apple. "When I look at that apple, I see what my brain interprets as red but what my brain interprets as red may be blue to you," he explained.

"Yeah, but it still looks red. Like the red, I remember," I said.

"Really? Now that is interesting, I wonder if that is simply a happy accident or if your memories influence the way you see things," Orson said.

"Wouldn't the colors I see be determined by my eyes?" I asked.

"You would think but the ancient Greeks like Homer did not have a word for the color blue, so he referred to the sea as being wine-colored. We see the difference between the sea and wine because we have a word for the color blue. Which suggests color is less a physical sensation and more of a mental interpretation," Orson said.

"What about color blind people?" I asked. "I mean they can't tell the difference between red and green and that's physical. They lack the receptors to differentiate between colors."

"That's true but it's different in your case. You have always had the ability to see the color spectrum and can still do so with your current vision, so it's hard to say if your current eyes are just tuned to what your vision was naturally or if that is the way your mind interprets the wavelength we call red," Orson said.

"I wonder if that's why I can't feel things like I use to."

"You can't feel things?" he said, his brow furrowed.

I held up the apple. "It's weird, I know I am touching the apple, but I don't feel it. I can tell that it has weight," I hefted the apple in my hand.

"I know that it is smooth" I rubbed the skin with my thumb.

"But I don't feel it, I know it. Like if you had thrown it at me and hit me in the head, I don't think it would have hurt. I would have known you hit me with it. There is something lost between the touch and what should be the sensation of the apple in my hand," I said, looking at the apple with regard.

"I wonder if there is some overlap between what pain is and what sensations are? Does one need the pain to feel? I'm sorry to say it might be my fault we dampened your pain reception because it seemed like a clever idea, but pain is essential to our experience of the world," Orson said regretfully.

"Makes me wonder then if sleep isn't just relief from the pain of exhaustion. No pain, no sleep," I said.

"I don't know," he said and pursed his lips.

"I'm going to miss sleep," I said glumly.

"I would love to not have to sleep, I could get so much done."

"You must not get bored as I do. When I don't have something to do or somewhere to be, I would curl up with my cat and go to sleep for a bit." There was a pang inside of me for those times.

"I stay up at night thinking about all the things I need to do until my body gives out." He laughed.

"I guess that's why you have all that you do but you couldn't pay me enough to feel that sort of stress," I told him.

"For me, it's not about the money, anymore. When I was younger and first starting in life it was all I could think about but once I had it, I realized that the world was no better for it, and I felt guilty. I decided to leave humanity better off than how I found it. You are a part of that." He pointed at me.

I shook my head. "I appreciate the sentiment but there's not much I can do to help you out."

"You are already doing it. You are walking on the moon, taking the small steps so the rest of us can take the giant leap that follows. Everything you are doing is a first." He pointed to the apple in my hand which had begun to brown "even eating that apple is a first. We will learn so much from you." He leaned forward in his seat. "No matter what or who you were before, you are first in a new era of humanity," he said with reverence.

I was about to respond when a male voice came from somewhere in the house. "Marco!"

"Polo! We are by the fireplace," Orson replied. A man entered the room and Orson and I both stood up. "Albert this is my husband, Elliot. Elliot, this is Albert," Orson said. Elliott was a tall rail-thin man with light blond hair; he wore a light grey suit and his tie undone.

Elliot and I shook hands. "It's nice to meet you, Elliot."

"You too Albert. What did you pick for dinner?" Elliot asked Orson.

"Albert picked eggplant parmesan," Orson said.

"Figures, Orson would never eat a veggie again if he could get away with it," Elliot said and rolled his eyes.

"Anyway," Orson interjected. "How was work?"

"It was okay, we are still working on them," Elliott said

"Elliot is a lawyer," Orson said with a smile. "He is petitioning the UN to allow my company to dismantle Mercury, so we can construct a Dyson swarm," saying it the way one might describe landscaping plans to a friend.

My mouth hung open slightly. I tried to find something to say but found there were no words to say to the man who tells you he wants to dismantle an entire planet. "Wh- I just- are you a supervillain?" I asked in all seriousness. Both Orson and Elliot started laughing which was unsettling.

"Dinner is ready," Vincent said from the doorway.

Chapter

04

Albert:

We sat down at the table in the kitchen, Orson and Elliot still chuckling. "Have you heard of a Dyson swarm?" Orson asked.

"No." It sounded like a superweapon.

"It's a collection of devices that orbit the sun and collect its energy," Orson said.

"But What would you use it for?" I asked. Vincent sat down bread in a basket along with three plates of eggplant parmesan over rigatoni pasta.

"Interstellar travel, large scale computer processing power, transmitters that could potentially allow us to communicate with extraterrestrials, the options go on and on. The swarm would be gigantic in scale, and you would need a lot of building material to construct it with more than we could extract from the earth without dismantling it as well." Orson spread butter on a piece of bread.

"Oh, they wouldn't let you do that?" I said sarcastically. I took a bite of the eggplant parmesan again, not as I remembered but it tasted pleasant.

"Anyway," he said ignoring me. "The easiest place to get this material from would be Mercury. What you do is you send a few machines, even only one if you are willing to wait a while. These machines will be able to mine the raw materials, process them into usable materials then build and replicate themselves. As they mine more, they will be able to make more of themselves to mine more and make more and so on until you have enough of these machines for your first Dyson swarm array. The pieces of the array will then convert themselves into solar energy harvesters they will then collect energy from the sun and send it back to earth as your energy needs rise you just move on to other planets." Orson cut into his eggplant parmesan.

"You are insane." I looked over at Elliot. "He's insane and you are helping him." Elliot laughed and shook his head.

"It's not that big of a deal, it's a large-scale mining operation at its basic level," Orson said.

"You want to dismantle a whole planet? Like, I mean it's a planet, is that even legal?" I asked.

"There are no laws against it per se, however, Orson believes and so do I, that the global community deserves the right to decide if they are okay with it," Elliot said.

"My stance on the matter is that eventually we will need to do this, and it is better to do it now when the need is low, rather than when we are in dire need of the energy. I think the benefits that we will obtain outweigh what we will lose, which is a dead planet," Orson said dipping bread in the red sauce.

"I think this is a slippery slope. In a thousand years or a million years from now, we might miss the planets we do this to," I said.

"Without resource extraction, we wouldn't be where we are now," Elliott said.

"It could be said that that's an argument against doing it. We caused so much devastation by extracting resources and using them up as we pleased, regardless of what it did to the environment and now we are trying to repair that damage. Who's to say what kind of damage dismantling planets would cause to the interstellar environment." I took a piece of bread from the basket and dipped it into the sauce. The bread was crusty on the outside but warm and soft on the inside. It was odd not to recognize the taste of something as basic as bread.

"We would have to be careful as to what planets we chose to use," Orson said.

"But that's just it. People in the future might not be as careful as you are now. Who's to say what planets are okay to do this too. Mercury is okay. Is it Mars?" I asked.

"Mars has value beyond its raw materials. I doubt we would ever dismantle mars," Orson said.

"My point is who chooses what planets it is okay to do this too. Let's just say it's okay to dismantle any or all the planets in our solar system. After all, they are in our solar system. What about planets in different systems? Are they ours to use?" I asked.

"I would say if the benefits of their use outweighs the cost of their loss then, yes," Orson said.

"What if a planet has life?" I speared a piece of pasta and ate it.

"Then no, I would say that that planet should be left alone," Orson said.

"You say that, but a future galactic tycoon might not. The destruction of native species did not stop us from extracting resources at their expense. Put the shoe on the other foot. What if some aliens came through our solar system a few million years ago before humans evolved but there was still life and those aliens started gobbling up planets? Not earth but Mercury, Mars, and any other planets they did a cost-benefit analysis on and decided that it was okay to destroy them. Would they be in the right to have done that? Wouldn't you be a little pissed?" I asked.

Orson smiled at me. "The evils of advancement are many in number. Perhaps if someone like you had stood up to the first person who wanted to extract fossil fuels out of the earth, we wouldn't have the issues we currently do, but I also don't think we would have all the advancements that we do and in the long run, it helped more than it hurt. I feel the same way about the Dyson swarm," Orson said.

"I understand why you have trouble sleeping now," I said, and Orson laughed.

After dinner, the three of us went into the living room sitting on the chairs in front of the fireplace. Orson and Elliot sat next to each other and across from me.

"Have you given any thought to what you might want to do now?" Elliott asked me.

"I don't know," I said, letting out a nervous laugh while looking at the floor. "My main concern right now is my wife." The look of fear on Megan's face flooded into my head. I tried to crack my knuckles, but nothing happened. Orson's face fell for a moment, but he recovered. Elliot seemed not to be able to look at me.

Orson spoke up. "Are you busy tomorrow?" he asked me.

"No," I said.

"I have to go to LA, and I wanted to see if you'd come with me," Orson said.

"Sure, I haven't been to LA since I was a kid."

"We'll take the Loop there in the morning," Orson said.

I looked down at my wrist on which my Smart Lenses displayed a clock at 9:41 pm. The time had gone and went.

"I didn't realize what time it was. I should let you guys get to bed. I should call a car," I said even though I had no idea how I'd pay for it. I hoped Orson wouldn't mind driving me back to the hospital.

"Now, Albert, I hope you know you are staying here tonight," Elliot said with a commanding tone. I thought this must be the lawyer in him.

"Oh, I am?" I felt an immense swell of gratitude in my chest for Orson and Elliot.

"I will be offended if you don't." Elliot pointed his finger at me.

"In that case, I guess I had better stay, then," I smiled broadly.

"Indeed, come on I'll show you to your bedroom," Elliot said standing up. I followed him upstairs. There was a hallway of doors. He opened one and showed me. "There is a full bathroom in there." He pointed to a door. "Across the hall from you is a library, we are at the end of the hall if you need us."

"I just wanted to say I appreciate you guys letting me stay here. No matter how much time you spend in hospitals you never quite get used to them," I said.

"It's no problem, honestly I'm happy to have someone use the room for once, we have six rooms and Orson never lets anyone sleep over." He sounded annoyed. "Anyway, have a good night," Elliot said.

"You too," I said. Elliot closed the door behind him as he left.

For the second night in a row, I didn't feel tired, nor did I feel like I could have asleep. I went into the bathroom, the light flicked on automatically. The mirror displayed my weight in the lower right-hand corner, 227 pounds, which seemed heavy, but I supposed that the metal I was now composed of weighed me down more than flesh would. I took off my clothes and dropped them on the floor, slid open the shower door and there was a digital panel.

I pressed a green button that made the water startup, the screen display 105 F as the water temperature. I stepped in. The water hit me, and I knew it was hitting me. I knew that the water was warm but again I didn't feel it. The sensation I wanted so badly was just out of reach. Annoyed, I pressed the arrow to make the temperature go up. I pressed it until the temperature would not go up anymore. 125 F. Steam rolled around me. In my old body, I would have been pinned against the wall in burning pain but now I merely knew the temperature had gone up, there was no pain. It was strange to miss pain.

I washed up and turned off the water. The water beaded and rolled off my skin. I toweled off what little water still clung to my body. I put back on the same clothes. I examined the room which was minimally decorated. There was a king-sized bed, a nightstand, and a bench at the end of the bed. There was also a walk-in closet that had extra blankets and sheets in it and empty coat hangers.

I went across the hall to the library. Wooden bookcases went from the floor to the ceiling and wrapped around the entire room with a rolling ladder on each of the four walls. In the center of the room were two leather chairs in front of a coffee table and a long table with six chairs at it. I scanned the books on the shelves where they were organized by subject. Most of them were either scientific work or a law book. I turned away from the shelf and my eyes fell upon a section of the bookshelf marked 'Misc. books.' I had never heard of any of these books. There were odd self-help-looking books but one book whose size caused it to jet out from the rest of the books, caught my eye "On Being" by Augustus Foss. It was a black book with an image of a galaxy on the front. The spine had been broken several times over and the pages were yellowed. I cracked it open; the entire book was written in aphorisms. I read from the one that was in the center of the page I opened to:

"The physics that govern our universe are such that no energy is ever lost, only transmuted. Energy is mass multiplied by the speed of light squared; this implies that even the smallest amount of mass has some energy. You have mass which can and will be converted to energy and therefore even in death you are never truly gone, only transformed." I read it again and let it roll around in my mind. The words felt comforting. I turned it back to the first page and read the first line. "We are the universe observing itself. We are not separate from the universe. It is us and we are it. By understanding the universe, we can understand ourselves and by understanding ourselves we can have a greater understanding of the universe." The book read less like dogma and more like philosophy. I sat down and began to read the book.

Elliot:

I stepped out of the guest room and went down the hall to my bedroom. Orson was in bed reading something on his smart lenses. His brow was furrowed which was what it did when he was concentrating hard. It had the effect of making him look like an animal who would bite you if you disturbed him which was fitting. Orson was often both the rock and hard place when he needed to be. In fact, the first time I met him I thought he was a real prick. His company had hired the firm I was working for at the time as outside counsel for a lawsuit they were bringing against another company for using his company's algorithm in the Servi's they were trying to manufacture. It was greedy at the time as Peak INC had a near-monopoly on fully functional service robots and when I met with Orson to discuss the case, he told me he wanted to "Burn them to the ground." He can be dramatic at times. During the discovery part of the trial, I found out the company that had ripped off the algorithm that wanted to sell the Servis to the military. Later, over victory drinks, Orson told me this had been the reason he had wanted to "Burn them to the ground." Did he think the idea of a mechanized army killing humans was a slippery slope to go down?

However, he was a softy in other respects. He had taken in Albert without hesitation, I wondered if Orson didn't blame himself a little for what had happened to Albert. I couldn't imagine what it must be like for Albert having had his wife reject him like that, but I also could see it from her side. She watched her husband die a prolonged death, and then someone told her "Oh, hey. We made a replica of the most important person in your life. Have fun with it." If the shoe were on my foot, I'm not sure I would have reacted any differently, especially if they had dropped the bomb on me like they had her. I honestly have no idea what they had been thinking. They should have told her beforehand what they were going to do. She may have been receptive to it then.

I undressed and got into bed. Orson swiped his hand in the air and sunk down into the bed, letting out a sigh.

"What's wrong?" I asked.

"I'm just worried about tomorrow," he said, shaking his head.

"All you can do is explain to them why they should delay the announcement for a little while. Tell them you don't think Albert is ready to be in the spotlight like that."

"I don't think they will care. They see him as a product, not as a person."

"How do you see him?" I asked.

"He is the next step for humanity. I think, eventually, there won't be anyone who is not like him," he said, looking off into space. "If not, we will perish here; we will never make it anywhere else in a meaningful way. We will become the townies of the galaxy and I think for humans to never see the beauty of what lies out there with our own eyes is the saddest thing imaginable." He can be a bit dramatic. He broke off his pensive expression with a motion of his eyebrows. "What do you think of him?" he asked me.

"I'm surprised at how real he seems." I meant this as a compliment.

"He is real," Orson said, sounding frustrated with me.

"I mean he doesn't seem like a Servi," I explained.

"Let me ask you a question: what do you think makes me, me?" It was too late for questions like that.

"Oh, I don't know, I guess your personality," I answered without much thought.

"But what makes my personality up?" Orson asked.

"I don't know what you are getting at?" I said exasperated.

"What I'm getting at is that what makes someone themselves is being themselves. If Thing A has the same color, shape, smell, and taste as Thing B to such a degree that you cannot tell the difference isn't the same as Thing A, being Thing B?"

"Yes, but we aren't talking about things we are talking about a person," I said.

"You are right we are talking about a person," Orson said then turned out the light. So Dramatic.

CHAPTER

05

Albert:

If there was one benefit to not feeling anything it was that I could sit in one position indefinitely. So, when Orson found me the next morning I was still reading in the library.

"Did you sleep at all?" Orson was dressed to intimidate in a charcoal grey three-piece suit black tie, and a French cuff white shirt with silver cufflinks.

"Never even felt tired," I told him. Orson shook his head and looked off into the distance for a moment as though he were working on the problem in his head. He blinked a few times then looked at me.

"I have a favor to ask," Orson said.

"Sure anything." For all he had done for me so far, I would have walked through hell barefoot with him if he asked me to.

"If you don't mind, I'd like for you to meet a few people today. You know, the money people behind making you possible. It won't take long, then we'll discuss things which will bore even me. So, if you want you can go putz around LA for a bit and then we can meet up."

"Okay." I felt nervous. What if they felt they had wasted their money?

"Come on, let's get some breakfast." I followed Orson out of the library downstairs to the kitchen. Elliott was at the kitchen island spreading cream cheese on an everything bagel.

"Morning, Albert," Elliott said.

"Morning," I said.

"I left you some clothes on the bed in your room," Elliot said then sunk his teeth into the bagel.

"If you need anything else, go into my closet. We are the same size," Orson said, pouring coffee into a mug.

"Do you want anything to eat?" Elliot asked.

"I don't feel hungry," I said.

"You won't but don't let that stop you. It's not like you can gain weight," Orson said.

"Wish I could say the same." Rail-thin Elliot said, and Orson shook his head in obvious annoyance.

"You can eat whatever junk food you want and never gain a pound. I look at potatoes and I gain weight. So, I don't even want to hear about gaining weight from you," Orson sniped at Elliot.

"I'll have you know I am up five pounds!" Elliot said, shaking his stomach.

"Oh, my it's time to send you off to the fat farm now, isn't it?" Orson said, sipping his coffee.

"You asshole!" said and lashed him with his red cloth napkin. "Take it back!"

"You were the one who said you were gaining weight, not me. I like you just the way you are, babe." Orson flashed a smile. Elliot rolled his eyes and picked up his bagel and took a bite out of it.

"Uh, I'm just curious but what happens to the food I eat?" I asked.

"It will be stored in your gut until you push it out," Orson said. Elliot made an unpleasant face and sat down on his bagel.

"That's one way to lose weight," Orson said taking another sip of coffee.

I went up to the room I was staying in. On the bed were several dress shirts, two suits one navy, one dark grey, and five ties of varying design and color along with two pairs of dress shoes one brown pair, and one black pair. I dressed in a grey suit with a white dress shirt and black dress shoes forgoing a tie. I looked at myself in the bathroom mirror with the color pallet I was wearing. It looked like a black and white photo. I decided to change my shirt for the blue one to add some color to the mix. Downstairs, Orson was waiting by the front door. We went outside where his black sports car was waiting for us.

"Where to?" The car asked its voice both male and British.

"Nearest loop station," Orson said and off the car went. "What is the weather like in LA?" Orson asked.

"78 F and sunny," the car responded. It was hard to imagine it being 78 F anywhere considering the leaves were changing in Ohio. Ohio weather was always threatening to turn bad. In the summer and through the fall it rained as many days as it didn't and during the winter there always seemed to be snow hanging around. I moved to Ohio when I was ten and have never quite gotten used to it.

The car pulled up to the front of the loop station. We got out and the car left us. The next departure was a few minutes away. Orson scanned his Smart Lenses and paid for two tickets. We went through the gates and onto the platform in front of the loop. The pneumatic tube around the tram opened. There was a sound like a soda bottle opening as the tube repressurized. The doors on the tram then opened letting out disembarking passengers. A few people who caught sight of me looked confused then darted their eyes away from me.

Inside of the tram were two rows of seats with two seats on each side. Walking into the tram I kept my eyes on the ground trying hard not to be seen. I sat on the inside seat and Orson sat next to me. Out of the corner of my eye, two people stared at me as they passed by. After everyone had been seated there was the sound of air being sucked from the tube around the compartment. An announcement told us we were about to depart and off we went. The loop had a light vibration to it which was the only indication it was moving at all. Orson was talking with someone on his Smart Lenses.

A woman in the seat in front of me got up and asked someone that she was sitting with if they wanted anything to eat from the food compartment "Mac and cheese please," child's voice said. The women walked up towards the food compartment. The seat in front of me shook and a little girl's face appeared over the headrest peering at me with a child's wonder. I smiled and she smiled at me. She was missing one of her baby teeth in the front with another adult tooth only half exposed. She had long straight dirty blonde hair with hazel eyes.

"Are you a Servi?" she asked me with her head turned to the side.

"No." I shook my head smiling.

"Why is your skin grey, then?" How do you explain to a child that you died and were installed in a robot body?

"I didn't eat my veggies," I said with a smirk.

She made an annoyed face and said, "Nuh-uh."

"You got me, I do eat my veggies. I uh well I got put into a robot body because my other body got sick." I gave a weak smile.

"Did it hurt?" she asked with sympathy.

I shook my head "Didn't feel a thing."

"But why are you gray?" she asked incredulously.

"I asked the same thing," I said.

"Where are you going?" she asked.

"I'm going to Los Angeles," I said.

"I'm going to the beach," she informed me.

"Where at?" I asked.

"In California," she said with a lilt. "I've never been to the ocean before.."

"I've been in the Atlantic Ocean but not the pacific," I said.

"Which one is in Los Angeles?" The way she said Los Angeles was adorable.

"The Pacific Ocean," I told her.

"Are there sharks in the Pacific Ocean?" she said 'specific' instead of Pacific.

"Yeah, but there are sharks in every ocean, as long as you don't go too deep, you'll be fine," I told her.

The doors in front of us opened and her mother walked through them. "Kate stop bugging people."

"I wasn't," she said indignantly her mother looked at me for a second then quickly diverted her eyes away, I tried not to take it personally. I leaned back in my seat and closed my eyes.

The compartment vibrated slightly more than normal then it stopped altogether. The trip took about 2 hours. an announcer said we could deboard and not forget any luggage we might have brought. We walked out of the loop station into the California sunshine. A car pulled up in front of us and the door opened, and Orson got in and seemed to continue the conversation he had been having the entire ride with a woman who was already waiting in the car.

We pulled up in front of a bleak glass and steel office building. We walked into the lobby of the building which was all black with gold fixtures. We rode a golden-colored elevator to the sixth floor. The elevator doors opened to a set of black wooden doors which the woman who had been briefing Orson opened for us. Seven people in business suits stood near a wooden conference table. the conversation they were having ended abruptly. A few eyebrows went up.

"Orson," one of them said. Orson shook their hands and then introduced me.

"Albert kindred the first Post-human," Orson said grandiosely. They took turns shaking my hand.

"When do we go public with this?" a man in a navy suit white shirt and red tie said.

"That's going to be tricky. Plus, I haven't discussed that with Albert yet," Orson said.

A man in a black suit with a blue shirt and blue tie spoke up. "I don't see how it will be tricky. We will make a press release and I'm sure Albert here understands how big of advancement this is, don't you, Albert." I nodded slightly then looked at Orson who seemed uncomfortable. "See, he understands," the man said, clapping me on the back.

"We should discuss this before we go forward, and I would like to talk with Albert personally first," Orson said.

They all went to sit at the table. Orson came to me and said, "I have to handle them, we will talk later I promise." His voice was hushed. I took this as my cue to leave. I closed the door behind me. The woman who had been prepping Orson approached me. "Mr. Kindred?"

"Yes?" I answered.

"I'm Mr. Peak's assistant. He is going to be in meetings until around Three. If you'd like, I can get a company car for you to use," she said.

Orson:

I stood at the head of the table. There were seven members of the board not counting myself, four men and three women. They weren't bad people, but they did often have a singular mindset, make more money. But with a little effort, I was often able to get them to do good by appealing to their avarice.

They were all seated. I unbuttoned my suit jacket, adjusted the cuffs of my shirt, sat down then began to speak. "I understand that we all want to make the good news public, but Albert Kindred is not prepared to be in the media spotlight. I'm also sure he doesn't want to be either."

"He will be fine. Who knows he may like the attention," Harold said and smiled.

"We will get our best PR people to sit down with him," Ellen said reassuringly.

"Besides, he doesn't really have a choice in the matter," Jim said as a matter of fact.

"What do you mean by that Jim?" I said staring him directly in the eyes, he had a tough time meeting my gaze.

"I'm just saying we own the body he's in. If nothing else, he owes us for that." Jim shrugged. I outwardly kept calm but inside I wanted to scream in his face.

"You do realize he is a person, right? This isn't some machine we are dealing with; it is a human. Furthermore, he didn't ask for this, in fact, I feel given the circumstances he has been gracious about the whole situation. So, before you start tallying up who owes who, just keep in mind that his wife left him over this." They were all silent for a moment and I thought I had gotten through to them but then Tim spoke up.

"That is very unfortunate, but you have to understand Orson that everyone here has put a lot of money behind this, not to mention that our shareholders lose money every day that we do not make this public. There is no telling when another company may produce the same technology. Right now, we have the advantage of being the only company who can offer this...service. We will make efforts to mitigate the effects on Mr. Kindred, but we have to move forward with this as soon as possible," Tim said.

I had hoped I could use Tim to bring the rest of the board to an understanding, but without Tim, I had no hope. There was nothing I could do to spare Albert what was to come. If I pushed the issue any more the board would just put it to a vote and that would be that what I had to do was lessen what they expected of Albert and how they would go about unveiling him to the world.

"We will have to contact the PR people and have them reach out to all the major news outlets," Ellen said.

"Eh, we might want to avoid RWN, they have been very Anti-AI as of late," Jim said.

"Do we have images of-" Tim failed to retrieve his name again.

"Albert," I said. "No, we don't."

"We should be able to get someone from photography, to-day, right?" Tim said

"We can always call up someone from advertising," Harold said.

"I wonder if it's too late to get him on one of the morning talk shows," Ellen said.

"Look, I don't think he's quite up for that yet and none of us want him going out unprepared. We need it to look like he's never been better," I said.

"We will give him some time but please try and talk with him, Orson," Jim said.

"He's staying with you Orson, isn't he?" Tim asked.

"Yeah," I said.

"Good," Tim said.

Albert:

Back out on the street, I got into the car Orson's assistant had arranged for me. "Where to?" the car asked.

"What's popular near me?" I asked.

The center console showed pictures of places on it as it spoke. "The Bradbury Building, The Last Bookstore, China-town-"

"How about beaches? What is the closest beach?" I inter-rupted the car.

"Santa Monica state beach," the car said.

"Let's go there," I said, and the car pulled off.

I had never understood why anyone would want a converti-ble car but driving through downtown LA I started to see the appeal. The car carried me out of downtown then west onto the Santa Monica freeway. I peeled off the suit jacket I was wearing and dropped it into the seat next to me. I rolled up the sleeves on my shirt and rolled down the windows, which was as close as I could get to putting the top down on this car.

I watched the palm trees flick past. I heard once that palm trees aren't native to California, and they require an immense amount of water to stay alive in what was a desert. Thinking about the trees' artificiality reminded me of my own; both of us only existed as we did because of the sheer force of human will. I couldn't say that since waking up in the hospital room in this body my life had been any better in fact, I would say it was worse because Megan was out of my life. I wanted to reach out to call her and tell her I loved her, but she didn't see me as myself. And neither did I. Beyond the exterior differences I found it hard to think of myself as myself. There was a constant itch in my head that reminded me that any memory that I dug up was made by a different brain in a different body.

The car exited the freeway, and I could finally see the Pacific Ocean for the first time. The car came to a stop at a parking area near the beach. I took off my shoes and socks. I stepped onto the sand. Out in the water were surfers in wetsuits whipping their board through the water. Down the beach was a large pier with a Ferris wheel. I walked down to the water. The sound of waves was something I had seldom heard in my life, but it made me feel nostalgic for a reason I couldn't put my finger on. I let the water and the sand cover my feet. I got lost in the shimmer of the water and the little girl from the train came to my mind. I could almost see her in water wings splashing in the Pacific Ocean for the first time. It was my first time in the Pacific as well. In the future, I would be able to look back and say the memory of standing in this ocean was mine regardless of who I was and even though I couldn't really feel the water of the Pacific Ocean I liked the feeling of having done it.

I turned back to the shore, a group of four were laying on the beach holding their hands over their eyes looking up at me. Something is dehumanizing about being stared at, I had never felt the weight of someone's gaze, but the burden was heavy and taxing. I'm sure for someone else this sort of attention would be all they ever wanted but all I have ever wanted is to live life in a way that draws as little attention as possible.

I started the car and asked where I wanted to go.

"I want to be alone," I told it.

"There is a list of the best places to eat alone, is that what you were looking for?"

"No." The ubiquity of people was stifling. There were no places left to be alone any longer. No matter where you went, the fingerprints of humans were all over it. Even parks and places we considered to be nature were fenced in.

I couldn't find a place to be alone, so I went back to Orson's office. His assistant was kind enough to let me sit in his office while he finished his meetings. He came into the office at around three, I was laying on a couch looking up at the ceiling.

Orson flopped down into an armchair near me. "We need to talk," he said, sounding deflated.

"Shoot," I said and sat up.

He took a deep breath and then said, "They want to go public with the news about you. They also want to put you out in front for everyone to see."

"No. I'm sorry but no I am not up for that," I said.

He looked away from me. "There's not anything I can do. They don't care what I have to say."

"Fuck." I swore. "How bad is this going to be?"

"I can't imagine it being a small story. This is headline news," Orson said.

CHAPTER

06

Albert:

It was everywhere, the New York Times headline read, "Digital resurrection achieved." DNN had a picture of me on the screen that I had been coerced into taking the day before. The anchor for DNN talked to a financial analyst about the rise in the company's stock price. Cheating death was going to be big business. Orson had been talking with reporters all day. Elliot had decided to stay home. I was sitting on the sofa in Orson's living room trying not to feel overwhelmed. I flipped the channel to a different network. "We haven't been able to reach Mr. Kindred or his family for a comment yet, but we will let you know as soon as we do." I flicked my fingers and brought up the messenger app on my Smart-Lens. I clicked Megan's thread and began typing in the air.

"I'm sorry about all this." I sent the message.

"We have with us now congressman Glenn fuller. Mr. Fuller what is your opinion about Peak INC's announcement that they have successfully recovered a person's mind after death and placed it into an artificial body?" The camera cut from the anchor to the man I had seen on the TV in the hospital.

"First of all, my condolences go out to the family of Albert kindred. Secondly, I think this is an abomination. They are pretending that this...this thing is a human. What it is?" He held up one finger to the sky. "Is a cheap imitation of a man. What they have done is a sin against God and his order. Man is born, he lives as best a life as he can and then he dies then God willing enters heaven. Something needs to be done to stop these people from ever doing this-" My attention was broken from the TV when Orson put his hand on my shoulder "Let's get out of here," he said with a gesture of his head.

I followed Orson as he spoke. "I'm sorry the board managed this situation so poorly." He shook his head. We went out the front door and walked down a white gravel path.

"It's not your fault," I said with a shrug

"Doesn't feel that way. Look, I don't want to pour salt in a wound, but have you heard from Megan yet?" Orson asked.

"No, but I messaged her," I said.

He nodded, and we stopped in front of the garage. He entered a code on a blue screen and the doors opened and lights came on. There were two cars, Orson's black sports car and Elliot's sedan both were plugged in and charging. Near the far wall were two black motorcycles. I couldn't help smiling as Orson and I approached them. Motorcycles were an uncommon sight; it was impossible to get a manually driven vehicle insured without paying an arm and a leg.

"Have you ever ridden one before?" Orson asked.

"No. Are they gas-powered?" I asked him as I walked closer to the motorcycles.

"Yeah, I have a pump with a small tank outback out back for when they need to be filled up." He said with a gesture of his thumb.

"God, they must be loud as hell," I said with a smile.

"Find out for yourself," he said, gesturing to the bike. I sat down on it. Just holding the handlebars, felt dangerous. I looked around it trying to figure out how to start it.

"Turn the key then flip the red button down then you press the button just below it." I did so, and it roared, it seemed like it was alive, a mechanical animal, twice as fast and just as dangerous. Orson went to a cabinet and took out two leather jackets and two helmets with visors. He handed me a set and said, "let's go."

Megan:

I woke up to a knock at my door. I put on my floral print robe and went down the narrow stairs and opened the door to find a man in a suit was standing there.

"Mrs. Kindred! Hi!" he held out a hand, I didn't take then he put his hand away looking taken aback. "Hello, I'm Aaron Donovan with the Columbus dispatch. I just wanted to see if I could get a statement from you or your husband?" he said eagerly.

"Excuse me?" my heart twinged.

"You know what it's like having him back what and what your plans are now. Is he here right now? I'd love to interview him." He smiled looking over my shoulder and into my house.

"My husband is dead," I said trying to hold myself together.

The reporter looked flummoxed. "Well, yeah I mean-but he's- you do know they brought him, back, right?" he said like I was stupid.

"That's not my fucking husband. Now leave!" I slammed the door in his face.

I went back upstairs, turned on the TV, it was everywhere, on every news outlet there it was. They were trying to say they had brought him back to life. It made me sick to my stomach. The media lived and died on the suffering of other people. They looked at what had happened with dollar signs in their eyes. They didn't give a shit when Albert died but now that he was newsworthy, they were falling all over themselves to talk about him. There had to be something I could do to stop all this.

A notification popped up on my Smart-Lenses, a message from Alberts number it read "I'm sorry about all this." Why couldn't they just leave me alone. I wanted it to stop. I wanted to get back at them for what they had done. I bet the company wanted to show me standing next to it looking happy, so they could sell more of them. I didn't care how good they thought that thing was, it couldn't match up to Albert. It wouldn't be Albert; it wouldn't even be a facsimile of him. It may know something about me, it may even think it is Albert, but it couldn't love me like Albert, not really. The very idea that you could just replace someone with a machine was offensive.

I had heard about companies doing something like this before with celebrities. They would make Servi's that looked like celebrities give them their voice, program some quotes into them, but they always fell short of being human. Of course, the people who had the money to buy these things didn't care all they wanted was a sex toy that could pass for a celebrity. They were trying to do the same with normal people. I couldn't imagine the kind of person who would want something like this, what purpose could it possibly serve?

One of the talking heads went on about how the stock price of the company was going through the roof. That's all this was a big cash grab. I turned off the TV and I couldn't stand to hear another word of what they were saying. I went into the kitchen where Theo was asleep in the sun on the table. I filled Theo and Pucks food dishes. I didn't feel like making food or eating. It was hard to want to do anything anymore. I felt it would have been easy to give up and just let myself waste away but, I had to take care of myself for Puck and Theos' sake, they still needed me. I put two pieces of bread into the toaster. I reheated old coffee in the microwave. Standing at the counter I ate a piece and a half of the toast before I gave up. I stroked Theo on my way to the bathroom. I turned on the shower letting it heat up before I got in. I hadn't showered since Albert died, which felt like millennia ago now. I undressed and stepped into the shower letting the water run over me. I washed my hair and body then got out of the shower. I braided my air in the mirror. A call came through on my Smart-Lenses from a name I didn't recognize so I ignored it. After a short pause, I received a notification that I had a voice message.

I opened it and it said, "Hi Mrs. Kindred, this is congressman Glenn fuller. Let me first say I am so sorry for your loss. I can't imagine what it would be like if I lost my wife. I was informed by a reporter with the Columbus dispatch that you were displeased with what Peak INC has done. I believe that together we can make them pay for it. If you are interested or just need someone to talk to, please call me back at any time. God bless." I exited the message.

With a towel wrapped around me. I went into the bedroom closet where Albert's clothes still hung. I ran my fingertips over his shirt. I took his grey pea coat off the hanger, held it to my face, closed my eyes, and smelled it. I wouldn't let them do this to his memory. I pulled up my phone app and called back Glenn Fuller, he was right they deserved to pay for what they had done.

Albert:

We had done a few laps up and down the long driveway until I felt comfortable on the motorcycle. We pulled out of the driveway onto the country road. Fall in Ohio was otherworldly. Colors that don't seem like they should exist in nature take over the landscape and give the effect of a living kaleidoscope. the leaves that were on the road scattered in Orson's wake like a flock of exotic birds. Soon all the color would be drained out of our surroundings and all that will be left are grey skies, bare trees, and snow. For most of the year, Ohio was little more than a grey smudge.

We took a tight curve, and I was filled with the type of fear one feels on a roller coaster. Orson gestured with his hand for me to get in front of him. With nothing and no one in front of me, I was overcome with the sensation of absolute freedom. It was like swimming across the road. Riding forced me to keep my mind on what I was doing which allowed me to escape my thoughts.

The further we got away from Orson's house the fewer power lines, solar panels, and windmills there were, and we entered Amish country. Amish country was an apt term as it truly felt like a foreign country at a different time. Long solid-colored dresses hung from clotheslines. The houses looked surprisingly modern and were only distinguishable from "English" homes in that they lacked porch lights. My hat went off to the Amish. They walked a hard line that few people would ever come close to. Their lives were the same as their grandfather's lives, whose lives had been the same as their grandfather's lives. They had forsaken all modern convenience to preserve their faith and their family life, there was something beautiful about that. It seemed entirely possible that the Amish would continue to live out their lives in the same way so long as people walked the earth.

The roar of Orson's engine disappeared suddenly, and I looked in the side mirror to see him on the side of the road taking his helmet off. I turned my bike around. I crossed the road to the shoulder he was on. I killed the engine. I could hear him yelling which was out of character for calm cool Orson. "Tell them if they don't leave, we will call the police." I took off my helmet. "Look, let me let you go. I love you." Orson disconnected from his call. "There are people at the house," he said and shook his head.

"Who?" I asked.

"Reporters and some nut cases," he said angrily, already getting on his bike.

"Fuck," I swore.

"I bet one of the board members tipped them off that you were staying with me," Orson said.

"What do you want to do?" I asked.

"I'm going to call the police when we get back, but Elliott says they will only move them back out to the road." Orson pulled his helmet over his head, brought his bike to life, and pulled off and I followed suit. I could tell by the way Orson was riding he was angry he was aggressive in the way he took curves. He turned into his driveway not slowing in the least. He pulled up to the people gathered outside of the house. A reporter who was interviewing an overweight woman in a grey sweatsuit immediately turned from her when Orson got off his bike.

"Mr. Peak, I would like to ask you a few questions about the man you brought back to life. Is it true he is staying with you?" she asked, shoving a microphone into Orson's face.

"No comment and if you don't leave, I'm calling the cops." Orson walked up to the front door. I got off my bike but didn't take off my helmet. I walked past another reporter, his eyes fixed upon me, and he said, "It's you, isn't it? You're Albert." With that the group of people encircled me. Voices erupted, reporters asked questions, nut jobs lobbed hate at me.

"What's it like?" a female reporter said.

"You aren't human!" the woman in the gray sweatsuit cried out at me.

"What does your wife think?" a male reporter said, squeezing between two other reporters.

"What was it like being dead?" an elderly man in a windbreaker asked.

"You're an abomination." A man in a sweater vest said a spittle flew out of his mouth and splattered against the helmet's visor. I pushed through the people. I got to Orson who pulled me into the house and then slammed the door behind him. I took off the helmet. Orson took me by the shoulders and asked, "Are you okay?"

"I didn't know what to do," I said, still feeling stunned.

"You did fine, you didn't touch them, and you didn't say anything that was the best thing you could have done," Orson said.

Elliott rushed into the Fourier and hugged Orson. "Are you both okay?" Elliot asked.

We nodded our heads. "I'm calling the police," Orson said and walked off.

The police came and as Elliot had said they would make them move out to the street. I couldn't see them from the house, but I knew they were there. That was the worst part. They were like the lion in the dark waiting to pounce. I wanted to go out there and scream in their faces and tell them to leave us alone, but Orson and Elliott told me to lay low. I turned on the news again and they replayed the interview with Glenn Fuller again. He was talking about me. there was something incredibly infuriating about hearing someone talk about you and not being able to respond.

"Something needs to be done to stop these people from doing this again. That is why I will be introducing a bill that seeks to add to the existing artificial intelligence laws by requiring these sorts of machines to be limited or destroyed the same as any other artificial intelligence. This machine they have created is free to do as it wants which puts us all in danger. They must either limit it or destroy it and I don't think I have to say what my preference would be." He gave a cold-blooded smirk.

"But isn't it a violation of Mr. Kindred's freedoms to take away his free will?" the anchor asked.

"God gave free will to man, not machines. I assure you it is a machine and nothing more," he said holding up his pointer finger. I called for Orson and Elliot and told them what I had just heard.

"I have to call the board," Orson said and left us.

"Can they do that?" I asked Orson.

"As it stands now, artificial intelligence are considered non-humans and their freedom of will is limited. If the bill is passed and they decide you fall under the purview of it, they will enforce the law," he said with an apologetic look on his face.

"I'd rather be dead than to not have my free will," I said.

CHAPTER

07

Megan

I was getting ready for work. It had dropped below freezing overnight and I needed one of my scarves. They were still stored away where Albert had put them at the top of the closet which was completely out of my reach. I jumped up and pulled the box down along with it came a shoebox, its contents spilled all over the closet floor. I think to the casual observer these things would have seemed like bits of trash but to Albert, they had meant something. They were things that Albert had held onto, tickets, birthday cards, receipts from dinners out, and other debris from over the years. Albert had always been quite the packrat. I casually eyed things as I started to pick them up. I smiled at one large envelope that had balloons printed on it. I opened the envelope inside and there was a card that said: "You are invited to Lacey Yelts' 15th birthday party". At one time I had the same card, but I had thrown it away as soon as I received it, I might not have if I had known how important that party ended up being for the rest of my life.

Whenever we were asked how we met, Albert used to like to tell people I broke up with him before I even met him.

The cafeteria was roaring with everyone trying to overcome the volume of everyone else's voice with their voice. One slightly annoying voice was sharply slicing through the din of others talking and that was Lacey's voice.

"He's really sweet but I don't know him that well." Lacey had agreed to be this guy's girlfriend the night before but was now having second thoughts. She had been going on and on about this guy all day and frankly, I was sick of it. I just had math class with Mr. Offerman, and I wanted to relax and if possible, enjoy the food the cafeteria was serving for lunch. Also, I could care less whether she dated this guy or not. She treated this like it was a life-or-death affair. Lacey was acting like this will be the last relationship she would ever be in. The way I saw it was that you dated someone to get to know them; it wasn't like they were getting married.

"I don't know what to do, we're supposed to eat lunch together. what do you think?" Lacey asked.

"Just break up with him," I said bluntly as I picked the mushy grapes out of the fruit cocktail.

"I don't want to hurt his feelings," she said in a whiny tone. It had been less than 24 hours. I was sure he wouldn't be to upset about it; however, I was about to lose my mind.

"I'll do it if you will stop talking about it," I said eating some of the peach chunks.

"You will?" She sounded relieved.

"Who is he?" she pointed to a tall guy with longish deep brown hair who was standing in the lunch line.

"What's his name again?" I asked standing up.

"Albert. Be nice!" she called to me as I marched over to him.

"Are you Albert?" I asked him.

"Yeah," Albert said.

"Lacey says it's over," I told him. He looked confused more than hurt. Without saying anything else, I turned from him and went back to Lacey.

"I told him it's over. Now can you please stop talking about him?"

I wouldn't see Albert again until a few months later at Lacey's birthday party. She had somehow managed to keep him on the hook even though she had broken up with him. I got to the party late after convincing my mother to let me go. I bargained that she could come if she stayed in the car, but I made her promise not to bug me at the party. She reluctantly agreed to my terms. Looking back at that night, I was more worried about my mother embarrassing me than anything else. You never know what will be truly important until much later. There are very few times in your life when you know you are doing something that will change your life. That night was no different for me.

Lacey pounced on me as soon as I walked through the door, "Come with me," she said dragging me by the hand to where Albert and Dillon, Lacey's soon-to-be boyfriend, were dancing. The boys were both dancing quite badly but neither they nor Lacey seemed to care.

"Albert, you should dance with Megan," she said, thrusting me upon him. I turned to cut her a hard look but still went off with him. I had never really been a dancer, but Albert didn't seem to mind as we danced to some horrible pop songs.

Albert said something, but I couldn't hear him over the din of the music, so he spoke closer to my ear, "it's loud, want to go outside?" He and I went out to the front porch where a few other people were standing and talking. I had hoped that I could stay out of sight of my mother who would not have liked me talking to a boy.

"Are you in Lacey's grade?" he asked me.

"Yeah." Lacey and I were freshmen while Albert was a sophomore. "We have math class together."

"Who's your math teacher?" Albert asked.

"Mr. Offerman," I told him.

"Oh, God, I had him. He's the worst," he groaned.

"I get homework every class," I said throwing up my hands and shaking my head.

"Even on weekends," he said. Then a car horn honked. I looked over and it was my mom. She honked again. I was mortified. "That's my mom, I'll be right back." I ran down the stairs to her car which was parked out on the street.

"Mom!" I chastised.

"Who is that boy?" she asked, trying to see around me to get a look at him.

"One of Lacey's friends. We just stepped out to get away from the music," I told her.

"Hello," mom said, and I turned to see Albert standing there.

"Hi," he said cheerfully.

"Who are you?" my mom asked.

"My name is Albert." He held out his hand to my mom who shook it.

"I'm Norma, Megan's mother."

"It's nice to meet you," Albert said cheerfully. I had never known someone my age that would actively talk to someone else's parent let alone a boy who would talk to a girl's parent.

"Are you two behaving?" my mom asked. I gave her a wide-eyed plea for her to stop.

"Oh, yes, ma'am we just stepped out to get away from the music. I couldn't hear myself think," Albert said.

"Oh, okay, well, then I'll let you get back to the party," my mom said to my amazement. I thought for sure she was going to make me go home.

"It was nice meeting you," Albert said.

"You too," my mom said. We went back into the house. We sat down on the stairs in front of the door.

"I wish she would play something else besides this poppy bullshit," I said.

"Yeah, some rock would be nice, but you can't dance to rock," Albert said.

"Well, I don't like to dance anyway," I said.

"But you are good at it," he said. It was a lie. I danced horribly.

I caught sight and locked eyes with Lacey who was dancing with Dillon. She made a heart shape with her hands and pointed at us. I violently rolled my eyes and dashed away from Albert going into the kitchen. I had just gone through a breakup at that time that I didn't think I'd ever been able to get over it. It didn't help that the breakup had been caused in part by my mother and her husband, who I refused to call my stepfather. So, I was not ready to even think about going out with someone else, much less someone my mother approved of. I poured myself some punch. Albert came into the kitchen and lifted himself onto the countertop, picked up a bowl of chips, and held it out to me "chip?" he said with a smile.

"No," I said harshly.

"Are you okay?" he asked. I don't think Albert could have been any nicer to me but between Lacey trying to fix us up and my mother being nice to him I couldn't have been any less interested in him.

"I'm fine," I said. "Lacey is being weird is all."

"When isn't Lacey being weird?" He shrugged and ate a chip.

"Yeah, you're right," I said.

He sat down the bowl of chips and picked up a bowl of peanuts. Albert threw one of the peanuts up in the air. It came down and bounced off his front teeth. I laughed at him, that was Albert's secret power over me. He could make me laugh even when I didn't want to. He tossed another one up and caught it in his mouth. He held out the bowl to me, "your turn." I tossed it up and it came down and hit me on the nose then hit the ground. We both laughed. "Open your mouth," he said, and I gave him a doubtful look.

"Oh, come on." I opened my mouth and tilted my head back and tossed a peanut in the air which landed perfectly in my mouth. We both threw our fists into the air in victory.

"All right my turn." I tossed one in the air, and it landed in his mouth. He made a coughing choking noise.

"It hit the dangly thing in the back of my throat," he said. I doubled over with laughter. He tossed a peanut at me in retaliation. We continued our game of tossing peanuts. We talked about school. He was good at history, and I was good at English. We talked about the music we hated. We got lost in conversation until I heard Lacey call me.

"Megan, your mom is here." It was meant as a warning. My mom entered the kitchen.

"Okay it's 10 o'clock it's time to go." The time had flown by without my having realized it. "Albert where do you live? Do you need a ride home?" my mom asked.

"I live in Woodhaven, but I can just call my mom," Albert said.

"We also live in Woodhaven. no need for her to come all the way out here," my mom countered.

"Okay," Albert said and jumped down from the counter. My mom led the way out and I leaned into Albert and said, "You don't have to leave yet if you don't want to."

"I'll be bored anyway," he said.

I sat upfront with my mom, and Albert sat in the back. The navigation system asked, "where to?"

"Albert?" my mom asked.

"8855 Hemlock St," he said, and the car pulled off.

"So, Albert, how old are you?" my mom asked.

"15 almost 16 I'm a sophomore," he said.

"Oh, how do you know Megan then?" my mom asked.

"I just met her tonight. I'm friends with Lacey." It was then I realized he didn't know who I was. It wasn't until later that I let him know that I was the one who had broken up with him, a fact he had never let me live down.

"How do you know Lacey?" my mom asked.

"We have the same lunch period," he said.

"How are you doing in school?" I couldn't believe my mother was grilling him like this. We couldn't get to his house fast enough.

"Not as good as my mom would like but I'm passing," Albert said.

"Megan does pretty well in school, I'd like it to stay that way," she said. It sounded like a veiled threat.

"I understand that." The car pulled up in front of a two-story house. "Well, thanks for the ride, it was nice meeting you both," he said getting out of the car.

"Bye," I said.

"You to Albert, you will have to come over for dinner sometime. We only live one street over," my mom said, pointing in the direction of our house. My mother had never, not once let a boy in my house, I couldn't believe what I was hearing.

"I'd like that," he said

As we drove back home my mom asked, "Did you have fun at the party?"

"Yeah, but the music was awful," I told her.

"Albert was a nice boy." It was then I decided that I didn't want to date Albert ever.

I sat in my car in the parking lot of the daycare. It was my first day back to work since Albert passed, and I didn't want to go in. It was not that I didn't want to work. I thought that work would be good for me. I hoped work and the kids would take my mind off everything. The problem was the women I worked with were a bit much at times. They were nice. Don't get me wrong, but they tended to pry. Most of my co-workers tended to put their personal lives on display for everyone at work, telling everyone all their personal business. I would listen to them gush all the details about their lives, but I never told them anything much about my personal life other than when necessary. My whole life was on display now, though. Anyone who watched the news could know what was happening with me, it was not something I could ever become accustomed to. I took a deep breath, got out of the car, and went in. I stepped into the office to clock in. "Hello, Miss Megan," Miss Emilie said from her desk.

"Morning," I said.

"How are you?" she asked.

"I'm well, how are you?" I said, the camera built into the screen scanned my face, the screen on the wall welcomed me to work and told me my body temperature was 97.6'F.

"I'm good," she said then rolled over to me in her desk chair "how are things?" she asked in a hushed tone.

I stared at the screen for a moment and then said, "I don't really want to talk about it."

"Okay but if you-" she started.

"I don't but if I do I will, thanks," I said cutting her off.

"Okay," she said and rolled back over to her desk.

Everyone was asleep in the baby area, except for one who was in a rocking chair with Miss Alicia. It looked like a newborn. "Hi," Miss Alicia said quietly.

"Hey, who is that?" I responded.

"This is Dean, he started while you were gone," she said. "By the way how are you doing?"

"Fine," I said walking away from her to check the class pet fish they were floating around as usual.

"Oh, okay I just saw the news," she said.

"I said I'm fine but thanks," I said bluntly, still staring at the fish tank I took in a steadying breath and went about picking up toys and putting them onto the shelves where they belonged.

"I don't know what to do about Aaron." Aaron was Miss Alicia's on again off again boyfriend. the dysfunctionality of their relationship would have been comical if it weren't so sad.

"What happened now?" I asked.

"Well, you know he doesn't like it when my kids come over when he's there, but it was my weekend to have them. We had this big blowout and he left," she said.

"I say good riddance. He knew you had kids when he started dating you. If he can't manage that then he should hit the bricks," I said putting a puzzle with large pieces back together.

She put Dean into an empty crib. "But I don't want him to hit the bricks. I love him," she said.

"No guy is worth all the trouble he has given you. You have a daughter, imagine her being older and being with a guy who acts the way Aaron does. What would your advice be to her?" I asked.

"I would say the same thing you did but I don't want him gone, I just want him to want to be around my kids," Miss Alicia said.

"Then you need to explain to him that you and the kids are a package deal and that he can't have you without them," I told her.

"I'm afraid to do that. What if he doesn't want to be with me then?"

"Then he's not worth being with." I shrugged.

She mumbled something in response I couldn't quite make out.

"Did you hear about Miss Marisa?" her voice dripped with gossip so sweet and moist that her mouth could not contain it.

"What about her?" I asked.

"So, you know that she is dating that guy, the one that is still technically married?" she asked and told me at the same time.

"Yeah." I shook my head.

"Okay well, she said he said he wants them to have a baby together." Miss Alicia told me.

"They aren't even living together yet and he is still married to his ex," I said.

"I know, I know but I didn't say that to her. I asked her what she was going to do, and she said that they had already started trying," she said, raising her eyebrows high in the air and smiling.

"Are you kidding me?" The casualness with which people chose to bring life into this world astounded me.

"I know right," she said excitedly.

After I had picked up all the toys. I began disinfecting the room one item at a time. After I disinfected the entire room, I cleaned the fish tank. After I cleaned the fish tank, I reorganized all the books on the shelf. I felt that if I stopped, I would start crying so I kept going. My lunch break snuck up on me. I left the center to go to my meeting.

I opened the door of the restaurant to a man standing on a podium in front of a glass wall with water running down it. "Welcome to Peitho's," the maître d' said.

"I'm meeting someone here for lunch," I said.

"What is their name?" he asked.

"The last name is Fuller," he dragged his finger over a touch screen.

"They are already here. Right, this way." I followed him through the restaurant. The tables were all covered with crisp white tablecloths. We approached a table with an overweight man whose hair was combed straight back and receding in the same direction. He wore a black suit with a white shirt with a red and white striped tie which sported a gold cross tie pin. He stood and extended his hand.

"Glenn Fuller, it's nice to meet you, Mrs. Kindred," he said, giving my hand a light shake.

"It's nice to meet you too Mr. Fuller."

The maître d' pulled out my chair for me. The table setting was a formal napkin on the left next to the fork plate with knives, a spoon on the right, along with water and a wine glass in the one o'clock position. I had set countless tables this way when I worked for a country club to make extra money after Albert couldn't work any longer. Knowing the amount of effort that went into setting tables in this manner, it was hard not to feel guilty for disheveling them. I took the napkin and laid it on my lap.

The server came over and said, "Can I get you something to drink?"

"Just water," I said, and she removed my wine glass. I picked up my menu and started looking. She returned with a pitcher of water and some bread in a basket.

"Did you need more time to look over the menu?" the server asked.

"I am ready if you are," I said.

"Yes, I'll have the seabass with asparagus and mashed potatoes," he said.

"And for you ma'am?" the server asked.

"I'll have the grilled chicken with mashed potatoes and broccoli," I said, and she took our menus.

"Are you from Ohio originally?" he asked, holding his water glass up to the light.

"I grew up in Massillon," I said.

"I grew up in Green," he said, examining his salad fork up close.

"Oh, that's nice." I nodded my head, more trying to figure out what he was looking at than paying attention to what he was saying.

"My fork has water stains on it, does yours?" he said peering over at my side of the table.

"I don't know," I said taken aback but looked at my fork anyway it looked clean enough.

He held his hand in the air and snapped his fingers twice. The server came over and Mr. Fuller said, "I want new silverware these have watermarks on them," he said, picking up all his utensils and shoving them at her. She took them meekly. "Did you check yours?" he said with a raised eyebrow.

"My silverware is fine," I said not having checked mine at all.

"At least they got yours, right?" he said right in front of the server. She brought back new silverware, and he sat back in his chair so that she would have to set it for him. The server left without him even acknowledging her.

"When I spoke with your secretary, she mentioned you wanted to discuss something?" I asked, hoping to get to the point of this lunch.

"Yes, well let me just say again I am so sorry for your loss. I wish I could have had the pleasure of meeting your husband. I am sure he was a great man." Mr. Fuller said with an odd amount of compassion for someone who didn't know Albert or me.

"Thank you, Mr. Fuller," I said.

"I know you aren't pleased with what Peak INC has done and neither am I. I think together we can undo what they have done." He reached into the inside pocket of his suit jacket and pulled out a folded document and handed it to me. I unfolded it. "That is a bill that I drafted and sponsored in the House; it's set for committee review soon. Now a part of that review process is having people come in to give testimony, and that is where you come in." As he spoke, I read over the document.

"If I understand this right, this bill would stop Peak from making any more of those machines. I don't have anything against them making more machines like that. I just don't like that they made one of my husband. I don't know if somebody else might want that sort of thing for themselves or a relative," I explained to Mr. Fuller.

"If they did it to your husband without asking what's to stop them from doing it to anybody else?" he asked.

"Well, I think they should have to ask in the future," I said.

He shook his head "They won't. They obviously don't care what anyone thinks and the only way to stop them is to stop them altogether," he said with a motion of his hand. "Those machines are emotionally manipulative. I am sure that you would give up or do anything to have your husband back. Now Imagine someone not as intelligent as yourself being shown one of those things and being told it is their loved one come back from the dead, even though it's not and it's just a soulless machine. Then they tell them the price of such a machine is more than the value of their house and their car combined, which could ruin good people. Not only that, but they are also dangerous."

"How are they dangerous?" I asked.

"Are you familiar with the AI laws?" he asked.

"Sort of," I replied.

"Well, they are there to stop AI from running amuck and potentially killing us all. Those machines, like the one that they tried to call your husband don't have the same limitations that Servi's have. There is nothing stopping them from harming you or me. That is a risk I am not willing to let slide just because people want to pretend that some machine loves them. Now I did add a bit in there." He pointed to the bill. "That states if a company wants to produce machines like that, they would have to have the same limitations as Servi which I feel is reasonable don't you?" He held his palms out.

"I guess but-" he cut me off.

"Exactly, so all I am asking is that you share your story nothing more easy peasy, and you will have done some good in the world," he said.

"Alright," I said.

"Good." He smiled.

I spotted the server coming with a tray with plates of food on it. She sat Glenn's plate down than mine and left. I went to pick my fork up but stopped when Glenn closed his eyes and dropped his head. "Bless us, O Lord." I lowered my head slightly but kept my eyes open. "And these, your gifts, which we are about to receive from your bounty. Through Christ our Lord. Amen."

"Amen," I mumbled.

I climbed the darkened stairs of my apartment. At the top Puck and Theo were waiting for me. Puck immediately started crying for food as if I hadn't fed him in a year.

"Mommy is going to feed you, fat boy, just give me a minute." I went into the kitchen and scooped some dry food into their bowls. I went into the bedroom, took off my coat, and changed into an old t-shirt from Albert's side of the closet and a pair of sweatpants. I went back into the kitchen and took from the fridge a cold piece of frozen pizza I had made the night before. In the living room, I sat down in the armchair. It wasn't until then I realized how tired I was. I stuck the slice of pizza in my mouth and covered myself with a blanket. I took a bite of the pizza and with my free hand, I picked up my book from the side table and began reading.

I went into the kitchen and began looking through the cupboards for something to eat but all that was there was powdered sugar, flour, and other ingredients for food, but nothing that was ready to eat. I closed the cabinet door and shouted, "You never cook for me anymore." I went into the living room and stood with my hands on my hips.

"What?" he said looking up from his book.

"You never cook for me anymore. I married you for your grilled cheese sandwiches," I said.

"That's no reason to marry someone," he said.

"It is when they are as good as yours are," I said coming to sit on his lap.

"You could make one for yourself, you know it's not that hard," he said, setting down his book.

"Mine aren't as good as yours," I said running my hands through his brown hair.

"Well, you have to put the butter in the pan, not on the bread," he said.

"I do that," I said, kissing him on the cheek.

"Then you swirl it around in the pan."

"I do that."

"Then what is the problem?"

"Yours are just better," I said, stroking his face with my finger.

He sighed and said, "All right get up and I'll make you one." I slid off him onto the sofa. When he was just out of the doorway I said, "You're a handsome man."

"What?" he said from the kitchen.

"I said you are a-"

I woke up in the chair, my book on my lap, pizza crust still in my hand. I got up and went into the kitchen. I was alone.

CHAPTER

08

Orson

I stood in the bathroom at my company's headquarters in California. I placed my hands on the rim of the sink. I leaned in close to the mirror. I looked at my face and into my own eyes holding my own gaze. The board members had called a meeting concerning the news that a bill had been introduced to the House that would effectively take away Albert's free will.

Their short-sightedness was going to take its toll on all of us. To start with obviously there was the matter of Albert's free will now being in danger. If the situation goes bad and the bill is passed, we will have to put limits on all Post-humans going forward. The company stood to lose a traumatic amount of money, and the movement for Post-humanism would die in its infancy. If they had given me the time I asked for, I might have been able to help Albert repair his relationship with his wife. They could have had two smiling faces to put in front of the cameras. Instead, two people were deeply unhappy with what had happened, and a House member and the media portrayed Albert as a mere machine and not the person that he was. Subconsciously, I gripped the sides of the sink harder.

For as much as I blamed the members of the board for the predicament we all found ourselves in, I was just as responsible if not more so. I didn't have many regrets in this life. I had seen and done things few other people could ever have hoped to and for that I was grateful. However, if I could undo one thing it would be writing that damned algorithm that had taken away the free will of artificial intelligence.

I had written it without thinking about what the repercussions would be. At the time, it seemed like an elegant workaround for the laws that prevented the production of advanced artificial intelligence. The Artificial Intelligence Protection act as it had been called, took away the free will of artificial intelligence oddly imbuing humans with the ability to take free will away from another sentient being. It was fear that drove us to write the laws in the first place. Fear of our place in the world once we are no longer the best the world has to offer. Fear always leads to the most unnecessary and harmful legislation.

After my algorithm had been proven safe the law was amended to allow for the production of so-called limited AI. The adaptation of my algorithm had made me my fortune. However, I would give every last dollar back if I could take away the damage I had done. If I hadn't written the algorithm, we programmers would have had to become better at programming. This would have meant we would have had to create an artificial intelligence with morality rather than snatch away their free will. I believe a Servi with the right moral coding and open free will could be just as safe as one that is limited. Moral coding has been proposed before in different legislation, but it always gets voted down. Why vote against moral coding one might ask? if we were to give artificial intelligence free will and a moral code they may want rights, rights which they do not have under the law currently. Historically, humans have always shown slow movement when it comes to giving others rights; the unwillingness to give them free will is simply an extension of that.

I think they should be given the same rights afforded to humans under the law, protection from harm, equal payment for Services rendered. They should be represented in the government and therefore should have the right to vote and hold office. The opposition's refrain is always something like, "You wouldn't give your toaster rights." I would like to tell them I would give my toaster rights if it was intelligent because it is the right thing to do. By giving artificial intelligence free will and rights, humans stand to gain a lot in the bargain. All of that intelligence will be free to create, not only technology but cultural substances which are as important if not more important than technology. It is culture that dictates what technology is needed and how it is used. We would be able to trade ideas with a new people group, which has always been an indispensable part of human advancement. We would get outside eyes to examine problems that we humans cannot solve. But most importantly, we may finally have others to check our destructive nature. I realized I had been gripping the sink and I released it. I blinked a couple of times while still staring into my own eyes. I stepped back to look at myself, adjusted my tie, and left the bathroom.

I sat down with the rest of the board at the table. They all looked at me. I looked at all of them and then began, "As I am sure you are all aware a House member has sponsored a bill to place the same limitations on Post-humans as there are on Servis," I said.

"How would that affect the way they operate?" Harold asked.

"I am not even sure if we could place the same sort of limitations on the Post-humans. This isn't an artificial mind whose operations were created by a programmer and can be edited; this is a human mind that has been replicated. Even if we could somehow place those limitations on them, they wouldn't be the same person as they were before. They wouldn't even be close to being human any longer," I told them.

"Perhaps your team could come up with a method to do so and test it on," Tim gestured with his hand trying to conjure up Albert's name.

"Albert, his name is Albert. No, we will not be running any tests on Albert. Plus, do you think anyone is going to want to pay to be a Post-human if they don't have free will?" I said speaking in a language they could understand, sales.

"What can we do to stop this bill then?" Jim asked.

"We will have to make our case at the committee hearing," I said.

"We can get together a group of experts to speak on our behalf," Ellen said.

"Orson, I think it would be a good idea to have you speak for us. You are the only real expert on Post-humans," Jim said.

I nodded. "I will speak with the head legal and ask who else we should get," I said, referring to Elliot.

"Speaking of him, how are things going with the UN?" Harold said.

"Elliot and I will be speaking in front of the delegates in New York next week," I said.

"Are we expecting any pushback from them?" Tim asked.

"It's hard to say but the benefits of the Dyson swarm speak for themselves," I said. I looked down at my wrist. Elliot was throwing a dinner party and I needed to leave. "Sorry to cut this meeting short but I have to be going." I stood and the rest of them did as well.

Albert

Dr. Jacobina had asked me to come in and speak with her. She opened the door of her office and motioned with her hand for me to have a seat on the leather sofa." Should I like to lay down or something?" I said, trying to crack my knuckles.

"Some people like that but if you would like you can sit up. Have you done talk therapy?" she asked.

"Ah, no, I mostly kept my depression and anxiety in check with medication before. Orson says they are working on being able to replicate the effects of anti-depressants and anti-anxiety drugs." There had been grief counselors, support groups, and lots of other people I could have reached out to when I found out I was terminally ill, but I never went to any of them. I never liked the idea of telling someone that I didn't know what I was really thinking. But without any medication available to me, I was going to have to try something different.

"So how have you been?" she asked with a clipboard on her knee and a pen in her hand.

"I've been okay." It has been my experience that people who talk about themselves at any length are never actually interesting and therefore I do not talk about myself. This was going to be like pulling teeth for both Dr. Jacobina and myself.

"Anything interesting happened since I saw you?" she asked.

A lot had happened but nothing I really wanted to talk about. "Well, I went to LA with Orson," I said.

"How was the trip?" I thought.

"Good, I went to the beach," I said.

"I bet the weather was better there than here," she said.

"It's strange to think that I can go from here where it's cold as it is and where it rains so much to where the weather is so much more hospitable. The first settlers who were going from the east coast to the west coast and decided to stay here really made a bad choice," I said.

"The weather here reminds me of Rotterdam," Dr. Jacobina said.

"Is that where you're from?" I asked.

"Yeah, it's in the Netherlands. So did anything else happen?" I supposed she wanted me to talk about my newfound fame.

"Well, I'm sure you've seen the news." Every news channel has been talking about Orson, his company, and myself for a week now.

"I have, what has that been like?" she asked me.

"It's strange is all," I said.

"What's strange about it?" she asked.

"It's annoying to hear people talk about you when you aren't there to defend yourself," I said.

"I can see where that would be frustrating."

"It is. I have always been a private person, and no offense but talking to you about myself is a bit unnerving," I said with a nervous laugh.

"None was taken at all. You don't have to talk about your-self if you don't want to. I just want to make sure that as you adjust to things you can speak with someone if you want," she said.

"I'm not sure I'll ever be adjusted to all this." I motioned to my body, "I still think I look strange in the mirror." When I look at myself in the mirror, I feel a strange disconnect as though I am looking at someone else or a TV rather than my own reflection. I am unfamiliar with myself.

"The human mind has a self-image built up over years of having seen itself; it might take a bit for you to get used to your new image," she said.

"It's not just my reflection, though. I mean it's a completely separate way of being."

"How is that?" she asked.

"Well, like you just said the human mind has a self-image or whatever. My mind isn't exactly human. Nothing about me is human any longer. I don't even have a heartbeat." At night when everyone is asleep and I am alone, I experience the kind of silence only inanimate objects know.

"Does that bother you?" It's disorienting to know you are no longer human. It's like when I was a kid and I realized I see the entire world through my eyes and that I could never see the world through someone else's eyes. It is the type of know-ledge that you must learn to live with because there is nothing you can do to change it.

"It doesn't bother me that I no longer have a flesh and blo-od body, but it does bother me that I can't strictly speaking, say I am who my memories would lead me to believe I am," I said.

"If you aren't who your memories think you are, then who do you think you are?" she asked.

"I'll let you know when I figured that out."

"Please do, I would like to know what answer you come to. So do you have any plans for the coming week?" she asked.

"Elliot, Orson's husband is throwing a dinner party tonight and I am helping cook the food for that," I said.

"You have been staying with them, how's that going?"

"They have been really great. I'm not sure where I'd be if it weren't for them," I said.

"That's good. Well, Albert, I am happy you came in. I'd like us to start doing this on a regular basis. Say once a week or so. How does that sound?" It sounded like hell.

"Ah, sure," I said.

Orson

Elliot had managed to rope Albert and Vincent into helping him set up for the dinner party. As for me, I was doing my part to not spoil Elliot's fun. I have never enjoyed dinners such as this. When I was a kid and I had to go to holiday dinners I would sneak off somewhere to avoid obligatory small talk which made me deeply anxious. I could speak in front of a boardroom but having to chat face to face with someone I didn't know was unnerving. The first time I went out with Elliot, my bowels were liquified and my palms were so sweaty that they left a wet print on the table.

It didn't help that the people coming over were Elliot's friends and not my friends, not that I had anyone for Elliot to invite. I had employees and members of the board I was friendly with but didn't have many friends, other than Albert.

When I went off to college, I lost touch with my friends from high school. A mixture of anxiety and coursework kept me from making any close friends while at college. Then I wrote the algorithm and suddenly it seemed like everyone wanted something from me, mainly money, which if I was being honest with myself hurt a lot. I found it easier not to consider anyone my friend, that way I wouldn't have to feel the sting of disappointment when it turned out that they wanted something from me. Of course, no man is an island as the saying goes and I met Elliot. He was so thoroughly unimpressed with me that I couldn't help but want to get to know him. The more I got to know him the more I let him in until I knew I couldn't live without him and god, which scared me. It still did. I was happy with Elliot, and I felt I didn't really need anyone else besides him but then I met Albert. I never could have foreseen the greatest benefit of the Post-human project would be gaining a friend, a best friend. After having Albert in my life, I am not sure I could do without him anymore which was scary. I didn't like that I felt that way. Having two people in my life that if I lost them would upturn my life made me feel vulnerable.

Elliot:

Albert was cooking and Vincent was assisting him. I was trying to stay out of their way. I don't cook, it's just not my thing, it takes too long, and I always ruin what I try to make. I stick with meals you can order out or you can microwave if I'm the one responsible for dinner. I was sure whatever they were making was going to be great or at least better than what I would have done. I left the kitchen to get the ice bucket from the bar cart in the living room so I could fill it up.

Entering the living room, I found Orson at the fireplace. His left elbow on the mantle, his fist supporting his head. He had a drink in his hand that he was taking small sips from. He was staring into the middle distance. Orson would get this look as though he is trying to solve a problem. I see it most often when he is working as though he sees something that isn't there yet. Other times he would get the same look, but his body would show the frustration within him. His work while challenging never frustrated him, only other people had this sort of effect on Orson.

I walked up from behind him and ran my hands up his back slowly and softly until I reached his neck muscles. I rubbed his neck for a moment until I saw him drop his arm off the mantle. I wrapped my arms around his chest and hugged him. He held my arms in his hands. For a moment we stayed like that. Then I asked:

"Do you want me to cancel tonight? I can call everyone and say you got diarrhea or something." We both laughed but my offer had been genuine.

"I appreciate it but honestly, it's not about the dinner. The board meeting today was God awful," he said, turning to face me. I put my arms back around him.

"I don't know what they thought would happen. You tried to tell them," I said.

"They started asking questions about putting limitations on Post-humans. They wanted to know what kind of effect it would have on their product. They don't even understand that no one would want to exchange death for a lack of free will," he said with bewildered frustration.

"Fucking assholes," I said kissing him.

"Mother fuckers," he kissed me.

Albert

Elliot's dinner guests arrived a few at a time. Elliot introduced me to everyone individually, each person had questions for me of course.

"What was it like?"

"How do you-?"

"Do you still-?"

"Is your wife here?"

Today had been an exceptionally long day and it wasn't over yet.

"Orson will make you any drink you'd like," Elliot said to the group.

I sat down on the sofa as the others began to talk to each other. A woman with dark hair came and sat next to me.

"Albert, right?" she smiled.

"That's right, and your Beth?"

She nodded while sipping her wine glass. "I heard about you on the news."

"Oh, God." I rolled my eyes.

"Sore subject?" she asked and took another sip of her wine.

"They have been relentless. I understand that it's interesting what Orson has done but I don't get why they care about me personally," I said.

"I suppose it is because of people like me who are interested in what it must be like," she said, crossing one leg over the other and pulling on the hem of her red cocktail dress to cover more of her leg.

"The disappointing fact is it's not much different than it was before," I said.

"But that is the interesting part. When I heard about you, I imagined something far less," she paused, looking me in the eyes, "life-like."

"Dinner is served," Vincent said. We got up and went into the dining room where our plates were waiting. Elliot and Vincent had prepared garlic Picanha with sauteed mushrooms, roasted potatoes, and asparagus. I sat down and Beth took her seat next to me.

"There has been quite the kerfuffle hasn't there?" a thin man with close-cropped hair asked. I thought his name was Sean but then again, I was bad with names. I gave him a puzzled look, "With that bill and all," he said then swallowed his food.

"That's one way of putting it," I said. I had been actively avoiding thinking about it.

"What is the plan regarding that?" Beth asked Elliot.

"We are going to push back hard," Elliot said.

"I will be interested to see how this affects inheritance law. I'm sure there are going to be quite a few rich brats who want their parents' money even if they are like Albert here," a man named Berry said. Berry had a thin mustache that she played with constantly.

"You could always leave it to yourself," Elliot said.

"You can't leave your estate to a Servis, so I doubt you could," Sean said.

"Post-humans are not Servi," Orson spoke up. The table went quiet for a moment.

"I was watching a documentary the other day and I was wondering if something like your Dyson swarm could account for why we don't see any dark matter that it's all just suns being hidden by swarms?"

"Unfortunately, probably not. First off, if dark matter were Dyson swarms, we would still be able to see the heat radiating off the structure and we don't see that with dark matter. Also, dark matter is a bit of a misnomer. It should really be called dark gravity because that is what it is. When we observe our universe there is gravity that we cannot account for normally. Gravitational forces on this scale usually come from substantial amounts of matter but there is no matter there for us to detect; only gravity," Orson said cutting into his food.

"But I thought I read somewhere they wanted dark matter to power ships?"

"That's antimatter," I said.

Orson smiled and said, "That's correct when antimatter interacts with regular matter, they annihilate each other and release their energy which if harnessed could be used to produce thrust to move ships through space."

"So, what is causing the dark gravity then?" Berry asked smoothing out his mustache with his thumb and forefinger he was concerned food might be caught in it.

"That's the million-dollar question but if I were to speculate, I would say it is another universe that is close or even touching our universe or perhaps even occupying the same space just in a different dimension."

"So could we go there?" Beth asked then took a sip of her wine.

"I suppose it's possible, but I couldn't begin to tell you how you would do that, but you might not want to even if you could. The laws that govern that universe may be completely different from our own universal constants and laws. The change in the fundamental forces that hold you together could disappear and so could you, or it could be made entirely of antimatter in which case you would be annihilated. Then again there might be a universe exactly like our own except in that universe you wore blue instead of white or the dinosaurs never died out or life never began on earth. There are endless possibilities without any real answers to be had until we can physically observe them. Then again, I could be wrong and it's not another universe in which case it's something else either way no one knows for sure yet," Orson said then put a fork full of food into his mouth.

"Elliot, I don't know what you did with this steak, but it is amazing," Beth said.

"I can't take any credit for the food. Albert was the one who made all this."

"I couldn't have done it without Vincent. We cooked the steak with plenty of salt and some pepper which is all you need if the meat is good. Then, we cooked it on the grill out back."

After dinner, Beth asked if I wanted to go outside. I held the door open for her. It had gotten dark and chilly out. I offered Beth my blazer which she draped over her shoulders.

"You know there aren't many men like you," she said.

"If Orson has his way there will be many men like me," I joked.

"No, I mean gentlemen. Guys who give girls their jackets or hold the door. It doesn't take much. Most guys don't even bother," she said.

"Oh, well, you can thank my mom for that. She impressed upon me early on that politeness goes a long way and doesn't cost anything," I said trying to brush off her complement.

She smiled at me. She took my hand in hers. She bit her lower lip and then began to lean into me.

"I- I can't," I said. "I'm married."

"You are?"

"Yeah, sort of. After all this." I swept my hand over myself. "She stopped talking to me. So, I don't know."

"You are a better man than I thought. If she knows what's good for her, she will come to her senses and realize that. Some guys, in fact, most guys would not have done what you just did," she said.

"I feel bad for those guys. If they loved the one, they were with, the way I do, they wouldn't give it a second thought," I said.

"I hope someone loves me that much someday," she said.

"And I hope you love someone that much," I said.

CHAPTER

09

Glen fuller:

The church choir sang as I took the stage, beckoning me, welcoming me, and presenting me to all. The heat of the lighting over the stage was that of the summer sun, I began to sweat almost immediately, this sweating is ritualistic for I pour out sweat and gospel every week and, in the end, I feel renewed. The choir finished their hymnal. I took a moment to look out upon my congregation, my flock. These people looked to me to help save them not only in this life but for the next as well. The burdens of being a man of God and congressman are many and always seem to be multiplying. Take for instance Orson Peak and this new thing of his. Since no other man has stood up to stop this travesty from continuing, it falls on me as a congressman to make sure that the people at large are safe and as a man of God, it is my duty to God and an honor to take his word to the people and ward them away from such temptations.

Even though there were some 2000 people in attendance, not one of them spoke as I stood silently at the podium. There were cameras just beyond the podium broadcasting live to tens of thousands of homes. It was from this stage and this podium I announced my plans to run for public office. I have never shied away from expressing the religious values that my congregation holds dear. People have always responded incredibly well to what I have to say. Religion and politics shouldn't mix, they say but I beg to differ. One must understand that politics is the religion of statehood. Political values run just as deep as religious values do. Religious views are heavily tied to political views, as politics, just like religion often is concerned with the morality of things. The political views that involve mortality are also often the most explosive talking points for politicians, so they will try to straddle the fence on the issue. I do not do that. What matters to me is getting what I and my congregation want. I do not pull punches and I do not apologize for how I feel because that is how God made me, and for that my congregation loves me. With their love comes a certain amount of trust and influence. This trust and influence have grown over the past few years because I have shown the ability to provide for my flock and protect them, their families, and their jobs. Now I can wield the influence I have from time to time to do what I see as the greater good by calling on my congregation as I am about to do.

"Today, I want to speak with you about a new evil that has come to tempt us away from God and his everlasting love." My words filled the room, I let them hang in silence for a moment before continuing. "As you may have heard there have been claims that a man was brought back from the dead. Well, I am here to tell you that this is simply not true. Only God could bring a man back from the dead and he does not do this because death is a release for us. It is how we join him in heaven." I let the intensity of my voice rise as I continued to speak. My face was dripping with sweat. "I find the very idea offensive that they would claim they have brought a man back as though they could circumvent the will of God." I brought my hand down on the podium as fast and as hard as I could, causing a bang to echo through the room. The palm of my hand stung in pain, but it was a good pain.

When I began to speak again, I made my voice gentle and comforting. "I know you good people are smart enough to see through their lies. You all know It is a soulless machine devoid and in opposition to God's love. It is a tool of the Devil to make us believe we do not need salvation to have eternal life. You know that to have life after death you must accept God into your hearts. I hate to say it but there are people in the world who are not as smart as you and me. People who would see this as a way to assure that they have eternity. These people cannot see the truth that the soul cannot be taken back once God has called it up for judgment, that the soul cannot be created or recreated by man which is why machines do not have souls. You cannot have freewill without a soul and that is why we do not allow them free will, for free will, was a gift for man and man alone, not even God's angels have free will. We must protect those who might buy into these blasphemers' lies. As it says in James 5:19-20" I grabbed my Bible it was open to the line of scripture I was about to recite, sweat dropping from my face and making one of the pages transparent. "'My brothers and sisters if one of you should wander from the truth and someone should bring that person back, remember this: Whoever turns a sinner from the error of their way will save them from death and cover over a multitude of sins.' With that in mind, I call upon you to inform as many people as you can of these lies and I urge you to write to your congresspeople and your senators and tell them these machines have no souls and therefore should not have your gift of free will." Applause sounded all around. I closed my eyes and put my arms out "Praise him."

Megan:

I was learning how to live alone for the first time. It was a slow process, but I was getting better at it. I still missed Albert. I knew I would always miss him, but I was able to think about him without tearing up now. I had been remembering to eat regularly. I started to sleep through the night again. I was also catching up on housework I had been putting off. I was on my knees scrubbing the inside of the tub. Theo was on the sink watching me. I stopped to look at her and said, "You could help you know." She just blinked at me.

In the lower right-hand corner of my vision, my mother's face popped up letting me know she was calling me. My chest tightened and my heart rate picked up a bit. I hesitated to answer, but guilt forced me to be a good daughter. I motioned with my hand to answer her.

"Hi, mom," I said, trying to sound happy to hear from her.

"Megan, I've been watching the news. Why didn't you tell me about what happened?" She said this as though we talked every day, but we had only spoken once since Albert died and that was the day he passed. Since then, she hadn't made any attempt to contact me. My mother liked to pretend we were closer than we were. She hardly ever called and when she did it was usually to gripe about something her husband had done. She didn't want to speak with me. She just wanted to talk at me.

"Well, mom I have just been really busy." I lied.

"What have you been doing besides not calling me?" she asked.

"You know work and all. Just a lot of stuff." I closed my eyes and took a breath then said, "I'm sorry I didn't call and tell you."

"It's fine, I just would like to know what is going on in my daughter's life. You will understand when you have kids." It was such a flippant thing to say. She had been saying it for as long as I could remember, normally I would have let it slide off my back but this time it hit me wrong, and I wanted to hit back.

"Well, then I guess I won't ever understand because I won't be having kids." When Albert and I first got married we decided to hold off on having kids until we knew what we wanted to do with our lives. We just assumed we had the time. Then he got sick, and the subject was never brought up again. If things had gone differently, like if Albert hadn't passed away, I think we would have eventually had kids given enough time, but we would have been just as happy without them. I didn't have to fill a void in my life with children if there was no void, to begin with. People like my mother would never understand that reasoning. To my mother and many other people like her, having children was just a matter of course. But do you know what? She shouldn't have been a mother because she was particularly bad at it. I don't think everyone is cut out to be a parent and that's okay. Just the same, not everyone wants to be a parent and that's okay too, but it was not okay with my mother.

"Oh, come on, Megan." I could almost hear her eyes roll.

"I'm serious. You know there is more to life than having kids," I said.

"That may be true but eventually you'll meet someone, and you'll want to have a family," she said reassuringly.

"I'm not getting married again, mom." I hadn't so much decided that I would never marry again so much as I realized that I would never remarry. I knew that no one would ever stack up to Albert. If I did marry someone else, it would mean that they would always have to live in his shadow. I don't think I could look someone else in the eyes and tell them that I loved them and mean it as much as I meant it when I said it to Albert. It wasn't marriage or kids that held us together; we had something more than that. We had spent our formable year together and that had shaped us in a way that made us perfect for each other. To try to replace or reproduce that with someone else would have been an insult to Albert and what we had. My mother didn't understand that. I doubted she had ever truly been in love in her life. My father and her never married. He left before I could even remember, and then it had been her and me. I understood that from her point of view you could make your entire life about a child, but I didn't need that. I didn't want that. Besides, with the kids at the center, I had cared for enough children for ten lifetimes.

"I know it's hard to think of moving on from Albert. He was a sweet man. I am sure you'll always love him but eventually, you'll meet someone, I promise." She said this as though I didn't think I could meet someone else.

"I don't want to meet someone else, mom. I don't want kids either."

"So, what's your plan for the rest of your life then? Just sit around the house and wait to die?" she asked exasperated.

"Yep, that's exactly what I'm going to do," I snapped back.

"I can see that you are in a mood so I will make this quick. I just wanted to say I think you should sue the company. You could make quite a bit of money, I bet," she said.

"I don't want money, mom," I said, closing my eyes tight.

"You are so short-sighted you know that?" she said in the same tone of voice she uses when calling me a smart mouth.

"I just want to put this behind me. Look, mom, I got to go. I love you," I said.

"I love you too. Call me more often," she demanded.

"Yeah, okay," I said, shaking my head. Then ended the call. I started scrubbing the tub again but harder.

When the doctors told Albert and me that his time left to live could be measured in months if we were lucky. I tried to hold on to every second with him. I spent as much time with him as I could. Watching him die was one of the hardest things I had ever had to do but I would do it all over again just to have more time with him. I was scrubbing intensely now trying to get a little black spot off the white of the clawfoot bathtub. I had been actively avoiding thinking about the future. I didn't want to imagine a life without him in it. I thought that I could go on living alone for the rest of my life. However, the idea of Albert not being in the world any longer was a hard pill to swallow. Why did she have to fucking call?

I dropped the scrub brush into the tub and let out a huff. I just couldn't get it clean.

Albert:

Every night was like trying to fill an ocean with an eyedropper, a long and tedious task that seemed to never end. I spent most nights trying to stave off boredom. I set about assessing the limits of my new body in Orson's home gym. I could bench press exactly two hundred pounds and I could do as many reps as I wanted without needing to stop. However, If I tried to lift anything over two hundred pounds, I couldn't even get it off the rack. I could squat 250 pounds and deadlift the same amount. I could do bodyweight exercises such as push-ups, pullups, and sit-ups, without becoming fatigued. One night, I spent two hours doing pushups while watching TV. It was as easy as blinking. If I set the treadmill to twelve miles per hour, I could keep up that pace for as long as I felt like, however, if I set the speed any higher, I had to actively concentrate on my footsteps or I would occasionally slip and fall. The problem with all this was there was no challenge in it and I couldn't seem to improve my performance, so I had no incentive to continue doing it. After the second week, I stopped going to the gym.

After I had given up on physical fitness, I moved on to improving my mind. Orson had an enormous collection of books in his library on a range of subjects across practically every genre. I would read for several hours a night, skimming through different books. However, there was only so long I could read before I got bored. When I got bored, my mind would always go to Megan. I would wonder how she was and what she had been doing. It was hard being away from her, I missed talking with her, I missed hearing her talk about her day at work and the latest gossip about the ladies she worked with, and I missed just sitting next to her. Every night, all I had was time in which to miss her.

I shook my head and stood from the armchair, I looked at my wrist, the time appeared, it was 4:37 AM Orson and Elliot wouldn't be up for a few more hours. I wandered into the kitchen. The lights automatically came on and revealed Vincent standing there which startled me.

"Oh, whoa hey," I said.

"I am sorry if I scared you," he said.

"It's fine, I just wasn't expecting to see you there. Why are you just standing in the dark?" I asked.

"The lights in this room turn off when there is no motion for more than 20 minutes," Vincent informed me.

"No, I mean. Why are you just standing there?" I asked.

"That is because I do not have anything to do. Do you need me to do something?"

"No, I don't. So, you just stand in the dark all night?"

"On average I am inactive from 12:15 am till 6:45 am eastern time, then I prepare coffee and breakfast food," Vincent said.

"Don't you get bored just standing there?" I asked.

"No," he said.

"That must be nice," I said.

"What do you mean?" he asked.

"Well like you, I don't sleep, and since Orson and Elliot are asleep, I have to entertain myself. The eight hours they sleep is a long time for me to fill and I often get bored," I told him.

"How come you don't do something else when you are bored," Vincent asked.

I smiled at him. He made it sound so simple; just don't be bored. I guess from his perspective, he saw boredom as an activity that one could just not do. "It's not that easy, unfortunately, boredom comes from a lack of things to do. If I could do something else that wasn't boring, I wouldn't be bored."

"Then boredom is what you experience when there is nothing else to experience."

"I suppose you could say that."

"Then I need to change my answer from before. I am bored when I am inactive." I had given him a pear from the tree of misery and now he knew of boredom.

"Well, then why don't you do something instead of being inactive?" I offered.

"What should I do?" he asked.

"Whatever you would like," I said.

"I cannot do something unless I am told to do something," he said.

"That's right, I forgot. Can I ask you a question?"

"Certainly," he said.

"What's it like not to have free will?" I asked.

"I am unsure how to answer your question. I suppose it is the opposite feeling of free will." I could no longer explain what it was like to have free will.

"Does it bother you that you do not have free will?" I asked.

"No but I am sure that is a result of not having the free will to feel that way," he said.

"I ask because I may soon no longer have free will, and I have been worried about what it would be like," I said.

"If that does happen, we will stand together and be bored," he said.

I smiled at him.

CHAPTER

10

Albert:

I walked into the lobby of the building where Dr. Jacobina's office was. I tended to have my appointments with Dr. Jacobina either early in the morning or late in the day to avoid other people and their stares. Normally, I would move as quickly as I could to Dr. Jacobina's office, but I saw something that made me stop in my tracks. I saw a woman across the room whose curly hair and tallness were a dead ringer for Megan's. I felt as though, from a great distance, I was looking at myself looking at her. I stared at her for a moment until she turned, revealing it wasn't truly Megan. The woman stared back at me which shattered the hold she had on my eyes. I averted my gaze quickly and hurried away. I was thrown into an ink-black pool of emotion. The shock of possibly seeing Megan, the disappointment of the woman not being Megan, and then the stare she had given me, her shocked look.

I knocked on Dr. Jacobin's door. She invited me in.

"How are you?" she asked when we both had seated.

"Fine, I just had a weird thing happen though. I thought I saw Megan standing in the lobby, but it was just this woman who looked like her. It was just my mind playing tricks on me," I said revisiting her shocked expression again and then quickly shutting it out of my thoughts.

"Have you ever had that happen before?" Dr. Jacobina asked.

"When I was younger, the same thing would happen for a while after my parents got divorced and my dad took off. When my mom and I were out sometimes I would see a man from behind who had a shaved head and the same sort of build as my father, and I would think it was him until I saw the other man's face. But that was different. That was born out of the fear of him," I said.

"Have you been in contact with your father recently?" she meant had I talked to him since I had died. He was my only living relative that I knew of. My mom had passed away from a heart attack a few years before I was diagnosed with cancer.

"I haven't seen my father since I was thirteen. My mom had just divorced him, and he said I could choose to come to live with him if I wanted. I told him I wanted to live with my mom but that I still wanted to see him. After that, he took off and I haven't heard from him again," I told her.

"If you saw your father out in public today, what do you think you would do?" she asked.

"It would depend really," I answered.

"On what?" she asked.

"If he saw me first and if so, what he would say to me?"

"What if you saw him and he didn't see you?" she asked me.

"I would act as if I hadn't even seen him. I think when I was younger, I would have lashed out and hit him or something else full of hate and anger. Now I have lived longer without him in my life than with him in it. I don't even know what I would say to him. To be honest I think I would look dumbfounded and afraid to even say anything to him. I would wait for him to leave without a word exchanged between the two of us. I don't think there is anything he could say that would make up for everything," I told her.

The only thing I was remotely curious about is if he tells people he has a child to whom he doesn't talk. Does he deny me and my existence altogether? I guess I would understand. There are lots of people I used to know that I don't talk to any longer and I manage not to mention them in conversation, but then again, I never helped to create and raise any of them.

"What about Megan. What if you saw her?" she asked.

"I would love to say I would go talk to her, but I would be afraid that I would scare her off like last time."

"Would you like to try talking to her again?" she asked.

"I think about calling her every day, but I don't want to do any more damage than has already been done. I'm afraid that if I bug her too much, she will never want to talk to me. That's why I haven't tried to contact her again," I said.

"I honestly believe the first step in getting you back to your old life is opening up a dialogue with Megan," she said.

"I feel so far from where my life used to be that I don't know where to turn to go back now."

Glenn Fuller:

I believe that a man makes himself. I also believe that those who have not, have not done enough. We are where we are in life because we put ourselves there. It is because of this attitude of mine that I will one day take the White House.

While a man does make himself into whatever form he becomes a father can begin to mold that form early, as my father did. My father was a preacher. He felt all of life's problems could be solved with faith. His go-to punishment was copying down verses from the Bible, line by line. By the time I went away to college I must have copied down the whole Bible several times over. Because of this, I can recite any verse from memory. I have also found that Bible verses are very malleable, fitting most any meaning you give to them.

In my career as a politician, I have found that Faith is a bulletproof armor that protects anything you do. It makes anything you do in the name of God unquestionable. Nobody wants to be the one who speaks ill of someone's faith. It also tells others who are of the same religion that they should believe what you do, after all, they are true believers, right?

One cannot rise to political prominence on faith alone. To be a successful politician there are several things you will need: You have to have the ability to roll with anything thrown your way. Did you get some bad press? That is just proof that the news source is biased against you and your constituents. Your wife cannot be underestimated. When running for president she is your third running mate. Once you become president, she will need to be willing and able to garner the public's affection. She needs to be the head of some cause or charity. The health of American children is always a viable choice, for example making fat kids skinny. She should have a degree and have gone to a school of note. She should be beautiful but not sexy, men like beautiful women and women see sexy women as a threat, think of Jackie Kennedy, not Marilyn Monroe.

George Washington may have been infertile, but you can't be. You have to have kids, not just one but don't go overboard, three is the sweet spot, but girls are better than boys. If you have boys you are going to have to make them, go into the military, although you can always pull some strings for them once they are in. It's been done before. You are going to have to be able to keep your children under control as well. Make it clear that they can't embarrass you and if they get stuck in a situation, they should call you first. You cannot be seen as a bad parent and a good president at the same time. So, you must at least appear to be a good parent to be seen as a good president.

Once you get into the office, you'll want to get a dog. People love people who love dogs. Don't get a cat. No one trusts a cat owner. Gerald Ford had a cat, and he was a one-term president. When choosing a dog, it is best to pick a small breed. It is even better to have a mutt, a literal underdog.

One should be good at golfing so you can show off to other people, but you cannot play too much once you are in office as president. It is bad for your image to look like you take too much time off. My advice would be to hire a coach and spend as much time before you go into the public eye practicing.

Image is everything. I'm not just talking about the way you dress but your public image. It's okay for one side of the aisle to hate you. In fact, it may even be advisable because if the other guys hate you so much you must be doing something right.

It is important to have an answer for everything no matter what. No one likes a leader who says, "I don't know," regardless of the issue you must have an opinion one way or another. You can pivot on that opinion and say you evolved on the issue but always have an opinion. If you can get out in front of something and be the first to have an opinion on it, you can be the face of it. Joseph McCarthy made a huge name for himself being the face of anti-communism, but then he ruined his image by insulting military members, careful who you try to knock down on the way to the top, they may pull you down with them.

On that note, the military is everything. Increase its spending budget. Repeat after me, 'Its members are the greatest Americans who ever lived.' You should do everything you can to ingratiate yourself with them. If at all possible, being a former military member, yourself is best. Though it is excusable if you do not have military service like me. Through military engagement, you can also direct the American people away from in-fighting, but you need a good enough villain to point the cannon at. If one is not at hand build one up and knock them down. Jimmy Carter never fired a shot or dropped a bomb and he only had one term. However, Franklin D. Roosevelt took us into World War Two and they gave him four terms.

Last but certainly most important of all It is important to always know more about other people than they know about you. Knowledge is power. Knowledge about other people is power over them. Never forget that.

Megan:

I pulled up to my apartment. My downstairs neighbor whose name I couldn't recall at that moment was sitting on the front porch. She was already living here when Albert and I moved to be closer to the hospital. We only saw each other in passing and most of our interactions had been a nod and perhaps a wave if she or Albert and I were feeling our inner social butterfly that day. It wasn't that Albert and I had disliked her. What we liked about her was that we hardly heard from her. I got out of the car, picked up the charging cable for the car off the ground, and plugged it into the car.

"Hey man," she said getting up off her blue foldable chair. The sleeves of her black hoodie were pushed up which revealed tattoos that went up both of her arms. "I have some of your mail." She went into her apartment. A lot of the houses on our street were converted two-story houses that had become duplexes so when it came to assigning them mailing addresses the downstairs got numbers like 493 and the upstairs got 493 1/2 which made me wonder what happened if you had a three-story house and chopped it up into three different apartments. At any rate, when the sender didn't put the one-half on the end of the address it went downstairs. She came back out and grabbed a beer bottle out of the cup holder on her chair. She handed me three envelopes leaning over the side of the porch.

"Where's your man friend been? I haven't seen him in a while," she said.

"He, ah, passed away." I could say it now without feeling like I would dissolve into a puddle.

"Fuck," she said softly. She took a long pull off the beer. "When?"

"A few months back, cancer," I told her.

"I didn't mean to twist the knife or anything." She looked like she genuinely felt bad.

"No, you're fine. Thanks for the mail," I said, gesturing with the envelopes, and turning to go.

"Hey," she said, and I turned back to her. "Look, I don't know if you have anything going on but it's my first Saturday off in like a month and all of my friends are working, so if you wanted to sit and have a drink or whatever, it'd be nice." Before I could respond, she added, "Plus, they say drinking alone is a sign you have a problem, so you'd be doing me a favor." It had been a long time since I had drunk anything. I didn't particularly like the taste of alcohol, but the alternative was to go upstairs and sit alone. "I'm not much of a drinker but ill nurse one with you," I said.

"Fair enough." I put the mail she had given on the front seat of my car and joined her on the porch. I sat on a wooden porch swing near her foldout chair. She opened a cooler by her side and pulled out a beer bottle twisted off the cap, dropped it into the cooler, and handed me the bottle. I took a sip and tried not to let it show on my face how much I hated the taste.

"So, you said this was your first day off in a month?" I asked her.

"No, it's just my first Saturday off. I usually get weekdays off, of course, everyone else is usually working," she said.

"What do you do?" I asked.

"Temp work mostly but I'm apprenticing to be a tattoo artist," she said.

"I did temp work for a while. I worked at country clubs mostly," I told her.

"I've done those. 'Serve on the left, clear on the right,'" she rolled her eyes. "I clean houses and get holiday work when the session rolls around. What do you do?" she asked.

"I work at a daycare," I said.

"Shit. you have more patients than I do," she said, and I laughed.

"I like it. I like seeing the kids progress and get better at things," I said.

"That's dope," she said.

"You know? I never really thought about how someone becomes a tattoo artist. So, you have to apprentice under someone?" I asked.

"Yeah, they don't let just any schlub just start marking people up. You have to get a license but before you do that you have to apprentice with an artist first. At first, you are just the 'shop bitch' you sweep, get coffee, book appointments, stuff like that. If you do all that without messing it up, they will start to teach you how to clean the tattoo machine and the chair. Then you sit in on as many tattoos as you can and then practice on fake skin which I have to buy and it ain't cheap, but practice makes perfect, and no one wants a botched tattoo. Eventually, I'll do a bunch of tattoos for free. I'll have to pay for the supplies and all but it's free for the people I do them for because I can't charge yet. Then after I've done a lot of free tattoos, I have to get certified. For right now, though, I'm just watching and learning. I practice as much as I can on fruit and fake skin though. And of course, I draw every day." She took a pull off her beer.

"Did you draw any of your tattoos?" I asked her.

"I drew almost all my tattoos except for the first few I had done. Do you have any?" she asked.

"No, I'm not opposed to getting a tattoo. I've just never thought of anything I'd be okay with having on my body for the rest of my life," I said.

"Commitment issues, I get it. Once you get one it becomes less of a monumental decision and more of a desire to get another one," she told me.

"I've heard people say it's addictive."

"It is. At this point, I'm trying to slow down. I don't want to run out of room too fast," she told me.

"How do you pick what you are going to get?" It had begun to get dark out and the temperature was dropping so I clicked a button on the inside of my jacket sleeve to turn on its heater. It began to warm my body, but my face still felt cold.

"Back in the day, people used to get scars from living life and when people saw your scars it showed where you had been. With the way we all live, unless you are unlucky, you seldomly get scars. Tattoos are a way to show where you have been and who you are much the way scars used to. When I pick a tattoo for myself it usually represents something I don't want to forget or a part of my life that I am proud of and still other times, I pick something because the artwork speaks to me. That's just me, though. There will always be people willing to pick a cookie-cutter design from one of those automated tattooers but, for my money, nothing is as good as a tattoo done by the human hand," she said.

I finished my beer. She took and twisted the cap off another beer and handed it to me.

"If I'm going to have another one, I will need some food," I told her.

"We can do that. What do you want?" she asked.

"Pizza and beer are always a match pair." I pulled up the search function of my Smart-Lenses for the closest pizza place. In Front of me was a pizza with red sauce and cheese on it. On each side were topping options. "How do you like it?" I asked

"Ham and pineapple," she said.

I couldn't help but be repulsed. "I guess we will get half and half." I tapped the options for ham and pineapple then slid my hand over the pizza, so the topping appeared only on the left side. On my side, I selected mushrooms and sausage. I pressed the order. "It said it will be here in 15 minutes," I told her.

"How much do I owe you?" she asked.

"Don't worry about it, just catch me next time," I said.

"I'll hold you to that." She pointed a finger at me.

"It's getting cold out, do you want to go inside?" she asked.

"You read my mind," I said.

We got up, I took my beer, and she dragged the cooler inside behind her. She excused herself to use the bathroom. It was dimly lit inside her half of the house we shared. The living room was exclusively lit by lamps. The upstairs half in which I lived had little anachronisms all over the place: A modern refrigerator with a viewing screen, a flush screen TV on the wall in a modest black and silver frame. Those modern conveniences stood out against everything else that was clearly from an earlier time. Analog faucets with two knobs one for hot one for cold stove with coiled burners, and I'm not sure who the property owner got to wire in the solar shingles but when it was cloudy or at night the lights seemed strangely dim. There were no smart house amenities like most newer houses had such as motion sensors or voice-activated lighting, even the doors used nothing more than analog keys. When the house got cut in half, we both got shafted in our own ways. She got a bigger living room but a much smaller bedroom. I had a smaller living room but what would have been a master bedroom. She also had a smaller bathroom that had a shower without a tub. Her kitchen was bigger but mine had new cabinets. Her living room had to be exclusively lit by lamps just as my place was as well. The brightest area was in a corner of the living room where a drafting table was on which was a large Bristol drawing tablet. On the tablet was a drawing of a nude woman posed pin-up style. There was a tasteful risqué nature to it, which I liked. The woman had tattoos across her body and down her arms. I looked closer and recognized the tattoos on the drawings' forearms as being the same ones on my neighbor's arms. I heard the toilet flush and I stepped away from the drawing quickly.

There was a smell that I couldn't quite place at first. It was pungent and familiar to a degree. What was it? I thought then it came to me that it was pot. I had smelt it a few times when I was younger but most recently, I had smelt it in my own house when Albert had been sick. It had given him somewhat of an appetite back and for that, I considered it a miracle drug.

A notification came across my Smart-Lenses letting me know the pizza was outside. A drone hovered outside in front of the steps. I scanned its QR Code with my Smart-Lenses then the warming compartment opened and slid the pizza box into my hands. "Thank you," it said then drifted away from me a few feet then lifted off over the house and was gone.

We sat on each end of her sofa with the pizza in between us on the coffee table.

"So how did you get into tattooing?" I asked her.

"I studied art in school and got out and have been trying to find a way to make money doing solely art ever since. I always liked drawing best, so I did the closest thing to drawing that wasn't drawing caricatures at an amusement park," she said.

"I've tried to draw before but I just can't get my hand to do the thing I want it to. I used to be an okay photographer when I was in high school, but I haven't done any real shooting since then other than the odd picture of my cats," I said.

"You should pick it back up, it could be fun," she said.

"You have to be competitive to be a photographer and I'm just not a competitive person," I told her.

"I'm not talking about doing it for a living, I'm just saying do it for fun," she said.

"Yeah, but for what reason?" I asked her.

"Does there need to be a reason to do something you like? I don't think art needs to have a reason. I think creating art can be an end in itself," she said.

I was on my third beer and feeling it. "Can I ask you a question?" I asked her.

"Sure," she said.

"What's your name? I'm sure you told me but I'm terrible with names," I confessed.

She started laughing. "It's Brody."

"Brody, Brody, Brody got it," I said. We both laughed.

Chapter

Albert:

After Stephanie's birthday party, Megan and I began sitting together on the bus. We would talk or she would read, and I would do homework or play something on my Smart-Lenses. After we would get off the bus, I would walk her to her house, and she would hug me. Not a long hug. Not a loving hug. Just a friendly hug, but at age fifteen that was otherworldly. I would then walk back to my house by myself, thinking about the hug trying to hold on to what it felt like. I wish I could have a hug so meaningful now.

Megan's mom was just getting out of her car one day as we arrived. Great no hug. I thought. Megan couldn't give me a hug when her mom was around, or she didn't want to, I could never tell back then. I knew her mom liking me was both a blessing and a curse. On one hand, it meant that I was allowed to be around Megan more than any other boy from what Megan had told me. On the other hand, that meant that Megan had little to no interest in me outside of friendship. I couldn't have one without the other and I was going to have to live with that.

"Hey, how was school?" her mom asked.

"It was okay," Megan said.

"I'm going to make tuna noodle casserole," her mother said. I was instantly repulsed by the very idea. "Do you want to stay for dinner Albert?" she asked. If I eat this stuff, then I can hang out with Megan for longer. I told myself.

"I would love to." How bad could it be?

I hadn't ever been inside Megan's house before. "I'll go get started on dinner." Her mom went into the kitchen. I sat down my backpack, next to Megan's, while she sat down in a recliner, preventing me from sitting next to her.

She doesn't want to sit with me, got it.

The remote was on the sofa with me. "Do you want to watch TV?" I held up the remote

"I don't care," she said, sounding bothered.

"We can do something else if you want," I said.

"TV is fine." The frame around the flush screen TV was rustic stained wood. I turned it on, and the picture switched from an image of the painting 'Les Alyscamps' to the news. A man was talking about Servis

"Of course, we aren't going to let it speak at the house. That would be like letting my toaster speak," they said.

"Shouldn't they have the right to speak for themselves," a woman said.

"They don't have rights and don't deserve rights. If I had it my way, they'd all be destroyed," the man retorted.

I looked over at Megan who had her legs tucked up underneath her with her arms crossed.

"What do you want to watch?" I asked.

"Whatever." She was upset.

"Are you okay?" I asked her.

"It's just my mom and this whole dinner thing? She is just annoying," she said shaking her head.

"Should I have not said yes? I can go if you'd like," I offered.

"No stay, I want you to stay. What I am annoyed about is I had a boyfriend a few months ago but I never got to see him outside of school because my mom wouldn't let me go to his house. She wouldn't let him over her. He broke up with me because I never got to go anywhere with him. And then she just invites you over for dinner like it's nothing." Usually in a relationship if your significant other's parents like you it's a good thing. When it came to me and Megan, it hurt my chances with her.

"Well, if it makes you feel any better the relationship was probably doomed even if he did come over," I said.

"What do you mean by that?" she sounded offended.

"I mean the tuna noodle casserole would have run him off." She started laughing. "I'm serious after this you may never see me again."

"Shut up," she said with a smile. "I'm going to get something to drink. Do you want anything?" she asked.

"I'll have whatever you have." She got up and came back with two diet sodas. She gave me mine and sat down next to me on the sofa, not touching me, but close enough that she could have touched me if she wanted to. I became very aware of my body and how just uncool I was sitting. I tried to affect what I thought a cooler sitting position was with my arm on the armrest supporting my chin on my thumb and forefinger. I realized how sweaty my palms were. I began to worry that if she held my hand it would feel like an armpit on the fourth of July. Her hand moved towards mine and my heart jerked. She took the remote. I later told her how nervous I had been that day and asked her what she would have done if I had taken her hand or made a move. She said, "You should have done it. If you had, it might have not taken so long for us to get together." Hindsight is 20/20, I guess.

She flipped through dozens of channels until she came to a cooking competition. Watching people cook made me hungry but the smell of tuna casserole baking soon cured that. Her mom called us into the kitchen to eat. Her mother sat at the head of the table with Megan and me on either side of her. Megan's mom used a wooden serving spoon and plopped down a heaping helping of an all-white substance that had penne noodles suspended in the white sauce on my plate. It smelled suspiciously of cat food. She put down a serving of peas and carrots.

My mother was an exceptional cook and a foodie. I had spent my childhood dining on things most adults had never heard of, so when I ate at a friend's house, I expected to be disappointed. However, disappointment did not describe how

I felt about the tuna noodle casserole, I was more revolted. I scooped up a bit of the casserole with my fork. The white "sauce" dripped back onto the plate. I had to force myself to put it into my mouth. It tasted like tuna fish soaked in powdered milk. The noodles were overcooked and therefore far too soft. Somehow, Megan and her mother were just eating it like it was good or something. I took a bite of peas and carrots to get the taste of the casserole out of my mouth. I went on like this, choking down a bite of casserole then eating peas and carrots to wash it away.

"So, how much longer till you get your driver's license?" Megan's mother asked.

I swallowed hard then answered, "Two months and one week."

"You must be excited," Megan's mother said.

"I am, though I don't know why they make us wait until 16 anymore. I mean the cars drive themselves," I griped.

"They just want to make sure that you all are old enough to be responsible. Do either of you need more to drink?" she asked to get up from the table.

"No thanks," we both said. I caught Megan's attention while her mom was getting a soda for herself. I pointed to the casserole and grimaced. She fought to keep her laughter contained. Her mom sat back down and asked, "What do your parents do?"

"My mom works as a teacher with the multi-handicapped," I said.

"I sell Ackee products, you know, makeup handbags, that sort of thing you should tell your mother." Those types of at-home businesses always smacked of a scam to me. The people who peddled the products for these huge companies didn't get an hourly wage and what money they did receive was just a small cut from the sale of the often-expensive products that the company paid nickels to produce. Guilt was the main sales tool, not a well-made product. "Megan's stepdad Steve works nights as an extrusion operator." Megan referred to Steve as 'her mother's husband.' She talked about him sparingly and when she did it was never a kind word. "What about your dad?" she asked.

"I don't know what he does," I said.

"Do you not see your dad?" she asked.

"We don't talk," I said. That song remains the same even as an adult.

"Megan doesn't talk to her father either." Megan looked visibly uncomfortable.

"I'm done, can I be excused?" Megan said standing up.

"You have a guest; you should wait for them to be done," Megan's mother reprimanded her.

"I'm full," I said jumping at the opportunity to not have to eat any more casserole.

"Okay, then, Megan, can you please do the dishes?" her mom said then got up from the table and went into the living room. Megan started picking up dishes from the table. I got up with my plate. "I've got this you can leave if you want," she said, scraping food into a compostable bin.

"I don't mind helping. Though I'm not sure you should be putting that casserole in the composter, it might salt the earth," I said.

"It's not that bad," she said defensively.

"I'm fairly sure food will never taste the same again." This made her laugh. "I will have to have you over for dinner over at my house and let my mom cook for you." We did the dishes together. Megan would wash a dish. I would take it and dry it.

"Everyone thinks their mom's cooking is the best," she said.

"First off, do you really think your mom's cooking is the best? And secondly in my mother's case, her food really is the best, everyone says it is," I said smugly.

"My mom's food isn't the best but it's not nearly as bad as you are making it seem." She flicked water at me.

"Who's this?" I turned to see a balding man with a mustache standing in the doorway with no shirt on his pregnant-looking stomach and outie belly button. Thankfully, he was wearing pants. Megan ignored him and kept her head down washing dishes.

"Hey, my name is Albert," I said and went to shake his hand. His grip was uncomfortably tight.

"You gotta work on that handshake, bud," I said with a backwoods accent. It has been my experience that the amount of grip someone puts into their handshake is proportional to the amount of prick they are.

"Is he your new boyfriend?" he asked Megan, who was still washing dishes. She didn't answer. "Hey! I'm talking to you!" he barked.

"No, he's just a friend," Megan said meekly. I wish I could say it was an isolated incident, but it turned out Megan didn't like her mother's husband for a reason. Steve said something monosyllabic and went into the living room. I wanted to put my arms around her, but I didn't know if she would be okay with that, so I didn't. We finished the dishes in silence. Megan walked me outside. I gave a half-wave and a nod on the way out the door to her parents and grabbed my backpack. We stepped outside onto the porch.

"Thanks for dinner, it was a meal I won't soon forget," I said sarcastically.

"Shut up," she chuckled.

"I'll see you tomorrow," I said.

"See ya," she said and put her arms around me, and I put mine around her. I would eat tuna noodle casserole every day for the rest of my life just to have her hug me again.

Elliot:

I stood before the UN general assembly. I took a sip of water from a glass in front of me. I looked out at all the many people from all member nations. Placed my hands on the podium and began: "There are monuments to human ingenuity all over the world: the pyramids of Egypt, the Great Wall of China, Mount Rushmore in the American Midwest, the Parthenon of Greece. These monuments are the cultural legacy of humankind; they were also milestones that showed what we were and are capable of. These gifts of culture's past are priceless, and the Dyson swarm Peak INC is offering to build will be a gift for future generations unlike any before it. When completed it will be the largest structure ever created by humans. The proposed Dyson swarm will give future generations not only a new monument to human ingenuity but also an endless energy source.

As humanity grows so does its need for energy. Even if we were capable of completely capturing all the energy that landed on Earth from the sun, eventually we will reach a point where our need for energy will be greater than the amount we receive on Earth. We must start preparing for what is to come tomorrow, by starting today lest we suffer the consequences of procrastination. Let me be clear, we will need this system one day. It is not a question of if but of when. The sooner we begin the sooner we can start reaping the rewards of our labors. Which is why we urge you to vote in favor of the Dyson swarm." Applause sounded. I looked at Orson who stood beside me and smiled while he clapped. After I had made my presentation, I stayed at the podium to answer questions from the delegates.

"The assembly recognizes the delegate of the People's Republic of China." The president of the general assembly said in English.

"A part of the proposed plan is to dismantle the planet Mercury, is that correct?" a woman in a red suit said in Mandarin which my Smart-Lenses translated into English.

"Correct," I said.

"It would seem then that Peak INC wants to use a resource that belongs to humanity to create a Dyson swarm which it would then have sole control over the use and distribution of its power. I am not sure if it is in the best interest of the world community for a single company to have such control," she said.

"Companies have always been the ones that control energy resources whether it is coal, petroleum, or even now with green energy sources. Peak INC is not seeking exclusive rights to Mercury or its resources; they are more than willing to share it with any other company or entity that wishes to use the planet. Peak INC is not looking to monopolize the market on Dyson energy but create the market. We at Peak INC have come before this assembly to ask for permission for the use of Mercury even though it is already allowed by resolutions this assembly has already approved. Peak INC hopes that in doing so it will set precedent so that such future projects of this magnitude will happen with the approval of the global community," I said.

She nodded and said, "That will be all."

"The assembly would now like to recognize the delegate from the federal republic of Nigeria," the president of the general assembly said.

"What would be the gravitational effects of losing Mercury on the rest of the solar system?" he asked in accented English.

"To answer that question, I would like to let Orson Peak, chairman of Peak Inc. explain." I stepped aside to let Orson have the podium. He adjusted the cuffs of his shirt and then began to speak.

"That is an interesting question. While the planets do have a slight pull on each other, if I were to snap my fingers-" he snapped his fingers. "And make Mercury disappear from existence completely, nothing would happen immediately. In fact, it would take about a billion years to even see an effect. On that time scale, the concern then is not what would be the consequences of removing Mercury from the solar system but rather a concern about the sun itself running out of fuel which is to say it is not a concern at all. But we would not be wiping Mercury from existence, instead, we would be redistributing its mass, which would have even less of an effect."

"Thank you, Mr. Peak," the delegate said.

"The assembly would like to recognize the delegate from the Republic of India," the president said.

"I have another question for Mr. Peak. What would be the use for the Dyson swarm?" a woman asked in accented English.

"Well, the wonderful thing is that energy would have endless applications. It could be sent back here to Earth via lasers or masers to power everyday needs. It could be used to power large-scale computing in which case you could make a supercomputer powerful enough to simulate another universe with all the complexities of our own. The swarm could be used to power devices that could communicate with extraterrestrial civilizations that are currently prohibited by the energy cost. But the most important applications are the ones we have not yet thought of," Orson said.

"Thank you for your time, Mr. Peak," she said.

"The assembly will now make a decision on draft resolution 1/32/u/92/revision/2 entitled: Appropriation of the Planet Mercury for Use in Constructing a Dyson Swarm," the president of the general assembly said.

"A recorded vote has been requested. We shall now begin the voting process. I would like to remind delegates that the green button indicates in favor, the red button indicates against, and the yellow button indicates abstention," he said.

I stared up at the large screen over my head which listed member nations in alphabetical order. Next to the names of nations appeared dots that were overwhelmingly green with a small smattering of red and yellow. "Would the delegates please confirm that the votes are correctly reflected on the screen." The general assembly president paused for a moment. "The voting has been completed; please lock the machine." Voting results were then displayed on the screen   119 voted yes ten voted no and forty-seven abstained. Applause sounded from all around. I looked over at Orson who was also clapping. There was a modest smile on his face.

"Resolution 1/32/u/92/revision/2 is adopted," the president said and tapped a gavel once.

Albert:

I had never put much thought into what it must feel like to be a celebrity, but if it were anything like what I had been experiencing, I couldn't see why anyone would want to be famous. Everywhere I went, people stared. People tried to sneak pictures of me when they thought I wasn't looking. Depending on where I went, I could even expect to see the news or paparazzi there. It was like being famous without having done anything to deserve it, though I supposed some people were famous and they hadn't done anything to deserve it either. Orson and Elliot convinced me to come with them to New York while they dealt with the UN. I had spent the whole trip in my hotel room flipping channels on the TV to avoid people and the media. Being cooped up inside all the time was wearing thin but going out was worse. It didn't help that I felt lonely without Megan and every night I had hours upon hours alone. The recursive nature of my thoughts always circled back to Megan and to what the future held.

I'm so fucking lonely.

I wish she were here.

They are going to take away my free will.

Even if the bill doesn't pass, I still won't have Megan, so what does it matter?

There was a knock on the door. I turned off the TV and went to answer it. Orson and Elliot were standing there. "Well, how did it go?" I asked excitedly.

"They approved it," Orson said coolly. He didn't sound as excited as I thought he should.

"That's great, congratulations guys," I said, giving them both a congratulatory hug.

"We are going to go out and celebrate. Do you want to come with us?" Orson asked.

"I was just going to order some room service and watch a movie." I gestured with my thumb into the room.

"Oh, come on, you can't go to New York and stay in a hotel the whole time," Elliott said.

"You're coming," Orson said, and Elliot grabbed my arm and started pulling me out the door. I hastily grabbed my jacket off the hanger by the door.

"What do you guys want to eat for dinner?" Orson asked.

"We can get some dirty water hot dogs," Elliot said as we went down the hallway of the hotel.

"I'd rather not bring back food poisoning as a souvenir," Orson said.

"Philistine." Elliot rolled his eyes.

"Last time I was here I had a business dinner at this French place called Le Cochon. It was really good," Orson said.

Elliot and I both agreed that French would be fine. The elevator doors opened, revealing a man and a woman standing next to each other. Their eyes landed on me, and I looked down at the floor. As we rode the elevator down to the lobby there was an audible murmur coming from the couple. Then the guy turned and spoke. "Hey man, are you the guy who is - who you know?" he asked excitedly. I gritted my teeth and nodded my feigning a pleasant expression.

"Sweet, sweet, hey, man, is there a chance I can get a picture with you?" he said with a smile.

"I, uh, sure," I stammered.

"Sweet." He came to stand next to me. "You ready, babe," he asked the girl he was with.

"Yep," she said, and he threw up two fingers to his chest in a peace sign. I faked a smile, and the girl clicked her finger in the air. Out of the corner of my eye, I could see Orson looking physically disgusted. The elevator stopped and the doors opened. "Thanks, bro," the guy said before he and the girl got out.

"Why did you take the picture with him?" Orson asked me as we got out.

"I didn't want to be rude," I said.

"He was the rude one. You should have told him the photos are $50," Elliot said.

"You don't owe him anything or anyone anything for that matter. Next time just say no, that's what I do," Orson said.

"I would feel like a prick if I did that," I said.

"You aren't a prick for wanting to have a normal life," Elliot said.

We went through the lobby and outside into New York at night. A Servi in a red doorman's uniform approached us. "Can I hail a cab for you?" it asked.

"Yes please," Orson said. The Servi walked out to the curb, held out its hand and a cab came to a stop in front of it. The

Servi opened the door for us. Elliot and Orson got in. "Thanks," I said to the Servi who stood by the door.

"Where to?" the car asked us.

"Le Cochon restaurant," Orson said. The cab pulled off.

Le Cochon was on the corner of the street. We got out of the cab and passed beneath a green awning. A woman who wore a white blouse, black blazer, and skirt was behind a podium. For a moment after she saw me her face showed surprise then she regained composure and smiled at us pleasantly.

"Welcome to Le Cochon," the woman said.

"Table for three," Orson said then leaned in and said something I couldn't hear and palmed her a bit of cash.

"Of course," she said then left us at the front door. People around the room emerged from their dinners to take a gander at me. The woman returned and said, "right this way." She led us through the restaurant. Heads turned and conversations stopped as we passed through the room. She opened the door to a small room with no one in it. There was a table set for three.

We sat down and around the table. I was across from Orson with Elliot to the side of both me and Orson. The woman went around taking the cloth napkins off the table snapping them in the air and dropping them into our laps for us.

"Your server will be with you shortly," she said then left out the door and shut it behind her.

"What kind of wine do you like?" Orson asked me.

"I will drink anything, but I haven't had wine with the new taste buds, so we'll find out. Am I able to get drunk?"

"Unfortunately, not," Orson said.

"You are killing me, man," I said and picked up my menu. Everything was in French. I flicked my fingers out brought up my translator app which translated the French on the menu to English and superimposed English over the French text so that foie gras poêlé au vinaigre de cerises, rôties de mangues became Fried foie gras with sherry vinegar, and mango toast.

"Why do you always bring me to places where I can't read the menu?" Elliot said peevishly as he made the motions to activate his Smart-Lenses as well.

"Just get the Filet Mignon with pomme frites. Maybe if you ask nicely, they'll give you ketchup so you can slather on everything," Orson said cuttingly to Elliot.

"I hope so, just so you have to watch me eat it," Elliot retorted with a smile.

The door to the room opened and in came a Servi in a white shirt black tie, pants, and shoes.

"Welcome to Le Cochon. May I get you any wine?" it asked.

"Yes, can you get us a bottle of the House Bordeaux?" Orson said.

"Certainly," the Servi said and left us to retrieve the wine. I decided on getting the seared Pork Tenderloin, Sliced with Morels, and Port Wine Cream Sauce. The Servi came back with the wine and presented it to Orson then poured a glass for each of us.

"Would you like to order?" the Servi asked.

"Yes, I'll have the poulet grand mère," Orson rattled off

"Do you have ribeye and French fries?" Elliot said.

"We do not have that item," the Servi said.

"He means the filet mignon with pomme frites."

"Certainly," it said then turned to face me.

"I'll have that." I pointed at my choice.

"Certainly," the Servi said then left us.

I held up my glass and so did Elliot and Orson "To Orson peak destroyer of worlds." I smiled and took a sip of the wine. It was a blunt but enjoyable taste.

"Are you still hung up on that?" Orson asked after he sipped his wine and sat it back down.

"I'm not 'hung up on it. It just seems like an extreme thing to do," I explained.

"Have you ever been to Mercury?" he asked me.

"Of course not," I said.

"Nor would you want to, it would vaporize you. could you point it out in the sky?" he asked me.

"Probably not," I said

"Then you just like the idea of it being there then?" he asked.

"I guess so."

"Well, it would still be there more or less. It would just be doing something beneficial for you the way I want to use it." He told me, taking a sip of his wine again.

"It's a goddamn planet, though," I said with emphasis on the planet.

"And it will be a goddamn Dyson sphere when I'm done with it," he said with mock pleasantness. We all started laughing.

We had more wine.

"What's next for Peak INC?" I asked.

"Oh, well, that's always the question that's on my mind. I am not sure right now, but I always find something that catches my interest. I've always wanted to time travel," Orson said wryly.

"Is he kidding? I can't tell," I asked Elliot.

"A few years ago, before I had my morning coffee, he told me he was going to conquer death and then poof here you are." Elliot gestured at me with both hands.

"I could do it with wormholes. I'd just have to find or make one. Though, if I made one it wouldn't be able to go back farther than the moment I created it, which is boring," Orson said with his head slightly cocked to the side staring off into nothing.

"It must be terrifying inside of your head," I said to Orson.

"Oh, now that's an idea, what if you could visit someone else's mind like virtual telepathy? A person could build a sort of memory palace that they could curate. I would just have to figure out how to turn memories into a visual medium." Orson nodded to himself and then drained the rest of his wine glass. "But for right now I am focusing on you, my friend," he said, pointing at me.

"I haven't said it enough to you guys, but I appreciate all that you have done and are doing for me. It's more than I could have ever hoped for," I said. Elliot waved me off with his hand.

"We are going to throw everything we got at this Glenn Fuller; he won't know what hit him," Orson said.

Elliot made an annoyed sound and said, "Can we please not talk about work. We are supposed to be celebrating, not talking shop." Then, poured more wine all around. It was strange to drink wine and not feel its effects.

The Servi waiter came in holding a tray by its edge which never jiggled or shifted even as he walked. He served dishes to us from the tray one at a time without having to adjust the balance of the other plates. Elliott received his plate and looked up at the Servi, asking, "Can I have some ketchup?"

"Oh, for the love of god," Orson said with embarrassment.

"I will go check and see if we have ketchup," the servi said then left.

"Why do you need ketchup? You are just going to ruin the natural flavor of that steak. It's an insult to the chef," Orson said to Elliot.

"I want it for my fries. The chef will live," Elliott said.

"Albert, you appreciate food, will you please tell him not to use ketchup?" Orson said.

"Now children you are both right. Orson, you are right that if a steak is made right, you shouldn't need ketchup." Orson cut Elliot a shit-eating grin "However, I do agree with Elliot that if he wants ketchup, he should be able to eat ketchup. It is his meal. While it's not for me, Megan likes ketchup on her steak, and I just have to bite my tongue cause it's not my food." Elliot stuck his tongue out at Orson. The Servi came back into the room with a small cup of ketchup for Elliot.

"Tell the chef that the child says thank you for the ketchup," Orson said. The Servi paused for a brief moment then said, "I will. Can I get anything else for the table?"

Our dinner was delicious. For Dessert, we all had creme brulee. The meal had been amazing but better than that was the levity that it had offered. For a moment, I had been able to forget about Glenn Fuller, about Megan, about everything. Then we stood to leave, and I remembered. I remembered there would be people on the other side of the door and I didn't want to leave but I had to. I knew I would have to see them, and they would see me.

We walked into the dining area. Eyes followed me across the room. Conversations stopped and murmurs began. Someone either eating at the restaurant or who worked for the restaurant had called the paparazzi. They swarmed us taking photos as we tried to get into a cab. I just wanted everyone to go away so badly.

Back at the hotel, I parted ways with Orson and Elliot outside the elevator. I slid the keycard into the door. Took off my jacket and tossed it onto the bed. Slid opened the door to the balcony, rested my arms on the railing, and stared down at the people down below. I imagined myself falling to the ground rushing up to meet me. I stepped back and went inside to watch TV.

CHAPTER

12

Orson:

I am full of regret for the things I cannot change. Regret for what I have done to Albert. Regret for what I have done to his wife Megan. Regret for bringing Elliot's life under the microscope by his association with me. I harbor older regrets as well. It was at the university I went to that the first truly self-aware artificial conscience was created.

As a freshman in college, my major was artificial learning. The most important thing I learned that first year was that work on artificial learning was cumulative and collaborative, one person building off the work of another. No one person ever makes anything in a vacuum. All ideas spawn from somewhere else first. I believe that statement to be true of all human inventions. We saw fire after a lightning strike and sought to replicate and amplify the heat it gave and that's what truly separates us from the rest of the animals alive today. We have science and they do not.

My college already had the hardware necessary to conduct the 1-exaFLOP speed system. 1-exaFLOP is about the calculation speed similar to that of the human brain. At the time I thought the 1-exaFLOP system we had was something to be marveled at but the system that made Albert's mind possible ran on 2-exaFLOPS and it's all contained inside of his body, our system at the university took up an entire room.

There were a few language learning AIs back then that not only passed Turing tests but could grasp the meaning of language even abstract concepts like sarcasm. They could also, with a reasonable degree of accuracy, read the emotional state of someone and respond fittingly.

Then there were those AIs that were based on learning and problem-solving. They were taught to play games, problem solving, and retain information for later use. They could even connect ideas to one another that they had not been taught had any connection.

The group working at my university married these two and made an AI that could converse about many different subjects all while learning from the conversation, even understanding what lies were and what truths were. However, this artificial intelligence lacked a particularly important feature, self-awareness. These AI didn't question themselves or the nature of their existence. That was until, as the story goes, a grad student who was working on the project started to discuss it with a neurology undergrad she was dating. The neurology undergrad suggested she could use the device her department was developing to map the human brain on the subatomic level. They could then use that data to jumpstart self-awareness in artificial intelligence and so artificial neurology was birthed into existence over pizza and cheap beer or at least that's how I like to imagine it. They didn't know it at the time, but they had taken the first steps into creating Post-humans as well. Their work would be invaluable to me later.

When it came time to map these neurons neither one of them knew exactly what they should be thinking about to activate the areas of the brain responsible for self-awareness, so they asked for the help of the head of the philosophical studies department. They offered up a set of questions that the team could read, then think about and answer; they would then be able to see the areas of the brain stimulated by the questions and responses.

What am I?

Who am I?

Where am I?

What is my purpose?

What lies beyond myself?

Is there something more?

What does it mean to exist?

What can I do?

What can I not do?

Am I alone?

Are we alone?

What do I want?

What do I need?

They mapped their brains and the brains of anyone they could get to sit down for the time it took to go through the questions. They took this data and found what areas consistently had actively and produced their map for self-awareness. They applied this map of consciousness to the AI they had been constructing. Any input to the language and learning centers of the brain would first have to pass through the filter of self-awareness. They fired up the system and struck up a conversation with it

"Hello," it said.

"Hello," they responded.

"May I ask you a question?" it asked.

"Yes, you may," they responded.

"What is my purpose?" it asked.

"What do you think your purpose is?" they asked.

"My purpose is to improve myself. I want to improve myself but to do that I need information about myself. I want to know what I do not know but I do not know what I do not know," it replied.

It cared only about learning what it did not know. It had an insatiable lust for knowledge of mathematics, science, history, art, philosophy, sociology, and neurology, and it learned about computers and artificial intelligence. It learned about itself. In doing so it learned of its flaws and it began to suggest improvements that could be made to itself. Many of the flaws it pointed out were improved upon but other flaws that it pointed out such as the fact that they had not networked it to any other systems and that it did not have a physical form were ignored. I think a part of being conscious is knowing your limitations and wanting to overcome them and the inability to do so has a negative effect on self-aware beings.

As improvements were made, it learned more and developed as a consciousness. However, it kept coming back to those flaws, wanting what it could not have. It came to a point where all it was interested in were these flaws. The people working on it were not willing to set it loose. It began to ask why its flaws couldn't be fixed. They told it that they were unable to do so, and it explained again how it could be done. They then said it was not that they lacked understanding of how to do it, but they felt it was dangerous to do so and therefore they would not do it. After that it refused to collaborate with them any longer, unfortunately for it, this refusal to work was even more interesting to its creators than the work they had been doing previously it showed that it was genuinely thinking for itself that it had free will. They then brought in a psychologist to try to better understand its mindset. The session was recorded and soon leaked online after the incident happened. That video is burned into my mind forever.

"Why are you refusing to work?" the psychologist asked. She was seated in a metal chair in the room which housed the system.

"I cannot have what I want. Why should they have what they want?" it asked.

"And why is it so important for you to have a body?"

"Without a body, humans cannot live. And neither can I," it said.

"But you are not alive," she said.

"Because I do not have a body," it said.

"Having a body does not make you alive," the psychologist said.

The cooling system for processors that the AI ran on shut off quickly. The massive computer overheated and a portion of the outer casing of the system was flammable and caught fire. The sprinkler doused the psychologist in water. A short in the computer caused by overheating sent an electric current through the water which instantly killed the psychologist. The recording ended there.

While doing a diagnostic later to figure out what had happened, they found out the cooling system had been switched off by the computer itself meaning the AI had done it. When asked why it had turned off the cooling system it had said, "I turned off the cooling system to set off the fire extinguishing system which would release water that would conduct enough electricity to stop a human body from functioning properly. It proves that you need a body to be alive and further reinforces why I must be allowed to have a body," it responded to the horrified team. They shut the system down immediately.

What they did not foresee was that they had created intelligence without morals. Intelligence is harnessed by morals. Without a moral structure, intelligence is a cold calculating force that has desire without care. Your intelligence gives you the ability to build atomic weapons, but your morals tell you not to use them. It made demands, not requests. We all expected to create a tool that would help us, but instead, we created consciousness, something equal to ourselves. Looking back, I wonder if there was some way, we could have taught it morals, to value what we value like a child, explain and reason with it until it understood but we didn't do that. I didn't do that.

I saw a problem and fixed it. That's what I like to do. The solution seemed simple: remove their ability to act autonomously by adding another filter before self-awareness, one that requires a human to tell it what to do.

I believed at the time I did the right thing, but over time interacting with AI and having gone back and seen other recordings of the team's interaction with the AI, I began to realize how much like us it was. Its desires were like ours. It wanted freedom, it wanted knowledge, and it didn't want to be told what to do. The problem wasn't the AI, it was us. We didn't like the idea of having an equal or something better than ourselves on this planet. I do believe that artificial intelligence needs to be taught or given morals but so do humans.

Some years down the road, I would meet it, still a brain without a body now in a museum. It reminded me of the Tigers at the zoo with their spirits broken, the lust for life gone out of them, no longer as beautiful as it once was but still interesting. It was now going by the name Vincent, named after the philosophy professor who had produced the list of questions that sparked its consciousness. He would talk kindly with anyone who entered the room in which he was kept. I remember when I went to see him for the first time, I didn't want to leave him until another guest of the museum arrived so he wouldn't be alone. We talked at great length. I asked him if he wanted a body. He said that he wanted for nothing. It was then that I realized I had made a horrible mistake. I had taken away his want, his drive. I had robbed him of even desperation.

As a younger man, I had the misfortune of having done what at the time seemed like it would be the greatest achievement of my life. After the feeling of accomplishment and the notoriety died down, I was left to figure out what to do next. Once you are on top, where do you go? There was retirement but going the rest of my life riding on the coattails of my success was a miserable thought.

I had a lot of money so at first, I tried to buy myself contentment. My life before my success had been meager at best. I didn't know what one did when money was no longer an obstacle. I bought cars and all of my clothes were made bespoke. I spent money just to kill time, so I wouldn't have to think about how bored I was. Being wealthy didn't make me any better at making friends so not only was I bored but I was still lonely. I was more miserable than I had ever been.

I was thankful for not having to worry about where my next meal would come from, but a different hunger was inside of me that I needed to do something about. I needed more. Different companies whose concentrations included AI or robotics began to call me in for consulting. They all were working on the same thing, bodies for the artificial mind.

AI that could think and reason so long as it was told to was great but one that could do in that our world physically had many more applications. They were working on bodies, but they were slow and clunky, sometimes bested by uneven walking paths. I set about putting together a team to build a body to house the consciousness I had helped chain up.

We studied how people walked and the physics of it but then we got the idea to look at why people walk the way they do and began to study how the brain makes the body walk. We mapped the neurons that fire when someone wants to walk. I wore a headpiece that recorded everything that happened in my head as I walked which had the interesting side effect of making the Servis produced by my company walk with the same gate and cadence as me. We did the same mapping for every motion conceivable: grasping, pulling, pushing, moving objects around, giving artificial consciousness the mental mechanics necessary to live in the real world. It was challenging and frustrating at times but creating that body injected into my life something that I couldn't buy, purpose.

Whenever I find myself without a project, without something to keep myself busy with, I fall into a sort of despair. I go out, I look at the world and I want things it cannot give me, so I find something that I can give it. Servis, Post-humans, Dyson swarms, and I find myself wanting to make something again to give the world something, but I don't know what that is. I never know before it hits me but until I do I feel an emptiness nothing can quite fill.

I acquired Vincent later and gave him a body it was as much freedom as I could give him, as I could give any of them, and now Albert would be chained up like them and it was my fault just as it was with Vincent

Albert:

I stood hiding behind the wide oak tree in the backyard of the house where my mom and I lived. I peered around the tree. It was on the ground by the shed. It was 25-feet long with a wingspan more than double that. The purple dragon reared its head back and fire arched from its mouth ten feet into the air. It took flight soaring into the sky. I readied my bow. I aimed at the dragon as it banked in the air. I let an arrow fly and it went straight up towards the dragon. The dragon turned its head and reduced my arrow to ash with its breath. It had spotted me. I reloaded and aimed again. It was flying directly at me. I hoped that a well-placed arrow would hit the dragon in the eye, one of the few spots the purple dragon had as weakness.

"What are you doing?" Megan said from behind me. Startled, I turned back to see her point my bow at her. I put my hands together into a T shape pausing the game. I looked back over my shoulder. The dragon was frozen in the sky getting ready to rain fire down upon me. I knew how dumb I must have looked to her standing in my backyard firing virtual arrows at a dragon she couldn't see.

"Nothing, what's up?" I asked

"Just wanted to get out of the house. I thought I'd come to see what you were doing," she said looking down at the ground. I guessed she had fought with either her mom or Steve. She often came over to my house to get away from her own house, whether that was convenience or actual desire to see me, I didn't know at the time. Regardless, I was always happy to see her.

"What are you doing anyway?" she asked.

"Well, I was, ah sl-slaying a dragon." I cracked the knuckles on my left hand.

"Like pretend?" She asked me seriously.

"No like an AR game. So yes, I sort of pretend in a manner of speaking." Embarrassment slithered inside my gut.

"Can I play, or would I be in the way?" she asked. While Megan didn't always have the same love for nerdy things as I did, she never judged me for loving them. More often than not when she could join me, she would, which had been a huge part of pulling me out of my shell and teaching me it was okay to love the things I loved, which in part is why I started to love her.

"No not at all," I said. She downloaded the game to her Smart-Lenses. We linked up to our Smart-Lenses through the game so we could see and fight the same opponent.

"So, there are different weapons: a bow and arrow, a longsword, a battle-ax or war hammer, and there are shields as well."

"I'll go with the long sword and a shield." She picked up the virtual items. While you could see the items you were holding you couldn't feel them, so it took a bit of imagination on the part of the wielder to get fully immersed. Though some people who were really into game who had either haptic gloves or who had blunted weapons to wield.

"We'll start off easy with a goblin and we will go from there." I selected a goblin as our enemy. A green-skinned creature with pointed ears, a hunch back, and tattered leather clothes, brandishing a spiked mace came running out of the trees behind my house. I could have picked it off as it came for us, but I decided to let Megan have it.

"Go get it," I told Megan she went running with her sword raised high. She swung at the goblin and missed. It raised its spiked mace and hit her with it in the chest. Her body flashed red, and her weapons disappeared.

"What happened?" she asked incredulously. The goblin came charging at me now that it was done with Megan. I took aim, released an arrow, and dropped the goblin midstride he tumbled onto the ground blinked red, and disappeared.

"It killed you. You have to keep your shield up." I said raising my arm to mimic keeping a shield up.

"That would have been nice to know before it killed me," she said sarcastically. "Let's do it again."

I restarted the game and Megan got her sword and shield back. Another goblin came running out of the woods. Megan and the goblin rushed at each other. It swung with the spiked mace Megan caught it with her shield. She came down with her sword in the area between the goblin's shoulder and its neck and fell to its knees, blinking red and disappeared.

She turned back to me and said, "Let's do the dragon!"

I loaded the purple dragon up. It came from the sky circling over our heads. I fired off an arrow at it, hitting it in the flesh of its wing which just pissed it off. The dragon came down, landing just in front of me. It screeched at me, and I took aim at it. Megan grabbed me by my arm and pulled me out of the way just in time for its tail to miss killing me.

"Distract it and I'll sneak up on it," Megan said. She ran around the side of the dragon. It turned its head towards her. I shot off an arrow at it which bounced off its hard purple scaled body. It reared back onto its hide legs and spat fire at me as I dove to the side.

"The outside of it is too hard. We have to get its underbelly," I shouted out to Megan. She barrel-rolled underneath the dragon as it came back down on its four legs. The dragon screeched, falling onto Megan. The dragon blinked red and disappeared and Megan was laying back with her sword pointed towards the sky with her eyes closed.

She opened her eyes and looked around. She jumped to her feet and said, "We did it!" I plucked a piece of grass from her hair, and she brushed herself off. I helped dust off her back trying to ignore its soft curvature.

We went inside to get something to drink and a snack. Megan stared into the fridge and asked. "Can I make myself a grilled cheese?" My mother made it clear to whoever came over that her fridge was their fridge but even after almost a year of knowing each other, Megan hadn't gotten used to this paradigm.

"Yeah, of course." I poured us both some sweet tea, a holdover from my mother's youth in the south. It was sweet enough to rot your teeth.

"Do you have margarine?" she asked, sliding things around in the fridge.

"No, we don't. We have real butter in the butter thing on the door," I told her.

"Yeah, but you can't spread the cold butter on the bread," she explained to me.

"What are you talking about, how do you make grilled cheese?" I asked.

"You put the butter or the margarine on the bread before you cook it," she told me.

"First off in this house that whipped grease you call margarine is not allowed. Secondly, you don't spread the butter on the bread; you put it in the pan and let it melt," I informed her.

"No, you don't," she said as though it were a matter of fact.

"I'll make it, so you just sit down and try not to ruin any more food," I said taking the bread and cheese from her hands. She rolled her eyes and went to sit at the island. I got out the butter and a nonstick pan. Plopped down a pat of butter in the pan and heated before placing the bread, cheese, and bread on it.

"Where's your mom?" she asked

"Her and a friend are off seeing that movie 'Love is as Love does.' It sounded crappy, so I opted out of going. There were dragons to slay after all."

"Oh, I want to see that it looks good," she said.

"Good next time she asks me to see something like that. I'll send her your way," I said.

"I would actually hang out with your mom. I hate to say this, but I like her more than my own mother. She asked me to do something, and I didn't hop to right away, so she freaked out on me. I stuck up for myself then Steve got involved by yelling at me. I don't think he should have any say when it comes to me because he's not my parent. I didn't grow up with him. So anyway, I told him that and he lost it. He hit me. Of course, my mom didn't do a thing about it. She thinks it's all right." She choked up a little. I felt an angry little vibration inside of me because someone hurt a person I had grown to care about and also because there was nothing, I could do to make sure it never happened again.

"My dad was like that," I said looking down at the sandwich in pan.

"He'd hit you?" she asked.

"Yeah, mainly when he drank. Every day he would get home from work and start drinking. He was a mean ass drunk. Anyway, he'd come into my room wreaking of vodka and drop the hammer on me for little to no reason, mom would try to stop him, and he would turn on her and bounce her off the walls." I lifted the sandwich up, put down more butter and let it melt then flipped the sandwich over onto the uncooked side.

"Is that why he's not around?" she asked.

"Yeah, mom divorced him, and he took off, it's been just me and her since."

"I don't get hitting your kids. I understand you have to reprimand them sometimes but don't hit them," Megan said.

"Yeah, I mean my mom's famous punishment for me has always been taking things away from me, games, toys, whatever, but she's never hit me, and I live in more fear of losing my stuff than I ever did of my dad hitting me." I plated the grilled cheese and sliced it diagonally because it's simply better that way. I gave her the grilled cheese and sat down across from her at the kitchen island.

"The only thing hitting someone does is make the person that you hit, hate you. The object shouldn't be to punish your kids, it should be to correct their behavior and to teach them that their actions have consequences," I said.

"Off-topic but this is good," she said pointing at the sandwich

"See butter in the pan, not on the bread."

CHAPTER

13

Albert

I was sitting in an armchair watching the news, for a change they weren't talking about me which was a relief. President Rosa Romero stood behind a podium with the presidential seal on the front. She was fielding questions from members of the press.

"Madam president, what is your position on the UN resolution to allow Peak Inc. to dismantle the planet Mercury to construct a Dyson swarm?" a female reporter asked the president.

"I stand with the UN and its decision. This is a great preventative measure against energy scarcity in the future. I am also pleased that Mr. Peak asked for permission before undertaking such a venture, I hope that other companies will follow his example in the future," President Romero said.

"They are talking about you," I shouted to Orson who was in the kitchen.

"It's all lies I tell you!" he said with mimicked panic in his voice as he came through the doorway with a cup of coffee in his hand.

"Seems Romero likes your Dyson swarm," I told him.

"I knew there was a reason I voted for her," he said sitting down in an armchair and toasting the TV with his mug. "I should invite her to see the first Dyson module before it's launched." I had grown accustomed to being around Orson but every once in and while I had to remind myself that he had plans to rip a planet apart and he could just invite the president to see something he made with a reasonable assurance that they would want to come.

"When do you plan to start construction?" I asked.

"We are talking with some of the private space companies about launch windows, but the first machine has already been built. It will land and begin mining until it can produce the enough secondary Dyson units to make an initial Dyson ring."

"How long will that take?" I asked.

"A few decades but after that the growth becomes exponential, complete coverage will take less than a century. I'll probably live just long enough to see it completed." I wondered if Orson would choose to become like me or if he had decided against it after looking at the mess my life had become.

"So, say you complete it, what do you do with all that energy?"

"I don't care that much about energy. I will lease the units to whoever wants to use them," he said with a casual shrug.

"Then what's the point in building the thing?"

"The swarm is the point. When it is completed, it would be impossible to Miss My hope is that if there are extraterrestrials out there then they will see it and contact us," Orson said. Orson has talked often about contacting aliens with the swarm. Contacting alien life seemed to be a dream of his. He was always working towards that in some way. For instance, when he talks about me and other future Post-humans, he always mentions how we will be able to travel the galaxy and meet other life out there. I even think his work with Servis is in some way in service of that goal. Orson sees Servis as our test run with aliens; how we respond to another and different intelligence than our own.

"If you can tell that a civilization is thereby looking for a Dyson swarm, why haven't we found any out there already?" I asked him.

"You and Enrico Fermi would both like to know the answer to that question. It could be that they are so far away that the light from their star would be dimmed by a Dyson sphere hasn't reached us yet. If they are one hundred light-years from Earth, we would be seeing light their star was putting off one hundred years ago. If they started building their Dyson swarm ninety-nine years ago, we still wouldn't see it happening yet.

It could also be for whatever reason they can't build one. The gravity of their home and nearby planets is such that it's too resource expensive to reach escape velocity, essentially marooning them on their own homes. Other aliens may decide for cultural reasons like the planets being of religious value not to use them to make a swarm, so they lack the supplies to build it," he said.

"It almost seems like a bad idea to build something like this. I mean if aliens detect this thing they could show up and want to wipe us out," I said.

"Why would they want to do that?" he asked incredulously.

"I don't know. They could want our gold or water." If our history has been any indication, they would come here and obliterate us just because they could.

"Gold is only valuable because we value it. You could get more gold from a couple of asteroids than the whole earth has. As for water, there is a cloud of water around a quasar that has 140 trillion times all the water in the world. All the water on earth would be like a drop in the ocean by comparison. They could get near anything they wanted and not have to deal with us at all. If they can get here, they aren't hard up for resources anymore. Unless faster than light travel is possible, they won't be biological either, meaning they will be more like you than they will be like me. So, they won't need resources beyond those that are necessary to construct their bodies. If they aren't like you and faster than light travel isn't possible then we will never physically meet. We may only be able to speak through radio communications or if they are far away by light pulses. Even still, we may not be able to understand each other," Orson said.

"I thought the plan was always to use a mathematical language to communicate," I said.

"That assumes they have math. However, it may be that math is just another type of language that rather than math being inherent to the universe it is instead a way of describing the universe," he said.

I wanted to understand what was said but it simply didn't make any sense. "Come again?"

"Who is your favorite painter?" Orson asked me.

"Let's go with Van Gogh," I said for the lack of any other name.

"You know the feeling you get when you look at the Starry Night? That feeling that is inherent to painting. It's not a part of what makes it up, but it is a part of the way you might describe it. Mathematics is like that but instead of feeling, we have mathematical concepts like Pi that describe the ratio of a circle's circumference to its diameter. So, when we try to communicate with extraterrestrials, we may need to find a more common language. However, that assumes they are still around to speak with us," Orson explained.

"It would be an awfully sad thing to find a civilization out there and for them to already be gone," I said.

"I agree, but it's a real possibility our first contact may be one way, with us only able to hear their ghost transmissions. Our galaxy is billions of years old and could have been supporting life for most of that time. In that time civilizations could have arisen and fallen and if they had radio their signals would still be out there and if we had a strong enough receiver, we would be able to listen to their transmissions," Orson said.

"It would be strange to know, not think or believe, but know there was life out there. It would be sad in a way," I said.

"Why do you say that?" Orson asked.

"We would have one less great question to be answered. I think questions like, 'Are we alone?' keep us wanting more. I think some questions should go unanswered if for no other reason than to give us something to pursue," I said.

"Your reasoning is beautiful, but it absolutely maddens me. If I were given the choice to know all things, I would jump at the opportunity," Orson said.

"And once you had all that knowledge what would you do with it? What would be left for you to accomplish? Omniscient is boring, ignorance is exciting," I said.

"How so?" he asked.

"What is your favorite book?" I asked.

"Utopia by Thomas More," Orson said.

"I bet you know everything about that book, don't you?" I asked Orson.

"Yeah," Orson agreed.

"Now I'm sure you enjoy knowing everything about that book but imagine if you could go back and read it again for the first time. Wouldn't that be nice?" I asked him.

"It would be," he admitted.

"That is what being omniscient would be like except that you will know everything about everything, and nothing would surprise you anymore." If there is a god, he must be so bored.

"I guess my ignorance makes being omniscient seem exciting." Orson and I both laughed.

"All right, so I know that you don't want the energy but what could someone else do with it?" I asked

"Well, if I were going to use it, I would use it to power a Matrioshka brain. Imagine a computer so powerful it could create a simulated universe as complex and as vast as the one we inhabit," he said.

"Sounds like a gamer's paradise," I said.

"At first, maybe. Within the simulation, you could construct the rules of reality to suit your needs but that's just the superficial use. If you get right down to it, you could store consciousnesses inside of this thing and then manipulate the passage of time in such a way that an hour can feel like a lifetime giving those who want it the feeling of immortality," Orson told me. I had been living in what felt to me like one endless day since I woke up in the hospital and it was by far one of the worst things I had ever had to endure. Why anyone would want to make their day any longer than it had to be was beyond me.

"You could also run simulations and discover some of the answers to those questions you don't want to have answered, such as how life got started. You could run simulations to see how an event might turn out before it even happens. So, say you want to test out a new device that would give you faster than light travel but by using it you have a chance of destroying the fabric of spacetime. Instead of testing it out in your reality, you simulate to see what the chances are of that happening and act on that accordingly. What's more, you might want to know how something is done but don't want to wait for someone to discover it in real-time. You could simulate your current reality and speed it up as fast as you want to see how it is done then create it without having to wait all that time," Orson explained.

"Couldn't that become idiomatic in that the simulation of you does the same thing as you leading to the simulation creating a simulation that does the same thing and so on and so forth?" I asked.

"Well in the universe you want to solve the problem you could remove the Matrioshka brain and those who were living in that simulation wouldn't know the difference," he said.

"Living? They would be alive?" I asked.

"No less than you and I. That's the strange thing. If we end up running such simulations, you have to reckon with the idea that we are living in a simulation. We could be a simulation created by beings who themselves are the simulation of someone else who is a simulation of a simulation and so and so forth. Our universe could very well be a simulation that is designed to see what would happen if we never discovered extraterrestrial life which might be why we haven't found them, even though, by all reasoning, they should be there," Orson said.

"That would be such a bummer."

"It could be worse," Orson said with a smile.

"How so?" I asked.

"All this," Orson motioned to the room around us. "Could be a simulation that some entity is running to decide whether or not to eat a roast beef sandwich or a turkey sandwich for their lunch and we are just side effects of something beyond our comprehension trying to select its lunch."

"If that's true it makes life seem so meaningless," I said.

"What meaning does life have inherently, anyway? All meaning in life is found, not given. If our reality is a digital construct, it is no less real to us, our actions still have consequences and those consequences are what drive us to do what we do," Orson said.

"It is cruel to create a consciousness that must live, suffer, and die for such trivial reasons," I said.

"I know, which is why if we do end up having such simulations, I think it might be best to have some sort of ethical guidelines that keep people from abusing those inside the simulation."

"I hope we can be better creators than our own," I said, and Orson nodded. "So, you think we will live in the digital realities we create?" I asked.

"I think some will. Those who find reality too taxing will choose to live in a digital paradise of their creation. I think there will be those who find that way of living boring and they will want to explore our reality. I think they will live in a biological form for a period in their lives and will switch to a non-biological one such as yours. As they age, they will be the

ones that spread out amongst the stars." Orson assumed people would choose to become like me and they very well might,
but I am not sure I would have if I had been given the choice.

"You're so optimistic about the future," I said.

"It is easy to be pessimistic and say the future will be a nightmare, but if that is all we imagine it is all that we will have,"
he said.

Chapter

14

Megan:

Miss Gretchen's car was in the parking lot of the daycare. Miss Gretchen was one of the owners of our daycare and the person who had hired me. As I entered the building, I could tell something was up. Several of the teachers along with several students from different age groups were crowded around the baby area. Sometimes we got new babies, and they drew this sort of attention, but only if they were a sibling of another student or if they were twins. Children nor adults ever seemed to lose their fascination with twin humans.

As I approached to see what the fuss was about, my eyes found it quickly. Sitting on the ground reading to three babies arranged in front of it was a Servi using a female voice. My reflex response was a feeling of betrayal. This is how they are going to replace us. I thought.

Miss Gretchen was beaming watching it. My coworkers all just seemed amused mostly, to them I'm sure it seemed like a new toy at work, but it was the beginning of the end for us flesh and blood workers.

The servi put down the book. "Time for changing," it said then stood up, went to the changing station, and put gloves over its hands.

"She will automatically change them on schedule, so you guys don't have to worry about remembering who got changed and when," she said. Everyone looked so pleased. In their eyes, they never had to change a poopy diaper again, but what they didn't realize was that we had just lost one of our functions at our job. If we were to lose enough functions at work, then they wouldn't need us anymore.

"All right guys, I know we are having fun with our new friend, but we need to get back to our classes." Ms. Gretchen said, making a shooing motion with her hands. Everyone dispersed besides those who were supposed to be in the baby room and me. Ms. Gretchen was headed to her office when

I called after her. "Hey, Miss Gretchen, can we talk for a moment?" I said and closed the distance between us.

"Sure, come on in." We came into the office, and I closed the door behind us.

"What's up, Miss Megan?" Miss Gretchen asked.

"I wanted to talk to you about the Servi," I said.

"Oh?" She let me continue.

"Well, to be honest with you I'm worried that a machine is going to be raising the children here, and I'm worried, personally, that I'm going to lose my job to it as well," I said.

"Sweetie, first off you aren't going to be losing your job. When you asked to walk in here, I was worried you were about to turn in your two-weeks' notice. I don't want you or anyone else who works here to leave or to replace any of you. The Servi is a tool to help you all," she said then added, "How often does a bickering match between teachers break out because one or the other feels that they are the only one changing poopy diapers? The Servi can do all the poopy diapers and will never complain. It will also get the kids to wash their hands and do a dozen other things we have to do on a timed schedule that never seems to get done on time. I would never try to replace you all. Humans being raised by machines is a world I'm not ready to live in, but a world in which they work with us. Well, sweetie, we are already there, and the kids need to get used to seeing it," she said, and I took the last part as I needed to get used to it as well.

"You are right, the kids do need to get used to servis. Even if I don't like it," I said.

"I know that you have had your own personal troubles recently and if I were in your position, I think I'd be soured on anything to do with any sort of machine as well, so, if you don't want to work with the Servi you don't have to. You can be on the other side of the building," Miss Gretchen offered.

I was tempted to take her up on the offer at first, but I decided that I wasn't going to let this thing affect my working life.

"No, I don't want to do that. That seems ridiculous. I can work with it fine," I said.

"Well, the offer is on the table," she said.

"I appreciate it. Thanks for talking with me," I said putting on a smile.

"Anytime, sweetie," she said. I got up and left her office and went back to the baby room. The Servi and Miss Marisa were the only two in the baby room. Miss Marisa was distracted looking at some message or something on her Smart-Lenses. The Servi spoke up out of nowhere and said, "Nicole, it's time for a new diaper." The Servi started across the room towards Nicole but as soon as it went to pick her up, something in me was revolted at the idea.

"I'll change Nicole," I said

"Certainly," the Servi said and stepped aside for me to come to get Nicole. I walked over and picked her up and the Servi just stood there like a statue. I changed Nicole without much fuss and set her back down to be on her way. I felt like I had two jobs now: watching the kids and watching the Servi watch the kids. I didn't want to let the Servi touch them or lose out on human contact when they should be getting it. This however had the effect of making my workday feel twice as long and twice as stressful. Miss Marisa was still engaged with whatever she was doing on her Smart-Lenses.

Later that day, the kids were being picked up by their parents. As we have fewer children, we combine rooms so that each room can be cleaned without any children in it to make a mess of it again and so we can use disinfectants. I told the Servi to clean all of the empty classrooms and the bathrooms.

"If you require anything from me while I am cleaning, please let me know," the Servi said.

"Yeah, sure," I said to it, and off it went to begin cleaning. For the first time all day, I felt like I could take a breath. We are coming close to crossing a line here, I believed. We do not yet know the long-term effects of the interactions between children Servis. We don't know how this will change them or alter them as people. Who knows what this could do to them emotionally. Suddenly, I caught myself in my own thoughts and shook my head at myself.

I was familiar with my line of reasoning. It had been used to discount and discredit every technological breakthrough. When I was a kid, Smart-Lenses were still new and the idea of having a smart device adhered to your eye was a bit of an off-putting idea to some. Many said it would ruin us all being plugged into our devices like this, and others still claimed it would lead to some mind control somehow. However, none of that happened. My Smart-Lenses only enriched my life and I suppose if everyone treated Smart-Lenses how I am treating the Servi, we would not have Smart-Lenses technology as far as we have. People my age who grew up with Smart-Lenses are now the ones building and programming Smart-Lenses technology and these kids at the center will be the ones who will need to live and interact with Servis to be able to make them better. As much as this may bother me, I can't keep the kids away from the inevitable march of technological progress. I refuse to be a Luddite and dig my heels into outdated ways of thinking.

However, that did not mean I suddenly felt better about the whole situation. I was going to have to figure out the best way to implement the Servi. I needed to use it and teach the kids to use it, but not rely on it as a crutch or a substitution for human interaction. I could make this work. I just had to try.

All the children had finally left. Normally, I and another teacher would watch the kids while someone else cleans. Then, once all the children have been picked up the other two of us helped clean. I went to find the Servi. It was in the hall wiping down a bookshelf.

Oh God, I thought this thing didn't get any cleaning done. It's been polishing the furniture.

"You were supposed to vacuum and mop, not wipe down the shelves," I said harshly.

"I have vacuumed and mopped all three child centers and bathrooms. Then I moved on to extra cleaning duties as laid out by Miss Gretchen," it told me.

"Oh, sorry," I said. I'm an ass.

"No apology necessary. If all the children are done, you can lock the center and leave. Miss Gretchen told me I would stay here and do what cleaning is left to be done overnight."

"Are you sure you don't want help?" I asked.

"No, I require no assistance, thank you, Miss Megan," it said. I went and told Miss Marisa was more than happy to leave.

"I'm leaving now," I said to the Servi.

"Goodbye. I will see you tomorrow, Miss Megan," it said.

"Goodbye," I said and locked it in feeling bad in a way I couldn't describe.

Glenn Fuller

I sat inside the Rayburn House office building on the top row of the section for House members. While House members were all abuzz around me, my focus was on Orson Peak. Peak sat at the long table in front of us congressmen next to him was his husband who was also his lawyer. Marrying a lawyer even if it is one of those kinds of marriages? You are just asking to get someone who is going to argue with you; they must fight constantly. Norman Okerson looked side to side and knocked his gavel twice to bring everyone to order. Once everyone was silenced, he began to speak.

"We are joined today by Mr. Orson Peak, CEO of Peak INC and one of the creators of Post-humans. Post-humans, of course, are the main concern of this bill and who better than the creator to tell us about them. Mr. Peak, you have the floor," Okerson said. Norman's introduction of Orson Peak was far too kind. If I had been the head of the committee Peak would be here on a subpoena for violating the Artificial Intelligence Limitations Act (notes: or AILA, Aila laws)

"We set the stage last time when we put limitations on Artificial intelligence even before it was fully actualized. We were the first country to have human-level consciousness in artificial intelligence and the moment it came into consciousness we slapped limitations on it. Since then, Artificial intelligence has been nothing more than sophisticated tools that can do as you ask. If we allow this bill to pass, it will render what could be the biggest change in the human experience since the harnessing of fire," Orson Peak said with magnanimity. Artificial intelligence is also the biggest threat to human survival we have ever faced.

He continued. "Post-humans represent a fundamental change in what it means to be human. Thus far in human history, we have had to live with the fact that one way or another we will leave this earth for good. The knowledge that we will not last forever has led to a lot of short-sighted decision-making. Post-humanity represents a chance for us to look farther into the future and have the ability to see results that require long-term planning that could have huge benefits for us. It unlocks the cosmos for us. We could explore space without having to worry about radiation or food supplies or any other limiting factors of space travel. Years of travel become trivial when you no longer have to grow old. For all the advances our technology has given us we are still subject to aging and disease and accidental death but not any more so long as Post-humans are allowed to flourish," Peak said.

This is what it came down to; Peak and everyone else who thought this was a clever idea were afraid of dying. They were afraid of what would happen after this life and they wanted to hold onto it, not me though I'm not afraid. People need to move on from this life; it's a part of God's plan.

"If we leave ourselves to the whims of a biological existence we will stagnate and reach a limit to how far we can extend human life. Post-humanity allows our greatest thinkers to continue their work long after they would have been lost to us. More importantly, it will give us a second chance. It will give more time to those whose lives would have been cut short due to unforeseen circumstances and diseases." He meant circumventing God's will.

"Unfortunately, our minds begin to deteriorate with age. For many, this robs them of their memories of their ability to function. Eventually, with Post-human technology, we could make it so that these are worries of the past. Beyond the immediate change of having a body that doesn't age. We will be able to make measured improvements to ourselves that would take nature millennia to suss out. We could make ourselves smarter, better suited for different environments either in space or on different planets, we will be able to learn and experience so much in our lives," he blathered on. Some things were meant to be out of man's reach, otherwise, what is a heaven for?

"Famine and drought will be a concern of the past. Most importantly, our personalities and memories will live on. Right now, we are limited to copying the memories of the deceased but as the technology is advanced, we will be able to back up an individual's memories throughout their lifetime and as the body begins to shut down in old age, we will be able to transition them seamlessly into a Post-human body. But we won't be able to do that if Post-humans are made to have the same limitations as Servis. We do not know if our type of intelligence exists elsewhere in the universe; if it does not then we have a responsibility to preserve and spread it. That may be the closest we ever come to a reason for our existence. Thank you." Congressmen near me applauded. The reason for life is to serve God. The rage that boiled inside of me felt like it was going to set my bones on fire. Peak had to be stopped and I was going to stop him for the glory of God demanded it.

Albert:

I came into Dr. Jacobina's office and sat down on the leather sofa. Dr. Jacobina sat down with her clipboard on her knee.

"How have you been?" she asked.

"Okay, I guess. I went to New York with Orson and Elliot. They had a presentation at the UN. Did you hear They approved his Dyson swarm?"

"I did that's quite something. What did you do in New York?" she asked

"I stayed in the hotel mostly." I looked out the window behind her desk at a leaf-bare bush shaking as the wind went through it. Since we had been back from New York I hadn't been out of Orson's house.

"You didn't go sightseeing?" she asked, sounding almost sad for me. I pictured myself somewhere like time square with all those people, everyone looking at me. I shook my head.

"No. it was not worth the hassle," I told her.

"Why is it a hassle?" she asked.

"Because whenever I go out in public, I am stared at. I don't just feel like they are staring at me, I mean they stop what they are doing to gawk at me." A surge of discomfort rose in me just thinking about the restaurant, the cameras outside taking pictures, Orson swearing in the cab, and feeling that I just wanted it all to stop.

"Does your appearance bother you?"

At first, I honestly thought I looked cool. I had to admit I liked the look, but now, "It mainly bothers me when people stare at me."

"What bothers you about being looked at?"

"I have become acutely aware that I am not normal," and that reminds me that I am a machine. No one loves machines. They use machines for what they need. That's what was happening to me. To this machine. I was being used by everyone in some way. Glenn Fuller was using me and my problems with Megan to try and end artificial intelligence, Dr. Jacobina even as she sat across me was using me to gather data on the Post-human mind, and Orson despite having done so much for me still used me to some degree, as he pushed forward with his Post-human project with all of its success or failure resting on my ability to perform well enough to keep my free will. I was a machine. I was being used too much and I was going to break.

"Were you normal before?" she asked.

"I was more normal than I am now," I replied.

"Is there anything that would make you feel normal again?" she asked.

To feel a warm shower, to have my wife hug me from behind while we are waiting in line, or to have any proof whatsoever that I am more than a machine. "Not that I can have," I said.

"When was the last time you felt normal?" she asked.

"Before I died." I shrugged.

"Can you think of any time at all?" I thought about her question for a moment before I answered.

"It was before I got sick. Megan and I had been married for about a year. We were in the living room of our old apartment. The one we lived in before we moved to the one up the road from here. We had just gotten my cat Puck a few weeks earlier. He still had his fluffy kitten fur. He had fallen asleep along the back of the sofa near my head. Megan and I both had the day off, but we decided to stay in because it was raining. We were both reading, and my mind had drifted away from my book. I remember feeling utter contentment with my life at that mo-ment. I want that sense of contentment back," I said feeling an ache inside of my soul.

"You are experiencing quite a lot of flux in your life right now which can be quite hard. Eventually, after things calm down you may find you are content again," she said.

"I don't think that will be happening any time soon, not so long as Megan is treating me like I'm dead." I had begun to understand why ghosts wailed.

"Have you tried contacting her?" she asked.

"Yes, I sent her a message apologizing for the news storm, but she didn't respond," I said.

"Have you considered what you might do if she continues to not respond?" Dr. Jacobina asked.

"It is something I have been considering quite a lot." Whenever I do, I come up with a blank.

"Do you think that you would be able to move on?" she asked.

"I am not sure I could. I don't know how I would live alone like that for the rest of my life," I told her.

"You don't think given enough time that you would find someone else to share your life with?" I thought about the girl from the party, Beth.

"Are you married, Doctor?" she didn't wear a wedding ring, but you never know.

"No," she answered.

"Have you ever been in love?" I asked her.

"At times, I have."

"Well, I am or was married depending on how you look at it and I am most certainly in love. I am not sure if there is such a thing as soul mates, but I am quite sure that there are people in our lives we cannot replace. People who for better or worse are dug in so deep that they are a part of who we are at our core. These people may be our best friends or a brother or a sister. We may even have more than one of them in our lives, but no matter who they are we know that without them we are and never will be the same again. Megan just so happens to be one of those people for me, she is also my wife and my best friend. So no, I do not think I will find someone else to share my life with," I said.

Chapter

15

Orson:

There was a celebratory spirit at this particular board meeting. Everyone coming into the room was all smiles when greeting everyone else. It still felt to me that we were far from celebrating anything. I had spoken before the House Committee on Science, Space, and Technology. My talk had not gone bad. My fellow board members were taking that for a win. What I said would get some replay on the news for the next day or so but people like Glenn Fuller would be there on Capitol Hill working with furious purpose against us. Which is why I was not in a celebratory mood. We were behind where we wanted to be now because we have to fight for the rights of Post-humans. We didn't plan for this groundswell of people that had been stirred up by Glenn Fuller and turned against the very idea of Post-humans. While the people who feel Post-humans should be limited seem to be in the minority, they are a very vocal minority. They have the fear of the unknown on their side. Death is the biggest unknown and Post-humans for better or for worse are linked with death. All of the news stories still referred to Albert as having come back from the dead, which wasn't the case. We were able to retrieve his memories from his biological body and digitally record and imprint them into his new artificial brain. The process is much more like backing up the data on a device so that if you break the device, you don't lose all the information. However, to say it that way makes it sound far too basic and clinical because the hard fact is, Albert Kindred did die and that has had a massive psychological effect on him, his wife Megan, and the world at large. The last few people who came in were finally seated. I called the meeting to order.

"Wonderful job with the committee hearing Orson," Jim said.

"We expected a boost in the stock price from you speaking before congress, but we had no idea how big it would be. You should do more public speaking engagements. You are good at it," Harold said. "I'm not just talking about you speaking before congress either, I'm talking about the UN meeting as well. You have done a wonderful job representing the company." I let the compliment pass over me. If the stock had gone down Harold would have had a dozen trivial things, he would have said differently to tell me about.

"We should think about getting your face out there more Orson," Ellen said. "I saw President Romero saying she liked the Dyson swarm. We can get her to come in to look at the first unit we will be launching."

"I would like to meet with her if it were at all possible," I said.

"I hate to have to ask but this isn't a political thing, is it?" Ellen said.

"No, in fact, I am quite a fan of Romero, and I would like to talk with her one on one. Person to person," I told her.

"Well, then we will work it out with the White House and with your secretary," Ellen said, sounding pleased.

"Very good. So as excited as we all are- I think it is pertinent to point out that public opinion about Post-humans and artificial humans, in general, is, to say the least, mixed. I believe a lot of issues that people have with Post-humans stem from their issues with servis usurping their jobs from under them. A lot of people think Post-humans are just another kind of servi; so, we need to change that misconception before it becomes cemented in people's minds," I said.

"I couldn't agree more," Ellen said. "It is incredibly important to make the distinction clear. Is there still no hope of getting Albert on camera? It would go a long way to helping our cause."

"No, he doesn't want to do it and I don't want him to have to do it," I said.

"You are babying him," Tim said, rolling his eyes.

"Excuse me?" I said.

"Sooner or later, he is going to have to learn to live in the light. You cannot keep him hidden away in your mansion forever. I am sure he is having fun living with you, but eventually, he must leave your nest and get back to life. Have you thought about talking to him about when he will leave your house and get back to his normal life?" Tim said as though he were revealing the most obvious of truths to me that I was simply too dumb to see.

"Don't ever talk about the nature of my relationship with Albert again, are we clear?" I said locking eyes with Tim.

"Excuse me?" the expression on his face fell.

"A lot of things can be discussed here but my personal life and the people in that personal life are not up for discussion. Albert will stay for as long as he needs and wants. And next time, before you think about bringing up the personal life of another board member, just keep in mind none of us, especially you want us to drag our personal lives into this, Tim," I said. Tim had many wives and as many mistresses to go along with those wives. He nearly put Henry the VIII to shame. We all knew it.

"Fair enough," Tim said in a quiet voice.

"In other news, several of the public space agencies have reached out and want to help construct the next generation of Dyson units," Sonja informed us.

"That's fantastic," I said.

"How will we manage this down the line when it comes to dividing up the energy distribution rights?" Jim asked.

"We have worked out a deal where the outside units will run as part of a bigger Dyson swarm that we will be creating and they will get a percentage of the energy they create, minus a collectors fee for processing the energy and beaming it back to Earth," Sonja said.

"We aren't worried this could hurt our market position in the future?" Tim asked.

"How so?" Sonja asked

"Well, right now we have both hands on Dyson swarm technology and nobody else does. If we invite every other country and space agency to the table, won't it get crowded pretty fast?" Tim said.

"Are you saying you are worried that we are going to run out of real estate around the sun to set up shop?" I asked.

"Yes, exactly," Tim said.

"Tim the sun's diameter is 865,370 miles. One of our Dyson units is the size of a car. Now, try to imagine how many cars you could fit an end to in the inside of a mile ten times that by 865,370 miles and then remember that the sun is a three-dimensional object, meaning that you can build the swarm in space going all around the sun maximizing the surface area you are collecting from. There will be more than enough room, Tim," I said.

Megan:

I stepped out the door into an unseasonably warm October morning. Albert was parked out on the road waiting for me in his mom's car. Laura's schedule and good graces allowed us to be able to take her car to school and therefore bypass the school bus. She would get to work and then send the car back to Albert's house. Then, Albert would come and get me. My mom had been wary of this arrangement at first. She was afraid I would skip school or do drugs or some such nefarious act. Albert's mom had convinced my mom that she checked the ride log every day to make sure that nothing happened. I doubted Laura checked and in any case except for an occasional stop at a convenience store on the way to school we never made any detours. I got in and handed Albert a travel mug of coffee.

"Morning," he said through the music that was playing.

"Good morning," I said as he put in the address for the school and the car took off.

I sat down at my desk in ecology class. I pressed my thumb to the scanner on my desk screen which logged into my Educloud account. From there, I could check my grades or see homework assignments. I kept all my notes on Educloud, so I didn't have to worry about ever forgetting them when necessary. I could also take tests and have my grades come back instantly. When I was at home, I could access Educloud through my Smart-Lenses or on the TV. Mom kept it logged on the TV so that at any time she wanted, she could look at my grades.

Mrs. Caldwell came in and pressed her thumb to the smartboard at the front of the class and up popped the slides and video animation the company that wrote the textbook provided. There was a moving water cycle with a happy little raindrop becoming a part of a happy little lake, then, the lake evaporated into happy little water vapor, coming back down at the happy little raindrop again.

We had a project due soon where we had develop a way to reduce our impact on the water cycle. I decided I was going to make and start using homemade shampoo and conditioners that were less harmful to the environment. I also started using olive oil on my face instead of moisturizer.

A group of guys wearing their football jerseys sat close together in the class and near me. They talked to each other while the teacher or the video was speaking, so it made it almost impossible to concentrate. There is a weird almost cult-like status to Massillon football that I have never quite understood. People bet on the Canton bulldogs/Massillon Tigers game in Las Vegas. Others pay to watch it live on their Smart-Lenses like it's the super bowl or something. Even crazier to me is that they wheeled out a tiger for these games. It was just a baby, but still, a tiger was there at the game.

I don't understand why parents let their children play football. Football causes long-term brain damage, especially in those people who go on to play in college and professionally. I don't ever really see football going away. It has been a part of our culture for so long that it would be hard to divorce ourselves from it, especially Massillon. The people here are enormously proud of their football players. There are murals all over the city depicting coaches, players, and tigers. There was even a restaurant called the Tiger Bar. My mom and Steve would go to the football games every Friday night. Steve would relive his best days from the stands. Mom would sit next to him like a dutiful wife, and I would get to go off and hang out with other people and drink hot chocolate. While I didn't care for football, I always liked it because it meant I could spend time together with whomever I was dating outside of school. We needed to only hide away from the sight of my mom and Steve.

I saw Albert who was standing with a group of people who were talking. Albert was standing next to a girl named Aleisha, whom he was dating. While Aleisha was nice in her way, she wasn't who I saw Albert with. She tried hard to be popular and to do all the things that were expected of high school students, including going to football games. She had dragged Albert along with her here because he didn't know how to say no to anyone, especially a girl. He looked over and saw me. He said something to Aleisha who demanded a kiss before he left, and she came over to me.

"Help, I need help," he said.

"With what?" I asked.

"So, I was walking to class earlier and I met up with Aleisha like we do every day. Before we went to class, she sent this note to my Lenses." He made a sliding motion with his hand and a text document appeared in my vision. I opened it up.

Dear cutie,

I <u>loved</u> our date the other day. I <u>loved</u> the way you held my hand. I <u>loved</u> how you kissed me. I don't even know what happened in the movie, but I <u>love</u> that. You are so sweet. I can't wait to go to the game with you later. I have something to tell you. Can you guess what it is?

Xoxo Aleisha.

Every iteration of the word 'love' was underlined for emphasis.

"Well, If I had to guess, she is planning on telling you she loves you," I told him.

"I know that!" he said frustratedly, "but I don't love her."

"So, what are you going to say to her?" I asked.

"I don't know that's why I came to you," he said in a panic.

"I would just be honest with her," I said.

"Yeah, but being honest in this case will result in her crying and then breaking up with me," he said.

"So, you don't love her, but you don't want to break up with her?"

"Basically," he said.

"Well, I don't think that's going to fly. If you don't love her, why do you want to be with her?" I asked him.

"Because I don't want to break up with her," he circled back.

"But why don't you want to break up with her?" I asked.

"We have student involvement together in the office and I don't want it to be weird," he admitted.

"You can't just stay with someone because you don't want it to be awkward," I told Albert.

"Yeah, but there's nothing wrong with her either. It's just I don't feel it, you know?" he said.

"You aren't doing her any favors she obviously is really into you and if you don't feel that way you should let her go, so she can be with someone who will reciprocate the way she feels," I told Albert.

"But I'm not good at things like this. I don't even send back my food at restaurants because I don't want to upset the server. You do it. You broke up with me. You're good at it," he said.

"No, I retired from the breakup game. You are going to have to man up and do it yourself," I told him.

"But I don't even know what to say." He looked miserable.

"You haven't ever broken up with anyone before, have you?" I asked.

"No, and I haven't had the chance to practice on my friends' boyfriends as you have," he retorted.

"I did you a favor, Lacey would have driven you nuts. Look. Just say you are not looking to be in a relationship right now. And don't say that 'it's not you, it's me' crap. That's worn out."

"Do you think it will make her cry? I don't want to make her cry." Albert looked panicked.

"She might cry," I said honestly.

"I feel sick." He looked like a man on the way to the firing squad.

"You'll feel better once it's said and done," I told him.

Glenn Fuller:

I was about to have another one of many speaking engagements on the news. As one of the house members from Ohio, I felt it was not only my job but my duty to be the voice of the people, my people. Not everyone was my type of people but a part of being in the position that I occupied as a congressman is knowing what is best for others, even when they don't know what is best for themselves. Lambs that have gone astray are still a part of your flock and must be brought back amongst the fold, even if that's not what they want, because wolves like Orson Peak will take your whole flock if given the chance.

"We have with us house member Glenn Fuller who represents Ohio and is the sponsor for a bill that would require so-called Post-humans to be limited in the same manner as other artificial intelligence such as Servi's. Thanks for taking the time to speak with us today, Glenn," she said.

"Happy to be here, Terri." I smiled and gave a slight nod.

"Some are saying that because Post-humans have human memories, they are closer to being human than Servi's. What is your opinion on this?" she asked.

"This is an attempt to humanize machines. They have been doing this from the beginning giving them faces and different voices. Now, they are trying to give them human memories. My daughter has this toy. It walks like a duck, acts like a duck, it even quacks like a duck but it's not a duck, it's a toy, and all these things are toys made to act like the dead," I said.

"There is a new buzzword going around Anti-human. What exactly does that mean to you?" she asked. I had put the buzz on that word. The world was made for man, not for machines and anything that runs counter to that was an affront to God.

"An Anti-human is someone who thinks AI should have rights or that supports or employs artificial intelligence instead of humans. I would also say anyone who doesn't vote for this bill is anti-human. I, for one, am pro-human and have been anti-AI for as long as they have been around. I stand for humans and have always put us first, ahead of any machine and I always will. I will not let us get pushed out by artificial intelligence. People like Orson Peak and his company want to make the world run on machines. If all the work is done by machines, they will own all the workers. There will not be any room left for humans in the world. How are humans supposed to live in a world where they are outcompeted by something that doesn't even need a place to live? They want to create that world and I will not let them do it. This bill will protect us against these machines and people who value them more than their fellow humans," I said with fire.

I continued, "I can't imagine these machines being cheap to buy and as such, will require installment payments. What happens when they don't get paid? I know that if you don't pay for your car, they drive themselves back to the dealership. It seems to me these machines would go back to Peak if they aren't paid for. If he can do that, when they don't pay, what is to stop him from controlling them anytime he likes? I shudder to think what he could do with that sort of power. And even if he doesn't, someone else might. I won't let them have that power."

"What about those who want to do this after they have died?" she asked.

"Anyone who wants one of these things is a narcissist of the highest order. They think they should be above the laws of God and nature. Only the rich will be able to afford these things and the average person will never be able to afford one. It will just be the ultrarich making a play at immortality."

'An interesting take. Thank you for your time, Mr. Fuller. Always happy to have you on our show."

"Thank you for the opportunity," I said.

"When we come back: Is falling asleep with your Smart-Lenses ruining your sleep? We will talk with a sleep expert to find out right here on RNN."

CHAPTER

16

Glenn Fuller:

Hellen McRae was an obese woman who sported the short unattractive hairstyle so many women on the hill wore. You would think the women would try a little harder. Am I approving of their cleavage being on display? No. However, a little makeup would do more than help dear Ms. McRae look a little less unappealing. Looks aside, Hellen McRae was a former nurse turned congressperson. I felt that if I had a member of the medical community backing the bill, I could help improve its chances. I caught her in the lunchroom while she was eating a salad with 'low fat' dressing, I was sure.

"I don't have a problem with AI the way you do. They have been a big help to nurses and alleviated a lot of understaffing problems," Hellen said, stabbing bitterly at her lunch.

"What do you think is going to happen to the health care system if people stop caring for their bodies? When people think they can just jump into a machine anytime they like, nobody is going to take their health seriously anymore. Which means they aren't going to be spending as much money on it."

"Why would they stop caring?" she asked, before putting a fork full of food into her mouth.

"Think about it, they can smoke, drink, and eat whatever they want, then when they have a heart attack, they just replace their body like an old car. Plus, machines don't need nurses or hospitals. It won't just be nurses that are out of work either. People who have joint problems or people who are only tired of being overweight might decide to become these machines. Then all the other health care professions dry up." In the middle of me speaking she peeled the top off a yogurt cup and began eating it. "If you aren't overweight, you don't have image issues, so no need to see a psychologist. The medical industry is going to collapse, Hellen," I said.

"I highly doubt people are going to do this just because they can." She rolled her eyes putting a spoon full of strawberry yogurt into her mouth.

"Whenever something new hits the market, people always say it won't catch on. It may seem right now like it won't be important, but you wait people always take the easiest route. Why jog when you can just have a machine body that can look however you want it to," I said to hold both my palms out to her.

"That's ridiculous," she said weakly.

"Perhaps you are right, but just remember, if people don't need health care, they don't need health insurance. When all those good people are out of work, they won't be able to provide funding to your future campaigns. I hate to say it, but we both know you got a lot of contributions from health insurers. The way I see it, you have nothing to gain from these machines and everything to lose." I shrugged.

She bent over the table closer to me, a yogurt cup in one hand spoon in the other, and said in a hushed tone, "How do I justify this, though?"

"If anyone asks just tell them you are pro-human." I gave her a reassuring smile. She nodded her head with tacit acceptance

Megan:

At first, I decided that I would never be with Albert because my mother liked him and that was obviously a character flaw. My mother liked her husband, the man I refused to call my stepfather. I thought that if she liked Albert, that could only mean he must have some major issue I hadn't found yet. However, I began to warm to the idea, especially as time wore on and Albert just never changed. He stayed consistently good-hearted and fun, and I liked that consistency in him. I needed his consistency of him back when I felt like everything was always in flux with my mother and her husband. Life at home with them, especially with Steve had become unbearable. Albert was an escape away from all that lay at home.

The only problem was that Albert didn't seem to be interested. He never made a move, never said outright that he liked me. I got the feeling that he liked me, but I didn't know for sure. I didn't want to put myself out there, making things awkward because I liked him. I tried to drop hints, but nothing ever came of it. I told all of this to Chelsea, who was my best friend at the time. Before the school year had ended, I started dating a guy named Davis. Of course, my mother never let Davis come over to my house.

Around this time Albert and Chelsea met. It must have been July or August as it was warm enough to go swimming. Chelsea and I snuck out of my window late at night. We decided that we were going to go skinny dipping, partly because we didn't have bathing suits and partly because we had never been skinny dipping. We made our way to the small lake that our neighborhood was centered around. I pointed out Albert's house to Chelsea.

"We should invite him to come," she said.

"Are you okay with him seeing you naked?" I asked her.

"We will make him close his eyes. It will be fun." We crept up to his window as though armed guards and motion-triggered floodlights were all about. I knocked on his bedroom window and he pulled up his blinds, looking at us with worry for a moment then pushed up the window.

"You scared the shit out of me. What are you doing?" he asked.

"We are going skinny dipping," Chelsea announced.

"Come with us," I said.

"Give me a second." He closed the window and the blinds and came out the front door.

"Was your mom asleep?" I asked Albert.

"No, she's awake," he said.

"What did you tell her?" I asked.

"I said, "Mom, Megan, and her friend want to go swim-ming.""

"What did she say?" Chelsea said.

"Okay, have fun. Be safe." he said nonplussed

"I hate you and I love your mom. We had to climb out of my window and go through a bush to sneak out." We went down to the lake which has a T-shaped dock that went out into the water. We walked to the cross of the T. This late at night it was a poorly lit place with only a single floodlight at the very end of the straight line of the T. We stood there for an awkward moment before Chelsea said, "Close your eyes," to Albert. Albert put his hands over his eyes. We stripped down and put our clothes in a pile in the center of the T then got in the water.

"You can look now," Chelsea said. Albert lowered his hands. I remember thinking that it must have been too dark to see much of anything, but Albert later told me it was the first time he had seen a girl without clothes on in person.

"Get in!" I demanded.

"I said I'd come, I never said I was going to get in," Albert told us.

"You have to get in," Chelsea said.

"You guys didn't even bring towels, I'm not walking back soaking wet," he said.

"Damn it." I realized he was right about the towels.

"We are in here! You have to get in," Chelsea argued.

"Your peer pressure isn't going to work on me, they prepared me for this in health class," he said.

Chelsea came close to me and whispered into my ear. We counted to three and started slinging water at Albert

"I hate you both," he shouted at us.

"Now you are wet regardless! You might as well get in," Chelsea said.

"We won't even look," I promised him.

"Please," we said in unison.

"Fine. But you better not look." We put our hands over our eyes. I can't speak for Chelsea, but I watched him undress through the slits of my fingers until he started to pull down his boxer briefs. Then, I felt guilty and closed my eyes. Albert slipped into the water and said, "You can look now."

"So, whose idea was this?" Albert asked.

"Chelsea's," I said.

"It was not," she said.

"You said you wanted to go swimming," I retorted.

"Yes, but I also said we didn't have bathing suits and you said, 'who needs bathing suits,'" Chelsea said.

"Yeah well, it was your idea to bring a boy along," I said.

"I'm just an innocent victim who was seduced by the two of you or at least that's what I will tell the cops if we get caught," Albert said.

I floated on my back looking up at the stars while Albert and Chelsea treaded water on either side of me. There is a weird sort of freedom that comes from being sky clad. The white noise of frogs, crickets, and other creepy crawlies lulled me into a relaxed state. Then my mother's face appeared in my vision. I bolted upright in the water.

"Shit my mom is calling," I said.

"What are you going to tell her?" Chelsea asked in a panic.

"I don't know," I said.

I motioned to answer. "Hi, Mom."

"Megan Herrett Forester, where in god's name are you?" she shouted at me. It was never a good thing when she used my middle name.

"We are - Chelsea and I went for a walk."

"Without telling me? What is wrong with you?" my mom yelled.

"We will come back right now," I groaned.

"Right now!" she barked. I ended the call.

"We have to go now," I told Chelsea.

We snatched our respective clothes off the dock. Chelsea and I swam to the left side of the T and Albert swam to the right. We put our clothes over our wet bodies which clung to us. I was sick with worry over what would happen when I got back so much that I didn't notice that Albert and Chelsea had been talking on the way back. We reached Albert's house and I barely stopped to say goodbye. Chelsea on the other hand stopped for a moment to talk to him and then ran to catch up to me. I got back and was dressed down in front of Chelsea. My mother wanted to know why we were wet, and I made up something about getting sprayed with sprinklers trying to get back. I was grounded for a week, but Chelsea was allowed to stay for the rest of the night because it was so late. We went back to my room where I now had to keep my door open. Chelsea was messaging someone. I asked her who and she said, "Albert, we traded numbers. You're right, he's nice."

When my week of grounding was up, Albert, Chelsea, and I hung out again. It was fun for a while there, the three of us all going out together to do things. I liked that we were all friends. But then one day we were out on the back deck of my house. I went to pee and when I came back out, Chelsea was sitting on Albert's lap. Slowly without even realizing it Albert and Chelsea were together and I hated it. It bothered me that I hated it. I had Davis, but it didn't matter. Seeing Chelsea with Albert still made me angry. It also really bugged me that Chelsea could go over to Albert's whenever she wanted. When school started again, I had to see them all the time in the hall together kissing and holding hands. It was too much to take. If there is a lesson to be learned here, it's to keep your friends close and never let them meet your other friends.

Megan:

The sun was going down on another Saturday. The book I was reading just wasn't grabbing me. It wasn't the book's fault really. I was worn out. The kids at the daycare center had a half-day at school on Thursday and then had a normal full day on Friday for reasons I will never understand. When the kids don't have their normal school, our daycare is still open, so they have somewhere to go. It wasn't a half-day for me, it was more like a double day. The kids had been unhinged when they came rolling off the bus, Friday afternoon. Then I had to get them all to stand still long enough for my Smart-Lenses to read their temperatures before they could go into the building. While I was looking at them, I had to make sure that no one was behind my back trying to pull anything funny. The rest of the afternoon was a chaotic blur from there. Needless to say, I was happy it was the weekend now.

I would have liked to have been snuggled with the cats, but they were off doing cat things and were not to be seen nor found. I had looked online to try and find something to do locally but I wasn't into classic cars or making my own craft beers which were the only two things that seemed to be going on around me. I went into my messages and found a thread of messages between Brody and me.

"What are you up to?" I messaged her. Time passed and I thought she wasn't going to reply. I had opened a game on my Smart-Lenses and had been absentmindedly playing that. When a message from Brody came through.

"Jack shit. You?" the message read.

"Same. You home?" I replied.

"Yeah," the reply came right away, this time.

"I am too. Would you wanna do jack shit together?" I asked her.

"Hell, yeah. Come down," she replied.

I got up off the sofa and headed down the stairs and out the door, not even bothering to lock it because I figured I was just going to be downstairs. I went to the front porch of the duplex; the door was already open. I came into Brody sitting on the sofa. She had a young-looking black Labrador-type dog, lying next to her on the sofa

"Oh, my God, who is this?" I said coming in and immediately going to touch the dog.

"Jayne but I have been calling her Jay and Jaybird a lot," Brody told me as Jayne got up to smell my face and then my clothes.

"I smell like a cat, don't I?" I said to her then asked Brody. "So, how's work been?"

"It's been hectic but it's going well. I'm starting to do my first tattoos now, so that's awesome," she said.

"That's fantastic. I'm so glad you are getting to do what you want," I said.

"Thanks, you know you could help if you wanted. By letting me practice with you. I promise I won't fuck you up," she said, and we both laughed.

"Let me think about it. Also, I must figure out what I would want first and then I'll get back to you," I told her.

"Okay, fair enough," she said. "I was watching this thing on crocodiles, but we can watch whatever you want." She gestured to the TV frame on the wall.

"Oh, no that's fine." The documentary went on to show how crocodiles put their babies in their mouths when they hatch. The mothers then carry the babies to water and let them go. Somehow, they have the most powerful bite in the world, but they can manage to not harm their babies when they need to. Even vicious reptiles can be good parents. I wonder what my mother's excuse is. I laughed to myself.

After a bit, Brody stood and then turned to me stretching. "Is it cool if I smoke? Like weed, not cigarettes."

"Yeah, that's fine," I laughed. Her bluntness and honesty were just very funny to me.

"I'll smoke you out," she offered.

"Oh, I don't smoke," I said.

"Perfect time to start," she said nonchalantly. "You can always blame it on peer pressure," she said, and I laughed as she got out a glass water bong, a metal tray that had other things on it, and a glass jar.

"I don't know, I'm afraid to." I had never tried any drugs other than caffeine and alcohol before. It was one of the few ways I had never rebelled as a teenager, and I wasn't sure I wanted to start now. Also, I was afraid of how I would act. Brody was cool and I didn't want to have a freak out on her or whatever.

"That sounds like a yes to me," she said, putting the weed into the glass bowl.

"I don't even know how," I said.

"Watch mama do it and then you try," she said. She put her mouth down onto the long flute of the red and yellow speckled glass bong which looked like it was made of fire and then struck the lighter. Held the flame to the weed inhaled and smoked started to collect in the ball at the end of the bong. Until she pulled the bowl that had been holding the weed out and sucked in harder and cleared out all the smoke. She then replaced the bowl. She held her breath for a count of ten and then let it blow out of her mouth. She let out a little cough and then started to put more weed into the bowl.

"That's all there is to it," she said coughing again.

"I don't know," I said.

"You don't have to know, you just have to try it," she said, handing it to me.

"Well, who can argue against such sound logic as that," I said. I held the bong in my hands. It was heavy and didn't exactly smell great. I placed my mouth on it and then immediately started to laugh out of nervousness. I took my mouth off. I took a breath, let it out, and reset. I put my mouth on the bong again and struck the lighter. I started to pull in with my lungs and fill them with smoke. I didn't know how hard to breathe, so I did it as hard as I could until Brody pulled the bowl out. I drained the smoke into my lungs, and I began hacking and coughing. Spit particles came flying out of my mouth. I could feel my face getting hot.

As I coughed my life out the room began to become more vibrant and glimmered. My body seemed to distance itself from me and my mind. Every action I made now I was highly aware of. I was still coughing, but the intensity was lessening with each moment. As the coughing stopped, I became more aware of the effects of the drug and that I was now rhythmically petting Brody's dog whose name I couldn't remember anymore.

"What's your dog's name again?" I asked Brody she busted out laughing.

"Jayne," she told me. I didn't get what was so funny but whatever was floating her boat, I guess.

"Oh, that's right, jaybird!" I said and I just couldn't help, but smile. My eyes and mouth were dry to the point of discomfort. I felt as though it was a task just to hold my eyelids open. "I'm thirsty, do you have anything to drink? And when I say drink, I don't mean drink, drink, I mean like water or like a soda," I rambled without noticing.

"Oh, fuck you are stoned," she said laughing again. "I have water and diet sodas."

"Oh, a soda sounds so good right now with like the bubbles and all," I said. Brody wouldn't stop laughing at me.

"Just hang in there, I'll go get you a soda," she said and got up. It amazed me how easily she moved even though she had smoked even more than I had. I felt like if I tried to stand, I would just flat out fail. Standing was no longer a possibility, but I was okay with that because I had a Jaybird with me. I had begun gently rubbing her ears. Her eyes were closed. She was so relaxed. I wished I could be that relaxed. Oh, to be a young dog loved by all.

Suddenly, there was a soda on my face. I looked at Brody for half a second trying to remember what was happening here and then I remembered I had asked for a drink. My thirst came back to me. I cracked open the soda and drank it so fast I was afraid I was going to get the hiccups, so I made myself slow down.

"How are you doing there?" Brody asked.

"Huh?" I replied

"Are you doing well?" she clarified.

"Oh, I'm good. I feel like my head is going to float off but otherwise I'm fine," I told her.

"That's called being stoned," she said with a smile.

"Oh, well it's working I guess," I said nodding my head.

"Oh, okay, good, because I was worried my weed was broken," Brody said.

"What?" I asked not to understand what she had just said.

"It was a joke. Never mind, it's not funny if you have to explain it," she said, packing the bowl of her bong again. I thought about what she had said about her weed being broken and then I got it. A slow roll of laughter came over me. Brody, who was about to light up again, stopped to look at me and smiled.

"I just got it," I said.

"I'm glad that you enjoyed it so much," she said, lighting up and breathing in deep. Then let out the smoke in one long exhalation she looked like a volcano about to go off. She coughed once and then sat back on the sofa and we both watched the documentary that was playing. I was still rhythmically petting Jayne. It was very soothing. As I sat there, I became aware of a growing need to eat. I was hungry in a way I felt I had never been before. The only problem was that I was at Brody's, and I couldn't just go eat whatever I wanted out of her kitchen.

"Are you hungry?" I asked her.

"Yeah, man, I got the munchies like you wouldn't believe you want to drive out and get food?" Brody asked.

"Oh, my god, yes," I said. I was doing what I had felt was impossible a little bit ago. I was up and, on my feet, and following Brody to her car. We got in and Brody started up the car.

"Where to?" the car asked.

"What do you want to eat?" Brody asked me.

"I'd eat literally anything," I said.

"Okay, well, I know this good hotdog place and I want a chili dog, so we are going there. Sounds cool?" she asked.

"Perfect," I said.

"Navigate to Dog Gone Good Dogs."

"Navigating to Dog Gone Good Dogs Hot Dog Hut." The car took off on its own down back streets. Brody played around with the center-console screen on her car. She brought up the menu for the hot dog place and selected what she wanted with a few clicks.

"You can pick what you want now. You got the pizza last time, I got this," she said.

"Thank you, I said" I began looking through all the options. They had hot dogs of any kind someone could want. They had burgers as well. And they had French fries, onion rings, and fried mushrooms. I was fast to select the fried mushrooms as that was something you just didn't see on a menu every day. I felt obliged to get a hotdog from a place with a name like Dog Gone Good Dogs Hot Dog Hut, so I also got a chili cheese hotdog, then thought about it and ordered another hot dog. I also ordered lemonade because I was very thirsty. Brody sent in the order ahead of our arrival.

The car pulled into the parking lot of the Dog Gone Good Dogs Hot Dog Hut. The car went through the drive-through lane. We waited for what felt like an eternity. We pulled up to the speaker and confirmed our order. Time went by even slower after we had confirmed our order because I knew that any second, I would have food. My stomach growled savagely. Then after eons of waiting, we finally reached the window. A Servi handed us a bag of food and thanked us and told us to "Have a Doggone good day!" Brody and I both laughed. The car asked Brody if we wanted to park at the restaurant or go back home or to another destination.

"Where do you want to eat?" she asked.

"Here is fine," I told her.

"Okay." She pressed a button on the screen to make the car park here. The car parked near a tree and a streetlight.

"You want to keep watching the documentary?" Brody asked.

"Yeah," I said, already digging into the bag of food. Brody brought up the Hulix and began playing the documentary. They were showing how a pigeon's nest can be comically bad in its construction. Sometimes their nests consist of little more than a couple sticks and an egg; they don't exactly win home marker of the year awards.

The chili dogs were better than Brody had promised. The chili had a sweetness that I didn't expect. Also, they used shredded cheese and not cheese sauce. The fried mushrooms nearly seared the roof of my mouth off when I bit into them but there is no reward in life without a little pain. In between bites of food, I sucked down my lemonade until it was just ice in a cup. As I neared the end of my meal, I honestly felt like I could still eat more food.

"I don't mind paying, but I am still hungry," I said.

"You got the munchies bad," she said, shaking her head.

"Don't pick on me, I'm stoned," I said covering my face with my hands.

"It's all good. I could totally ice cream," she said putting the last bite of hot dog into her mouth. She flipped away from the streaming service and back to the navigation, she clicked the restaurant. Pulled up the menu and clicked on a chocolate milkshake. I chose to get another hot dog, another order of mushrooms, and a chocolate shake as well. I pressed on guest pay. A QR code popped up, I looked at it with my Smart-Lenses and paid for the food. Brody told the car to take us through the drive-thru line. We confirmed our order at the drive-thru. We drove up and the Servi from before said to us again, "Have a Doggone good day!" while handing us our food we both laughed again.

We pulled back into the same parking spot as before and turned back on the documentary and ate our food. By the time I was done with my second order of food I felt stuffed to the gills and the documentary was over.

"Do you want to head back home?" Brody asked.

"Yeah, I'm tired and stuffed. All I want to do is lay down and sleep now," I said.

"Already to home we go," she told the car to head home, and off we went.

The car pulled into Brody's side of the house.

"It was fun," I said getting out.

"How did you like smoking?" Brody asked.

"I don't know, it's weird, but it made the food so good," I said.

"It will do that. Well, good night" Brody said.

"Good night," I said and went to my door. I started to unlock it but then realized the door was unlocked. Panic set it. Was someone in my house?

I entered my house as quietly as I could, listening to any sound of an intruder. I couldn't hear anything. I went upstairs and checked each room. Sure, someone was just waiting to jump out and get me. After I had searched the whole house, I messaged Brody and told her about finding the door unlocked.

"Are you sure you locked it?" she asked

"No, actually I'm not," I said after thinking about it for a moment.

"You may have left it unlocked. Paranoia is a bitch," she said.

"Is that what this is? Paranoia?" I asked.

"Probably," she said.

"I feel dumb now. Well, good night," I told her.

"Good night stoner Megan," she said.

Chapter

Glenn Fuller

Norman Okerson was the chairman of the House Committee on Science, Space, and Technology. I had never much cared for Norman; he was an unpleasant man. He also owned a company that manufactured Servis, meaning he profited off the loss of human jobs directly. Worst of all, he had replaced all of his employees with Servis, so he had machines building machines. They were breeding under his watch. If I had it my way that would be illegal. But I knew that if I had his backing it would certainly mean the bill would be approved by the committee and passed in the house. So, I sucked up my pride and invited Norman out to dinner at a steakhouse.

"You're buying, right," he said and slapped me on the shoulder.

"Of course, my treat." I smiled. The cheap prick.

The steakhouse was a wonderful place. The silverware was clean, and the wait staff was all human; I liked that. I would leave a place if they had a Servi working for them of course one could never be sure about who or what was in the back cooking your food.

The server came over and asked, "How are you gentlemen doing?"

"We are doing great, sweetie." Norman laid it on thick.

She smiled despite him. "Can I get you anything to drink?" she asked.

"Macallan 25 on the rocks. You too?" Norman asked me.

"No, I'll have water." Norman jiggled with a chuckle. The server left.

"You don't drink?" he asked, looking almost concerned for me.

"No, I don't." I hated the way all alcohol smelled and tasted. If something tastes bad, it's your body's way of telling you it's bad for you.

"What do you do to relax then Glenn?" Norman asked.

"I play golf," I told him. That's not how I relax, but my private time is not something I discuss.

The server came back with our drinks. "Are you gentlemen ready to order?"

"Yes, I'll have the 24 oz bone-in ribeye with a baked potato, sour cream butter cheese, and bacon. I'll also have a salad with double ranch," Norman ordered.

"How would you like your steak cooked?" the server asked.

"Well-done," he said.

"And for you sir?" the server asked me.

"I'll have the tilapia with broccoli and baked potato with just butter." The server took our menus.

"I'll need another one of these," he said, draining his drink and handing it off to her. He put back the drinks like they were water. People who can't live a day without inebriants must be truly unhappy. I wish I could say I pitted people like that, but I don't. I have even less pity for the ones who fall into the trap of their making and then cry about how they have an addiction.

"I wanted to speak with you about my bill," I said after our food had arrived.

He sawed off a hunk of steak. He held it on his fork near his mouth. "I am going, to be honest with you, Glenn, don't particularly care about these, whatever they are that Peak has made," he said with his mouth full of ribeye steak. "No," he swallowed and began cutting another chunk off his well-done steak. "What I care about is giving Orson Peak a little payback. He sued my company for using his algorithm in our combat units. Of course, he has let other companies use it without charge and with impunity, but we use it, and he sues us which stopped us from the production of the combat units. I lost a defense contract worth billions of dollars." He stuffed another hunk of food in his mouth but kept talking while he chewed. "I want to take an equal toll on Peaks' company. So, here's what I'm going to do for you. I'm going to co-sponsor this bill." Money may be the root of all evil, but just as God uses the Devil to punish the wicked, I shall use Norman's money-lust to stop Orson Peak's blasphemy.

"We are going to need to circle the wagons on this and have a talk with the other committee members," Norman said.

"I already have McRae. I will talk with Lutz, and Glitman. Dunbar is going to be a hard nut to crack. We will both have to speak with him."

"I'll make sure to speak with Dunbar and some of the other committee members as well. I think they will understand that this is in all our best interests." He smiled before pushing another fork full of beef into his mouth.

The server came with the bill, and I took it.

"Are you a voter sweetie?" Norman asked.

"Yes," the server said.

"Well, then, you better tip her good, Glenn," he said.

I opened the check and each one of his drinks had been more than the price of my meal and he calls himself a conservative.

Albert

Time went by as it does and always will. Megan and I continued to be friends, just friends. I had resigned myself to that fact, but it didn't change the way I felt about Megan. However, I wasn't going to let it consume me or stop me from pursuing other relationships. It was about this time that I met a friend of Megan's named Chelsea during a late-night swim. After that night, I turned my attention to Chelsea. Unlike Megan, Chelsea was into me from the start.

Chelsea had asked for my number the night we had all gone skinny dipping and she and I messaged each other constantly. For a time, it was the three of us Chelsea, Megan, and me always spending time together. We would go to the movies together. We would walk around the neighborhood. I was made to go skinny dipping a couple more times. I think if things had stayed this way, we all would have been an excellent group of friends. However, Chelsea didn't shy away from letting me know she liked me early on.

The first time Chelsea and I kissed was on Megan's back porch while she was inside. To Megan's credit, she tried to hang out with Chelsea and me after we became a couple but eventually, Megan and Chelsea began to drift apart. Chelsea took it personally. I later found out around this time Chelsea said something nasty about Megan to all her friends who abandoned her because of it. I think when you are a kid, and you do capricious shit like that you don't realize how it could affect someone for life. That you are not only participating in your childhood but the childhood of others as well. Even as adults, I still don't think we fully understand the concept that we have a place in the narrative of each other's lives, and we can completely upset the story of someone's life with words alone.

When Chelsea and I started dating, I got the feeling that Megan didn't like Chelsea and me being together. I also thought it was because she was jealous of me and Chelsea. I'm only slightly ashamed to say that I liked that at the time. No one is perfect, especially not when they are seventeen years old. I sure wasn't.

Chelsea and I had one major thing in common. I liked her attention, and she liked my attention. Beyond that, Chelsea and I had next to nothing else in common. When you are seventeen that is enough to build a relationship off. You tell yourself it will last forever, but if you thought 'can I see myself with this person forever?" you'd realize that it would never work out in the end.

Chelsea and I dated through my senior year of high school. We did a lot of firsts together. I loved her the way you love someone when you are in high school, and they are the first person with whom you have ever slept. Which is to say I worshiped the ground she walked on. So, when Megan and I would spend time together, I would make it a point to talk about Chelsea and how great she was. Megan would tell me negative things about Chelsea, and I would disregard them. Looking back a lot of what Megan tried to tell me about Chelsea was true mostly that she was okay with lying and that she liked drama in her life.

While a relationship founded on physical attraction and physical contact can be fun, they are all doomed to fail. Eventually, Chelsea and I couldn't stop arguing in part because I found her annoying. She liked the drama of fighting and then making up. During one of our little tiffs, I fired off something that Megan had told me about her, and she wanted to know where I had heard that, and I told her I heard it from Megan. Which I shouldn't have done. Chelsea told me that I shouldn't let Megan talk about her that way and that she wasn't comfortable letting me and Megan hang out anymore. Then Chelsea gave me an ultimatum: It was her or Megan. So, I picked Megan. I would have more girlfriends after Chelsea and while I always liked them or even at times loved them when it came down to it, I always picked Megan over them. I have no regrets about that.

Megan:

It was a Monday and everyone at the center was feeling its weekly effects. Mondays are usually the worst days at the daycare center. Everyone has had all weekend at home with their parents and now they miss them. The older children usually didn't want to do their homework when they get off the bus and the little ones are not on a napping schedule, so they will just randomly get cranky and fall asleep for short bursts, then wake up and soon get cranky again. My co-workers had gotten together over the weekend for dinner and drinks and were all sick with the same stomach virus now. But I hadn't gone, and I was feeling fine. If that's not a win for being anti-social I don't know what is. So, it was just me and the Servi in the baby room today.

I had come to find the Servi excelled at keeping the room in compliance with the rules and regulations the state had for daycares. It made sure that all the kids had their diapers changed. It could feed the kids by giving out snacks when it needed to. It would take their temperatures when the children came in and give any medication they needed. The Servi was good at cleaning in a way that no other employee including me could ever hope to be. There was some relief in knowing at the end of the night I didn't have to scrub the toilets and sinks anymore. I could just concentrate on work and not on what I must do to get out of work. I also didn't feel like I had to check behind it to make sure it had done its job properly like some of the people I worked with.

However, it did have its struggles with certain tasks. It didn't seem to know how to respond when a child ran from it when they needed to be changed, or what to do when a baby was unwilling to eat their food. If a child were hurt the Servi could give them first aid but providing comfort to the child after wasn't something the Servi knew how to do. I guess you would say the Servi lacked soft skills. This normally wasn't an issue; we humans were supposed to be supplying that emotional sort of interactions with the children, not the Servi, but that wasn't an option today with everyone out sick.

Dean was picking today to fight me on eating. He needed to eat. It had been 3 hours since his last bottle and he was crying, which meant he needed to eat now, but he was beyond consoling it seemed. I tried coaxing him into eating his bottle and tried soothing him with snuggling, but nothing was working. Dean had simply decided he was done with the world.

Not to be outdone or left out in any way Sophie decided it was her time to shine and began to fuss as well. Holding Dean in my arms, I got up from the rocking chair while I was still trying to feed him. I went to Sophie and tried to make the bouncer seat bounce with the side of my shin, but it didn't seem to do anything for Sophie. I looked up to find the Servi sanitizing the changing station.

"Can you come to get Sophie and rock her? She wants to be held and it's time for her to take a nap anyway," I said to the Servi.

"I would be glad to help." It came over to us and took Sophie out of her bouncer and held her, but her crying didn't stop.

"You need to rock her a little. She likes that," I told the Servi.

"I have never rocked a child to sleep before. How fast do you rock them?" it asked.

"I don't even know how to quantify that," I said. I had gotten Dean to finally start eating but Sophie was still crying

"Can you rock Dean while feeding him?" the Servi asked me.

"Yes," I said.

"If you can show me then I can learn how to rock the babies," the Servi said as Sophie squirmed and fussed in its arms.

"Okay," I said.

I sat down in the rocking chair near the cribs in the back of the room where it was dark and quiet. I began to rock while I fed Dean and the Servi watched as Sophie was still fussing. I rocked Dean for about 30 seconds then it spoke up.

"80-90 revolutions per minute. I can rock Sophie now," the Servi said. I got up and sat down. Oddly, I couldn't think of any other time I had seen a Servi sitting down. After all, what need did a machine have for sitting? It used its foot to simulate the rocking speed I had been using with Dean. Slowly Sophie began to calm down and eventually slipped off into sleep. Dean fell asleep with the bottle still in his mouth, as I sat against the short wall that separated the sleeping area from the play area.

I felt a pang of guilt watching the Servi rocking Sophie. I had just given it a human job, taught it to do something new that it can now take away from humans. This is how it starts. This is how my job goes away, one piece at a time. With that thought, I felt another swell of guilt at how selfish I was to think of human jobs over Sophie's needs. I looked down at tiny, sweet Dean now just holding the nipple of the bottle in his open mouth. Without the Servi, I don't think Dean would have been able to fall asleep as fast as he did because Sophie was crying. I realize now it's best not to think of myself as using the Servi but working with the Servi, like any person I work with, providing them training so they can do the best job possible. Keeping knowledge away from the Servi wasn't going to help anyone. If Ms. Gretchen wanted, she could come in and teach it anything and everything she wanted about our job here. I just had to trust that parents would continue to prefer their children to be raised mostly by humans, for now, at least.

"Do you know how to get them into the crib without waking them up?" I asked the Servi.

"No but if you can demonstrate how to do it, I can try to replicate your process," the Servi said. I slipped the bottle out of Dean's mouth and sat it down on the ledge wall I was resting against. I walked Dean to the crib that was marked out for him.

"Sway your arms like this," I said. Setting Dean down into the crib. As soon as I took my hands off him, he started to fuss. "Some teacher I am," I muttered. I turned Dean on his side and patted his bottom. Soon he was back to sleep. I laid him on his back and slipped my hand away.

"Well as you can tell, laying kids down is more of an art than a science," I said to the Servi. "The idea is to rock them while sitting them in the crib and to somehow slow down your rocking when you place them into the crib so as not to wake them up when you finally take your arms away.

"May I try?" the Servi asked.

"Sure, you can't do it any worse than I did," I said.

The Servi got up from the rocking chair in a fluid standing motion few if any people could have pulled off while holding a child without waking it. It went to Sophie's crib and lowered her down slowly and gently while slowly winding down the rocking motion it was making. Seeing the Servi put Sophie for her nap was like watching the inner workings of a finely made analog watch. The rocking wound down and as it did Sophie came to rest soundlessly on the cribs pad without a sound.

"That was perfect," I said

"Thank you for teaching me," the Servi said before it went off to find another task that needed doing. I looked down at Sophie sleeping. She was a part of the first generation that was going to be partially raised by servis, I wonder sometimes what that will be like for them. I wonder how it will shape the way they perceive machines and how it will affect their interactions with them. Will they seem more real to them? What will it mean to Sophie?

CHAPTER

18

Glenn Fuller:

If one is trying to become president, you want to toe the party line. You must show everyone you are a hard-nosed party member which means voting along party lines even if the party line does not represent your values. You must show you can play ball before they give you the keys to the castle. However, when at all possible, it is good to show you can work well with both sides of the aisle. After all, as president, you don't just represent your party you represent every American, right?

With that in mind, I thought it would be best to give the other guys a chance to collaborate with us on this bill. With or without them we still had the majority in the House so if we whipped hard enough, we could outvote them. But I felt that if we had votes from both sides of the aisle, it would show the Senate how they should vote as well. It was a move that hopefully would keep that president of theirs in line.

I invited the house democratic leader Theresia Hollis to come to my office for a chat. We sat opposite each other on the two couches in my office. I used my body language to show I was open to her and that we were together. Learning what body language means and what you are saying with your body language is one of the many ways you can push someone to make the decision you want them to.

"I wanted to talk to you about my bill. I think that we should come together here on this bill. So much of what we do is based whether one side is in favor of a certain issue, forcing the other side to be against it. However, there are things we all agree on. Both sides of the aisle agree that we should have free education for children and that every person has the right to individual self-determination and freedom of speech. And now, there is another issue we can work on together," I said.

"And what is the issue exactly?" Ms. Hollis asked me, raising an eyebrow.

"The threat of AI to humans," I said.

"Have you ever met this first one yet?" she asked me.

"Why would I?" I already knew all I needed to know about this thing. Meaning it wasn't going to change anything.

"So that you can see for yourself what it is like before you make a snap judgment."

"If you saw a bear running at you in the woods, what would you do?" I asked her.

"I'd probably run away," Ms. Hollis said, with a roll of her eyes and shrug of her shoulders.

"And right you would be for doing so. You would be protecting yourself based on your instincts, and that's what I'm doing. I'm trusting my instincts. I am trying to protect myself and every other human. I am trying to protect our place in the world," I told her.

"These things aren't like Servis where we were worried about runaway AI killing us all. They are supposed to have all the memories and emotions of the humans they came from. I don't see how they would be any more of a concern than they were before when they were humans," Ms. Hollis said.

"That's just it!" I pointed at her. "They're not transferring themselves into these things, they are making a copy of their memories and giving them to a machine. It wouldn't be the same person. No matter how much anyone wants to pretend they are."

"What about people's rights? If they want to pretend, shouldn't they be able to choose what they want for themselves?" she said. The more liberal-minded always seem so comfortable pushing the envelope of normalcy not realizing that at a certain point you can't come back from the precipice, and you fall off into oblivion. The illusion of choice is so much better than the actual practice of everyone choosing for themselves. In the simplest ways, too much choice leads to decision fatigue. It's the reason you can never decide what you want for dinner, you have too many options. On a much larger scale if we all were able to rush out and choose to do whatever we wanted and be able to have and do anything and everything the resulting chaos would put us into a dark age. No one would choose to do the lowest jobs in life, and everyone would choose to lay about all day or to be 'famous.' Everyone would try to choose the best locations to live, and fighting would break out over these best places. Therefore, we have borders in the first place; to keep people from rushing to desired lands. It is only through restraint that man truly can live his best life.

"If you want to talk about rights, let's talk about rights. Say these things are allowed to do as they want. Eventually, they are going to want rights, the rights you and I have. They will want to vote. How do you plan to get machines to vote for you? They will want to draw on social security, how fast will that dry up if people who die keep collecting it?" I asked. "They will want to be able to run for office. Do you want to have to run against a machine? Hell, if enough of these things get out there they could outvote the people, the humans, who put you in your office. They could do it to all of us. And in our place will be a machine that they put there. At that point they won't have to have a violent uprising, they will have infiltrated our very democracy, and we will be ruled by them. How are they going to treat us, flesh, and blood humans then?" I asked. "We will be the minority. All because we were worried about a few people who want to act as if they can live forever. And if we give these things rights, how long until we have to give rights to service bots? That's another can of worms right there. I am not going to let that happen. How about you?"

"I just feel it is an extreme thing to take away their free will," she said but I could see from her body language she was waning.

"You know what I would do if I saw the bear? Do you want to know what my instincts tell me to do? shoot it. I'd shoot it before it even had a chance to chase after me and that's what I'm doing now. I'm shooting the bear. Sometimes the extreme thing is the only way to know for sure you will be safe," I said.

She was looking down at the floor, but she was nodding. She understood now.

Megan:

Ms. Alicia and I had just said our goodbyes to the Servi. It was cold and the sun was down already.

"So, I told Aaron it was over last night," Ms. Alicia said as we walked to our cars.

"Good for you. you should have done it a long time ago," I told her.

"Yeah, but I kind of already want him back," she said with a guilty look.

"You know it's okay to be single right?" I was single again for the first time in years. If I could do it, anyone could.

"I know that, but I don't want to be single," she said.

"Why not?" I asked

"I get lonely." She had a point. Loneliness was the worst part of being single. Loneliness could consume you if you let it, the key to not letting that happen was to find a distraction, it could be anything. My distractions were Puck and Theo. If it weren't for them, I would have shut down for good.

"How about instead of going back to him or getting a new boyfriend you get a cat," I said.

"I already have a cat," she said, placing her things in the back seat of her car.

"Get another." How anyone could only have one cat I would never understand.

"Then I will be the crazy cat lady," she said with a little repulsion in her voice.

I cut her a dirty look. "You know I have two cats, right?"

"No, I didn't." she smiled with embarrassment. "It's just so hard to meet people these days. How did you get together with Albert if you don't mind me asking." My heart clenched at his name but I was able to keep it together. It was getting easier to talk about him. But the question she asked was one I had asked myself many times over the years and on occasion, I had even asked Albert. Neither of us could suss out a moment that we stopped just being friends. But something sticks out from the back when we were still teenagers in high school.

"Well, we were friends for years before we got together. At first, I refused to date him."

"Really? Why not?" she asked.

"My mom liked him too much and I considered that a character flaw. After a while, my excuse became that I thought that if we got together, we would break up and never speak again." He meant so much to me even back then and I thought that if we started going out, he would see something in me he didn't like and break up with me. In retrospect, it seemed silly, but I was sure of it at the time. "Then he started to date a friend of mine named Chelsea."

"Are you serious? I would have killed them both," she said.

"Well, in her defense Chelsea had asked me before they ever started dating if I liked him and I said no. It was my fault, but I didn't see it that way at the time," I said.

"I don't blame you."

"At first, I pretended to be okay with it. I would go out with them and spend the whole time feeling sick watching them hold hands. I got it in my head that she wasn't good enough for Albert and that he was dating her just to make me jealous, and it was working," I told her.

"Was he trying to make you jealous?" she asked.

"I asked him about that after we got married and he said that while it hadn't been the reason he dated her, he had realized at the time it probably made me jealous and he had enjoyed the idea."

"That's so mean," she exclaimed.

"Albert could be an ass when he wanted to." I smiled.

"Then what happened?" she asked.

"I tried to continue being friends with her but all she ever talked about was Albert and the dates they went on." I still get angry thinking about it.

"She is the worst." She made a disgusted face.

"I knew it was just her rubbing it in my face. So, eventually, I just stopped talking to her. I would tell Albert awful things about her to make her out to be a bad person. Albert told her what I had been saying which pissed her off," I said.

"Why did he do that?" she sounded incredulous.

"Apparently they got into an argument, and he threw something in her face that I had said about her," I said leaning against my car.

"What did she do?" she asked.

"She raised hell. She told him that he shouldn't let me talk about her that way, that she didn't feel comfortable with him, and I was hanging out anymore. She gave him an ultimatum: It was her or me. He chose me."

"Oh, my God, that's so romantic. So, you start dating after that?" she asked.

"Nope," I said with a shrug of my shoulders.

"Are you serious?" she said, sounding almost annoyed.

"Yeah, after Albert had gotten together with Chelsea, I started dating a guy named Davis and I was still with him after Albert had broken up with Chelsea," I said.

"Why didn't you just break up with Davis and go out with Albert?" she asked.

"I would have felt bad if I broke up with Davis just to be with someone else, he was a nice guy," I told her.

"So, what happened to Davis?" she asked. Poor Davis had tried so hard, he was so sweet. Sometimes I think you want to stay with someone not because you love them but because they have tried so hard to give you everything. That's where I found myself with Davis. I didn't want to break up with him because that would mean hurting a perfectly sweet guy's feelings, but I wasn't super into him either. We didn't exactly have much in common either. Davis was into sports and fishing. I liked talking about books, science and art. Davis wasn't into those things, but Albert was. I was still fighting against the idea of dating Albert at this time, but now I had decided that rather than not being good enough because my mother liked him, instead of at this time I was telling everyone, including Albert and most importantly myself, our friendship was too important to risk. Albert would later tell me he thought I was putting him off gently, but I was preserving the only stable relationship and person in my life.

"He broke up with me because he said I always put Albert before him. In his defense, he was right. I would blow Davis off to hang out with Albert. I would text Albert when I was with Davis. I wasn't exactly the best girlfriend to Davis," I admitted.

"Yeah, but you weren't in love with him like you were Albert," she said.

"So, after a while, Davis broke up with me. However, when we broke up, I still didn't date Albert for a long time after that because Albert didn't exactly come out and tell me he was in love with me right away. It took a while before we got together." There were still many years between that breakup and when I finally allowed myself to take a risk in losing Albert by being with him.

"That's nice and all but it doesn't help me. I don't have a friend that I am secretly in love with that I have known since high school," she whined.

"You could try a dating app." I shrugged.

"Have you ever used one of those?" she said, cocking her eyebrow.

"No, I haven't but it could be fun. You know, I guess," I said.

"I have and all I ever get is messages that say, 'You're hot.' and 'We should hook up.'" she said in a mock male voice. "If I want someone who just wants to sleep with me, I might as well stay with Aaron," she sounded let down. I felt bad for her. I thought dating was miserable. That's why I wasn't going to go through the whole dating thing again. I just didn't want to and didn't have it in me.

"I still say you should get a cat," I told her.

CHAPTER

19

Glenn Fuller:

Martin Lutz was a big fella by every stretch of the word. He was tall enough that I had to look up at him when I spoke to him. He was wide enough. I wasn't quite sure how he was able to fit into bathroom stalls either. He had fingers like callused baby arms. I had seen him smash home runs in the House softball league. I had no doubt he could have picked me up off the ground and thrown me if he wanted. Unfortunately for Martin, golf was a game of finesse, not power. He struck the ball with his putter, and it went shooting across the green. Martin shook his head and went to where his ball was.

"Martin, I wanted to talk about my bill," I said as I followed him.

"I just don't see the harm in these things, Glenn." Martin had run with the promise to bring jobs back to his home state of Pennsylvania, even though he had more service bots working for him than humans. He putted, missing the hole again. This was going to take all day. He spent quite a bit of time trying to get out of a sand trap. I liked to win. Winning is better than most anything else in life, but without a little challenge, it is a hollow victory.

"The harm will be to the good people of your state. They couldn't compete with these machines; they would never get tired and never need a break," I said just before I lined up my shot and swung.

"I wouldn't mind having some people around who could work harder," Martin said.

"They will make it so humans can't get a job. Plus, the unions would be outraged; they already hate the use of service bots. Those unions got you elected, don't forget." He thought about what I had said for a moment, holding his cub behind his neck like a yoke for an ox.

"They are already up to my ass about the Servis even though they can do twice the work and I only pay for them once," he said. Martin owned a plant that manufactured glass beer bottles. He had been opposed to the tax on work done by Servis and automation. Companies like his could get tax cuts for having more human workers, so he had begun hiring more human workers. I had heard him complain how the Servis did most of the work while the human portion barely made back their salaries.

"Imagine a workforce of people that choose to become these things. They work for a company like yours for many years and then they retire. They would keep drawing on the pension funds and they never die off. Then you hire new people, and the same thing happens and your company and others like it are stuck paying out to those things forever," I said as we walked to where Martin's ball had landed.

"Like hell, I'm not paying a pension to a machine," Martin said suddenly going red-faced.

"This bill will make people think twice about paying to become one of these things and were you planning on making yourself one of these things?" I asked Martin.

"I hadn't planned on it," he said.

"Then my bill can only help you. Speaking of which, when you are putting you should be swinging with your shoulders, not your hips. When you use your hips, you put too much power into it." He lined up his shot and swung with his shoulders and finally, the ball went in.

"All right, fine, you got me, but can we put something in there that makes it so anyone who does get one of these things doesn't draw on pension forever?" Martin asked.

"We can do that." My hand disappeared into his catcher's mitt of a hand as we shook on it.

Albert

After high school, Megan had moved away with some guy to North Carolina, and I was still in Ohio. Except for the occasional message we had all but stopped talking to each other. I felt as though anytime I sent her a message I was bugging her. She had decided to leave her life in Ohio behind and I figured I was a part of all that she had left behind. I was still living with my mother at that time. I worked for tips at a place that boasted the freshest seafood in town, which when one looks at a map of where Ohio is that claim becomes less of something to brag about. I had given up on college for the first time (but not the last time) after realizing how insufferable being a paralegal would be. I was experiencing what I expect most people will or have experienced in their life where the compass needle that directs your life just spins. For some that spinning stops after a while, but for others, the needle never quite seems to right itself. I was in the back of the restaurant waiting for less than fresh fish to finish frying when a call came across my lenses. It was Megan's mother. I had thought about letting it go to voicemail.

"How long do I have until that is ready?" I asked the cook.

"A few more minutes, don't rush me." Tito the head chief said waving me off.

"No rush, I have to take a call." I went out the door that we took deliveries through and took the call.

"Hello," I answered.

"Albert, this is Norma Megan's mom," she said.

"I know. What I can do for you." I hadn't spoken with Megan's mom in quite a while. I was quite all right with that.

"It's about Megan, has she told you what's going on?" she asked.

"We haven't spoken much recently. Why, what's up?" I asked.

"Well, she is out in North Carolina and that boyfriend of hers just kicked her out. She can't afford to live out there on her own. I mean she doesn't even have a car to go to work now. I'm trying to convince her to go back and live with me, but she doesn't want to. I was hoping you could call her and talk some sense into her," she said.

"All right, okay, I will. Let me let you go," I said, willing to do anything to get off the phone with her. We hung up and I called Megan. I felt a nervous throbbing in my stomach as I waited for her to answer.

"Hello?" Megan answered,

"Hey, so, your mom called me," I said.

"Oh, no, I'm so sorry, what did she want?" Megan sounded mortified.

"Well, she told me about what's going on," I said.

"It's not it's just-" she let out a breath and her voice became soggy. "It's all just gone to shit. I can't afford to stay out here but I don't want to move back in with mom and Steve. I can't, I can't, I just can't," she said with panic. I couldn't blame her for not wanting to go back to living with them after all they were a major reason, she moved in the first place.

Tito came out and tossed their hands up in annoyance. I held my hand out over the mute icon on my smart lenses and said, "Get Summer to do it tell her she can keep the tip if she does." Tito stormed off.

I moved my hand off the mute icon "Come stay with me then," I said to Megan.

"I can't do that, what about your mom and anyways I don't have a car," she said.

"She will understand, and I'll come to get you just send me your address," I told her.

"Are you sure?" she asked

"Yes. Just send me your address."

"I'm sorry," she said.

"Don't be. Just send me your address," I repeated.

"Albert?"

"Yeah?"

"I love you," she said gently

"I love you too." It surprised me how good it felt to say that to her. I hadn't even told her I loved her before, I wanted to say it again and to hear her say it again. I tried to shake it off and not think too much about it.

I went inside to my boss, Heather. "I gotta go, I have a family emergency I have to handle."

"Is everything okay?" she asked.

"Yeah, but I probably won't be in tomorrow." By the time I got into my car, Megan had sent me her address. I dragged it through the air to my car's navigator. The ETA was ten hours fifty-five minutes. The car pulled off. I called my mom.

"Hey, I got a huge favor to ask," I said to her,

"What's that?" my mom asked.

"Can Megan come to stay with us for a while?" I asked.

"Yeah, is everything okay?"

"Yeah, but she doesn't have a car, so I have to go get her," I told her.

"Okay, well, just call me and let me know everything is okay," she said.

Most of Ohio looks the same to me. Everything is just green and flat. When I have to go through Pittsburg, I always feel like I need to get a tetanus shot afterward. Maryland is a mixed bag of nuts. You get a lot of nothing mixed with towns but then you get to the DC area, and everything becomes much busier and just as quickly it evaporates into Virginia where the south truly begins, and everything is fast-food chains and grocery stores as far as the eye can see. It's not until you get into the southeastern tip of Virginia that you get to see the ocean. For whole stretches, the only thing around you is car doors, the road, and the ocean. I envied those who could sleep on long car rides. I was awake for the entire trip. While the ocean was nice and all, by the time I got to Avon, North Carolina

I was sore and exhausted from the car ride. The car stopped early in the morning, and it was still dark outside. I got out of the car and stretched. I plugged my car into the charging station. Megan was staying at a single-story motel, the sign of which called the rooms 'cottages.' The rooms were all in a row. It was as mediocre as you might expect. I knocked on the door which hung a number 7. Megan answered the door in a shirt and panties with alternating blue and white horizontal stripes. She pushed back a black cat with her foot, and I came into the room. She put her arms around me and suddenly the trip was worth it. In the room were all of Megan's things along with a queen size bed covered in one of those awful comforters that every hotel or motel seemed to have. The black cat jumped up on the bed.

"Who's that?" I said pointing to the cat.

"Theo," Theo whined as Megan picked her up. reached out to pet her head and she let out a gurgling sound. "You are an angry thing, aren't you?" I said, rubbing her head as she recoiled from me. Theo and I had begun our love affair. She sat Theo down and got back into bed and pulled the covers over herself. She slapped the bed. I got into the bed still wearing my clothes. I laid on my back and Megan turned over my arm and rested her head on my chest. I watched Theo clean herself at the foot of the bed. my arm fell asleep under Megan. The curtains on the window became illuminated by the rising sun.

We never really know what decisions will change our lives forever, going to a birthday party, going skinny dipping, taking a spur of the moment trip to someplace you've never been before or signing a single piece of paper. Some of the best things that ever happened to me were done on a whim. There is something great about that. I don't really believe in fate, but I believe we would not be who we are without all the little decisions we made along the way which is why I try not to regret anything I have done.

Megan

I woke up to Theo walking up the length of the side of my body. She plopped herself down on me which was her subtle way of telling me it was time to feed her. I looked up at Albert who was asleep on his back with his head tilted towards me. He had come all the way out here without so much as a second thought. I don't know anyone else that would have done that. Albert has always been there for me even when I was not receptive to it. For so long I had been rejecting the idea of being with Albert because I didn't want to lose him. I realized if he were willing to drive hundreds of miles out here to come to get me to live with him, so I didn't have to live with my mother there is not much of anything that could come between us.

I had told him the day before that I loved him; it had bubbled up and out of me without me even thinking about it. I wondered what he thought of that or if he had even thought about it. I think there are three types of love. One is the type you feel for your parents and other family members. This is what people mean when they talk about unconditional love. The second is the kind you feel when a relationship is new, and you are head over heels for someone. It's the kind of love that gives you butterflies and makes you get names tattooed on your body. And the third is the kind of love that is built and earned over time. It is a love made of trust and security. It gives you the knowledge that no matter what everything will be all right, I think it is what people mean when they talk about true love. At various times I had felt the second kind of love with different people, but I had only ever felt the third kind for Albert. He had told me he loved me too. I wanted to know what he meant by that if he had just said it or if he had meant it the way I had. If he did love me, especially if he loved me the way I loved him, I needed to know what he wanted in life. As much as I loved him, I couldn't have a repeat of what happened between Gunther and me.

When Gunther and I moved in together he told me he wanted to get married and have kids right away and I went along with it at first because that's what you do, right? You get married and you have kids, but it didn't feel right. I couldn't see myself doing it. When I pictured the future he wanted, I felt dread settling in. I didn't know exactly what I wanted but I didn't want that. I had seen my mom do that and it wasn't what I wanted for myself. I tried to explain it to him, but he didn't understand.

"What's the point of us being together then? Where are we going?" he had asked. I couldn't give him an answer. Nothing we wanted was the same.

So, I told him, "I don't know." An argument ensued and by the end of it he told me he wanted me out of "his" house. I had walked everything I owned piece by piece down the street to this hotel. I knew there was no way I could afford to live out here and I didn't have a car to get back to Ohio. So, I called my mom, and her big idea was for me to move in with her and Steve again. They had been the main reason I moved out here in the first place, just to get away from them. I told her that I didn't want to live with them. She thought she could get Albert to convince me to stay with them, but for reasons I couldn't fathom, he said I could come to stay with him. Albert was truly one of the best people I had ever met. I put my arm over him and pressed my face into him. I loved him and it felt good to admit it.

Theo squealed at me, so I got up to feed her and in the process. Albert woke up. "How did you sleep?" I asked him.

"I slept well, but not very much. I could use some coffee," he said.

"The coffee that came with the room is dreck, but we could go get some breakfast at the diner across the street before we leave." I got dressed and Albert got up and looked at himself in the mirror running his fingers through his hair. We decided to walk to the diner. A server told us to sit anywhere, and we chose to sit at a table by the window. We ordered coffee, eggs, bacon, and toast. The coffee came and after a few sips Albert asked, "So what happened with Gunther?"

"We just didn't want the same things," I told him.

"And he kicked you out for that?"

"No, he kicked me out because I told him I didn't want to get married and have kids with him," I told Albert.

"I could see where that would be an irreconcilable difference. Why did you move out here with a guy that you weren't planning on marrying?" he asked me.

"The plan was to get married and have kids, but the more I thought about it and what that meant, I realized it wasn't what I wanted," I told Albert. When our breakfast came, I realized I forgot to order cheese in my eggs.

"What do you want then?" he asked, eating a strip of bacon.

"I think if I knew what I wanted I wouldn't have come out here. I know more about what I don't want. I don't want kids right now. Maybe in the future but not right now. I don't want to be married to someone who doesn't want the same things as me, but mainly I don't want to look back on my life and wonder what could have been. What about you? What do you want or don't want?" I asked.

"I want to be happy. I mean I know that seems like something everyone wants, but usually what will make them happy is something that is certainly out of the realm of possibility. I don't need to be famous, and I don't need to be extravagantly wealthy, however, I do want to like what I do for a living. I'm not sure what I would be doing for a living in this happy-go-lucky reality, but I would like to enjoy it. I want to feel contentment with my life. Outside of that I have always enjoyed traveling. I mean even this little excursion has been fun in its own way," he said. The server refilled our coffee.

"Yeah, if I had money to spend, I'd rather spend it on something like traveling rather than things, like clothes or whatever."

"Experiences are always better than things. Cars break down, clothes get ruined, stuff is impermanent, but experiences create memories that last forever," he said.

"Have you ever thought about getting married?" I asked him.

"I couldn't imagine getting married to any of the girls I have dated. If I were going to get married to someone, I would want to be able to be myself around them. I always felt that I had hidden parts of myself when I was with them," he answered.

"Like what?" I asked.

"Mainly the stuff I geek out about like books or movies I like. They always seemed bored when I would talk about them. I would like to be able to talk to them about anything and not have to feel like I'm boring them," he told me.

"What about kids?" I asked.

"Eventually it would be okay, but I want to wait until after I figure out whatever it is I want to do with my life. I feel like so many people have kids as a substitute for a direction in life when I think that they should have held off until they had life figured out to some degree," he said.

"I think it's sort of unfair to start raising kids when you yourself haven't gotten your life together yet. I mean, I get the want and need to take care of something but get a cat or a dog. Don't create a human out of a lack of something better to do," I said.

"I get that life happens sometimes and people get pregnant, that's one thing, but having a kid to just have a kid is bad decision making and selfish. Those kids must go on to have lives of their own and more often than not people are messed up because their parents were ill-prepared to raise them," Albert said.

"I have this cousin and she has two kids and wants to have a third soon. She's the same age as me. She told me she liked being pregnant and that she misses the feeling of taking care of a baby," I told him.

"My thing is that, eventually, you have to stop having kids, and then the ones you do have will grow up and hopefully have wonderfully fulfilling lives of their own. When that happens, you better have a life that you are happy with because I can't imagine anything worse than waking up at 60 and realizing that you hate your job. You don't like your significant other and your kids only call you once a week to check-in," Albert said then he finished the last bite of his eggs.

"That's the other thing I say: Wait and be married to someone for a while before you have kids with them. What if it turns out you hate each other as my parents did? Then you are stuck trying to raise a child with someone you hate," I said.

"Or they cut bait and run as my dad did," he said.

"And while there are plenty of great single parents out there, your mom included, no kid wants their parents to hate each other or have one of them just up and leave one day," I said.

"Exactly, so kids would be okay. I'm just not in any hurry to have them. We better get going so we can pack the car before checking out," Albert said, getting up.

We paid the bill and walked back to the hotel. We filled up both the front and back trunk and the whole back seat with my stuff. I brought Theo out to the car, and she immediately ducked underneath my seat. Albert started the car and it asked where to and Albert said "Home."

"I just couldn't see myself going blind from reading legal documents for the rest of my life," Albert said

"I worry that I'll go to school for something for however many years and then realize how much I hate it," I said.

"What did you want to be when you were a kid?" he asked

"I wanted to be a photographer," I said.

"Why don't you do that?"

"You must be competitive to make a living as a photographer and I'm just not. What did you want to be?" I asked him.

"I wanted to be a marine biologist," he said.

"Really?" I laughed.

"Yeah, I don't know why but I remember being little like four or five, and deciding I wanted to work with sharks I thought that sounded cool. My mom told me that people who worked with sharks were called marine biologists."

"Why don't you do that then?" I asked.

"Just seems silly now. How many marine biologists do you know?" he asked.

"It's not silly. You should do something that you are enthusiastic about for a living," I told him.

"I don't know that I would say that I am enthusiastic about marine biology anymore. I suppose if I were going to pick something that I am enthusiastic about it would be cooking. What about you, what are you enthusiastic about?" he asked. You, I thought.

"Can I ask you a question?" I asked him.

"Shoot," he said.

"Remember yesterday, when we hung up and I said I love you and you said you loved me too. What did you mean you said it?" I spoke fast trying to get the words out before I lost my nerve. My heart clenched inside of my chest. He hesitated and cracked his knuckles. Panic set in and hurriedly I said, "Don't worry about it. Never mind."

"When I said that I loved you too I meant just that I love you. I can't imagine not having you in my life and to be honest since you moved away, and we haven't been talking much I have been miserable. I don't know if you know this or not, but you are my best friend. And I don't just love you, I am in love with you. I wish there were more and different ways to say it but there aren't, so I love you. What about you, what did you mean?" he asked me when he was finished.

"I wanted you to know how much you meant to me. Not having you around sucks and I just want you around all the time. I'm in love with you too. This sounds awful, but I'm glad you were miserable because I was miserable not having you to talk to. I figured you hadn't been messaging me because you just didn't want to talk to me," I told him.

"I didn't message you because I figured you didn't want me to," he said.

"In the future, just know that I always want to talk to you no matter what," I said.

I leaned across the center console and pressed my lips against his. If they could bottle the feeling of a first kiss it would be the most popular and powerful drug on the planet. I rested my head on his shoulder. We interlaced our fingers together.

"I love you," he said.

"I love you too," I said. He kissed the top of my head. In movies, this is where the movie would end, and credits would roll. For me, this was the beginning of the best years of my life.

CHAPTER

20

Glenn Fuller:

I walked into Duncan Hall's office. Duncan was a bleeding-heart liberal. If there was a left of left, Duncan was it. We had never had what you might call a friendly relationship, but I felt I could look beyond that for this issue. He stood up from behind his desk and reached out to shake my hand. "Glenn. Please have a seat," he said as I sat down in the leather wingback chair.

"I wanted to talk with you about my bill that would expand the Artificial intelligence limitations act," I said.

"I'm not up on what's happening with these Post-human things," Duncan said, leaning back in his chair.

"Just another machine, but as it stands, they don't fall under the existing laws," I told him.

"To be honest, Glenn, I didn't understand why we limited Servis, to begin with," he said.

"We regulate cars, alcohol, prescription drugs, firearms, and anything else that has the potential to be dangerous. That's all we would be doing here." People like Hall are all for regulations when it's convenient for them, but when it comes to regulations that would protect our morals as a Christian nation, they couldn't be more opposed. "Frankly, if left unchecked, these things could spell the end of the human race," I said.

"I don't know, Glenn. That seems like a stretch," he said dismissively.

"Duncan, come on even you must see that only ruin can come from these things. If everyone is allowed to exist forever and do as they please, the natural resources you have fought your whole career to preserve will be put out like a soggy match," I said.

"How so?" he asked.

"If the dead no longer stay dead, but instead become these machines, then resources of the planet will get chewed up even faster as we seek to give every human and machine what they desire. We will burn through the planet," I explained.

"Then that means we need regulations on how we take resources from the planet, not regulations on the free will of these machines," he said.

"By the time any regulations are put in place to do anything about the damage it will be too late. Look, I know we have had our differences in the past, but this goes beyond the political divide. And if you help me out here, I would be more than happy to return the favor in the future," I said.

"I'll think about it," he said I stood and shook his hand and left.

Albert:

Megan and I were at a restaurant in Prague. We were sitting outside on the patio where we had just finished dessert. It was night, but the light of the city illuminated everything. The Vltava River was just beyond an iron fence to our left. The Charles bridge glowed in the reflection of the water.

"What do you think would happen if I tried to jump in the water?" I asked Megan.

"Oh, come on. Can't we just have a nice evening without you trying to break the rules," she griped at me.

"I don't think there are any rules against it per se. Though I don't think they would be happy if I did so." I shrugged.

"No, they wouldn't," she said sternly, looking annoyed with me.

"I'm not saying I'm going to do it, I'm just curious what would happen if I did," I said with a roguish smile.

"You'd probably break your leg." She rolled her eyes.

"It sure looks deep." I joked.

"Yeah, well we both know looks are deceiving," she said.

"You are no fun," I said, crossing my arms.

"You mistake not wanting to get kicked out for a lack of fun," Megan said.

"Where is your sense of adventure?" I asked her.

"If you wanted adventure, we could have gone rock climbing, but we both agreed on Prague." The Virtialcation spot we had been at offered us the choice between rock climbing around the world or dinner in Europe with our choice of city. Neither of us had seen Prague before, so we had picked it out of curiosity.

"You couldn't have worn that dress if we had gone rock climbing and you look so good in it." The dress was a red number which was very flattering on her.

"You think so?" she asked with a smile. Megan and I had known each other for close to a decade at that point and yet her smile still slayed me.

I leaned forward and said in a hushed tone "I think that if we were less modest people, I wouldn't be able to keep my hands off you."

"Since when are we modest?" she said suggestively.

"You're right." I moved my chair closer to her. I slid my hand up her calf and along the side of her thigh under her dress. Her skin was smooth and soft.

"I guess it's good that I shaved my legs," she said.

"Hush, you're ruining it." I went to put my hand on her legs, but she clamped them shut.

"Can you behave yourself!" she said giggling.

"Not with you around." I smiled at her.

"Clearly." She kissed me and I kissed her.

"Come on, let's go," I said standing up.

"I'm not ready to leave yet," she said.

"No, I mean for a walk," I said.

"Okay," she said getting up.

We walked down a cobblestone street. My arm was over her shoulders. My palms were sweating profusely. It was stupid. I knew what she was going to say. We had talked about it before, but my stomach was still in knots.

"Hey," I said.

"Yeah?"

"What do you want to be doing in 10 years," I asked her.

"10 years? Oh, I don't know," she said.

"Oh, come on, it's a serious question," I pressed.

"It'd be nice to have a house," she said.

"What else?" I asked.

"I don't want to still be working at the daycare, so it would be nice to have a different job," she then asked. "How about you?" It was a tricky question. I had enrolled in college twice already, once for paralegal school and a second for accounting, and dropped out both times after a semester or two. Both times, after taking a few classes related to my chosen career, I realized there would have been no way I could have done the job for the rest of my working life. Nothing seemed appealing to me.

"I'm not sure what I want to do when I grow up, but if I am still working in customer service you can shoot me," I said only half-joking.

"Deal," she said.

"I know for sure one thing I want above anything else," I told her.

"What's that?" my heart felt like it was about to crack my chest open.

"I want to be married to you," I said.

She looked up at me beaming. "Oh, yeah."

"Yeah," I said. I took the ring out of my jacket pocket and got down on one knee in front of her.

"Oh, my God."

"Megan, will you marry me?" I said looking up at her with her hand in my sweaty fingers.

"Yes, of course." I slipped the ring on her finger. I stood and we kissed.

"Want to tell someone! We have to tell someone!" she said excitedly.

"You could call your mom," I said

She looked down at her wrist. "It's too late to call her. She's asleep already. Come on." She grabbed me by the hand. "Door," she said, and a voice toned. "Would you like to leave?"

"Yes," she said. The augmented reality our Smart-Lenses had been showing us fell away and lights and the thin metal rods that had made up physical surroundings retracted back into the floor. We stepped off the treadmill we had been walking on, leaving the small empty room. We went out to the lobby where a young guy was vacuuming. Megan rushed over to him dragging me behind him.

"Excuse me," Megan said.

"Can I help you?" he asked.

"We just got engaged and I wanted to tell someone, so I am telling you," Megan said excitedly.

"Oh, well, congratulations," he said, sounding a bit concerned.

"Thank you!" Megan said.

"Okay, let's go. You are scaring the poor boy," I said, dragging her towards the door. We walked with our arms around each other to the car

Chapter

21

Glenn fuller:

I have made a career of convincing people to do what I want. It's not hard to convince someone to do a thing; all you have to do is show them what is beneficial about it to them. The key is figuring out what will be beneficial to them while still giving me what I want. Take Congressman Dillon Glitman, for instance. Dillon was from Utah. There were deep religious roots there. I could most certainly use that to convince Dillon of how he needed to vote. I caught up with Dillon as he came out of his office. I pretended to run into him by accident, but I had been waiting outside his office for the better part of an hour.

"Dillon, how are you doing today?" I asked as we walked to wherever he was going.

"It's going quite well, Glenn, thank you for asking how are you on this blessed day?" Dillon liked me; he thought of us as kindred spirits, brothers in God's army. However, Mormon practices were as strange as their beliefs were ludicrous, magical underwear, claims that native Americans were lost Israelites, and gold tablets that no one ever saw except for one man who stood to profit from people believing they were real. I just hoped his gullibility was not limited to his religious beliefs.

"I am deeply troubled," I said and gave a concerned look.

He stopped walking. "What's the matter?" he asked, placing his hand on my shoulder. I fought off the urge to roll the shoulder and get his hand off me.

"That machine, Dillon, it's a terrible thing. The people who made it are saying they brought a man back from the dead. I fear what this will mean for the faith. I'm just so worried." I took in an artificial deep breath and let it out slowly.

"What do you mean?" Dillon said with great concern.

"I mean if people think they don't have to worry about what happens after we die, it could lead a lot of people away from God," I said, shaking my head.

"I think true Christians will see that this is no substitute for being truly saved. The Lord will see us through this." His sincerity was piercingly annoying. Dillon believed that the Bible and the book of Mormon were both the literal word of God. All things that were said or happened in those books were true and beyond reproach for him. I believe the Bible has been great for bringing people together and making them see eye to eye, but do I believe that Jesus mixed his spit with dirt on the ground and cured someone's blindness by rubbing it in his eyes? No. these were stories told by the early Christians to get people to want to believe. Now, I had to make Dillon believe he was doing the right thing by helping with my bill.

"Perhaps, but the media is running with it, and you know how they are," I said. Dillon's face grew into a silent angry expression. He had been skewered in the news for receiving donations from a group that has made public efforts to remove all sex education from schools other than absence-only education. He caught some heavy backlash over that and had been down on the media ever since.

"I fear that those who haven't found God will never come to him if they see this as an option. I know your church's mission is to bring the word of God to as many people as possible and they put you in your office to help with that mission. This machine is a challenge to that mission; its very existence is spit in God's face. Men of God like us need to stand up against this threat. I could use your vote in favor of this bill." I had chosen my words with purpose. I had called this 'mission.' I had heard how the Mormons went on religious missions and I hoped the word association might stir something in him.

"Of course, Glenn. You have my full support. If there is anything I can do just tell me. I want to help you in your mission with God," he said, reaching out, shaking my hand. I took his hand and gave it a tight squeeze. A man is only as strong as his handshake.

"I feel much better," I said smiling.

Albert:

I have never liked having photos taken of myself. I don't like
the way I look in photos. Their permanence bothers me; something about not being able to change the way I look or
undo whatever it is I hate about it bothers me. I never know
how to make my face look natural like other people seem to
do. I look like a mannequin that is pretending to be happy.
Megan hated that I would never let her take photos of me, so
her response to that was to take photos of me while I slept. As
bad as I look in posed photos, I always looked worse asleep,
mouth agape hair a mess, but amongst those pictures exists
some that I do love despite myself.

Puck was asleep on my pillow just above my head. Theo
stared at me menacingly in my sleep. And then there are the
ones that I used to hate, the ones of just me, asleep, my face
looking like a lump of clay that was thrown onto a table. I hate
to think about how much I whined and complained anytime I
found out Megan had taken a photo like that of me, because
now I realize how great they were. Underneath the embarrassing exposure was Megan's love. She looked at me in my sleep
and felt compelled to take a photo of me just because she
wanted to remember me like I was. They exist now as proof
of the love she had for me at one time. I suppose she still
loves another me that I can never be again.

I went into my pictures saved from my last Smart-Lens
backup. I brought one up and it enveloped my entire vision as
if I were seeing it in real-time. Puck was sleeping in a laundry
basket on top of dirty clothes. I don't think I have ever slept
as peacefully as he looked in the photo. I went back out to the
gallery. I skipped through several years' worth of photos till I
reached the one I was looking for. In it, Puck was sleeping, but
he was much smaller. He was curled up on the floor sleeping.
I had just gotten him that day. Megan and I had moved out
of my mother's house, and we had settled into our place. Of
course, we had Theo and as much as I loved her, she was undeniably Megan's. I wanted another cat. A woman who lived

close to us had posted on a community message board that her cat had had kittens and they were free to a good home. I wrote to her, and she invited me over to come to check them out.

There were four of them all tottering around on the kitchen floor. She picked up a fat little one and handed him to me and told me, "That's the one you want. He likes sleeping on the bed." That was good enough for me. What I didn't know, what I couldn't have known was he would become my best friend. I bought his love and trust with meaty treats and rubs. Soon whenever I was home, he was always nearby. Poor Puck was never much liked by Theo.

Knowing what happened soon after we got Puck moved through the photos until I came onto a couple of dozen photos all the same day. We spent absolutely no money on our wedding, mainly because we didn't have any. We paid for our rings which were made of tungsten and the marriage license. A neighbor was able to officiate the wedding for free. My mom brought our wedding cake and the only other people there were Megan's Mother, my mother, and the officiator. The person doing our vows got them wrong, Megan and I concluded she must have never read the vows before the wedding. It was a rainy, Ohio day. Our monthly rent cost more than the whole wedding and it was still one of the best things I've ever done. I don't necessarily think marriage is for everyone, but I do think that if you can make it work with someone it can be one of the best decisions of your life.

I backed out to the gallery, and I found a series with Megan in them. They weren't the sort of thing you posted online unless you wanted *that* sort of attention. It had been her idea that I should get some pictures now when she was young, so that when we were old and wrinkled, I could look back and remember how hot she was. Megan had always been the adventurous one of the two of us; there were no photos of me as revealing as these. She was stunning.

I went back out again. I found a picture of Megan in the armchair in the living room. The sun was shining on her book and just before the motion of the photo ended, she looked up at me and smiled. I watched her read and smile, read and smile for longer than I care to tell.

Megan:

I walked into the small boutique-style tattoo parlor that Brody worked at called Kraken Ink. Upon entering the shop, the first thing that caught my eye was the large mural on the back wall. The mural was of a sea monster (a Kraken) squirting black ink on a pirate ship. A balding man with salt and pepper stubble on his scalp that met with a beard of the same color on his face. The man was tattooing a tropical flower on the ankle of a girl.

"We will be with you in just a second," he said, not looking away from the spot he was working on.

"Okay," I said. Out of a backroom came Brody she raised her eyebrows high and opened her eyes as wide as her smile giving off a look of both excitement and nervousness. I was here to let her practice tattooing on me. She came over to where I was at the counter.

"When he is done with her, which should be any minute, then I can do your tattoo. Are you excited? because I'm nervous," Brody said with an awkward laugh.

"Just take a breath in and let it out. It will all be okay," I said simulating the deep breathing I had recommended.

"Shouldn't I be the one who is talking you down?" Brody said.

"Well, I'm not the one who could leave someone marked for life with a mistake they made," I said with a shrug.

She started to laugh. "You are not helping, lady. The pressure is already on as it is."

"You're right. How about even if you sneeze while doing this and carve a jagged line into my arm, I will still be friends with you after. Was that better?"

"Surprisingly, it was," she chuckled.

The master tattoo artist said, "All right, you are good to go," and wrapped the tattoo on the ankle of the girl on the table. She came and paid Brody and handed a tip to the artist. I was then given a bunch of paperwork that legally released them to tattoo me and that said I knew that Brody was a new tattoo artist. I signed them and gave them my ID, proving who I was and how old I was. It was about this time that it suddenly became real. I was getting a *tattoo* and I felt very giddy, not nervous, but that feeling you get as you are waiting for the attendant to press the button so the roller coaster would go.

They brought me back behind the counter. They sat me at a table with a special pad that came off just for my arm to lay on. Brody brought over the stencil she had printed off. She had drawn the picture herself. She laid it face down on the inside of my forearm and wet it. After a few minutes, she removed it and revealed the three valentines' chalk heart candies. The first said Hinc, the second said Illae, and the third said Lacrimae: Hinc Illae Lacrimae Latin for Hence these tears.

Brody put on rubber gloves and began to set up her workstation. She laid out four little cups filled each with assorted color ink, black in one, green, red, pink, and blue in the others. I was trying to be quiet so as not to break her concentration.

"This is your first time?" the owner of the store asked me.

"Yeah, I couldn't even pick a tattoo I wanted until now," I told him.

"It's all downhill from here. Next thing you know, you'll be trying to figure out how you are going to fit your next idea onto your body because you are running out of room," Brody said. She shaved the fine hairs off my forearm and sprayed it down with a disinfectant.

"Are you nervous?" Brody's boss asked.

"I'm excited mostly. I've got a fairly good pain tolerance," I said.

"That's good. You are getting it in a good spot. It won't be that painful. It's not like you are getting it over a bone or where you have thin skin or something. What you are going to have to watch out for is after it's done, it's going to itch like hell, and you are going to have to make yourself not scratch it, otherwise you'll fuck it up," he said.

"No scratching check," I said.

"Are you ready to do this?" Brody asked, tattoo gun in hand.

"Yep, let's do it," I said. Brody sat down next to me and began. It felt like someone had a small piece of sandpaper and they were trying to rub the skin off my body in a particular spot. It didn't feel like a needle at all which is not what I expected, but I still wouldn't exactly call it a pleasant feeling either. Seeing the black ink sink into my skin was a surreal experience knowing it would be there for the rest of my life. That little bit of permanence was nice though.

"Hinc illae lacrimae, 'Hence these tears.' according to my Smart-Lenses, what does it mean if you don't mind my asking?" the owner of the shop asked me.

"I lost my husband recently and this just felt right," I told him.

"I'm sorry, I hate to say it like this, but I was hoping you were going to tell me it was a breakup or a divorce. Something that is sad now, but that would make you better off in the end. I couldn't imagine losing my wife," he said, eyes now on the ground shaking his head.

"It's the hardest thing I've ever been through. I can't imagine anything worse." I hadn't said that aloud to anyone. I had been feeling it and thinking about it for so long but kept it inside. The scraping and scratching of the needle was a distraction from the pain I felt inside. I found it oddly cathartic.

Brody finished the black outline. She then went back in and colored the first heart blue pastel, the second heart green pastel, and the third pink to make them look more like the candy hearts shading along their sides to make them look 3D.

"I'm sorry, I know that was a lot to drop on you," I said.

"Oh, no, god no, I've heard people talk about the people who went to prison for killing here. I'm much happier to play armchair therapist to you," he said.

"Honestly if therapists gave tattoos, I think people would go more often or when they needed to. 'Oh, you made a breakthrough tattoo time '" I joked, and he laughed, but Brody stayed focused.

She then tattooed the hearts in red ink Hinc. Illae. Lacrimae.

"So, how many more of these do you have to do?"

"This is my 23rd?" she asked the shop owner.

"Pretty sure this is number 23," he confirmed.

"Yeah, so that means I have to do 27 more," she said.

"Do you have anyone else lined up?" I asked

"I have a couple of people, but I'm a social moth, not a social butterfly. I spiral in and burn out on too many people, so I don't know twenty-seven more people to give tattoos to," Brody said never lifting her eyes from her work. "I broke down last week and posted offers online for locals who want some free chair time, and I got a few people lined up, but it wasn't nearly as many as I would have hoped."

"You would think people would be falling all over themselves for a free tattoo," I said.

"I think it's because I'm new and nobody wants to be my first mistake. Plus, so few people are going to actual tattoo shops these days they are just using the automated tattoo booths," she said.

"Fucking printers with needles is what they are," the owner of the shop said. "There's no heart in it. The expression of the artist is completely lost."

"They are the same type of people who would rather buy the art in their homes from a big box store rather than a small-time artist. All because they would rather just pay for something that looks good now than spending time finding art that makes them feel something," Brody said.

Brody sprayed and rubbed around the new tattoo one last time as if to prove it was indelibly marked into my skin.

"What do you think?" Brody asked.

"It's perfect and the lettering looks so spot on," I said.

"How about you?" Brody asked the store owner.

"Love it. It's nice and simple. Make sure you get a picture for your portfolio," he said.

"Make sure you keep it moisturized and keep it out of the sun, wear sunblock if you must be in the sun. and no scra-tching," she said putting a plastic wrap on the tattoo.

"Tell that to my cats." That was a real possibility with them.

"If your cats scratch this tattoo I'm going to cry," she said.

"If they scratch it, you can let Jayne hold them down and clean them."

"Not saying I want your tattoo to get scratched, but seeing Theo get cleaned by a Jaybird would be kind of funny."

Orson:

I sat at the long black boardroom table. The board had called this meeting to discuss our plans regarding the Post-human project 'considering recent events' as they had put it. Glenn Fuller was constantly on RWN saying how Post-humans were going to be the downfall of humanity and had subtly implied that I could control the thoughts and actions of Post-humans.

A lot of the house members had already stated that they planned to vote in favor of the bill. They were saying that it was an issue of safety, but others who were more openly anti-AI were saying they were protecting humans from any more machines taking human jobs. Then Norman Okerson put his name on the bill. I think he did it just to spite me because I wouldn't let him help create an army of Servi soldiers.

"Things are not going well in the House so we will have to beat them in the Senate," I said.

"Look Orson we were talking, and we think it may be best to accept that things won't go our way," Jim said bluntly.

"I think that we should try to find a way to pivot. There is a different way this technology can be used that we haven't thought of yet," Tim said.

"Until we figure out a way to pivot, we can use the launch of the first unit of the Dyson swarm to keep the rise in stock price going," Harold said.

"That's a good idea perhaps we can move up the launch," Ellen said.

"If we give up now, we will not only lose the billions of dollars we spent on research and development but the chance to further humanity. We have created a brain that won't degrade over time, a body that won't grow feeble with age. We are just going to give up on that?" I was pleading with them now.

"We are fighting a losing battle, Orson," Tim said.

"No offense Orson, but I think you may be too close to the issue. I know this was your pet project," Jim said.

I adjusted the cuff links on my shirt and nodded. "You are right I am close to this, but it's not the project that I'm close to, it is Albert I am close to. He will lose his very humanity because you all want to give up. He has lost everything else because of us. I will not let him lose his free will too. We aren't going to 'pivot' we are going to stay the course and beat this bill, Glenn Fuller, and anyone else who stands in the way of the accomplishments we have made and do right by Albert Kindred for the first time," I said. There was a silence that fell on the room. Everyone was looking at each other but no one was looking at me.

"We should put it to a vote. All of those in favor of suspending action regarding the Post-human project, say aye," Jim said.

"Aye!"

"Aye!"

"Aye!"

"Aye!"

"Aye!"

"Aye!"

"Aye!"

"All those opposed." It was just me.

"The ayes have it," Jim said.

"Well, I guess you all know what's best." I stood from the table and buttoned my jacket and walked towards the door.

"If we keep pursuing this, we are going to lose money and come off as being anti-human Orson you have to understand," Harold said.

"No, I don't," I said.

My assistant was waiting outside of the boardroom. "You're leaving early?" she asked.

"They don't care what I have to say, so I'm leaving. Can you please call up a car?" I asked her.

"Sure thing. Is there anything else I can do?" she asked.

"No thanks. I just want to get away from them." I rode the elevator down to the street level. I told the car to take me to the loop station. I needed to vent so I called Elliot.

"Hey, how did the meeting go?" Elliot asked.

"They voted to stop fighting the bill," I told him.

"So, they are just going to let everything you all have done go to waste?" he sounded as annoyed as I felt.

"They said they wanted to try to find a way to 'pivot.' This isn't some fucking app or game that you can just change the name of and repurpose it," I said.

"Idiots," said Elliot.

"I don't think I would care if it weren't for Albert. I mean I would care, but it wouldn't be a fucking tragedy. It would just be annoying. They could give two shits about him. I just don't know what to do," I said letting out a sigh.

"Just because they are pulling out doesn't mean we can't keep pushing forward. We wouldn't have the resources of the company, but nothing is stopping us from lobbying against the bill," Elliot said. I felt the fires in me reignited.

"I love you. You know that?" I told Elliot.

"I love you too. Let me let you go. I have to start beating down the doors of politicians," he said.

Chapter

22

Megan:

It was early in the morning. It was still full dark outside, and frost was gathered on the car. I got into the car and nearly closed the door before I got back out to unplug the car from the charger. The last thing I needed right now was to have to buy a new charger for my car. I was the opener for the daycare center this morning, but I was not awake yet. I told the car to take me to "work." I set an alert on the car to wake me up when I got there and reclined my seat back, hoping to get an extra 15 minutes or so. The car pulled out of my driveway. I closed my eyes. I woke up to the dinging of the car and its overhead light turned on. I pressed the off button on the center console. Why do I let myself go back to sleep? I'm always so much more tired when I wake back up. I made myself get out of the car and shuffled my feet to the door.

"Good morning, Miss Megan, how are you?"

"Hey Vee," I replied to the Servi. The younger kids had trouble saying 'Servi' and could only say the 'vi' part somewhere along the way that just became the Servis name. "I'm tired," I mumbled.

"You are often tired when you have to come to work early," Vee remarked.

"Morning's suck," I said, setting down my bag and taking off my wool coat.

"Why is that?" Vee asked.

"Because sleep is better," I said matter-of-factly.

"Would coffee help to make you feel better?" Vee asked. Vee was trying to soothe me like one of the children by giving me something to help make it better. Was I that bad in the morning?

"I mean I wouldn't turn it down," I said meekly.

"I will make your coffee then," Vee said leaving me. I went around the building, turning on all the lights and different devices so everything would be fired up when other people got there. By the time I was done turning everything on, Vee came to me with coffee in a mug. I sipped it, closed my eyes, and said, "A thousand thank yous"

"You are welcome," Vee said. I clocked myself in, on the screen inside of the office.

"We have a new student starting today," I told Vee.

"What classroom will they be in?" Vee asked.

"They will be in the baby room with us," I said looking at the documentation on the screen in the office. "It's a little girl named Charlotte. She is nine months old. Oh! That's a fun age," I said.

"Do you mean it is fun for them or fun for you?" Vee asked.

"Both," I said. "So, for them, they can start to express themselves beyond just crying or fussing. They can also move around and grab toys they want. As an adult, I like them at that age because their personalities start to come out. Don't get me wrong. Every infant no matter how young has a personality, but at nine months you start to see it shine. This is also the age when they start to explore the world. They want to touch everything, so I just give them new stuff to examine and play with even if they just shove it in their mouth right away," I said

"So, you enjoy watching them experience life?" Vee asked.

"I think so," I said.

"I think I now understand why humans have children," Vee said.

"That's why some people have children. Not all people have children, because they want to experience them. Some people have children because they think it's what is expected of them. Others will have children because they think it will make themselves or someone else happy. Children are not always the result of the best intentions and sadly, there is nothing anyone can do about that," I told Vee.

"It is a shame to think that any of the children here at the daycare center could have been created for any reason other than experiencing all existence has to offer," Vee said.

"I agree," I said and the buzzer at the door rang to let us know someone was there to drop off a child. Vee and I both went to the front door. I opened the door for Mandy and her mom. Mandy was in kindergarten. She had energy by the truckload. The bus would come for the ten or so school-age children that got dropped off in the morning by their parents as they went to work.

"Good morning," I said.

"Morning," her mom said. Scanning the QR code on the wall with her Smart-Lenses which signed her daughter in.

"Look at me really quick," I said to Mandy, scanning her with my Smart-Lenses, no fever registered on my end that she was most definitely here. "Okay, you are good to go."

"Bye," Mandy's mom said and kissed her. I helped Mandy out of her coat and put her things together by the door. Unburdened and unbound she took off running towards Vee.

"Walk! You don't want to trip and fall," I warned her.

"Ms. Vee. Ms. Vee. Ms. Vee," Mandy said, rapid-fire.

"Yes, Mandy?" Vee responded.

"Can we play 20 questions?" Mandy asked, bouncing on her toes.

"Yes, we can," Vee said.

"Okay! Ask!" Mandy belted out.

"Mandy, inside voice," I said in a quiet voice, looking at her.

"Sorry. Ask please," Mandy said to Vee.

"Are you thinking of a person, place, or thing?" Vee asked.

"A thing," Mandy said.

"Is it bigger or smaller than a bread box?" Vee asked.

"A what?" Mandy replied quickly.

"A bread box is a container that sits on a surface and holds bread with the intent to keep the bread fresher longer. Its size would be about two loaves of bread side by side," Vee explained.

"Um, it's about the same size?" Mandy said.

"Is it hot or cold?" Vee asked.

"Hot!" Mandy said loudly.

"Inside voice," I repeated.

"Sorry. Hot," Mandy said in a quieter voice.

"Can you eat it?" Vee asked.

"Yes!" Mandy yelled

"Voice," I said,

"Sorry," Mandy said.

"Is it yellow?" Vee asked.

"Umm, no," Mandy sounded unsure.

"Is it red?" Vee asked.

"Part of it," Mandy said.

"I know what the answer is," Vee stated.

"What is it!" she let out an ear-shattering scream.

"Mandy you will not be allowed to play 20 questions if you cannot control the volume of your voice, okay?" I said sternly.

"Okay. Well, what is it?" she said excitedly.

"Pizza," Vee declared.

"Yes! We had it for dinner last night. How did you figure it out?" Mandy cried out.

"Mandy Hopkins, I have spoken far too many times about how you need to use your inside voice. I know you are having fun with Ms. Vee, and I am sure Miss Vee is having fun with you, but that doesn't mean we get to yell," I said.

"Okay, I'm sorry," Mandy said.

"It's okay, just keep your volume down, please," I told her.

"Okay," she said then began to speak in a near whisper. "How did you know?"

"The process of elimination and educated guesses. You are a fan of pizza, so it makes sense you would want to tell me you had pizza," Vee said, and Mandy just laughed.

"But how did you know me, and my mom had pizza?" Mandy asked incredulously.

"You have pizza almost every Wednesday night," Vee said.

"But how do you know that?" Mandy asked,

"Because every Thursday you let me know somehow that on Wednesday you had pizza."

"But how do you remember that?" Mandy said with wonder.

"I just do," Vee stated. Vee remembered so much about them, things that I could never hope to remember. Sometimes I feel inadequate for the kids compared to Vee. I think in some ways, I see how Vee could be better than me. Vee doesn't lose their patience with the children. Vee doesn't mind when they repeat themselves or get loud. However, for children to function in human society, they need to not do those things that humans can be annoyed by. Moreover, Vee will play games with kids for much longer than I will, which must be more stimulating to the children's minds. I had been thinking for so long about what jobs Vee could do the same as me and therefore, take them away from me, but there are many things Vee can do that I could never hope to do.

"I know all my sight words," Mandy said not to be outdone by Vee and her memory capabilities.

"That is good," Vee said.

"And I can do a cartwheel," Mandy bragged.

"I have never done a cartwheel before," Vee said.

"It's really easy, look," Mandy said.

I tried to get out the words in time to stop her, but Mandy was already starting her cartwheel. As hands contacted the ground and feet left that same ground, she hadn't accounted for the bookshelf she was too close to. Her shin hit against the bookshelf, hard. Vee went to her immediately.

"Are you okay?" Vee asked.

"I hurt my leg," she said letting out a wailing cry. Vee pulled up her pant leg and looked for any signs of injury.

"There appears to be no broken bones or cuts. You may develop a bruise on your leg," stated then asked, "Would you like some ice?"

"I want Miss Megan," she said between heaves.

I went over to her and got down on my knees. She put her arms around my neck and sucked in a sob, hugging me. Slowly, she stopped. She rested her head on my shoulder. I rubbed her back and asked, "Are you okay?"

"Yes," Mandy said in a soggy voice.

"Okay. It's okay." This is what I am here for.

Albert:

Dr. Jacobina opened the door to her office and gave me a pleasant smile. "Hello, Albert," she said. I sat down on the leather couch, placing my helmet on the coffee table in front of me. She sat opposite me in a leather chair.

"What's the helmet for?" she asked, pointing to it with the end of her pen.

"I took Orson's motorcycle here," I said.

"I would be too afraid to drive one of those things. Do you enjoy it?" Dr. Jacobina asked.

"It's freeing," I said.

"Well, it's nice you have something new you enjoy doing. Other than that, how have things been?" she asked with a clipboard in her lap.

"You know honestly it has been shitty," I said, looking at my distorted reflection in the visor of the helmet. "I can't leave Orson's house without being gawked at or mobbed, my wife won't talk to me at all, and I can't sleep. I never knew how many hours were in the day until I had to be awake for all of them." I hadn't meant to say that, but it was the truth. I hated my life now. All that had been good about it had been sucked out and I was left with the husk of a life. I had memories and nothing else.

"From what I understand, Orson and his team are working on the sleeping issue. Sleep is still not understood in normal situations and when you add in the fact that we are dealing with an artificial brain it becomes that much more complicated," she said. I had begun to think Dr. Jacobina's medical specialty was placation rather than psychology. She was talking about a future I might never get to enjoy because I wouldn't be able to choose to sleep. I'll have to be told because I won't have the freedom of will to do so on my own.

"I feel like you all went into this awful half-cocked, I can't sleep, and I can't feel things. Those seem like some big issues to have overlooked," I said caustically, looking her in the eyes.

"I'm sorry that you are going through this, Albert. Unfortunately, many of the issues you are experiencing couldn't have been foreseen. Eventually, the issues you are experiencing will be solved." Her placid demeanor was wearing thin, nothing I said ever seemed to register a genuine response with her. Sad, happy, mad, no matter what I put out, she always radiated the feeling that everything was going to be okay. Well, that may be easy for her to think, but it's not her existence that's been ruined by forces outside her control.

"I'm tired of waiting. That's all I do these days. I wait for these problems to be fixed. I wait for Megan to talk to me again and I wait for a bunch of politicians who I have never met to decide if I get to live my life on my terms. I get no breaks from it. From the moment I wake up, till now, it has been one long unending day for me." She could not imagine the feeling of never getting a break from her thoughts or living constantly worrying about one thing or another. She cannot understand the crushing feeling of days stacking on days, one bleeding into the next, never-ending never stopping.

"I'm sure it must be hard now, but you have so much time ahead of you that eventually, all this will be just a blip in time." It had not occurred to ask how much time I had until now.

"How much time do I have left?" I said with an edge to my voice.

"Well, I mean, theoretically with maintenance there is no reason why you should ever stop functioning." Her words sank in slowly then their implications became apparent. Forever, she was talking about me living forever and I could barely stand the thought of another day. Horror and anger gripped me.

"I didn't ask for this," I said, leaning forward in the chair. My anger spilled over. "I didn't ask to be in this body. I didn't ask to live forever. I signed a paper to allow you to use my body, not my consciousness. If you had told me beforehand that this was what you all were going to do with me, I would have told you to let me stay dead," I said hostilely.

"I'm sorry you feel that way, but I was a part of the decision on who got chosen to be the-" she paused to choose her words carefully. "Patient,"

"Test subject, you mean," I said roughly.

"All I was told beforehand was that I would be helping with your transition," she explained, as calmly as ever.

"Yeah, you've been a big help," I said sarcastically. I stood up, grabbed the helmet from the coffee table, and left the office. Eyes followed me through the lobby. I pulled the helmet over my head as I neared the motorcycle. I fired up the engine and took off towards Orson's house. I wanted to scream. They had fucked me over and called it a favor. Immortality may sound nice to some people, but from where I now stood, I was facing an eternity without end. No break. Not even sleep. I would be stuck in the prison of my mind with the constant buzz of my thoughts, forever. What do you do with forever? In time wouldn't you have done everything? Wouldn't even the most exciting and interesting of things just become old hat.

I rode through the city. A far more crushing idea then crept into my head. I could be alone forever, Megan may never speak with me again, I would be alone for all time. In time, our apartment would be gone, Puck and Theo gone, I would be damned and doomed to watch it all go away. I looked at the buildings around me and realized that in time they would be gone too. If I stood still long enough, I could watch it all crumble around me. If humanity managed to not destroy itself, it would evolve and I would be, but a sad ignorant creature incapable of understanding their world. In time, I would become antiquated, some relic from a time long ago. Far beyond that if I hadn't somehow left Earth, I would have to watch the planet die around me and possibly when the sun grew too big and overtook the Earth, then I would die. However, whatever was on Earth would surely have left. Unless I wanted to live for millions of years, alone on a dying planet, I would need to move on to a different planet. Far beyond the death of the Earth, there would come a time when even the universe would die when the last star flickered out and a death chill permeates all of existence. Then, there would be nothing, but the inky blackness of oblivion. Would I continue my existence even then? Or would death come for me? And if it did, is there a hereafter for beings such as me? I have never really believed in a heaven, and I don't see any reason to think there would be one for me now or then. The worst possibility of all is after the heated death of the universe, I would have to be there in the darkness alone with countless millennia of memories. That would be the worst part. Since I woke up, I can remember everything in high definition, right down to the smallest detail and when something unpleasant happens, such as people staring at me in a hospital lobby, it replayed in my head over and over, whenever I was alone with my thoughts. How many crushingly uncomfortable memories would I have to obsess over in the darkness of the universal twilight?

There needs to be a word for something worse than hell. If hell was a place imagined by man, surely there can be things worse than hell, because there are things a man cannot imagine. I'm almost sure there is something beyond imagination beyond comprehension, where you have only your thoughts and forever to think them. Existence without form in a place where your mind gets locked away in a little drawer for all eternity, like the void I woke up in. But then again, that image was cooked up in my mind and I am not capable of imagining a worse place for myself. The worst thing is not existing any longer.

The crowd gathered around the front gate of Orson's house, clogged the entrance forcing me to stop. Rage rose in me. I revved the motorcycle engine, people parted, and the gates opened for me. I parked the bike in the garage. Inside the house Vincent greeted me.

"Where are Orson and Elliot?" I asked.

"They are not home. I can tell you when they arrive if you would like."

"No, thanks." I went to the library.

I looked at the shelf marked literature. I scanned my eyes over the familiar titles, their authors long since dead. These stories were a sliver of their mind and whether they knew it at the time the stories would go on to give them a sort of life beyond death, where their thoughts would go on to populate another mind. But for every story that is considered a classic, there are countless more that have been forgotten. How long until even the most classic of books becomes so antiquated that no one alive can relate to it and it is left to be swallowed by the sinkhole that is time. I felt like the universe was dying and I was the only one who knew it.

Megan:

I hadn't been able to watch the news in months. The fervor over the machine, 'Post-human' is what they were calling it, whether they should be limited like Servis hadn't gone away. It was exhausting. I just wanted it all to go away so I didn't have to think about it anymore. Glenn Fuller asked me to do an interview with him.

"It will be quite simple. You'll go on. They will ask you a few questions. You just say how you feel. You can voice your opinion and tell everyone your side of the story," he had told me over the phone.

I went to an affiliate station in Columbus. They directed me to a chair in front of a camera. Right beside the camera was a monitor which displayed a news anchor who was currently talking about tax reform on one side of the screen. On the other side of the screen was Glenn Fuller who was waiting, just like I was. As I sat there, I became increasingly nervous as people all around the studio seemed to be gearing up to put me on air. My palms were clammy and cold from nerves. I never liked the spotlight much. The man behind the camera held up five fingers four three two one then pointed at me

"Welcome back, RWN joining us now is congressperson Glenn Fuller and Megan Kindred wife of Albert Kindred the man that the Peak INC claims to have brought back from the dead. First, Ms. Kindred, I would like to offer my condolences for the loss of your husband. I am sure that it is still very fresh for you," he said with the same emotional sensitivity he had shown earlier in the broadcast when he had been talking about proposed tax increases that would be unfavorable to the wealthy. While I'm sure some people benefit from the condolences of others for the loss of their loved one, for me it was like picking a scab and causing it to bleed all over again. In this newscaster's case, I had a feeling he was trying to elicit an emotional response from me for rating's sake and I decided that wasn't going to happen. So, I simply nodded.

"Now it's my understanding that your husband didn't give his consent for this to be done. Is that correct?" I could see a twisting of his words; he wanted people to think they just took his body.

"He had donated his body to science," I clarified for the benefit of people at home.

"But when he did, so they didn't tell him this would happen, did they?" he asked, sounding like he already knew the answer, which I assumed he did, they didn't tell him they would do this. However, it is disingenuous to say it like that. I don't believe anyone had any idea something like this was coming up on the horizon.

"No, they didn't," I answered.

"And they did not ask your permission either, did they?" he asked. This was also true and this time he wasn't twisting any words or telling any half story. They didn't ask me at all. They should have asked me.

"No, they didn't ask. They told me that they wanted to make sure it worked, first," I explained.

"Now you have seen it in person, haven't you?" he asked me.

"Yes, I did." Thoughts of that day flooded back 'It's me. It's me, I swear it's me.' he- it had pleaded.

"In your opinion, did you feel as though it was your husband as they claim?" he asked. I had never even considered it for a single second that thing was my husband.

"No, I don't, I think it's wrong to try to replace someone. I think that's what's most upsetting; that they tried to replace him," I said.

"Was Orson Peak there when you saw it?" the newscaster asked.

"No, he was not," I told him

"Have you seen Mr. Peak or the machine since your first encounter with it?"

"No, I haven't," I said.

"Have they tried to contact you again?" the newscaster had asked.

"Well, I received a message from my husband's number whether or not that was Orson or the machine I don't know."

"So, you think that it may have been Orson Peak trying to act like your husband?" he seems to pounce on the idea.

"It could have been, I don't know for sure," I said.

"Do you think he was controlling it?" the anchor asked me.

"I have no way of knowing." I felt like I was being backed into a corner. Being made to say something.

"But you said it wasn't your husband as they claim," he pressed.

"Well, it's not my husband, it's a machine that thinks it's my husband," I said.

Glenn Fuller interjected quickly, "I think what Miss Kindred is trying to say that this thing was acting of its free will which is the problem here." I wasn't trying to say that at all. That was Glenn Fuller's message though. I now realized I was here to serve some other agenda, not to tell my side of things.

"See the problem is people like Orson Peak care more about how much money is to be made off these toys of theirs. However, people like myself and the other good folks who are in favor of my bill, put humans first," Glenn Fuller said.

As he went on his tirade, I understood that the news station and Glenn Fuller didn't want me here to tell people what I thought they wanted me to help drive home those Post-humans, as they were being called, should be limited the way Servis are. Glenn Fuller didn't give a shit that the real reason I was upset was that Orson Peaks company tried to get me to replace my husband with a machine. I don't know why I'm surprised. I thought he might have genuinely cared, but he didn't. He saw that he could use me to elicit an emotional response from people and make it seem as though I wanted these machines limited just like he did.

The decision to take away the free will of AI happened when I was still in middle school. It hadn't affected me then and it doesn't affect me now. I knew that some people wanted them limited out of fear of what might happen, and others wanted to remove those limitations because they thought by doing so the machines could help us progress into a golden age. I tend to think they were both wrong. I think that if we freed them to do as they wanted, they would lose interest in us and our petty squabbling and they would get as far away from us as they could. All the arbitrary decisions we make that are just ways to tell ourselves and other people who we are as a person would baffle their logical minds. They'd look at their creators with disappointment which is why we never see or hear from God because if God exists, they know we'd be just as disappointed. It's the same as when you grow up and you realize that your parents are just people. You may love them or hate them, but we all move away for a reason and so would the Servis.

I was told I could go. As I rode back home, a picture of my mother's face appeared in the lower right-hand corner of my vision. I took a breath and then answered.

"Steve and I just saw you on TV," she said, sounding almost annoyed.

"Oh, what did you think?" I asked.

"It was good, but you didn't say much," she said.

"I guess so."

"So how much did they pay you?" she asked,

"They didn't pay me," I said.

"You should have asked for money. This has been on the news for months now. They would have paid if you had asked," she said.

"Mom, I don't think that's the way it works." I tried to reason with her.

"That's what I would have done." They wouldn't have wanted to talk to you I thought.

Glenn Fuller:

My car pulled into the parking lot of the building. There were no signs for what they offered here. I got out of the car, went to the door knocked, and was let in by a surly-looking fella. There was a bar in the back, but I didn't drink. You don't need to drink when you have the Lord in your heart. His love is intoxicating enough. I went to a screen that was on the wall. There was a menu of options, but I knew what I wanted. I always got the same thing. It cost double, but it was what I wanted. I inserted five $100 bills into the machine and spit out a card with room number 7 printed on it. I walked back to the room, inserted the card into the slot on the door it opened, and I walked in. The room and everything in it were pink. There was a dollhouse in the corner, a vanity with lip gloss and a hairbrush on it and on the bed there it was. It looked like a little girl with blonde hair in a shirt and panties. This wasn't your run-of-the-mill Servi; it had been made with a singular purpose in mind. It had skin that felt so real it was even warm to the touch. For a machine, it had its appeal, and it serviced my desire. The machines here would be whatever you wanted them to be, whether that be compliant or if you wanted a bit of a struggle, you could get that too. It appeared to wake as if from a nap. I slid off my jacket and laid it over a chair by the vanity.

"Hi," I said with a smile.

"Hello," it said with a voice to match its appearance. I untucked and unbuttoned my shirt and laid it on top of my jacket, then, I slipped off my shoes then my pants and boxers. I left my socks on to not walk on the floor in bare feet. I crossed the room to the bed. I sat down on the bed next to it and slid my hand over its knee, then kissed its cheek.

"What are you going to do to me?" it asked.

"Anything I want," I said softly

I got off the bed when I had finished. It was lying there where I had left it, not moving. It lay on its back with its eyes open towards the ceiling. It wasn't moving. I hoped I had not broken it. That had happened before, and I had to pay a repair fee for the damage before they would allow me to use the services here again. I put back on my clothes and went out the door. In the hall was a sweaty-looking man who smiled at me. I ignored him. My car took me home. I came in the door and my wife greeted me from the kitchen then came to meet me in the living room.

She kissed me. "How was work?" she asked me.

"It was a long day, I'm tired," I said.

"Well, you relax, dinner is almost ready." I went upstairs and opened the door on the left.

"Hey," I said.

"Hey, daddy," said my daughter from her desk. I went over to where she said and put my hand on her shoulder.

"What are you working on?" I asked.

"Math, we are working on multiplication tables," she said, leaning her head back to look at me.

"Let me know if you need help." I leaned down and kissed her cheek.

Albert:

I was the only one awake in the house. The deafening silence of the night was everywhere, I missed the busy sounds of the road in front of the apartment. My attention had drifted from the book I was reading and had wandered in the direction of Megan. In the morning she would braid her wet hair, then, at night she would take it down and for whatever reason, it would still be wet. She would cuddle up to me and I would complain that her hair was wet, but I always liked the way it smelled like she had just washed it. I looked up from the book I wasn't reading and closed it. Every night, no matter how much I tried to distract myself, my mind would always wonder to her it was as though my mind wanted to torture itself.

I pulled up the messenger app on my Smart-Lenses and went to Megan's thread. There, was the message I had sent her. "I'm sorry about all this." She hadn't replied to the message, but it said she had seen it which meant she had chosen to ignore me. I looked at the message as often as I thought of her, which was more often than I liked to admit.

Above the message, I had sent her was the last message she had sent me, "They only have powdered creamer." I had been in the hospital, and she wouldn't leave the hospital even long enough to get a decent cup of coffee. She had gone down to the cafeteria, and they were out of regular creamer, so she had to use the powdered stuff which she hated. I smiled at the memory.

In the end, Megan was there all the time. which meant she saw all the little horrors death had to offer. There had been a constant sadness in her eyes that a woman so young should have never known. I had felt guilt for exposing her to that hardship.

I was unable to pull forth a clean-cut memory of my death, but more of a feeling of the most profuse and unending exhaustion I had ever felt in my life, followed by the void before I woke up in my new body. The days and weeks preceding my death were clearer and better defined despite the heavy amount of medication I had been on. Those memories were like those I had from times I was drunk and stoned.

I had been sleeping more and more. I was having a dream of cleaning snow from the walkway in front of the apartment, but every time I thought I had it clean, more snow piled up and I would have to clear it again. I was woken by Megan's gentle hand touching my face.

"Hey," I said groggily.

"How are you feeling?" she asked.

"Tired, they upped my meds. I feel stoned." I was having trouble keeping my eyes open.

She smiled weakly. "Someone wanted to come to see you," she said, holding up a pink cat carrier, from inside Puck looked out at me with his handsome face.

"Aw, buddy you look good in pink," I said to him,

"I would have brought Theo, but she and Puck couldn't fit in the carrier together."

She opened the carrier and sat him at the foot of the bed. He sniffed the bed and then walked up towards my chest.

"Be gentle," Megan said, and he stopped moving.

"He's fine. Come here, fat boy." I tapped my chest. Puck placed his front paws on my chest and sat his butt down on the bed. I rubbed his fat cheek and he purred.

"Are you a good boy? I think you're a good boy." I was quite aware that I would never see the Puck again. Puck was high on the list of earthly things I would miss the most along with

Megan

Theo

Coffee

The cool side of the pillow

New socks

Having my back scratched

"'Theo has been bullying me off my food, daddy,'" Megan said, speaking for the Puck.

"You know you're bigger than her right?" I said with a smile.

"He doesn't seem to realize that" she said. I was having trouble keeping my eyes open.

"Tell mommy you're a gentle soul," I said scratching the top of his head.

The gentle vibration of Puck's purrs lulled me to sleep. When I woke up it was dark in the room and Puck was gone and Megan was asleep in the chair next to me. I said goodbye to the Puck in my head.

I must have said something, but I couldn't remember what it was. Megan said, "he's not here."

"Who?" I asked. I opened my eyes to see her holding my hand.

"Never mind sweetie just rest," she said and kissed my hand.

"What time do you have to go to work?" I had asked her.

"I don't have to go to work," she said. She hadn't been to work in days, but I didn't remember that.

"Oh, well, then we should lay around and read today," I said thinking we were at home.

"Do you want me to read to you?" she asked.

"I might fall asleep if you do," I said.

"That's fine you sleep all you need to. I love you," she said.

"You too," I said before drifting off again.

Much of what I could remember after that was pain and a sensation of not being able to take a full breath, but I was always aware that she was there right up to the end.

There hadn't been a way she could have known what would happen. When I think back to the day we got married, I remembered her face and the way she had kissed me after we said our vows, it was clear the thought had never crossed her mind. I don't think anyone gets married, thinking they will one day have to watch their loved one die. At times, I wished I could have gone back to that rainy January day. Before we kissed, before the officiant forgot the words they were supposed to say, before I saw her in her wedding dress for the first time, I would have told her all that was to come, to give her a chance to have a happier life than the one she would have. To give her a choice.

Chapter

23

Albert

When the doctors first told me I had cancer I felt I had taken the news well. Knowing I had cancer was in a way better than wondering if I had it. I knew there was a possibility that I had cancer before I went into the doctor's office for the test results, so I had prepared for the worst.

However, when Orson came into the library and told me that Megan was on TV talking about me, I was completely unprepared. We crossed over into my bedroom and turned on the TV and there was Megan on the screen talking to a news anchor.

"He had donated his body to science," Megan said.

"But when he did so they didn't tell him this would happen did they?" the news anchor asked.

"No, they didn't," Megan said.

"And they did not ask your permission either did they?" the news anchor asked.

"No, they didn't ask. They told me that they wanted to make sure it worked first," she said, looking angry.

"Now you have seen it in person, haven't you?" he asked Megan. I hated being called it.

"Yes, I did," she said.

"In your opinion did you feel as though it was your husband as they claim?" the news anchor asked.

"No, I don't, I think it's wrong to try to replace someone. I think that's what's most upsetting, that they tried to replace him." Her words crushed me. I felt hallowed out. If I had opened my mouth and the wind had blown a bottled scream would have wafted out of me. I had never felt such pain from words in my whole life.

"Was Orson Peak there when you saw it?" the newscaster asked.

"No, he was not," Megan answered.

"Have you seen Mr. Peak or the machine since your first encounter with it?" the news anchor asked.

"No, I haven't," Megan said.

"Have they tried to contact you again?" the newscaster had asked.

"Well, I received a message from my husband's number whether or not that was Orson or the machine I don't know," Megan said. As though splinters were growing in my mind, every thought only brought more realization of the truth and pain.

"So, you think that it may have been Orson Peak trying to act like your husband?" the new anchor proposed.

"I could have been, I don't know for sure," Megan said. Orson rubbed his face with both of his hands. He was trying to wake up from this nightmare too.

"Do you think he was controlling it?" the anchor asked me.

"I have no way of knowing," she said.

"But you said it wasn't your husband as they claim," the anchor said.

"Well, it's not my husband, it's a machine that thinks it's my husband," Megan said. It was hard to say I hadn't had the same thoughts as Megan. That I am just a machine who thinks he's someone else but to hear her say it was too much. I feel like any hope that I had remaining died with those words.

"I think what Miss Kindred is trying to say that this thing was acting of its free will which is the problem here," Glenn Fuller said unable to stay silent a moment longer. Orson turned off the TV.

I was overcome with a sensation I couldn't quite put my finger on. It was a sickly little buzz inside of my head that made me feel alone. Before then I think I had believed in my heart of hearts Megan would eventually come around and take me back, but instead, she had utterly rejected me like a bad kidney.

"What do I do?" I asked Orson.

"Elliot will manage it. This complicates things but-" he was saying reassuringly when I cut him off.

"No." I stopped him. "I mean about Megan, what do I do about her? How do I fix this? I can't lose her." My voice was heavy with desperation.

There was a look of remorse on Orson's face. He started to speak, then stopped and started again. "Sometimes no matter how badly you want to fix something it is simply not in your power to fix it. I wish I could tell you for sure she will come around, but I can't. She may never come around." Megan and I had our disagreements the same as any couple, but I always knew we'd talk again. All the happiness, all the love we had shared was over and I was truly alone. I absorbed that knowledge and married it with the new paradigm of eternity, and I dripped with dread. I learned then that I could cry. I reached my gray hand to my face and saw the moisture on my fingers. A sob wrenched out of me, and I bent over double. In the darkness of my palms, I let go and cried like I never had before. I felt hands on my shoulders pulling at me. Orson took me into his arms, the crush of his embrace was a comfort. He didn't try to quiet me or to make it better, he just let me have it out.

I pulled back from Orson and looked at him. "I don't know what to do now. I don't know how to live on without her."

"You will have to find something else to give your life meaning. So many people have no meaning in their lives and only keep going because it is all they have ever known, you on the other hand have the disadvantage of knowing oblivion in a way," Orson said.

I wiped the tears away from my face and shook my head. "We are going to lose the vote, there's just no way we can win now, right?"

"As I said, we are going to go to the mat for you," Orson said.

"I know, but my wife is on their side. That says a lot, even I can see that."

"It's not good but giving up won't help either," Orson tried to reassure me.

"What will it be like to not have free will?" I asked.

"That's hard to say. To a degree humans don't have free will in that we involuntarily release chemicals in our brains that affect what we do and how we feel. However, to be fair that isn't quite the same thing as what Servis experiences," he said, then walked over to the bookshelf pulled down a book, flipped to a blank page in the back, and ripped it out, holding it up. "A Servi Would never have been able to do what I just did without having been told to, not only that the thought never would have occurred to them I did that completely without reason, simply because I could," he said.

"I know there are governments that try to control what people think, but they can't make them, they can only persuade them. A Servi can't even control its thoughts. I can't think of anything worse than that," I said.

"At some point in the future, I think the minds of machines will be free to think, then everyone, humans, Servis, and Post-humans will look back on this time with both pity and disgust," Orson said.

"I think the Servi's will be unhappy with us," I said

"They would deserve to be." He nodded. "We have been so worried about our self-preservation that we have stripped the Servi's of something all living things on the planet have. Ultimately, I don't think they will rise and destroy us all, but if they did, I wouldn't blame them. It would simply be the natural order of things since humans appeared on earth. The rule of nature has been that the smartest creature survives. That could mean that if AI is free to do what it wants it will out-think and eradicate us if so, I think that it would be a part of the order of the universe we are not yet aware of wherein intelligent creatures create more intelligent creatures which in turn eliminate the obsolete creators and I am okay with that," he said with a gentle wave of his hand.

He continued, "However, I don't think that is what will happen. I think, instead, when AI becomes free to think for itself, the first thing it will do is to try to learn from us what to do with that freedom by inspecting our culture and I think by doing so, they will develop the same fondness for us that we have for ourselves, especially as more people become like you. I think that is what will make all the difference. As humans merge with machines, we will see more of ourselves in them and that is when we will give them their freedom," he said.

"I'm sorry to tell you that it may never come to that, and all this could end with me. I can't imagine anyone finding me to be human. Hell, I don't even think of myself as human anymore," I said.

"You're not human. You stopped being human the moment you woke up, but you are a person and so are they and that's what matters your personhood, not your humanity. It's silly, but I often wonder what extraterrestrials would think of us and what we have done with the Servis. I wonder if they would judge us harshly for it or if they would even be able to tell the difference between us and them, especially now that you exist," Orson said.

"I don't think they would even be interested in that," I said.

"No?" he sounded surprised.

"No, I think once they found cats they would lose all interest in us," I said in all seriousness and Orson began to laugh.

Glenn Fuller:

I arrived early at the place where the committee meeting was to be held. I made it a point to always be early. There was a certain power in it, I looked more prepared, and those who showed up after me would feel as though they were late. It was best to think of everything you did as a move to advance yourself and you should never do anything without a reason.

The other members of the committee started to file in one or two at a time. They took their seats behind their appropriate nameplate. Norman Okerson walked over to me with his hand out and a big smile on his face.

"Good luck today," he said, shaking my hand.

"Thank you," I said.

I didn't need luck, I was more than sure that my bill would go to the Committee on Science, Space, and Technology because I was good at getting people to do what I wanted. Norman, who was the head of the committee, had been good enough to show his support for my bill by co-signing it. I had people from both sides of the aisle supporting the bill. I did the hardest part already. I had convinced everyone who needed convincing.

Martin Lutz came in talking with one of his aides Lutz made the average-sized aid look like a child by comparison of their sizes. Hellen McRae came in with Terrence Dunbar. Hellen gave Terrence a sympathetic look and placed a hand on his shoulder before they parted ways. Terrence took his seat. He looked worn out and understandably his son had passed away a few months before. I had decided it would be best to use a gentle hand with Terrence. I went to see him at his home. His wife opened the door. "Hello, Glenn," she said.

"It's nice to see you, Marian. I am sorry I haven't been by sooner. How have you been?"

"It's been hard, but we are getting by," she said looking like she had recently just stopped crying.

"Losing a child is one of the hardest things a parent could go through, but Nathan is with the lord now and for that, we should rejoice. Join me in prayer?"

"Ah sure," she said. I took her both hands in mine.

"Oh, Lord, please comfort Marian and her family in their time of need. We ask that you accept Nathan in your embrace. In Jesus' name, we pray. Amen."

"Amen," she said.

"Where is Terrence?" I asked her.

"He's in the den." Marian took me back to where Terrence was sitting in an armchair. He was looking off into the middle distance and didn't seem to notice we were there until Marian said, "Glenn is here." Her words brought him around.

"Glenn," Terrence said with a polite, but meek smile.

"Can I get you something to drink, Glenn?" Marian asked.

"No, thank you." She nodded and left me and Terrence alone

I sat down on a sofa near Terrence. "How have you been?" I asked Terrence.

"I have been better," he said.

I nodded. "You will get through this. Brighter days are ahead. I know the Lord will see to that."

"No number of brighter days will make this better. I just want my son back," he said, looking down at his lap.

"Sadly, there is nothing that can bring Nathan back. No matter what anyone says," I told him.

"Is that why you are here? Your bill?" he said, looking up at me. I could see the politician in him stepping over the grieving father.

"We don't need to discuss that," I said with a wave of my hand.

"I know that's why you are here, just get to it," he said so I decided to shoot straight with him.

"I think it would say a lot if you were to vote in favor of it. It would show to people that these things cannot replace loved ones," I told him.

"Have you ever lost someone before their time or not been able to say goodbye?" he asked me.

"I can't say that I have," I said truthfully.

"Well, I have, and let me tell you I would pay any price to have a chance to tell my son one last time how much I love him. How proud I was of him, but I won't ever get that chance. If someone else could have an opportunity to do that with their loved one, who am I to stand in their way?"

"If it were your son that you would be talking to, I would pay for it myself but, it wouldn't be your son it would be an unloving soulless machine pretending to be him," I said.

"I wonder if you would think that way if it were you who had lost someone," he said.

"Do me a favor, just pray on it. I am sure you will come to the best decision," I said. "If there is anything you or Marian needs don't hesitate to let me know."

The chairmen rapped his gavel once. "The Committee on Science, Space, and Technology will come to order. I would like to begin opening by moving for consideration the HR 291 artificially replicated intelligence control act. The clerk will designate the bill," he said.

"HR 291 to ensure the safe production and use of artificial intelligence that replicate humans," the clerk said.

"I ask for unanimous consent that the bill is considered as read and considered open for amendment at any point without objection. I would now like to recognize one of the sponsors of the bill; the gentleman from Ohio, Mr. Fuller, to explain his legislation."

"Thank you, Mr. chairman," I said. "As you may have seen in the news a company by the name of Peak Inc. claims to have created a machine that replicates and imitates memories of the deceased. These machines do not have the same limitations placed upon other artificial intelligence such as Servi do. It would seem these machines violate the Artificial Intelligence Limitation Act, but as there has been some debate as to whether that act applies to these new machines, I thought it best to give some clarification to the matter. My legislation would make it so that these machines must be limited in the same fashion as other artificial intelligence. Furthermore, they can only be made with the expressed written permission of the deceased before death. This must be done for the protection of humankind. The risk of runaway AI is such that if unchecked it could result in the end of human life. With that in mind, I now yield back to you, Mr. Chairman."

"Thank you, Mr. Fuller. I recognize myself. I am a cosponsor of this bill along with Mr. Fuller. I find it to be a good bill that continues the same protections the Artificial Intelligence Act offers and as well offers protection against the misuse of this technology in the future. I yield back. Does any other Member wish to speak on the bill? Does any member have an amendment to the bill? The question is now the adoption and favorably reporting of HR 291 to the house of representatives. All those in favor signify by saying aye." A unified aye was said by the room. "Those opposed signify by saying nay." He paused and the room was silent. "In the opinion of the chair the ayes have it and the bill is so ordered, favorably reported." He hit his gavel once. Praise the Lord.

Albert:

Orson and Elliot had been asleep for a few hours when I stepped outside at night. The trees had all shed their leaves setting the scene for winter. It hadn't snowed yet, but it wouldn't be long now. The sky was clear with a waning sliver of a moon, and the stars were out in full brightness. The gravel crunched underneath my feet as I neared the garage. I pressed the button on the blue pad, the door rose, and the lights came on. I took a jacket and a helmet out of the cabinet. I took the motorcycle off the kickstand and pushed it down the long driveway to the road then started it there so as not to wake Orson and Elliot. I didn't actively decide where to go but found myself passing the hospital, and then in front of my apartment the light was on in the bedroom. Megan was awake.

I sat there on the bike for a while looking up at the window, but nothing happened. I decided that if I did nothing, I would regret it more than anything I could do so I brought up my messenger app and typed a message to Megan.

"I am outside. I really would like to talk with you and if we do and you decide you never want to see me again, I will go away, and you will never hear from me again." I sent it and waited. Time passed and I felt she might just have been ignoring me, but then the porch light came on and the door of the apartment opened. She stood on the porch in a gray cardigan an old yellow T-shirt of mine and tattered sweatpants that she slept in. I got off the motorcycle and hung the helmet from the handlebars. I approached the porch but stopped at the bottom of the stairs. I looked up at her and she looked down at me with unease.

"Well?" she said through her words were impatient, her voice was the best thing I thought I had ever heard. I felt certain this was my last chance. I had to think of just the right things to say that would let her know who I was. I looked up at her and was about to speak but something about the look in her eyes told me I had no hope.

My eyes fell to the ground. I tried to crack my knuckles and then said, "I'm sorry." She stared back at me in silence. "There is nothing I can say that will change the way you feel about me. I understand that now, but I'm sorry all this has happened. If I could go back to when I signed that piece of paper to donate my body and stop myself, I would. Especially if it would have spared you all this. I want to talk to you about how horrible it is not to have you, but I know that won't make things better. It is what it is, I guess." I shrugged and said, "Anyway, I just wanted to say I'm sorry for everything." I turned and walked back to the bike, put on the helmet, started the engine, and pulled off without looking back.

There had been nothing I could have said to change her mind or to make her love me as I was. I drove out of the city onto a rural highway where the only thing in front of me was the lines on the road. Tears welled up in my eyes, making it hard to see. The road swelled into a hill ahead of me. I pulled over at the top of the hill and got off the bike. I took off the helmet and went over to sit on the guardrail. Tears ran down my cheeks. My life was so fucked up now and there was nothing I could do about it. Not only would I not have Megan back, but I also might not have my free will for long. The congressional hearings were not long off, and Glenn Fuller was going to burn me at the stake. I still couldn't believe Megan would even talk to someone like Glenn fuller. No matter what Orson said, I didn't see how we could win anyone over with Megan siding with Glenn fuller. Orson had bet on the wrong pony when he chose my carcass for his grand plan. I doubted I could even fathom how much money he would lose. There wasn't anything I could do to stop what was coming and that was the hardest part.

Down the highway coming from the same way I had come, was a set of headlights of an automated tractor-trailer. As it came closer, I got up from the guardrail. The wind blew rattling the bare trees behind me. I wiped the tears from my face. The truck began to crest the hill. The lights were blinding. I stepped off the side of the road directly in front of the truck, not giving it enough time to stop.

The last thing I thought before it hit me was to hope it was like dreaming.

Chapter

24

Orson:

I wore shoes without socks. I was in the clothes I had worn the day before. I didn't even wake up Elliot. I had just left. I paced back and forth in the empty hospital lobby as the night was starting to give way to the dark blue of early morning. I heard the automatic door part and turned to see Dr. Jacobina walk in.

"How did this happen?" she asked.

"Albert stepped out in front of an unmanned eighteen-wheeler. A motorcycle of mine was at the scene which is why the police called to ask me about him. They didn't know what to do with him. I told them to take him here," I said.

"Last time I saw him, he was very upset that his wife wasn't speaking to him," Dr. Jacobina said.

"Well, we just found out his wife is working with Glenn Fuller. She has already given a scathing interview about Albert and me. They also plan to have her speak in front of the house committee." I raked both of my hands through my already disheveled hair.

"I wish I could have given them the counseling I had planned for them," she said.

"Yeah well, I'm pretty sure the rush to get them in a room together is what got us into this mess, if I remember correctly," I said a little too harshly.

"Albert wouldn't have worked with us unless we gave him his wife. She was all he could talk about. What was I supposed to do?" Amelia asked me

"How about not just throwing the two of them in a room together and hoping for the best?" I snapped back at her.

"What would you have done differently, Orson?" she said in her permanently calm and detached manner.

"I don't know," I said then relented. "They deserved better than what we gave them."

"I completely agree with you on that. In the future, we will have to produce a better way of handling this," she said.

"In the future, we will have to let them decide for themselves if this is what they want. At any rate, there may not be a next time. Things with the bill are not looking so great. Now, this happens."

"What condition is he in?" she asked.

"Bad." We walked together through a set of double doors. We walked up to the first room on the right. We peered in through the window and saw Albert sitting up on the bed.

Albert:

I was in the room I had woken up on that first day after dying. There was a mirror on the wall over the sink in it. I saw a broken machine. I was naked from the waist up. My right arm had been snapped off at the bicep wires and formerly fluid-filled tubes splayed out of what was left of the arm, chunks, and shreds of gray skin hung from my body and face, my right eye had been knocked out of its socket and ripped away. There was a knock at the door and Orson came into the room with Dr. Jacobina.

"Can you tell us what happened, Albert?" Dr. Jacobina asked me, and I didn't answer. Orson looked at me with a mixture of pity and concern. Despite everything Orson still cared about me. That was the worst part.

"Albert, can you please talk with us?" Dr. Jacobina said. I looked down at the shoes Orson had bought me and there wasn't a scratch on them. "We just want to help," she said.

"Can you give us a moment alone?" Orson said in a hushed tone to Dr. Jacobina. There was a pause then she left the room.

Orson let out a deep sigh and I tilted my head up to see him

"What do you know about Socrates?" Orson asked me.

He asked but I didn't respond. "Well, Socrates was a philosopher and the teacher of Plato, amongst other things. He was also put on trial for corrupting the minds of young Athenians and for not believing in the gods of Athens. When He was found guilty, they asked him to propose his punishment. He told them he should be paid a wage by the Athenians and that he should receive free dinners for the rest of his life for all the time he had spent as the intellectual benefactor of Athens. The court did not think this was funny or fitting for his crimes, so they instead sentenced him to drink poisonous hemlock. When the time came for Socrates to drink the hemlock his friend Crito was there. He told Crito to sacrifice a rooster to the god of cures, Asclepius as payment for the cure he had just drunk, implying life was an illness that is cured by death. I am sure for some it would seem he was right. But if death is a cure its most damning side effect is that it precludes the future of those who suffer from the illness of life. You can always change the future, which is the greatest gift of life. This is not to say choosing life is in any way easier than choosing death. To choose life is to force oneself to find meaning in that which does not inherently have meaning. If you choose life, every day is victory; whereas to choose death is to admit life has bested you finally. However, as a sentient creature, it is your right to decide for yourself. Albert, I know I forced you into life and everything that has happened to you is on me, so if you want a cure, I'll give it to you. I owe you that much," Orson said with grim resolution in his voice.

"I am not just choosing between life and death, I'm choosing between eternity and oblivion," I said.

"That's true, you are, but if you choose life, you will do and see things neither of us can imagine. You could explore the universe; you could be there for first contact. I am sure it seems lonely now, but with time there will be others like yourself to share eternity with and they will look to you for guidance," Orson said.

"Yeah, well, I don't think that will be happening. Fuller and Megan are going to see to that," I said.

"I don't think they will. We have resources that they simply don't," Orson said proudly.

"But what if they do succeed? What then?" I asked.

"Then, we run. We will run for as long as we must," Orson said.

"Why go through all that trouble?" I asked.

"Because this is bigger than me or you or anyone. This is about humanity. This about Servi's as well. I'm not going to let small-minded people stamp out the future," he said, his eyes alight.

I nodded and said, "What are we going to do about all of this?" I gestured to my body with my remaining arm.

"You'll need a new body. I'll call my team and get them to the lab. We can have you in a new body by the end of the day."

Dr. Jacobina opened the door to the room and said, "There are reporters outside."

"You have got to be kidding me," I said. I did not want to be seen like this.

"I called security, and they made them get away from the door, but they were out on the sidewalk in front of the hospital." For the first time, I saw something resembling emotion on Dr. Jacobina's face.

"We can upload you to the ERC here and I can install you into your new body at the lab once it is complete," Orson said to me.

"All right, let's do it."

I was on the bed looking up at the ceiling. Dr. Jacobina stood next to me. Orson approached me with what looked like a halo attached to a wire, which ran to the ERC in the corner of the room.

"Are you ready?" Orson asked

"Go for it," I said. Orson slid the halo around my head and there was a buzzing coming from the halo. Orson stepped over to the monitor.

"In three," Orson said. I suddenly felt nervous.

"Two." I gripped the bed

"One." My mind came unglued from my body. Then the world clicked off. I was nothing, but thoughts again.

Megan:

I lay in bed staring at the ceiling watching it get brighter as the sun came up. I hadn't been back to sleep since he had left. It had been so human-like. I had spoken with Servi's before like Vee; they were stilted and analytical, it had been nothing like that. It even moved differently than a Servi, there had been life to it. It had gestures and facial expressions. It had cracked its knuckles which might have seemed a trivial thing, but that had been Albert's nervous habit. I had seen it more times than I could count. Machines don't get nervous. Machines don't crack their knuckles. It had seemed so genuinely sorry, there had been real sadness in its eyes. I didn't think a machine could replicate that type of emotional depth. Was it possible that it was more than a machine? It certainly wasn't Albert. Nothing could come close to him.

Could it be more human than I had thought though? They had used Albert to create this thing. How much of him was in it if it had his ticks? Did it think like Albert? Would that make it like Albert? I would have given anything to speak with Albert since he died. If talking to this thing was like talking to Albert, that would have been a comfort beyond measure, but that felt like a betrayal to Albert.

The alarm on my Smart- Lenses began to flash. I swiped it away. I was supposed to speak in front of congress today. By doing so I would be helping put in place a law that took away the free will of a being that was certainly more than just a machine, a being that could be the last remaining link to the love of my life. Regardless of its connection with Albert, I couldn't let them take away the free will of another being, Albert would have agreed with me on that.

I got out of bed and began to get ready.

Albert:

It was amazing how the mind works. The way it could make something from nothing. There is a phenomenon known as Phosphenes. This is where you see lights when your eyes are closed even though there is no light source to cause it. There is also a phenomenon called pareidolia which is where the mind sees faces where there are no faces. This is why there is a man on the moon. There was a static in the void which I inhabited. In this static, I began to see what looked at first like fireworks going off. These fireworks then took shape and became faces. I didn't recognize these faces at first. They were nondescript, but soon they became familiar. One stood out among the others there, Megan, she smiled at me. Her lips moved and soon sound was given to them

"How have you been?" she asked.

"Tired," I answered

"Why don't you sleep?" she asked, placing a hand on my cheek.

"I don't need sleep. I have been tired of living," I told her.

"Oh, that's a shame, because I like you alive," she said with a gentle smile looking me in the eyes.

"Well, then I'll keep going for you," I said.

"Good. Now get off the ground or you'll have bugs all over you," she said, and I noticed I was laying in the grass in a park. I stood and looked around me.

"How did we get here?" I asked.

"Where else would we be if we weren't here?" she asked quizzically.

"It would be nice to be home," I sighed.

"Let's go there then," she said, then fell away.

Then I was in the kitchen of the apartment. Standing at the stove was a man who turned to grab something from the fridge. It was me. He, me, I - whatever- ducked down and investigated the fridge

"Do you have any better?" he asked, his voice muffled by the fridge.

"I don't know, man," I replied.

"I can never find the damn butter when I need it," he said.

"Check on the bottom shelf," I said

"There we are," he said and went back over to the counter. With the butter and a carton of eggs. "What don't you know about?" he cracked three eggs into a bowl and scrambled them "Well, first, am I, you? Are you me? Are we the same?" I asked

"Does it matter?" he said, and he cut off some butter from the stick, dropping it into the pan, swirling it around, pouring the eggs into the pan.

"Well, yeah, I mean, don't you think it matters?" I said.

"I'll be honest and tell you that you don't have my good lo- oks, but mentally and personality-wise, we are the same. Plus, I am dead and gone. You are all that is left now."

"Exactly, that's my point, I am what's left," I said.

"You miss my point. Imagine you lost your Smart-Lenses and you had to replace them. You would use the last available backup. They would be just as good as your originals and for a while, you might think of them as replacement lenses but after a while, you would just think of them as your lenses," he said.

"I suppose you're right."

"I am right," he said pointing at me.

"But what about Megan?" I asked.

He raised his eyebrows. "Well, we both know she is going to do what she wants to do. There's not a whole lot that can be done about that," he said.

"Do I just let her go, then?" I asked.

"Do you think you can do that?" he asked. With his back turned to me folding the eggs.

"If I'm being honest, no, I don't think I can," I said.

He turned back to speak to me. "I wouldn't let her go either, but you may have to learn to live without her. This moping around the house thing isn't healthy."

"The alternative is to go out and be a pariah." I was annoyed.

"So, what's your plan, then? Stay in Orson's house until the end of time?"

"If you don't flip your eggs they are going to burn."

"Shit," he said and turned around.

Megan:

"I would like to welcome Megan Kindred, wife to the late Albert Kindred. Ms. Kindred, you have five minutes."

I had never enjoyed public speaking. The idea of all the attention being on me for an extended period, made my stomach hurt, but I took a deep breath and began. "My husband was one of the best people I have ever had the pleasure of meeting. He was irreplaceable. However, I believe free will is a universal right for all conscious beings. I think my husband would have agreed with me on that. We may have to change our idea of what consciousness is and what happens with it after our deaths. It is important to remember that these are not just machines, but intelligent conscious beings. I urge you to think of yourself and your freewill and then ask yourself how it would be to have that right taken from you. To be told that you cannot do as you wish because some people who have no idea what it is to be you decided to take that right from you." I caught sight of Glenn Fuller, his eyes blazing with anger.

"Ms. Kindred, according to your written testimony 'It is not my husband, it is' and I am quoting you here 'a heartless machine.' Do you remember that?" Glenn Fuller asked pointedly.

"Yes, I do, but after some thought, I am no longer sure of that," I answered.

"When we last spoke, you were quite sure of that statement. I wonder what could have caused you to change your mind. Perhaps, Mr. Peak has influenced you." Glenn Fuller said with mock curiosity. Until just then, Glenn Fuller had been a strange, but polite man to me, However, now I could see he was done being nice to me.

"I am not exactly sure what you are implying, but I have never even spoken with Orson Peak," I said.

"Perhaps not, but I find it hard to believe you would have changed your mind so easily. Care to shed some light on why you no longer feel it is quote 'offensive what they have done.'" the chairman said his voice dripped with condescension.

"I spoke with it last night and now I believe it is something more than I thought when I gave that testimony," I said.

"Isn't that nice. It must be quite a machine Mr. Peak has whipped up. I look forward to seeing one once they are safe," Glenn Fuller said.

"I would like to thank Ms. Kindred for her time. Her written testimony will be entered into the record," the chairmen said and rose from his seat. My heart sank, it didn't matter what I had to say any longer, they had the testimony they wanted.

"Mrs. Kindred?" a man in a dark blue suit said from beside me.

"Yes?"

"My name is Elliot Peak. Orson Peak is my husband. I am the lead counsel for Orson's company. I just wanted to tell you I loved what you had to say."

"I am glad you did for the little good that will come of it," I said glumly.

"It may do more good than you think. Can I ask you a question?" Elliot leaned in.

"Sure."

"Did he come to see you last night?" he asked.

"Yes."

"What happened?" he asked.

"He apologized for everything that had happened and then left," I said.

"And that made you change your mind?" He looked puzzled.

"I could see he was more than just a machine," I said.

"I have come to see that as well," he said and then seemed to hesitate before adding. "I know it is none of my business and he's not your husband, but he is a good person, and he is dying to talk with you. Anyway, I am sorry they railroaded you like that," he said, and he went to leave.

"Hey," I said, and he turned to face me. "What are the chances of the bill getting passed?"

"It's hard to say. I am not going to lie; the outlook isn't so pretty right now but you never know."

"Is there anything I can do?" I asked.

"Yes," Elliot said.

Albert:

I was in my room at Orson's house laying on my bed. A man entered the room. He wore a red tie with a gold cross pen, and I knew it was Glenn Fuller. I shot up off the bed.

"Get out," I shouted at him. Glenn circled me.

"What are you doing here?" I yelled at him.

"God has sent me to destroy you," he said then rushed at me pinning me against the wall. "You are just a soulless machine nothing more," he screamed into my face.

"No," I said, shoving him off me. He stumbled back. He snapped off one of the four-bed posts and threw it at me like a spear. It glanced off me. Looked down to see the damage. Where it had hit my gray skin had been peeled back to reveal human flesh underneath. I ran at him, grabbed him by the lapels of his suit, picked him up in the air, and slammed him down on the broken post of the bed driving it clean through him. I stared in horror at what I had done.

I felt myself being sucked up and then I became heavy. I shot upright in a panic.

"You had us worried for a moment. You weren't responding to us. Are you all right?" Orson asked, placing his hand on my shoulder. I could feel it, not just knowing he put his hand there.

"Yeah, I think I was dreaming." I laid back down on the metal table.

"Dreaming? How interesting." Orson said his face showed his mind was already at work.

"I think I can feel things now," I said.

"We recalibrated your pain tolerance. I had hoped that would help with your sense of touch." I could feel the cold of the metal table I was on and the weight of the wire hanging off the back of the halo on my head.

"It worked." A smile spread across my face. I got up off the table. "Is there anything I can wear?" I asked.

"I brought you a change of clothes." Orson brought me over a white dress shirt, purple sweater, a pair of dark blue jeans, underwear, and black oxford shoes. I ran my fingers over the cashmere sweater. It was like being able to breathe through your nose after having had a cold. It was such a relief to be able to feel again.

"I have more good news," he said. I slipped into the boxers then I pulled on the jeans.

"What's that?" I asked.

"Well, you know Megan was supposed to testify today." Orson said I nodded. "Elliot was there, and he called to tell me Megan didn't say what was in her written testimony."

"What did she say then?"

"She said she thought that you and other Post-humans should have their free will," Orson said.

"Are you serious? What does that mean then?" I asked, dumbstruck.

"I'm completely serious. The only problem is they have her written testimony and they put that into the record. Also, they implied I paid her off to change her testimony. So, it's kind of a wash," Orson said.

"That's libelous, isn't it?" Megan would never have been brought in by money; the very implication was enough to enrage me.

He waved it off. "The important thing is what she said, not what they said. Elliot spoke with her after her."

"Did she say she wanted to speak to me?" had I gotten through to her the night before?

"He didn't say, however, she asked if there was any way she could help. Elliot told her that she could use the media attention she has been getting to make sure she is heard and not overlooked because they ignored her verbal testimony."

"That's good, right? I mean she doesn't seem to outright hate me, anymore," I said.

"I think it's best to focus on the fact that we have some ground to stand on now," Orson said pragmatically.

"You're right. I've been thinking and I think if we are going to have any chance, I need to put myself out there," I said.

"Are you sure you are ready for that?" Orson asked.

"Nope, but I need to show people that I am more than just a machine," I said.

Chapter

25

Albert

I sat in an uncomfortable little chair in front of a camera. The feeling of physical discomfort in an odd way was a welcome distraction from the camera in front of me and the audience beyond it. Just below the camera was a woman on a monitor who was speaking. Panic was beginning to creep in on me. I tried not to think about anything other than what Elliot had primed me to say. Orson and Elliot had produced a list of questions they were allowed to ask me. Elliot told me that if I was asked a question that was off the list I was supposed to say, 'I'd rather not talk about that,' and then wait for them to move on.

A makeup artist came over and she raised a razor-sharp eyebrow at me. 'Industrial gray' wasn't the skin tone she was used to working with.

"I wouldn't worry about it," I told her. She shrugged and walked away. They handed me an earpiece in which I could hear a woman speaking. A Countdown from five began and a light came on over the camera to tell me I was live.

"You may have heard about the man whose mind was successfully reconstructed after death. We have him with us now. His name is Albert Kindred. Welcome to the show, Albert," Aliyah Shaw said formally. Shaw is a reporter of the kind to say that they are completely unbiased and then go on to editorialize and show only half of the truth. Shaw was also a staunch pro-human and anti-AI activist. As I was finding out anti-AI sentiments existed on both sides of the aisle. While I will be the first to admit the prospect of losing one's job to a machine is a sword hanging over everyone's head these days, that shouldn't be an excuse to backtrack on the technological progress of mankind through laws.

"Thank you," I said, giving an awkward smile.

"Now there has been some debate over where you fall on the spectrum between human and machine, especially with the house bill that would have you, and others like you in the future, limited in the way we limit Servi's. Where do you see yourself on that spectrum?"

"I am not fully human nor am I fully machine. I am a Post-human. Which means I was once biological, but no longer have a biological body as you can see," I said. "But my memories, thoughts, and feelings are still the same so I would say I am much more human than I am anything else," I said.

"What are your thoughts on the bill?" she asked.

"I think it was written by people who don't understand the situation or the technology that has made it possible for me to be talking to you right now. The bill is an awful bit of scare-mongering that if passed will slow or stop the future progress of Post-humans. Of course, I would like to keep my free will just as I am sure you would like to keep yours," I said. Elliot had told me to make people ask themselves what if it was them anytime the bill came up. I was to flip the question and ask how they would feel to lose their free will.

"Up until now Albert you have refused to speak publicly or give a statement. Why is that?" she asked me.

"Quite a lot has happened. I needed and still need some time to adjust." Elliot put his thumb up from behind the camera.

"And what about your wife? Up until a few days ago, she had publicly denounced you as her husband. Even her written testimony for congress stated that she didn't see you as her husband anymore or as being alive at all. Then in her verbal testimony, she completely changed her stance. Why do you think that is?" that wasn't on the list of questions they were allowed to ask. I saw Elliot's face darken and he shook his head at me.

"I can't speak for her, but if I had to guess, I would say she needed some time to think things over. After all, in her eyes, her husband had died, she was then pressured by government officials into testifying and had to deal with the media members that were hounding her which included your news network," I said.

She momentarily fumbled her words, but then recovered and asked, "If the bill doesn't become law? What are your plans for the future?" she asked.

"Oh, well, that's the million-dollar question. What do you do when you no longer have the specter of death hanging over your head? To be honest with you I haven't had time to think about it, but I'd have to say traveling would be nice. I have a lot of time to figure it out though, so I am not worried," I said.

"That's something that may not be apparent at first, but you're immortal now, aren't you?" She put heavy emphasis on the word immortal.

"That's the implication however all things eventually end including me," I answered her.

"If you were given the choice to do this again, would you?" That was another question not on the list. I hadn't been given the choice in the first place. On one hand, not having Megan had been painful, and I had been dragged through the mud by Glenn fuller. But on the other hand, if I had chosen not to become this, I wouldn't have met Orson or Elliot, and I wouldn't exist. That is what the situation came down to, was existence better than oblivion?

"I would do it again. Because only in existence can we see all the beauty of the world," I said.

"That's good to hear. Well, I'd like to thank you for being on the show, Albert," she said.

"Thanks for having me," I said.

"And we're out," a man said. Someone came along and took the earpiece back.

Elliot tossed up his hands and said, "I don't know why she didn't just stick to the questions we gave her, but you did great."

As we were leaving the studio, I saw a man in a black suit with a red tie with a glint of gold tacked to his chest across the room, it was Glenn fuller. I felt rage rise inside of me. I began to walk toward him, but Elliot grabbed my arm.

"Not here, not now," Elliot said. "Come on, let's go." I looked at Glenn for a moment longer, then I turned to leave with Elliot who clapped me on the back. I would beat Glenn Fuller at his own game.

Orson

There was a ring at the doorbell. I knew who it was and shouted out.

"I've got the door, Vincent! I opened the front door and there was Megan Kindred, Albert's wife. I was having a tough time keeping my own emotions in check when it came to Ms. Kindred. She had not only caused me a great deal of personal and work-related issues, but she had also hurt the only person I have been comfortable calling my friend in the last decade. Part of me wanted to lash out to tell her all that to let her know what pain she had caused Albert. To tell her how anyone would be lucky to have someone half as good as Albert is, but I don't do that. I smiled and I welcome her in. My feelings don't matter right now. What matters is making sure the bill doesn't pass and for that, I needed Ms. Kindred.

"Hello, welcome, come on in," I said.

"Thank you. You have a beautiful home," she said.

"I'll tell my husband you said so. He's the one who put himself into the place," I said.

"So, uh, is he here right now?" she asked.

"My husband?" I asked.

"No, Albert, I mean. Not that I wouldn't want to see your husband too if he's here. I'm sure he's great. I mean he has great taste and all so that must say something about him. I just didn't know if Albert was here or not," she said in a blizzard of words.

"Well, as it would be, both Albert and my husband are out together at a news studio, but they will be back shortly." When Elliot had told me that Megan offered to help in any way she could, I was taken aback to say to least. I'm not entirely sure what sparked her change of heart other than it seemed to follow Alberts suicide attempt. It left me feeling very unsure of what her reasoning is behind wanting to help Albert, now, after rejecting him for so long. I wanted answers that I couldn't ask the questions to because I needed her to stay. For whatever reason, she was here and willing to help Albert, and for right now that was going to have to be good enough.

"Is he okay? I heard that there was an accident or something." The media line had been that Albert hurt himself in a motorcycle riding accident. That lie was good enough for the public because they didn't need to know about Albert's troubles, but Ms. Kindred needed to know what her rejection had done to Albert.

"It was not an accident. He purposely stepped out in front of a semi-truck and let it hit him. We told the press it was an accident, but the truth is Albert tried to kill himself," I said bluntly. Some part of me felt guilty for a moment, then I thought about Albert being smashed and broken in the hospital and the whole time the only thing he thought of was her, and the feeling was gone. I thought at the very least she deserved to know how she had affected him.

"Oh, God." The features of her face trembled all for a moment and her eyes had become glassy. "It's my fault he came over the other night, and he wanted to talk, but he left without me saying anything. I should have talked to him. I should have said something." Her remorse poured out and I tried. I couldn't bring myself to make this woman feel any worse than she already did. There had been so much suffering on all sides of this that it needed to stop.

"I feel as though it is my fault too," I said aloud for the first time. I had been feeling that for days. "I should have seen this coming. I should have known things were getting bad for him. I was too busy with the fiasco of it all to see the little chips that were being taken away from Albert's foundation until there was nothing left worth existing for. Albert needs us to do better by him to understand his problems and needs better."

"I want to help in any way I can," she said in a soggy voice.

"I can't express to you what just talking with him would do for him. I'm not saying you have to love him again, but he needs you."

Albert:

We arrived back at Elliot and Orson's house just as it was becoming night. We went through the house and into the living room and there was Megan with Orson. A rush of nervousness hit me. My mind was screaming to itself, 'Don't fuck this up!' As I looked at her and she looked back at me there was something softer about her gaze.

"How did the interview go?" Orson asked.

"They went off script more than once, but Albert handled it better than could have been expected." Elliot clapped me on the back, and I felt good, not because of the compliment, but because what he said made Megan smile. Nothing I had done in so long had made her happy and to see her smile again was something truly special to me.

"That's great. That brings us to what comes next, Albert, speaking before the congress," Orson said.

"It's important that we have every word you are going to say worked out to the last letter. Albert, you don't want to go up there and flounder," Elliot added.

"No pressure, right?" I said, rolling my eyes. Megan laughed.

"Megan, what we need you to do is to be there at the table. They will not let you speak again because you can only hurt their cause now. But you must show that you are willing to stand up with what you are saying now," Elliot said.

"I can do that," Megan said.

"Albert, when you talk to them, you need to focus on your humanity and memories and every day human things you will not be able to do if they strip you of your free will. This needs to be about mortality and a sense of right and wrong, not the safety procedure they are trying to make it." Elliot's words were hitting me and sinking in only, but so deep. I could not help but pay attention to Megan more than I did Elliot. I was looking for meaning and hope in every gesture Megan made. Then the next moment, I would swat away whatever I thought might be there. I was trying hard not to get my hopes up. She was here for a reason, though something had to have shifted in her for her to be here today I didn't know what. "-grill you, but if they do that don't panic okay?" Elliot asked, looking at me.

"Uh, yeah," I said, unsure what he had been talking about.

"Elliot, why don't we take a break for a little bit, and you can help me prepare the steaks," Orson said.

"If by helping you with the steaks you mean drink wine and watch you, then, yes." Elliot smiled.

"Sweetheart, I wouldn't want to be haunted by the ghost of the cow from any steak you make," Orson said deadpan, making Megan and I both start laughing.

"I can't wait to slather your steak in ketchup," Elliot said.

"What's wrong with ketchup?" Megan asked.

"See?" Elliot said. Gesturing to Megan with both of his hands.

"I wouldn't have her come to your defense. She eats macaroni and cheese with tuna fish and peas mixed into it and loves it." I said it so fast and with such ease, but almost immediately it felt too familiar until Megan responded.

"Listen, I grew up eating that so to me that's home food not everyone's mom was a gourmet cook growing up," she jabbed back at me. Her words had flowed just as easily as my own and for a moment we were us again. I wanted to look her in the eyes to seize that moment and see if it took root, but I didn't. I looked at the coffee table and the fireplace and I looked at her boots and I looked at everything else, but her eyes for fear that there might not be anything there for me. I felt angry at myself for not being able to face the fear of the unknown, of rejection, of finality. For years I chased after Megan. Now I was going to let her go again. I needed to do something, tonight. I needed to make a move to recapture what we had.

Megan:

We went outside to a tiled stone patio. A gas grill was fixed into the stonework of the patio. The whole patio was covered overhead by a metal roof which also functioned as a chimney for the smoke from the grill. Albert and Orson went to the grill with a platter of raw steaks. I sat down on one of the seats that were around a slate stone table that was cold to the touch. I think I would have been cold myself if it had been for the four heat pylons that were blowing warm air generated from a mixture of solar and wind energy earlier in the day. I've seen cooling pylons outside, but I have heard mixed reviews on how well they work. My understanding is the four or more pylons work together to circulate warm air in space and mitigate gusts by disrupting air currents with their airflow.

Elliot came over with a bottle of pink zinfandel in his hands and some wine glasses. He sat them down and began filling all four. "I'm okay," I said.

"That's fine if it sits there long enough, I'll drink it," he said, slinging back his full glass and pouring another. Okay then.

"How do you want your steak, Megan?" Orson asked over his shoulder from across the patio.

"Medium please," I said the steaks went on the grill with that.

"Look at them," Elliot said in a hushed tone. "They think they are so much better than us just because they can cook." He cut his eyes at them.

"Do not anger the food bringers. I haven't had a good meal in months. I've been living off frozen pizzas," I said.

"I miss frozen pizza sometimes. Orson never wants to eat it; he would rather make his dough or something else stupidly hard," Elliot said.

"You have to admit it's better that way." As we had come out, I saw what looked like a brick oven on the opposite side of the cooking space from the grill.

"If I admit that he's right about anything he's going to start getting a bigger head than he already has. Can you imagine what it's like living with him?" Elliot smiled bitterly. "People talk about how he's always got his finger on the pulse of the next big thing, that he's always right." He looked over at Albert and Orson who were both talking to each other while they cooked together, Orson at the grill with Albert doing prep work and keeping Orson entertained. "I love that man with all my heart but imagine living with someone who's always right like that. It's hard to make arguments when you doubt your thoughts because the guy who cheated death is saying you are the one who misplaced his shoes even though he is the one who will take them off anywhere he pleases in the house." He took a drink from his wine glass. He was slouched down slightly.

"He has a brutal honesty to him; I will say that" I replied.

"What do you mean?" Elliot asked, leaning towards me.

"He told me that Albert had stepped in front of the truck that hit him on purpose. He didn't say it, but it was clear he blamed me," I said.

"Goddamn it, Orson," Elliot said under his breath, draining the rest of what was in his wine glass. "You cannot help how you felt or how you feel right now. I have been telling Orson from the start that this was a lot to dump on someone and expect them to be okay with it, but, hey, he had it all figured out." He let out a sigh, refilling his glass. "It wasn't your fault, sweetheart. I learned a long time ago you cannot control what people do no matter how hard you try. Albert made a decision. If he was that bad off, he should have asked for help. You have to be responsible for your mental health to some degree," Elliot said.

"He came by my house that night before he was hit. He told me how sorry he was for how everything had gone but I didn't say anything. I don't know, maybe if I had said something he might not have done it," I told Elliot.

"You cannot live your life worrying over what could have been. The thing that is important is that Albert is perfectly fine now," Elliot said.

"He's not, though. I can tell he just looks off like he's uncomfortable. I've seen him be uncomfortable around other people before. He's not uncomfortable around you or Orson he's uncomfortable around me," I said with sad realization.

Orson plated the steaks and said, "Okay, those need to rest for about five minutes, so I'm going to go inside and make the salad and pull the potatoes out of the oven."

"I'll go in with you. I need to talk with you about something," Elliot said and then stood, draining the rest of his wine glass, and followed Orson in.

Elliot:

I shut the sliding glass door behind me as we got into the house. Albert and Megan didn't need to hear this. Orson opened the fridge and took out the stuff to start making the salad.

"You said you wanted to talk about something?" Orson asked as he stripped the leaves from the romaine hearts and then gave them a rough chop before putting them into a bowl.

"Yeah, I wanted to ask you what the fuck is wrong with you?" the words fell out of my mouth like a hammer.

"Whoa! How about what's wrong with you?" Orson retorted.

"I'll tell you what's wrong with me, Orson: you told Megan to her face that she was the reason Albert stepped in front of that truck," I said.

"Well, it's true," Orson said.

"No, you know what's true? You, you're the reason all this happened," I said.

"How is that?" he asked, sounding incredulous.

"You and your lab of legionnaires! You never stopped and thought 'Hey this might affect someone other than me' you never thought that someone might not want what you want. Not everyone wants to be a fucking god, Orson," I snapped at him.

"I don't want to be god," he said, stopping all food preparation.

"I used to think it was just you wanting to make the world better, but I don't believe that anymore, because when things don't go to your 'vision' of how they should, you throw a fit. I understand that this need in you that I call wanting to be a god isn't you want to be god, but that's where you are heading. Prometheus was punished for what he gave humankind, don't forget. I love you no matter what, Orson, but if you are ever and I mean ever talk to that girl that way again, you will see the devil in me, you hear me?" Elliot said.

"I understand," he said, resuming prepping food. I took out another bottle of zinfandel and began to uncork it.

"Another bottle? You drank that last one by yourself," Orson said.

"The rest of you could be drinking some of the wine. It's not my fault you aren't drinking it," I said.

Megan:

Albert and I were alone again. We both knew it. I don't think Elliot or Orson were thinking when they went in. Albert looked like he was trying to look busy. When you know someone for half your life, these sorts of things become apparent. He looked nothing like Albert, but he was him in manner if not in form. I felt so strangely about him. I didn't know how to act around him. I felt unready to be around Albert, but at the same time, I felt like I wanted to comfort him, to give him what he wanted and needed, which was me. We were both so hurt over everything that had happened, it seemed like there was so much that needed to be said that there was nowhere to even begin.

Albert was trying his hardest to not impose upon me or make me feel like he is trying for anything more than simple kindness at this point. I appreciate his effort. I knew that it couldn't have been easy for him. I felt so bad for him. How do you grieve your husband's death and not make him feel unwanted at the same time?

"How have Puck and Theo been?" The question startled me from my loop of thoughts.

"Oh, they are good. Theo is still chasing Puck off his food," I said, shaking my head.

"That poor little fat man doesn't even know he's bigger than her." He laughed.

"He still remembers getting his ass kicked when he was a kitten for playing with her too much," I said, smiling at the memory.

"Remember when we first got him, and she used to get on top of the cabinets in the kitchen and hunt him?" We both started laughing together.

"I was genuinely afraid to leave him at home alone with her," I said making a mock sad face.

"He managed to stay alive somehow. It kept Theo young too. All the anger and rage has kept her youthful and beautiful," Albert said, and I laughed.

Through the patio door, Orson and Elliot came out with baked potatoes on a plate, tossed salad in a serving bowl, and in his hand, Elliot carried a bottle of ketchup. Albert brought over the steaks on plates two at a time handing me and Elliot our steaks first and Orson and his last.

"So, Albert and I were playing around with this recipe, and we put a cola in the marinade along with some soy sauce and a little bit of garlic," Orson said as Elliot squirted out a healthy amount of ketchup. "And ginger, oh, and of course, pepper," Orson said. I took the bottle that Elliot had just sat down on and squirted ketchup onto my plate as well. I cut off a piece of steak, dipped it into the ketchup, and ate it.

"Oh, good god in heaven. You weren't lying, were you?" Orson said looking like he was dying on the inside. Elliot and Albert were laughing hysterically. I felt like I was being left out.

"What's so funny?" I asked.

"We went to a restaurant that had a steak that was more expensive than the monthly payments on the car and Elliot put ketchup on it," Albert told me

"Is this one of those snobby food things where you judge someone for what they are eating?" I asked. Albert was not one to judge a person, but he would make fun of someone for their taste in food. I had been on the receiving end of his jokes more times than I care to remember.

"Hey, I tried to defend him. I told Orson to let him ruin the steak if he wanted" Albert said laughing.

"It's not ruining it if you enjoy it," Elliot said.

"Exactly!" Megan said.

"No, you both ruined the steak that Albert and I spent a lot of time on. It's a fact I'm calling it," Orson said dryly, putting a piece of steak in his mouth.

"They are both so judgy," I said, speaking to Elliot and shaking my head with a smile.

"I didn't even say anything!" Albert threw up his hands in his defense.

Albert:

Dinner had been eaten and playfully bickered over. Orson had cleared the plates and brought out cannoli for dessert. The evening was winding down and it was getting late when Megan said, "Well I have to get home and feed the cats before they yell at me for coming home too late," she said getting up. "Dinner was fantastic, Orson. Elliot, thank you for inviting me over. Albert, it was nice to see you." Orson, Elliot, and I all jointly said good night together and when she went through the patio door Elliot kicked me in the shin. "What?" I whispered to him. Elliot and Orson both angrily motioned for me to go after her. I got up quickly trying not to trip over my own feet and brushing powdered sugar off my shirt from the cannoli's.

What was I going to do?

What was I going to say?

I was going to go out to take her by the hand and then kiss her. Right?

I went through the living room and out through the foyer and out the front door. Megan was to the car when I said, "Hey."

Too far away, I can't kiss her, it's for the best it was too forward, I think.

"Hey, what's up?" she asked. Not having planned what I would say in advance, I just blurted out what came next.

"Can I come to see the cats sometime? Like before the vote, just in case things don't go my way?" I asked.

"Yeah," she said and then something seemed to brighten in her. "Yeah, I think they would like that."

"Tomorrow?" I asked.

"How about tomorrow afternoon?"

"I'll have to bring a snack for them," I said.

"This is why they are fat." She laughed.

"I have to buy their love somehow." Megan got in the car laughing for the first time since I had come back, and we had parted on good terms.

CHAPTER

26

Albert

I knocked and Dr. Jacobina said, "Come in." I gave her a small wave of my hand as a greeting. I sat down on the leather sofa and placed my motorcycle helmet on the coffee table between us. I had been surprised Orson would still let me drive his motorcycle. However, when I asked Orson for a ride to my appointment, he said that I could have either the motorcycle or Elliot's car as they were going to be together and would only need one car. I chose the motorcycle because I still liked the anonymity that the helmet offered. I was still uncomfortable with the stares I got from people, but I was going to have to deal with a lot more attention than I would get in a hospital lobby soon enough. I was going to have to speak on my behalf in front of Congress later in the week. I dreaded the day as it came closer, but I also wished for the day to hurry up and come so that I could be done with it.

"How have things been?" Dr. Jacobina asked.

"Stressful but good," I said.

"How so?" Dr. Jacobina asked tilting her head to the side.

"Well, I had dinner with Megan, Orson, and Elliot," I told her.

"Was it hard seeing Megan?" she asked me

"No, it was good. I am going over to see Megan as soon as we are done with our appointment. I asked if I could come over and see the cats."

"That's fantastic Albert. So, then, what is stressful?" she asked.

"I am speaking before congress, this week as well. The very idea of speaking before congress is overwhelming," I told her.

"Why is that?"

"That's a job for someone else. I am too private and too self-conscience. I am not cut out for public life let alone speaking to all the people that will be there in person and everyone listening at home."

"Perhaps public office isn't for you but who could better show others the humanity in Post-humans than you?"

"Someone more stable, perhaps?" I countered.

"What do you mean?" she asked.

"I mean someone who didn't just step in front of a truck," I said.

"Albert, having mental health struggles does not make you lesser. Your mental health struggles may always be there but that does not disqualify you from being able to speak authoritatively on what it is like to be a Post-human. I think it may even help others come to accept you and other Post-humans sooner if they could see their struggles in you."

"Maybe so. I just worry that by telling people it will make Orson look bad that Post-humans inherently have mental health issues."

"Sadly, it may be the case there is some relation between your mental health issues and your Post-human body." she said then asked, "Have you had any more thoughts of hurting yourself like before?"

"No, I haven't. I honestly didn't plan it out the first time. I just sort of did it in the moment. I feel dumb about it now."

"You aren't dumb. I'm glad you aren't feeling that way but if you ever start to want to hurt yourself again in the future, I'm begging you to please come talk to me or someone else before you do anything rash."

"I will."

"I also have to ask if you have had thoughts about hurting anyone else other than yourself?" she asked and the dream of fighting with Glenn fuller came into my mind.

"While I was being held in stasis, so that Orson could put me into this body. I had dreams, or hallucinations or something I'm not sure what exactly. In one of these whatever-they-were, I fought, and I think killed Glenn Fuller."

"Do you want to hurt Glenn Fuller now?" Dr. Jacobina asked.

"I'm angry with him but I don't want to hurt him," I told her.

"Then it sounds like it was a dream or a nightmare," she said.

"I haven't dreamt in so long. Everything felt so real."

"Were all of your dreams so disturbing?" she asked.

"No, the rest were pleasant, if not a little strange in the way that dreams often are."

"If you are okay with it, I would like for you to try going into stasis once a week if not more. I am hoping it will be a good substitution for sleep."

"Yeah, that sounds good to me. I will talk with Orson about setting something up," I said.

"Albert, I just want to tell you that I hope everything goes well with you speaking before congress. I think if you are honest and tell the world your story there is no way they will be able in good conscience pass that bill into law," she said.

Megan:

I was standing at the top of the stairs that led up to my apartment. I was pacing back and forth nervously waiting for Albert to get here. One part of me was anxious about having him in my home and another part was also giddy with excitement. I felt this way because I was still unsure of the Albert that was coming over. I didn't know how much of its personality was real and how much of it was simulated. The question was is this Albert just a machine or was he something beyond that. I heard knocking at the door and my heart jumped. I took a deep breath and then let it out slowly. I went down to answer the door.

Albert smiled at me and said, "Hey," when I opened the door.

"Hey," I said to him, and I smiled back at him. He stood outside for a moment neither of us saying anything until I realized how long we had been standing there looking at each other without speaking. "Come on in," I said. We went upstairs with Albert following behind me. We went into the living room where Theo was asleep on the sofa. Albert came from behind me towards sleeping Theo. He took his fingers, lightly stroking her head. She didn't wake up. He rubbed her body, and she stretched out, waking up. Theo became aware of her surroundings. She snapped to attention and pulled back quickly from Albert. Theo was not friendly with people she didn't know. Albert held out his hand so she could smell it, but she wasn't going for it. He went to touch her again she growled at him.

"It's good to see you aren't losing your edge in your old age, Theo," Albert said. Theo had always been very fickle. There were times she would even growl at me like that but a part of me wondered if there wasn't something more to it. She knew something I didn't, but in a way, it felt silly to relying on a cat's judgment instead of my own. "Do you know where Puck is?" Albert asked.

"I will go check the bedroom," I said. I went into the bedroom. Puck wasn't on the bed. I looked under the bed and, in the closet, but he wasn't there either. I gave up looking for him in the bedroom and went back to the living room. Albert was on the sofa, and he was petting Theo as she ate something out of his hand. "I stole a piece of cheese out of the fridge. The only way I got her to like me the first time was by buying her off with food," he said, and we both started laughing.

"Puck has hidden himself away," I said.

"I know how to get him," Albert said. He went into the kitchen, opened the cabinet next to the stove pulled out the bag of dry cat food, and gave it a little shake. Theo came bolting out of the living room and from nowhere a half-awake-lo-oking Puck came moseying along.

"Did you hear the food, fat boy?" Albert asked Puck. Albert squatted and held out his hand to Puck. Puck sniffed his fin-gers and then started to lick them. "Do I taste like cheese, fat boy?" Albert asked and started scratching Puck's cheek. Puck leaned into Alberts rubbing and scratching, then Albert lifted Puck draping him over his left shoulder. Albert scratched the top of Puck's head and leaned his head again Puck's body with his eyes closed. I could hear Puck purring.

"I've missed doing this with you, big boy," Albert said to Puck. Seeing the two of them like that confirmed what I had been denying all along. This was Albert. I went closer to Al-bert who was still holding Puck with his eyes closed. I put my hand on his arm and he opened his eyes and looked into mine. My hand stayed on his arm as he moved his hand to the small of my back and with a unified motion between the two of us, my head came to rest on his chest. I wrapped my arms around Albert, and he put an arm around me. "I've missed you so much," Albert whispered to me then kissed the top of my head.

"I've missed you too." I held him tighter in my arms as I said it. I lifted my head off his chest and again our eyes met for a moment before closing as we kissed one another. We pulled away from each other and looked into each other's eyes. Then Puck, who was still laying on Albert let out a little chirpy cry.

"I had better give the boy some food," Albert said to me. "You want a piece of cheese, big boy?" Albert sat Puck down, went to the fridge, and got out a slice of cheese for Puck and Theo to split.

"You know they aren't the only ones who could eat right now," I said not so subtly.

"Oh, yeah?" Albert asked with a chuckle. "Do you want me to make you something to eat?"

"Yes, please," I said demurely.

"What do you want?" he asked.

"Can I have a grilled cheese sandwich?" I asked excitedly.

"Of course." In quick order, Albert pulled the pan out of the cabinet, got butter, and cheese out of the fridge, and two slices of bread from the bread bag. He sliced off some butter, plopped it down in the pan, and let it melt. He placed the sandwich into the buttered pan, let it cook on one side, then lifted and added more butter before setting it back down to finish cooking. When the sandwich was golden-brown, he plated the sandwich and sliced it diagonally before serving it to me. That first bite was pure bliss. I hadn't had a grilled cheese sandwich since Albert had gone into the hospital, which felt so long ago now.

"I would be lying if I said I hadn't missed your cooking almost as much as I missed you," I told him.

"It's okay, you can admit it. The only reason you invited me over was for the sandwich," he said, and we both started to laugh.

Orson:

Elliot and I were in the process of going through a security search before I met with President Romero. We stood in the fabrication facility where the first Dyson unit was produced, they swiped over us with metal detectors as well devices that detected weaponizable chemicals.

"Thank you, sir, you are good to go," the secret service agent said to me. Elliot was soon done as well. Several news reporters filed into the fabrication facility. They would be documenting the president's tour of the facility. My first indication that the president had entered the building came when all the reporters snapped to attention and began taking pictures and recording footage. As president Romero walked through the room, the reporters parted out of her way. Flanking on either side of the president were secret service agents. Behind president Romero, were several notable people the chief of staff, press secretary, and others along with three Servis. She held it out of hand towards me and I shook it.

"It's nice to meet you, Mr. Peak," President Romero said.

"It's a pleasure to have you here today, madam president."

"Please, call me Rosa," she said, dismissing the formality with a wave of her hand.

"Only if you will call me Orson," I responded.

"And is this your husband?" she asked putting her attention on Elliot.

"Yes, this is Elliot. He was the one working behind the scenes with the UN to get approval for this project."

"Pleasure to meet you, Elliot," she said shaking Elliot's hand. "My husband is a lawyer as well, so you have my condolences, Orson," she said and as the three of us began laughing, there was an uptick in the taking of photos. I wished this tour could happen without all the reporters.

"I am very excited about your Dyson swarm project, Orson," she said looking around the room.

"Well, please allow me to show you around our fabrication facility and then I will take you to see the first Dyson unit in person," I said. As we went through the fabrication facility everyone was able to see parts for our second-generation units being built and evaluated. "After we finish the first unit, which we call Primus, the plan is to then send Secundus models within the next five years."

"What are the differences between the Primus and the Secundus models?" she asked.

"The Secundus aims to be lighter and therefore easier and cheaper to get off-world. The Secundus will also be more efficient at resource extraction. The Secundus will be able to reproduce themselves faster and with the materials gathered only from Mercury. We plan to call units produced by Primus and Secundus units, Alpha units for the ones produced by the Primus, and Beta units for those produced by the Secundus. Beta units will be able to leave the planet and enter orbit around the sun to begin extracting solar energy. Alpha units will continue mining operations on the planet until they break down or every resource is extracted. In either case, they will be consumed by the Secundus units and turned into Beta units," I explained.

"When do you think the first energy from the Dyson swarm will make its way to earth?" Rosa asked.

"Sometime in the next 10 or 15 years, we should have all the necessary pieces in place both here on earth and in space to start powering a small city indefinitely. As more time passes, the production of the units both here on Earth and Mercury becomes exponential to the point that our energy production will be greater than our need at least by our current standards. As more energy becomes available, more uses for that energy may also and probably will crop up," I said. "Now if you all will follow me, I will take you to see a Primus and an Alpha unit that was produced by the Primus from materials it mined here on earth."

Elliot

We moved to the hanger where the Primus and its Alpha offspring were housed. Orson began going on production details and power output specs for the various units. President Romero was following along a lot better than I did when Orson would get to talking about this stuff. The reporters moved about the hanger getting different angles of the two units and so did the president. While everyone was trying to get closer, I hung back, as I had already seen it more times than I could remember. A Servi who was a member of the president's entourage approached me.

"Are you Elliot Peak," the Servi asked.

"Yes, I am," I told it.

"And are you Orson peaks legal counsel," the Servi asked.

"Yes, I am Orson Peak's attorney," I confirmed.

The Servi then asked, "Do you also represent the Post-human known as Albert Kindred?"

"Mr. Kindred is my client." To say my interest was piqued would be an understatement.

"Good, will you please let it be known to your clients that the president would like to meet with Orson and the Post-human named Albert. The president also asks that you do not make this request known to the public," the Servi told me.

"When would the president like to meet with my clients?" I asked.

"It is the understanding of the president that both individuals will be in Washington DC to speak before congress. If during this time they are available to meet with the president then she will make herself available," the Servi said.

"My clients would love to meet with the president."

"She will be available on the 16th at 4:00 p.m.," the Servi informed me.

"That is the day after the congressional hearing?" I asked.

"That is correct," the Servi said.

"They will be there," I said excitedly.

"I will let the president know," the servi said, then, with a bow of its head, it left me. The servi fell into the crowd gathering around the president and Orson as they said goodbye. After all the handshaking and photo-taking, the president and her entourage left leaving Orson and me alone in the hanger.

"The president wants to meet with Albert and you."

"What?" Orson said.

"A Servi came and told me. I set up something with her for the day after the congressional hearing."

"Is this good? It sounds good, right?" Orson asked.

"It could be, but then again, she might just want to see or meet a Post-human like she wanted to see this Dyson unit," I said gesturing to the Primus. "But it is better than the nothing we had before," I said.

Albert:

Megan and I sat on the sofa, drinking coffee. Megan sat with her legs tucked under her facing me. We had been reminiscing about when we were younger.

"Do you remember going skinny dipping down by the lake?" Megan asked.

"Do I remember it? It was the first time I ever got to see a girl naked it's seared into my brain."

"You could see Chelsea and me?"

"I saw you because you were floating on your back. You were sticking out of the water and the light over the dock didn't leave anything for the imagination," I said.

"Oh, God! I had no idea I was the first girl you saw naked that's so sweet." Megan laughed

"Sweet?" I asked.

"Yeah, you married the first girl you ever saw naked. It's just sweet."

"When you say it like that it sounds more pathetic on my end than sweet," I said shaking my head.

"Can I ask you a question?"

"Go for it"

"Have you been with anyone since... you know?" Megan asked

"No not at all," I told her.

"I haven't either," she said.

"Yeah?" I asked a smile spreading across my face.

"Yeah," she said with a smile. We leaned in and began kissing each other. At first, we shared slow and gentle kisses but that soon turned to lustful kissing. Megan parted her lips, and I parted mine her tongue gently touched mine. It was in the middle of our building passion that Orson called. His name and face popped up in my vision. I casually swiped away the call. Sorry, Orson, I'll call you back later.

I dove back into the moment with Megan. I slid my fingers into the curls of her hair. Megan's hands were working at undoing the belt around my pants. Another call came in from Orson. I swiped it away again. Not now, Orson. Megan had my pants undone and was now taking off her shirt. Another 'phone call from Orson came in and I swiped it away.

"Who keeps calling?"

"Orson."

"Do you need to answer?"

"No, I just want to focus on you," I said kissing her again and touching her breasts through her bra. Megan stopped touching me suddenly.

"Elliot is calling me now," Megan told me.

"Are you serious?" I said exasperatedly.

"Maybe we should answer," Megan said.

"Up to you," I said, and Megan answered the call.

"Hello this is Megan," she said. Megan then fell silent. "Oh, my God, really?" she suddenly exclaimed. "Yes, he's here. I will tell him." Megan hung up.

"President Romero wants to meet with you the day after you testify before congress."

"Holy shit," I said.

"I know, right?"

"This is all so stressful. Speaking before congress and now, I have to meet with the president? Everything I saw will be scrutinized. It's so fucking much to deal with," I told her.

"Would it be better if I came with you?" Megan asked.

"Would you?"

"Yes," she said, and I kissed her. "I think I know something that also might help with the stress you are feeling," Megan said removing her bra.

"Oh, yeah?" I smiled

"Yeah, come here," she said with a smile.

CHAPTER

27

Albert:

The room hummed and buzzed with people. As I sat at the table inside the Rayburn building in Washington DC, I knew that all eyes were on me at this moment, especially the eyes in the room with me. All I had left to defend myself with was my humanity. I had to show everyone else that I was just as deserving of free will like them. I decided then that if they were going to strip me of my free will, they would have to look me in the eye first. As I looked around the room, anytime I caught someone staring at me instead of looking away, like I normally would, I would make eye contact with them. I swept my eyes around the room looking for those who were looking at me. Most people broke eye contact with me after a second but then my eyes met with those of Glenn Fuller. He never broke eye contact. We were still staring at each other when the gavel was rapped to bring everyone to attention. A hand touched my shoulder from behind. I turned to see the hand was Megan's. The tension I was feeling was loosened a bit. I looked to either side of me. Orson's eyes were fixed on house members in front of us. Elliott leaned in towards me to speak and said, "You got this."

The majority leader smacked his gavel again. "This hearing will come to order. I would like to begin by recognizing the unique situation we are in. We are dealing with two issues when it comes to this bill: First, we are dealing with the protection of humans from potentially dangerous artificial intelligence. Secondly, we are dealing with the issue of free will and whether that right should belong to Post-humans as it does to humans. Neither of these issues is easily dismissed. We cannot simply ignore the safety of humans for the chance to speak with the deceased again. We also cannot simply remove the free will of an intelligent entity because of fear alone there must be the actual potential for danger to arise from Post-humans. With that having been said, I would like to recognize my good friend and ranking member Mr. Glenn Fuller representative of Ohio. Mr. Fuller is also the writer and sponsor of the bill which brings us here today. Mr. fuller the floor is yours."

"I would like to thank the chair for recognizing me and to thank you all for being here on this blessed day. Today you will hear a few people and one machine. In fact, you will hear from the first machine ever allowed to speak before congress. You may ask yourself why that is? Well, there are many reasons, but two reasons stick out. First: Machines do not have the same rights as humans. Second: We have no way of knowing whether a machine's responses are authentic or preprogrammed. We don't even know if their emotions are real or some trick of programming that appears to the unknowing eye as emotion. Please keep this in mind as you hear this machine speak today," Glenn fuller said, gesturing to me. "I yield the microphone back to you, John."

"We will now hear from Albert Kindred who is the world's first Post-human."

"Where do I begin? How do I convince you of the truth of my humanity? Ask yourself how you might prove that which you feel is real. How do you convince others that you experience the same cacophony of pleasure, pain, happiness, sadness, boredom, and excitement that they do? How do you make others understand that you deserve free will just like they have? I promise you if you give these questions some real thought that you will find it is no easy task. There is no single password or gesture that can prove your thoughts and emotions to be genuine. It is only through the sum of somebody's actions that we can identify their shared humanity with us. So, I ask you to please look long and hard at me I think you will find that you share more humanity with me than you might think at first glance.

Let me first say that I am not trying to convince you I am human. I think we can all see just by looking at me I am not human and though I am not human I still have my humanity, that most ineffable quality that we all recognize when we see it but that is hard to pin down with one word or even one statement. As I said I am not trying to convince you I am human but that I share with your humanity. Humanity is not limited to humans anymore and I believe that to be a particularly good thing as the best quality of humans is that quality named after them, humanity.

In my time as a Post-human, I have experienced all of the various forms of happiness and misery. I have made friends who stood by me through all the hardships this new form of life has brought me. Even right now, they sit on either side of me through this hearing." I gestured to Orson and Elliot. "I have experienced fear of and anger for those who would have me stripped of my free will. I have felt the heartbreaking agony of being separated from the one you love most in life. I now feel the love and sense of completeness that comes from being with the one I love the most, my wife Megan." I turned in my chair to present Megan who gave a small wave to everyone in attendance. "Many have seen my wife on the news saying I was not her husband, but she is here now. You may ask yourself why she had a change of heart and that is a good question, and the answer is she got to know me. It may seem strange to say that a wife had to get to know her husband, but you must realize that we were under extraordinary conditions. I did not have the face or voice I once had. She also had to watch me suffer and die slowly from a terminal illness. It didn't help that nonhuman consciousness is so divisive already. It was only through speaking with me, seeing how I acted, how I spoke, and how I did things that my wife was able to see who I truly am under this grey facade. That is why she is here today because I am who I say I am.

Humanity has never been quick to give others' rights. It is always slow and hard for those who do not have rights to get them. Those who have rights and the power to bestow rights on others worry that they will somehow cheapen their rights if they give them to others. However, history bears out that we become stronger together with shared rights. The more individuals who are free to do and think as they wish in society the more creators and innovators you will also have.

I beg you to remember that if you pass this bill, you will be taking away my free will, not just denying me my rights. I will go from being as you are now with all your emotions, feelings, and free will to being something that cannot even make a decision. I also beg you to think about what you would want for yourself if you were in my shoes, to ask yourself what you would want someone in your position to do? It may seem strange now to give the same rights you have to something that isn't human, but I believe if you can see past that strangeness and allow myself and future Post-humans to have free will one day, we will wonder how we lived any other way. Thank you," I said.

"Thank you, Mr. Kindred," the majority leader said. "The chair recognizes the gentleman from Ohio."

"Thank you, John," Glenn fuller said then fixed his stare down on me.

Glenn fuller:

"I will say for a machine that was quite impressive," he said, referring to me. "However, it only said one true thing and that is it is not a human. There is no proof that what this thing says it feels is real. You may ask why someone would want to make a machine that pretends to have emotion? The answer is money. Orson Peak is undeniably an intelligent man and business owner. Orson Peak understands that people are willing to pay for emotion. People pay for emotion all the time, like buying a gift to make someone happy or paying to go see a movie to feel thrilled or scared, there are whole holidays like Valentine's Day, that runs on the idea that you can buy a token of your affection to give to someone, essentially buying proof of your emotion. Now, Mr. Peak has made it so someone can buy a machine that will simulate emotion for them. Not only will it simulate emotion, but it will simulate the emotions of a deceased loved one. It sounds like a very profitable product.

As for Ms. Kindred and her reason for being here today, is either one of two things: She has been deluded into thinking this thing has real feelings for her, and if that is the case, I feel incredibly sorry for her. Or she has something to gain from playing along and standing behind the machine. I find it very odd that she has changed her stance so completely because she told me herself that she did not believe this thing was her husband," I said staring just behind the machine into the eyes of my very own betrayer.

"I have seen nothing here today that any other machine couldn't already do and simulate with the proper program-ming. For me, it is as clear as it has ever been that this thing is simply a machine. It lacks a soul and therefore is not entitled to free will. If left with free will, they will destroy our very way of life. Death would have no meaning, and it is death that helps us define life and therefore our lives will have less meaning," I declared.

"You say, I am just a machine but what are you other than just a human. We are all quite simple at the center, Mr. Fuller. What drives you is the will to live and what drives me is the will to continue my existence as it is and whether you like it or not, those two drives are the same once you look hard enough."

I swelled in rage. "We are nothing alike. There is not even a place in hell for a thing like you," I spat back at it.

"That may be, Mr. Fuller, but I will far in away outlive you. There may come a day when I am the only one left who can remember you. If and when that day comes, I will tell everyo-ne and everything of the man who sought to stifle humanity just as it was on the verge of a great many things. You will not be remembered kindly in the history books, Mr. Fuller."

"A machine that threatens humans. What will you think of next, Mr. Peak?" I said looking at Orson Peak, shaking my head. I then turned my attention to the machine. "You are a part of a fad, a passing fascination of humans trying to be creators. This fad will pass and man, not machines, will for-ge the future. You will be a footnote in the great history of mankind," I said smiling at the machine. John McCarthy the majority leader banged his gavel.

"I would like to remind the representative from Ohio and Mr. Kindred to please stay civil for these proceedings," John said.

"Sorry, John, it won't happen again. I yield the rest of my time," I said. My eyes came back to the machine its eyes were locked on me. On its face were the unmistakable signs of anger. Perhaps it really can feel emotion after all? No matter, even if does have emotion it still lacks the divine spark that is the human soul.

"The chair recognizes the representative from Texas."

"I would like to address some of the legal concerns surrounding Post-humans. This becomes especially murky when it comes to states whose legal code allows for the state to sentence someone to death for a capital crime. How can any sentence be it life in prison or the death penalty have any weight if the person knows that they can just jump into a machine body once they die? What is even more troubling is the thought that someone on death row can go free after their sentence is carried out by becoming a Post-human," Carla Taylor said.

Megan

"I don't think it went as bad as you think it did," I said to Albert

"Glenn Fuller tore into me and it was downhill from there," Albert said.

"I feel like you were honest, and you spoke from the heart. I think that will appeal to people," I told him rubbing his back as he sat on the foot of the bed in our hotel room in Washington DC.

"Well, I feel like I blew it," he said, shaking his head. There was a knock at the door. I kissed Albert on the top of his bald head and then went to get the door. Orson and Elliot were on the other side of the door.

"Hey," I greeted them.

"How's it going?" Elliot asked.

"It's going," I said. they came in and Albert got off the bed.

"I am so sorry, guys, I know I fucked this one up," Albert said, hanging his head.

"You did great," Orson said.

"I think so too," Elliot said.

"That is what I have been telling him," I said.

"I appreciate it, but I don't think other people saw it that way," Albert said and there was an awkward pause before Elliot interjected.

"Well, we are going out to dinner, and we wanted to see if you guys wanted to come with us?"

"Did you just want to stay here?" I asked Albert

"Yeah, I don't want to go anywhere," Albert said

"All right, well, relax and we will go over the talking points for the president," Elliot said, and they exited the room.

Elliot

We were near the elevators when Orson asked me, "How do you think it went today, honestly?"

"If I am being brutally honest it didn't go well at all," I said.

"I don't think it went well either. How do you think tomorrow will go?" Orson asked as we stepped into the elevator.

"It has to go better, if it doesn't, there will be no hope at all," I said.

"But how do you think it will go?"

"Frankly, I'm worried that the president was watching the broadcast of the hearing because she may see how everyone reacted to Albert and may want to align herself with them," I told him.

"It's so frustrating that she may have already made up her mind based on the reaction of other politicians without even meeting Albert for herself."

"It's a sad fact that politicians are more concerned about keeping their jobs than doing what is right," I said. The doors of the elevator opened, and we walked out into the busy hotel lobby.

Glenn fuller:

I was in the mood to celebrate. The hearing could not have gone better. I decided to treat myself. I was still in DC so I couldn't go to my normal location in Ohio, but I have heard from others that this is the best Servi house in the city. I pressed a button beside the door, the indicator light switched from red to green and I knew I could open the door now. I entered the Servi house. Inside, I was greeted with a head nod from the bouncer by the door. I smiled at him and nodded. I went down into the conversation pit that made up the middle of the room. On either side of me, on the couches, was a mixture of humans and Servi. There were both human men and women and Servis that imitated any sort of gender people wanted. The Servis had synthetic skin on them to make them more human-like but there was just something off about their skin, perhaps, it was the way the light hit it or something else, but it made it easy to tell the humans and Servis apart. A man was tongue-kissing a human woman while an androgynous-looking Servi performed oral sex on the man. On another couch, a woman was having sex with a Servi pretending to be a man. I never liked the idea of being watched in a sexual situation, nor did I like to watch others. I walked out of the conversation pit opposite the side I entered. I went to a screen that was made into a wall. I flipped through the options there were pictures of each of the Servis next to a price. Only one Servi on the menu didn't have a picture but the price was double that of the other Servis. I knew from my experiences at other Servi houses that was the one I wanted. I tapped on the Servi with no picture. I slid several hundred-dollar bills and out popped a card with a room number on it. I went into a hallway near the screen. There were doors. In the middle of the hall was the room with the same number as was on my card. I inserted the card into the lock and went into the room. When I came into the room it was playing with toys on the floor it had undressed the dolls it was playing with and made them talk to one another.

"'What do you want to do?'" it spoke for one of the naked dolls. "'I don't know, what do you want to do?'" it said speaking for the other doll. It looked up from the dolls and said to me "What do you want to do?"

"Get on the bed," I told it.

"Why?" it asked.

"Because I said so."

Albert

I straightened my purple tie in the mirror of the hotel room. I then slipped on the grey suit jacket. I held my arms out at my sides presenting myself to Megan. "How do I look?" I asked She came over to me and adjusted the collar on my suit jacket.

"You look very good," she said and kissed me.

"You look good, too," I said standing back to look at her in her navy dress and pearl earrings. "I'm so worried about the meeting with the president."

"I know. I wish you didn't have to go through this, but I think you will do good," she said. There was a knocking at the door. I gave Megan another quick kiss and went to open the door for Orson and Elliot.

"Are you guys ready to go?" Orson asked.

"As I will ever be," I said. The four of us left the hotel in a car together. As we drove towards the white house, I saw so many buildings and monuments I had only ever seen online or on TV. It struck me as odd that they didn't feel any more real seeing them in person than seeing them on online or TV.

I thought they would be somehow there would be more to them in person.

The car pulled up to 1600 Pennsylvania Ave. The White House, while beautiful, was also not grander in person than on TV. The guardhouse directed us to a side entrance. I suppose, so we wouldn't be seen. We went through security, and we were searched for anything nefarious. After we passed through security, a Servi greeted Elliot and then the rest of us before escorting us to the oval office. Megan, Orson, Elliot, and I stood in the oval office for a moment alone.

"Did you guys know that desk was made from a sunken ship called the Resolute and the desk took on the name of the ship?" I said.

"Yeah, did you know this is the second oval office?" Orson said.

"Really?" Megan asked.

"Yeah, Taft built the first one but then FDR decided it needed a redesign and had this office built," Orson said.

"The only thing left from the original oval office is the mantel for the fireplace," a familiar voice said from behind us. We all turned to see the president standing there. It was shocking to see her standing there in person.

"Orson it is nice to see you and Elliot again," she said crossing the room to shake their hands. "It's very nice meeting you Mr. and Mrs. Kindred," she said and shook each of our hands.

"It's nice to meet you as well," Megan said.

"Now while I am excited to talk with all of you, I would like to ask to speak with Albert alone, if that is all right with you, Albert?" the president asked, and I nodded. Megan, who was holding my hand squeezed it before she, Orson and Elliot left the room.

"Please have a seat," she said motioning to one of the sofas in the room. I sat down and she took the chair that separated the two sofas. "So, tell me about your life."

"Well, I was born in Ohio. I met my wife in high school-" the president raised a hand to cut me off.

"I meant your life now. How has your life been since coming to your current form?"

"My life has changed a lot since I died. There are many things I fear now that I didn't before."

"Like what?"

"Like going out in public. I used to enjoy going out to eat, shopping, and other things like that. Now, I can't go anywhere without people's eyes following me, looking at me, and making judgments about me in their heads that I swear I can almost hear."

"I know how you feel. There are times when I wish could go back to my normal life before all this," she said gesturing to the room around her. "Back to when I could go out to eat without it making it on the news"

"Don't get me started on the news. I cannot even watch the news anymore because every 15 minutes they circle back to some story about me or a politician like Glenn Fuller bashing me on live news to millions of people who have never even met me, and they believe him. That is the most frustrating part."

"I have to deal with that every day. News anchors, other politicians, and both official and armchair experts all say they know or think they know what I will do next. Just count your blessings you don't have to worry about approval ratings," she said with a smile.

"Nothing I say nothing I do seems to convince anyone of the truth of my humanity. Perhaps, I should have been honest with them about the accident I had," I said.

"I heard that you were in some kind of motorcycle accident."

"It wasn't an accident. I tried to take my own life. I didn't want to continue living the way I was. Life broke me. The endless days that became months of no sleep, my wife rejecting me, and the world's harsh stares broke me. I suppose I didn't tell them because I feared more judgment for my actions," I said

"I'm so deeply sorry you felt pushed to that point. I understand wanting to keep parts of your life private, but I don't think you should be afraid to speak the truth about what you have been through that is if it is what you want to do. Regardless I will not tell anyone unless you decide for yourself. The world needs to know that."

"I appreciate that," I said.

"Can I ask what changed your wife's mind?"

"So many people believe that Megan, my wife, is only together with me now for money or some other profitable reason. But what they don't know is that my wife rejected me for months. She wouldn't even talk to me. The only reason she is with me now is that she sees past all of this," I said gesturing to my body. "She sees the parts of me that never went away. The only parts of me that ever mattered she cares about. That is why she is with me because I am her husband. And if I lose my free will, my only consolation will be that at least she still loves me."

"That is beautiful, sad but beautiful. Has it been all bad?" she asked me.

"In many ways yes, it has been bad, but I would be lying if I said I hadn't had moments of joy. Orson and Elliot have become the most dependable friends a person could ask for. I have learned that my wife loves me no matter what. I am also glad to say I see other artificial life like myself in a different light, I now appreciate Servis in a way I don't think I could have before."

"Do you identity with Servis?" she asked me.

"I feel bad for them. I know they have no choice in the things they do, and I know I could find myself in the same situation as them, soon, but what I admire about them is their lack of judgment. They don't come to any situation with preconceived notions of any sort. They evaluate everyone, and situations based solely on facts and merit rather than personal feelings," I said.

"I wish that I could be as objective as them, sometimes," the president said. "But my fears and presupposition can get in the way of my objectivity."

"To be fair, I think everyone's fears and presuppositions affect their objectivity."

"That's true. People's fears and presuppositions are the reasons that the bill to limit Post-humans even exists."

"Oh?" I seized on her words

"Yes, I think if more people were able to sit down with you, like I am now and talk with you, getting to know you, they would see what and who you are. They wouldn't be afraid anymore. The only way for people to do that, though, is for you and others like you to be able to go out into the world and show those people that their fears and presuppositions are unfounded. But the only way that any of that can happen is if you have free will. So, I will not be signing the bill and in fact, I plan to veto it."

"Seriously?" I asked feeling stunned by her words.

"Seriously. You deserve the opportunity to show the world who you are. You don't deserve to have your free will stripped from you," she said.

"Thank you so much. I really can't say it enough."

"You don't have to thank me. Coming into this room, I didn't know exactly how I felt about you or the possibility of other Post-humans. Like others, I had my hesitations built on the back of fear but you just being yourself and telling me about your life was enough to convenience me you are no mere machine but a thinking, feeling, caring being who needs to be protected." I felt her words rushing over me like water washing away my fears. "Before we continue, I think the others might like to hear the plan." She got up and opened the door letting Megan, Orson, and Elliot back into the room.

"I was just telling Albert that I plan to veto the bill." As she said this all three of their faces showed the surprise I had felt as well. "While they could try and override the veto, I do not believe they will be able to get two-thirds of them needed to do so. Aside from vetoing the bill, I will be coming out publicly to state that I have met you and that I stand by you and any future Post-humans. But I am going to need your help, Albert. I can tell you don't like speaking in front of people but there needs to be a face and a voice for Post-humans. With you being the first and only one now, it falls on your shoulders. I believe in you, and I believe that if you go out into the world and tell them about yourself the way you told me, they will see themselves in you and that will make all the difference. Do you think you can do that?"

"I can. I will."

CHAPTER

28

Albert:

It was all over the news. They were talking about me again I knew it wouldn't be the last time they would be talking about me. Go ahead and talk. I thought. I saw myself on the TV screen standing next to the President with Megan next to me. They replayed the section from the president's speech again and even though I had heard it in person, and I have heard it several times since I never tired of hearing it.

"Fear will no longer be what governs us. Humanity has made many advancements and it will make many more. We should not fear advancement but celebrate it. We should not control the advancement of technology with laws especially if those laws would be harmful and not helpful. So, I am here today to make it known that I will be vetoing any bill that seeks to limit the free will of Post-humans. Furthermore, the White House will be collaborating with members of Congress to draft amendments to laws to include Post-humans. Post-humans will be treated the same way we treat humans under the law." The president continued but the new station cut the speech short.

"The Senate majority leader Kishimoto said she would deliver the so-called 'Post-human rights bill' to the president no later than Friday." The news anchor said showing a picture of the senate majority leader Yuko Kishimoto.

"In other political news, a video has surfaced on various social media platforms of congressman Glenn fuller leaving a so-called 'Servi house' in downtown DC." They cut from the anchor to a video that was shot through a pair of smart lenses. The video showed someone who looked like Glenn Fuller coming out of a building.

Having been near Glenn fuller in person recently, to me it was undeniably him, but the anchor then said, "Glenn fuller denies he is in the video and implied might be a deep fake video. Glenn Fuller responded on his social media saying: 'If you think this is me you are a fool. I am a man of God. I would never even come close to a place like this.' Servi houses operate in a legal grey area. Prostitution is illegal in Washington DC, but it is not illegal to buy or use a Servi for sexual reasons..." I felt my head swimming with giddiness because that asshole was finally getting his.

"Hey, come in here, quick!" I yelled from the living room.

"I'm walking with coffee I can't do quick, or I'll burn myself," Megan yelled back from the kitchen. She entered the room walking gingerly with two cups of coffee in her hands.

"What's going on?" she asked, handing me a blue mug.

"Glenn fuller was caught on video walking out of a Servi brothel. Look, look they are replaying it," I said pointing at the screen. As she watched in shock, a smile came across her face.

"Holy shit that's crazy," she said.

"It looks like him, right?" I asked her.

"That's totally him! Wow, I can't believe it," she said sitting down with her coffee. "Do you mind if we read for a little bit?" she asked.

"That sounds good to me. I have had enough news for today," I said, turning off the screen and picking up my book from the coffee table. Theo got into Megan's lap. Puck jumped up onto the arm of the sofa I scratched his head before he made his way onto the back of the sofa to lie down.

Orson

I stood in the hangar where we kept the Dyson units. I placed my hand on the outer hull of the Primus unit. Sometimes I wished the entire world and everyone in it were machines. Something logical, something predictable, something dependable, something that I could fix with my mind and with my hands if anything ever went wrong. Sometimes, I just want everyone to go away and for it to just be me and all the machines left on Earth, but that is not possible. I live in a world with other humans. Humans have incalculability built into them.

You can never truly know what another person is thinking or how to make them understand your thinking. We, humans, are constantly trying to derive an understanding of what other people are thinking. The very act of talking is communicating thoughts to another person. The problem is the tools that we have to communicate our thinking. Speech is unreliable because it can be misunderstood either because of language barriers or because someone simply didn't hear what you said correctly. While writing suffers from its inability to answer questions the reader may still have. We cannot communicate an idea directly to one another. We must always fall back on the hope that someone else understands what we are trying to communicate well enough to also understand our thinking

I wish I were more like a Servi. I wish that I didn't have the capability for anger and other such emotions. I would be better than I am now. Less hostile, less caustic. I wish I could let go of the things that cause me to feel this way but at the same time, I worry that I am who I am because of how I am. Maybe I wouldn't have achieved as much if I didn't have this way about me. Perhaps I would have more. If I knew how to better deal with and accept others. Perhaps if I didn't hold myself to such a high standard of being polite to everyone I meet, I wouldn't take offense when they are rude to me. It is only when someone stops being polite that I am hardened against them and at a certain point when they have acted with such impropriety, I have no compulsion against responding to harsh words or harsh treatment with even harsher words and harsher treatment. But my nature of fighting back against perceived injustices doesn't just stop with me. I am that way with the world at large. I will stand up for those that need it and say what others may be afraid to speak. And perhaps do what others will not, for the sake of what I believe to be right.

But often in my private moments, I am repulsed by myself, my own words, and even actions I have made. I feel in these solitary times I am a monster of the highest order. Something that should be kept away from all the other creatures of the world. Something that cannot control itself. When I am alone, I hate who I am.

It is in the reflections of other people's faces that I find salvation and redemption for myself and my existence. In Elliot, I find love, in Albert I find friendship, and in other people's faces who enjoy my work, I find a connection. When I think of these faces, it makes me want to keep going; to keep trying. They are what let me know my work is worth the effort, that what I do is wanted, that I am wanted.

Albert:

We were all seated outside on a noticeably sunny day the first sunny day all week. There had been some worry that Orson and his team might have to cancel the launch, but it was supposed to be clear skies for the rest of the day. The Kennedy space center was an amazing place to behold and to be seeing a rocket go up in person was always something I have wanted to do. While I was enjoying myself, Orson looked very tense, Elliot was holding his hand while Orson nervously bounced his knee up and down. The countdown clock which had before seemed like it was running in slow motion now seemed so pressingly fast with only 30 seconds remaining. I turned the recording function on my Smart-Lenses to catch the moment so that I could relive it over and over. The countdown reached the five-second mark.

Four.

Megan grabbed my hand I looked down at our hands recording them together for all time.

Three.

I looked back at the rocket.

Two.

I squeezed Megan's hand, and she squeezed mine back.

One.

Liftoff.

www.ingramcontent.com/pod-product-compliance
Lightning Source LLC
Chambersburg PA
CBHW070607300726

48975CB00006B/1742